THE
ADVOCATE'S
DEVIL

mc **Marshall Cavendish**
Editions

Text © 2002 Walter Woon
First published 2002 by Times Books International
Reprinted 2003 by Times Books International

© 2010 Marshall Cavendish International (Asia) Private Limited

This edition published 2010 by
Marshall Cavendish Editions
An imprint of Marshall Cavendish International
1 New Industrial Road, Singapore 536196

Other Marshall Cavendish Offices:
Marshall Cavendish International. PO Box 65829 London EC1P 1NY, UK • Marshall Cavendish
Corporation. 99 White Plains Road, Tarrytown NY 10591-9001, USA • Marshall Cavendish
International (Thailand) Co Ltd. 253 Asoke, 12th Flr, Sukhumvit 21 Road, Klongtoey Nua, Wattana,
Bangkok 10110, Thailand • Marshall Cavendish (Malaysia) Sdn Bhd, Times Subang, Lot 46, Subang
Hi-Tech Industrial Park, Batu Tiga, 40000 Shah Alam, Selangor Darul Ehsan, Malaysia.

Marshall Cavendish is a trademark of Times Publishing Limited

National Library Board Singapore Cataloguing in Publication Data
Woon, Walter C. M.
The advocate's devil / Walter Woon. – Singapore: Marshall Cavendish Editions, 2010.
p. cm.

ISBN-13 : 978-981-4302-65-4
1. Lawyers – Singapore – Fiction. 2. Singapore – History – 1867-1942 – Fiction. I. Title.

PR9570.S53
S823 — dc22   OCN613300884

Printed in Singapore by Times Printers Pte Ltd

To my parents Woon Eng Chwee and Lee Peck Har,
and to the memory of my grandparents
Woon Chow Tat and Cheang Seok Cheng Neo.

CONTENTS

The Body In Question

MADELINE. There's no mistake about it. That's her name in the papers all right. And that photo. Still as beautiful as I remember her. What has it been now? More than sixty years since the last time we met? Half a century? I can still recall the day clearly. It was the day she lost her husband.

It was 1937, some time in July. I can fix the date with some accuracy, because it was just after I started reading in chambers. Business was slack just about then, and we pupils were left much to ourselves. The three of us were lounging in chambers — myself, George (he was plain old George then, the "Sir" came many, many years later) and Ralph. They used to call us The Unholy Trinity.

Anyway, we were sitting around watching the pigeons dive-bomb the GPO. The little feathered fiends would fly round for a bit, then let loose before perching under the cool granite eaves. We watched the missiles with absorbed interest. We had a bet going. Each of us marked a circle in chalk on the five-foot way. Every direct hit in a circle meant a free drink at the Griffin Club, courtesy of the loser. George was having a bad time. My circle and Ralph's were plastered with little grey splotches. George's lay gleaming white in the sun, while he cursed each and every miss. It was a revelation. I hadn't realised that George was fluent in so many languages.

George had just let loose with another blistering string of oaths when the door opened and in trundled Moraiss, the chief clerk. Ralph and I buried our noses in *Archbold on Pleadings*. George, caught in midstream, shut his mouth with an audible snap. Moraiss cast a baleful eye over us. He was short — not more than five feet — and had skin the colour and texture of parchment. When he spoke it was like the wind rustling through dry leaves. Moraiss didn't approve of us.

"Mr d'Almeida wants you," he said, fixing me with his basilisk glare.

"Right-ho," I replied with an outward show of nonchalance. An interview with the All-Highest, no less. What little treats, I wondered, had he in store for me. Swallowing my trepidation, I fell into step behind Moraiss as he shuffled out of the room. It may have been my imagination, but I always fancied that Moraiss left the smell of mildewed books wherever he went. I followed him through the dim musty corridors, by scent as much as by sight.

We came at length into a panelled anteroom. The room was stacked high with books from floor to ceiling. Ancient tomes, grey with age, ready to flake into dust at the merest glance. My eyes skipped from spine to aged spine: *Moore's Privy Council Appeals*, *Leicester's Reports*, the *Straits Law Journal*, an original set of *Kyshe's Reports*. Books that were ancient when my father was young. The pungent, unmistakable smell of antiquity pervaded the room. What a fitting den for old Moraiss, who had quietly mummified in this dry forgotten corner of the world.

At the far end was a solid teak door, beyond which lay the Holy of Holies. There in majestic repose sat Clarence d'Almeida OBE, senior partner of the august firm of d'Almeida & d'Almeida, Advocates and Solicitors. Though he was nominally my pupil master, I had hardly seen Mr d'Almeida in the two months that I had been with the firm. Hardly is the wrong word. I hadn't seen him at all. When I joined the firm he was involved in the celebrated Opium Murders case, which shook several stuffed shirts out of office. I got the job because my father (of whom I have very little memory) had been a junior partner in the firm way back, so it was almost literally off the boat and into the office for me.

We pupils had been taken in hand from the start by Cuthbert d'Almeida, a perspiring butterball of a man, who bustled around the office exuding jollity and sweat in equal proportions. Cuthbert was Clarence's brother, but one would never have guessed. He was round, jovial and ubiquitous; a complete contrast to his brother. Cuthbert to us was always Cuthbert; his brother was Mr d'Almeida, with the "Mr" such an integral part of the name that we almost forgot that he had a Christian name.

Of Number One we saw nothing. To us Mr d'Almeida was just a brooding presence behind the door, with little time for mere mortals and none certainly for the likes of pupils. We all lived in awe of the great d'Almeida, whose advocacy swayed judges and juries throughout the Straits Settlements and the Malay States, and who had never been known to let a client hang.

Moraiss rapped ponderously on the door. Cued by an unheard summons he opened it and I stepped through.

The occupant of the high-backed leather chair was facing away from me when I entered, talking to a lady whose slender form was framed in the window. She stood gazing out at the waterfront, the light outlining her with a faint halo. After the gloom of the inner office the brightness from the high glass window was dazzling, and I screwed my eyes up involuntarily against the glare. The man in the chair spun around to face me. I had of course seen photographs, but the reality was to me quite startling. In my mind I had built up a picture of a Zeus hurling thunderbolts of rhetoric at a spellbound jury. The photographs in the old bound newspapers, yellow and fuzzy with age, were of a slim, black-haired man. I pictured him as tall, for some unaccountable reason. I wasn't prepared for the wizened gnome who gazed at me over a pair of old-fashioned horn-rimmed spectacles. He was about sixty, slight of build and conservative in dress. I suppose that I should have expected an older man; his brother Cuthbert was after all in his fifties. Unprepossessing though he may have seemed on first impressions, his eyes nevertheless gleamed and shone with a penetrating intensity and breathless fire.

"Ah, Mr Chiang, I presume," the gnome said to me interrogatively. The words were barked out in a staccato tattoo.

"Take a seat, take a seat." He gestured towards a leather armchair in the corner.

"We have a little mission for you," he continued in his rapid-fire tone, before I even had a chance to seat myself. At this point the lady in the window turned around.

"Dennis!" she exclaimed, in a voice that tinkled with fairy bells.

"Madeline!" I gasped, poised in the most undignified manner with my bottom lowered halfway into the chair. For a moment my mind ceased to work, stupefied by the unexpected vision. Then a hundred memories coursed into my consciousness, a torrent of bittersweet reminiscences.

I had been an aimless undergraduate when Madeline Strachan had suddenly materialised in my life. She had come up to spend a few months with her uncle, a semi-fossilised don at one of the smaller Cambridge colleges. We were introduced because we both had something in common. Her father had been in the Straits Settlements for many years and had gone native to the extent of having married a Chinese woman, who happened to be a second cousin twice-removed of my father's, or something of the sort. Anyway, the connection was deemed close enough to justify my invitation to tea. And there she was. I was instantly smitten. Smitten isn't the word — decapitated, more like.

Madeline was one of those fortunate alliances of East and West, a handsome delicate creature who inherited the best features from both her parents. She was pursued by every male undergraduate from a dozen colleges; and I was at the head of the pack, baying with the rest. I actively sought her, and she seemed to enjoy my company. I found that I was with her more and more, cutting lectures and supervisions with reckless abandon. We went walking and punting and dancing. We went to the theatre, to the movies. We cycled to Huntingdon and beyond. Then there was that unforgettable week in Paris (properly chaperoned, of course) — window shopping in the Rue de la Paix, lounging in the cafes on the Boul' Mich', watching the artists at the Place du Tertre. And when one glorious summer day she linked her arm through mine as we sauntered down King's Parade I was the envy of every red-blooded male in Cambridge. Then she was gone. The summer was over, and she went back to her father in some God-forsaken Scottish lowland town. Nursing my broken heart I threw myself back into my studies. Barely scraped a pass that year. But now, unlooked-for and unheralded, she had suddenly materialised again. What a fantastic, glorious opportunity....

"I see that you know Mrs Russell," said d'Almeida drily.

Mrs Russell...? I felt as if someone had just demolished my universe with a sledgehammer. I collapsed heavily into the armchair.

"Poor Dennis," laughed Madeline, not unkindly. "I'm sure you must have been as surprised as I was."

She glided over to me, holding out an exquisite hand. I shook it rather limply. My eyes were riveted on the little golden band that adorned the other hand.

"Yes... yes, forgive me, it was quite a surprise seeing you here unexpectedly like that."

D'Almeida glanced at me quizzically over his spectacles, but said nothing.

I forced myself to say the words. "Congratulations on your marriage," I said, trying to sound natural, "Who's the lucky fellow?"

"Alec," she said, "Alec Russell. Perhaps you know him?"

As a matter of fact I had heard of Alec Russell, though we hadn't actually met. Russell was the darling of the local amateur dramatic society and a star cricketer. His family had been in the Straits Settlements for nearly half a century, and it was said (not very loudly in his hearing though) that his dark hair and dark eyes were a little local colour introduced as a result of a trifling dalliance on the part of old man Russell in his forgotten youth. Untypically, young Alec had been brought up in the Colony instead of being hived off to England at a tender age. Alec Russell was popular with all classes, spoke the local lingo like a native, knew and was known by everyone in the Colony. I decided that I didn't care for the blighter.

"I thought you were still in Scotland," I said, still trying to suppress my emotions, "with your father."

"Well, when Daddy died I came out east to be with my Aunt Emily. She was Daddy's only sister, you know."

"I am sorry," I mumbled, painfully conscious of having put my foot in it.

"Don't be. I met Alec on the boat out. We were married a year ago last month."

A year ago. Barely a year after our glorious summer together. I sighed. How quickly some people forget.

D'Almeida eased himself into the conversation.

"I'm glad that you and Mrs Russell know one another. I think that you will not mind the service that I shall ask of you," he said. "We've been acting as executors of Mrs Russell's aunt's will."

I glanced at Madeline. D'Almeida saw my look and explained, "Miss Strachan passed away some eight months ago. She was fairly well off and left everything to Mrs Russell, to be held in trust until she attains the age of twenty-one. That age will be attained in one month's time, I believe."

He paused and glanced at Madeline, who nodded in confirmation.

D'Almeida continued, "I understand that Mr and Mrs Russell have formed a settled intention to leave Singapore once she comes of age, and so we shall have to liquidate the trust. The main asset is a house in Bukit Timah, which contains several interesting antiques. I'm sure you wouldn't mind accompanying Mrs Russell to the house to make an inventory?"

"It would be my pleasure," I replied sincerely.

D'Almeida smiled. "I thought as much," he said.

He glanced at the grandfather clock in the corner of the room. "It might be best to do this as soon as possible."

I took the hint and rose to leave.

"You drive, Chiang?" he inquired. I nodded.

"Take my motor," he said, tossing me a bunch of keys. "Faster than by cab."

He rose from his seat and escorted Madeline to the door. With old-world grace he kissed her hand as he guided her through the portal.

"Oh, Chiang," he called as I followed Madeline's retreating form, "the address." He held out a slip of paper. Sheepishly I came back and took it. "Try to be back before closing time." His eyes twinkled. Blushing furiously I trotted after Madeline.

On the way to the car I stopped at the pupils' room to pick up my things. Madeline sat just outside while I popped in. George, who has an uncanny ability to sense whenever there is a beautiful girl in the vicinity, was already at the door surveying our visitor. Ralph was peering out from under his armpits. Ignoring their nods and winks, I hurriedly shovelled my pad and pen into a handy briefcase, then beat a hasty retreat. I prayed sincerely that Madeline hadn't heard some of George's fruitier comments. There's no denying that my friends were a pair of lecherous toads (they still are, as a matter of fact, but it doesn't show so much now that they're old and respectable).

The syce had the car out in front of the building when we got down. D'Almeida owned an antique Rolls, kept in immaculate condition, with a rubber-bulb horn. I honked it twice, then roared off down the road. Turning past the GPO, I sped down Collyer Quay in a cloud of dust. The top was down, the sea breeze fresh. The slight overcast meant that we weren't fried to a crisp. Believe me, there's nothing more exhilarating than speeding along in a Rolls with a beautiful girl at your side, watching heads turn in the trolley buses. I thoroughly recommend it.

"Aren't we going the wrong way?" asked Madeline, combing back her hair from her face. She looked like a wood sprite with her long hair flying in the wind.

"No, we're just taking the coast road. It's more scenic."

"Isn't it longer than through town?"

"That too," I replied. She smiled, but said nothing.

The coconut trees whipped by. Occasionally we caught a glimpse of sparkling sea-green between the palms. The air smelt faintly of salt. The fresh breeze flecked the wave-tops with white horses. It was hard to keep my mind on the business at hand.

"This house of yours," I said, wrenching myself back to business, "isn't it rather out of the way?"

"It isn't mine," she replied, "Well, I suppose now it is. But we don't live there. We've got a little place out on the east coast. Near Sea View. Aunt Emily was quite a recluse. Didn't like people. Only really cared for her chickens."

"Chickens?" I raised my eyebrows.

"Yes, isn't it just too much? Can you imagine my dotty old aunt and her flock? She doted on them. She must have had a thousand of them, clucking around her place."

I paused a moment to reflect. "You don't seriously mean that I have to make an inventory of a thousand foul fowls?" I said slowly.

She giggled. "Course not, silly. There's loads of other rubbish all over the place. Aunt Emily was a great hoarder. I don't think that in fifty years she ever threw anything away. Mr d'Almeida seems to think that some of the stuff might be worth something. That's what we'll be looking at. So you don't have to count your chickens."

"That's a relief. I'm allergic to feathers."

"So am I. I don't like birds. Especially chickens. You know, their little beady eyes. They give me the willies." She gave a little shudder. "That's why I never went near the place. Well, hardly ever."

We passed several Malay huts on stilts. Little brown figures stood in the water pulling at their nets. The sun glanced off the endless strand as we flashed past.

"Who's been looking after the birds then?" I asked.

"Well, there's old Sarip. He's a sort of foreman. Aunt Emily had a small rubber plantation right next to the house. But I think there's a new man. Just after Aunt Emily died. I don't rightly know. Alec handles all those things."

"Alec runs the estate full-time then?"

"No, not really. He's a junior manager with Masterson & Co. He just pays the estate workers. Mr d'Almeida authorises the bank to let Alec have the money. In fact he's just collected this month's payroll today. But Sarip runs the plantation and the new man looks after the house."

"I haven't actually met Alec," I said conversationally. "I suppose we'll meet at the house?"

She frowned a little and her mouth puckered up in a pout. "No, I don't think so. Alec's not around a lot these days."

I pricked up my ears. "Been working late then?"

"Not exactly. Well, yes, in a manner of speaking. His company made him overseer of some mines or plantations or whatnots in the middle of the jungle. He's gone at the crack of dawn and doesn't get back till late at night. Even on weekends, would you believe. It's awfully trying." She folded her arms petulantly.

We lapsed into silence after that. What a prize chump this Alec Russell must be, I reflected. If I had someone like Madeline waiting at home you wouldn't catch me running off into the *ulu*. You wouldn't even get me out of the house. I let a wave of delicious recollection wash over me. The smell of new-mown hay warming in the sun.... Daffodils along the Backs.... Punting along the Cam.... The long walks to Grantchester and Girton and Cherry Hinton.... The spell was abruptly broken as I swerved violently to avoid a suicidal goat that ran bleating into the tangled *belukar* by the road. We turned from Reformatory Road into Bukit Timah Road.

"Just a little way along here, after the Ford factory," directed Madeline.

The track to the house meandered drunkenly off from the main road. The forest pressed in on both sides, smelling damp and alive. The sun hadn't yet baked the moisture out of the ground. Clouds of laterite dust billowed up behind the car as we drove, frosting the leaves with sugar-pink icing. Ghostly white butterflies swirled around us in drifts as we sped along. Once we left the main road the sounds of civilisation abruptly ceased. The purr of the motor seemed almost indecently loud in the silence.

We rounded a bend and there it was. The house lay on top of a small rise at the end of a drive flanked by flame-of-the-forest trees. It was a fairly large one-storey rectangular box, built on pillars of stone in the usual style. Behind were the kitchen and servants' quarters, connected to the main house by a covered way with a flight of stone steps leading presumably into the dining room. A garage lay off to one side. The grounds were about an acre in extent, terraced in a formal style. Balustrades edged the terraces and Grecian urns flanked the wide stairs that led from one level to the next. It must have been imposing when properly kept, but now it was unkempt and overgrown with *lalang*. I pulled up outside the colonnaded gates, not wishing to risk the Rolls on the pitted driveway.

The silence was deafening.

"Quite a tourist spot," I remarked, surveying the place. "You could commit a murder here and no one would know."

"I told you Aunt Emily was a recluse," replied Madeline, stepping daintily out of the car.

We walked up the drive. The flame trees were in bloom due to the long hot spell that we had just had. The ground under the trees was covered with an orange-red carpet of fallen flowers. The sunlight filtering through the boughs had a faintly sanguine tinge. I looked at the house again. The sun-bleached paint hung in shreds from the tightly shuttered windows. The gracious flight of steps leading to the wide veranda in front was cracked. Tufts of grass sprouted from the cracks. The bamboo blinds hung at drunken angles. Not the ideal honeymoon spot by any means, I reflected. The only sound was the scrunch of our feet on the gravel and the incessant "breeek-breeek" of the cicadas.

The sun was climbing up towards noon as we mounted the steps. Little rivulets of sweat were running down my spine. Madeline's frock showed little grey spots where it clung to her back. We stumbled gratefully into the shade of the veranda.

"Just a sec," said Madeline, fumbling around in her handbag, "I've got the keys in here somewhere."

I looked at the bag. It would have made a very decent knapsack for a fortnight's camping. I sighed. In my experience hunting for keys in a lady's handbag makes the usual silly pastime of looking for needles in haystacks seem easy by comparison.

Resigning myself to a longish wait, I leaned idly against the door. It creaked open.

"Funny," remarked Madeline as she stepped into the gloomy interior, "it's usually locked." I followed her in.

It took a while for my eyes to adjust to the gloom. The musty smell of long abandonment hung around the place. Sunlight shafted through the chinks in the wooden windows. Motes of dust twinkled in the shafts. The furniture was covered with white cloths. There was a faintly funereal air about the room. I shivered involuntarily. I'm not usually the nervous sort (just an average coward really) but the place gave me the shivers. Madeline however seemed unconcerned.

"Let's start in the master bedroom," said Madeline, "That's where most of the valuable stuff is. At least, if there is any valuable stuff, that's where it would be."

She led the way down a dark wooden-floored corridor. I was unconsciously walking on tip-toe. Her stilettos sounded deafening to my keyed-up senses as she clicked her way along the floorboards.

"Here it is," said Madeline, indicating a large wooden door.

I pushed it open. The sunlight streaming in from the open window was dazzling. I flung my arm up to ward off the glare. Then I saw him.

He stood there clad in a brightly-checked sarong, his brown body gleaming.

"Madeline!" he croaked, his mouth agape. His eyes were wild and his hair dishevelled. I'd never actually seen an *amok* before, but that fellow seemed to fit the bill. It wasn't the rather goggle-eyed glare or the wild look on his face. I think what convinced me was the *parang* in his hand. It looked very, very sharp and seemed disturbingly red at the edges. He began to move towards us, *parang* to the fore. It did occur to me momentarily that I might be doing the fellow an injustice, but I wasn't about to chance it. I did what any reasonable coward would do under the circumstances. Grabbing the handle I slammed the door shut. The Malay hurled himself forward and started hammering at the door.

"The bolt! The bolt!" I screamed, pawing the wood frantically, "where's the damned bolt!" The Malay was tugging at the other side of the door and bellowing like a berserk gorilla. I held on like grim death. "Find the bolt!" I yelled.

Madeline, who had been transfixed by the sudden apparition, suddenly came to life. As we played tug-of-war with the door she groped at the edge, her fingers desperately seeking the bolt. "It... it's not here," she gasped.

I had both hands on the handle, straining to keep the door shut.

"What kind of mental spastic of an architect makes doors without bolts on them?!"

Hanging onto a door without a bolt with a demented homicidal maniac on the other side has never been one of my favourite pastimes and I wasn't feeling very charitable.

The maniac on the other side was pulling with all his might and banging and yelling. "*Buka! Buka!*"

I knew enough Malay to know what that meant.

"Not by the hair of my chiny-chin-chin," I growled through clenched teeth.

Madeline grabbed the handle and began pulling. Her face was white.

"What's he saying?" she asked.

"I think he would like to come out and play," I gasped.

I had heard that *amoks* had superhuman strength. Believe me, you'd be surprised how much strength you have when you're scared out of your wits.

I hung on gritting my teeth. "What's in there?" I asked between grunts.

"Just the master bedroom."

"Is there another door?"

"No. Only to the bathroom."

"Windows? Can he get out the windows?"

Madeline shook her head. "They're all barred."

I nodded with satisfaction. At least he couldn't get at us. I relaxed momentarily. The door almost flew open. Recovering myself I yanked it closed.

"Find a stick! Quick!" I rasped.

"A what?" queried Madeline blankly.

"A stick! S-t-i-c-k. Plank. Wood. Anything to keep this blasted door shut." I wasn't in the mood to be polite to a lady.

She let go suddenly and I was almost pulled off my feet. With a prodigious effort I hauled the door shut again. My shoulders ached with the strain. I'm going to need longer sleeves after this, I reflected wryly.

Madeline rushed back bearing a stout broom.

"Shove it through the handle, quick," I commanded.

She pushed the broomstick through the handle, neatly skinning my fingers. What a relief! I sank down against the far wall. I felt that my arms would dangle in front of me like an orang-utan's when I walked. They ached like the devil. My fingers were raw where the skin had been rubbed off. My head throbbed. The madman was still kicking up an unholy row.

"Noisy little beggar, isn't he?" I remarked.

Madeline wasn't listening to me. Her eyes were riveted on a crumpled white bundle in the dark recess at the far end of the corridor. In the dim light we could see a red stain on the white. A white panama hat lay on the floor in front of it.

"Alec," she breathed. Then she fainted.

I REFLECTED on my problem. Here I was, trapped in a dank deserted grotto of a house out in the back of the beyond with a raving homicidal lunatic, a comatose woman who would probably have a hysterical fit when she came to and the minced remains of the woman's husband. As I saw it there were three choices open to me: I could act the hero and sort out the mess; revert to type and bolt quickly; or have a nervous breakdown. Having rejected the latter two options as impracticable and being of a quixotic nature, I decided that I had better investigate. (George attributed it to stupidity, but then George is not a charitable person.)

I edged gingerly towards the bundle. On examining the bundle more closely, I relaxed. There was nobody there — literally. It was just a pile of clothes, liberally soaked in a gooey red stuff. I didn't have to be a doctor to know that it was blood. It was still sticky. I picked up the panama hat. Neatly stencilled in the sweatband were the initials "A.R." A groan from behind me reminded me of Madeline.

She was about to scream when I reached her side. "It's all right, it's all right," I soothed, "It's not Alec."

"Not Alec? Are you sure?" she said in a slightly strained tone.

I nodded.

"Who is it then?"

She had me there. To avoid answering, I drew her towards me. It was only then that I was conscious that the hammering on the door had stopped. Instead there was a faint chopping sound. Even I as looked up, the sound stopped. There was a creak of floorboards being uprooted, and then a sharp crack.

"Good heavens, he's getting out!" I ejaculated.

Madeline looked at me with frightened eyes. Frantically, I cast around for a weapon. The only likely object was a cricket bat. Seizing it quickly, I braced myself for the onslaught. My eyes swept down the corridor. Only two doors — the one to the master bedroom and one other near the pile of clothes. A swift examination showed me that both doors were secure. So he could only get at us through the front door. If only I could meet him at the head of the steps, we might have a chance. With a reassuring pat on Madeline's shoulder, I rushed quickly into the front room and out onto the veranda.

I arrived just in time to see a brown figure scrambling over the balustrade into the first garden terrace. With a whoop I bounded down the veranda steps two at a time, swinging my cricket bat and shouting.

I have done many foolish things in my life, but I'm hard put to remember anything more foolish than what I did then. There I was, screaming like a dervish, pursuing an armed and dangerous loony with a cricket bat. Fortunately the fellow didn't seem to be too bright either, and was high-tailing it for the woods. I bounded across the first terrace, reaching the top of the stairs to the second terrace just as he reached the bottom. With a ear-splitting war-cry I launched myself at him in a flying tackle that would have got me my Blue for rugger. Our heads connected with a bone-jarring crack. My last thought was that the blighter must have a concrete nut. Then I passed out.

I REGAINED consciousness to find a bespectacled Chinese gentleman bending over me. "Who the devil are you?" I inquired testily. I had the granddaddy of all headaches and I was feeling peevish.

"I doctor," he replied enigmatically.

"Eye doctor? I don't need an eye doctor. My eyes are perfectly all right, thank you. Here, let me up." I tried to get up.

He pushed me down, clicking his tongue. "No, no. You lie."

This was really too much. "What do you mean, I lie? Are

you calling me a liar you quack? I tell you I'm all right. Where's Madeline? Let me up I say." I pushed him off roughly and struggled to my feet.

"Steady on, boy. No need to play rough, what?"

I spun around to face the speaker. He was a rubicund gentleman, fiftyish, with a white handlebar moustache and a Colonel Blimp figure — the very cliché of a colonial planter.

"And who the devil are you?" I inquired somewhat belligerently.

The man's brow clouded. He wasn't used to being addressed in such tones by mere orientals. But he kept his temper and answered, "Jefferies. Arthur Jefferies. I own the estate down the road." He held out a gnarled hand.

Somewhat abashed, I shook it. "I'm sorry Mr Jefferies. I've had a trying time and my nerves are a little frayed. No offence meant."

"None taken," replied Jefferies. "Rather rum doings, eh, what? How're you feeling?"

I looked around me. As far as I could make out I was in the master bedroom of Madeline's aunt's house. It was bare except for the bed on which I sat and a couple of dilapidated chairs. There was a gaping hole in the floor where the boards had been torn out. Madeline wasn't anywhere in sight.

"Where's Mrs Russell?"

"Resting," said Jefferies soothingly. "I met her running up the road on my way back for tiffin. Quite a state she was in, don't you know. Had the dickens of a time making sense of what she was saying. When I twigged, I called the police and brought Dr Soong here."

He indicated the Chinese doctor, who gave me a toothy grin and nodded. I nodded back. A sharp pain seared through my skull. I sat back heavily onto the bed.

"Take it easy, boy. Quite a knock you took." The pain subsided a little. Jefferies prattled on. "Who'd have thought old Iskandar would go off his chump like that?" He settled himself on the bed next to me and lit his pipe.

"Iskandar?" I queried blankly.

"The fellah you clobbered. Used to look after the place here. Always thought he was such a decent bloke, don't you know. So respectful, if you know what I mean. Always used to greet me properly." He darted me a look of reproof. "And a marvellous cook. You should taste his chicken satay. My word!"

"What about the body? Did they find the body?"

"Body?" Jefferies looked puzzled.

"Russell's. Alec Russell's body."

"Oh, that body." Jefferies exhaled a cloud of pungent smoke. As far as I could tell he must have been smoking old socks.

"No, 'fraid not. No body. But they're looking. There's a swamp behind the place, don't you know. And the estate. Thousands of places to hide a body. But it'll turn up. They'll find it by the smell. Never fails. Why, I remember once..."

I broke in before the flood of ghoulish reminiscences could start. "So there's no sign of Alec Russell?"

At that point there was the scraping of boots at the door of the room.

"Ah, the hero awakes," drawled a manicured voice.

The apparition in the doorway wore a khaki shirt and khaki shorts. A thin blond moustache teased its way across his upper lip. I surmised that he was a police officer from the pips on his shoulders and the swagger stick that he carried under his arm. Otherwise he might have been a gay boulevardier in fancy dress. He spoke, I noticed, out of the side of his mouth. He had an expression of ineffable superciliousness, much like a blue-blooded camel would wear on meeting a working-class dromedary. Having condescended to notice my existence, he went on talking to an unseen person outside the room.

"It's an open and shut case. This Iskandar fellow has done away with poor Alec Russell. The clearest case of murder that I've come across."

"That remains to be proven, Inspector," said a familiar voice.

There was a little bustle and in strode d'Almeida. His eyes twinkled as he looked at me.

"I hear that you've been using your head, young man," he said.

He turned to the Inspector. "I think we ought to hear what this young gentleman has to say before you condemn the accused — you will pardon me if I refer to him as the accused even if he hasn't been formally charged yet?" That was d'Almeida all over. Precise to the point of fastidiousness.

The Inspector harrumphed. I don't think he would have cared if d'Almeida referred to Iskandar as the Queen of Sheba. His aristocratic brow was clouded as he spoke to me.

"Well, go on then, spit it out."

I told them my story.

"There you are," said the Inspector with a note of triumph, "Cut and dried. Russell appears at the house around ten. Jefferies saw him as he drove up the road, isn't that so?"

Jefferies nodded, exhaling a cloud of vapour that would have made mustard gas smell like violets by comparison.

The Inspector continued. "He parks his car off the road where we found it, goes up to the house and there this Iskandar chappie does him in. Iskandar then disposes of the body, begins tidying up when he's interrupted by Mrs Russell and the boy."

I bristled a little at my description, but the Inspector continued heedless.

"He then makes a murderous attack on them, but gets cold feet when he finds that he's trapped. He bolts, your boy tackles him and we've got him."

The Inspector strode across the room to a cloth bag on a chair in the corner. "We've got the murder weapon, literally dripping with blood. We've got Russell's clothes, soaked in his blood. Opportunity, means and as for motive..."

He emptied the bag with a theatrical gesture. Two thick wads of notes fell out with a thump. "...we have this. Two hundred dollars meant for the estate workers. What could be clearer?"

I nodded in agreement.

But d'Almeida looked sceptical. "There is a reasonable doubt as to the accused's guilt. You do not have the body."

The Inspector rolled his eyes heavenward. He had a God-preserve-us-from-this-wog look on his face.

"Look d'Almeida," he said somewhat testily, "I know that you lawyer chappies are trained to see grey where everything is black and white but there's no doubt in my mind. The body will turn up and I'm going to see Iskandar swing for what he's done."

With that he marched out clutching the money.

"Well," said Jefferies, "I must toddle off now. My tiffin will be cold. And Mrs Russell will want seeing to. Coming, Dr Soong?"

Jefferies took his leave, followed by the egregious doctor.

We were alone in the room. D'Almeida turned to me. "What d'you think?"

Actually my brain hadn't yet recovered from the jolting around it had received and I wasn't thinking particularly straight, but I didn't want to appear uncommunicative with the man I hoped would be my future employer.

"I think that it seems to be a fairly clear case of murder as the Inspector says. He might cheat the noose with a plea of diminished responsibility, but I don't see how he can get around the facts."

"Facts?" said d'Almeida sardonically. "There aren't any facts. Just a pile of inferences drawn by that supercilious jackass in a Police Inspector's uniform. All we know for certain is that this man Iskandar had a *parang* and that there was blood on it."

"What about the money?" I queried.

"What about it? One, it's not a crime to have two hundred dollars. Two, we can't actually prove that Iskandar had the money; we can only infer this from the fact that the bag containing the money was in the same room as he was. Three, even if he had the money that doesn't mean that he killed Alec Russell."

"But the bloodstained clothes? Madeline identified them as Russell's."

"I don't doubt they are. That's what creates the doubt. What murderer bothers to strip the body before disposing of it? Why go to all the trouble? Separating the clothes from the body only doubles the chances of detection."

He had me there.

"There is something definitely wrong with this case," d'Almeida said as he began to pace around the room. "Too many unanswered questions. One, what was Russell doing here in the first place? Two, why did he bring the money with him? He was supposed to pay the estate workers. Why bring the bag to the house? And three, where has everything gone?"

He waved his hand around. It hadn't occurred to me before, but he was right. The room was empty.

"Let's look around," said d'Almeida abruptly.

He strode out rapidly. I followed.

We went through the rooms. The furniture was still there, but otherwise the place was bare. The dust lay thick on the covers. Old Miss Strachan was reputed to have been squirreling away knick-knacks for half a century. We opened the cupboards and rummaged through the bureau drawers. A couple of offended spiders scuttled off into more peaceful crannies. Of the old lady's hoard there was no sign. We went down the back stairs into the servants' quarters. Empty. Out in the yard was a large wire-mesh enclosure with a row of forlorn hen coops. Not a cluck interrupted the cicadas

"I don't understand it," I said, surveying the desolation, "Madeline told me that the old lady had a thousand chickens."

D'Almeida held his peace. We wandered to the kitchen. It was simply furnished, with a charcoal stove and two tables. A couple of cupboards stood against the wall. The stove was blackened and warm to the touch. This room at least showed signs of recent occupancy. The aroma of cooked meat still clung around the place. On the table lay a pile of coconut palm ribs of the sort that the Malays used to skewer meat and a basket of condiments and spices.

D'Almeida examined the contents of the basket. "What's this?" he asked sharply, pointing to a bowl of greasy white stuff.

I looked at it. Being single is an education. I knew immediately what it was.

"It's lard," I replied. "You use it for cooking."

D'Almeida nodded. He lifted the food cover that was on the other table. Four plucked white chickens lay there naked.

D'Almeida continued his examination of the room. In the corner next to the stove were two open bags of charcoal. D'Almeida bent down to examine the floor. In the charcoal dust was the unmistakable print of a shoe. He got up and slowly walked around the room. He opened the cupboards. There was the usual jumble of crockery and cutlery and a half-used bag of rice. Wandering out to the back of the kitchen we found a bicycle and a long pole from which two food carriers were slung. A basin of fresh blood was left out in the sun to congeal. D'Almeida dipped his finger experimentally into the stuff and tasted it.

I had been following all these antics with growing curiosity.

Suddenly d'Almeida rounded on me. "Well?" he said explosively, "what's the explanation of all this?"

I nearly jumped at the unexpected question. That was d'Almeida's way. He should have patented himself as a hiccup cure.

"Er...ah," I began, somewhat lamely, "it looks like Iskandar was helping himself to the Strachan chickens."

"Go on," said d'Almeida.

Gathering what wits I had, I continued.

"He... er... cooked the things and sold them."

A sudden thought struck me. "Satay. He made satay out of them. Jefferies said that his chicken satay was out of this world."

"Yes?" queried d'Almeida interrogatively.

I began warming up. "Iskandar had obviously been plundering the hen coop. He was selling satay on the side. He probably also sold all the loose things that he found in the house. Alec Russell came up unexpectedly, found the house empty and caught him with the last four chickens."

I lifted the food cover dramatically. "He accused him of theft and threatened to have him arrested. Iskandar then went amok, slashed Russell to death, disposed of the body and was cleaning up when we interrupted him."

"Interesting," said d'Almeida neutrally, "but it doesn't explain why Russell brought the money to the house."

I deflated like a punctured blimp. D'Almeida however seemed miles away. He hummed tunelessly and his eyes misted over. Abruptly he came out of his reverie and strode purposefully out of the kitchen. I was getting used to this. I trotted along after him.

We walked around the house and down the path in silence, passing the Indian constable who had been left on guard. Suddenly d'Almeida stopped. I almost bumped into him. His eyes were riveted on a hibiscus bush.

"Look," he said pointing. My heart pounded. He had spotted some vital clue. I strained my eyes to see what he was pointing at. A black-and-blue butterfly fluttered up.

"*Hypolimnas bolina incommoda*," said d'Almeida as the butterfly circled us, "it's supposed to be extinct in Malaya. I must write to the Raffles Museum."

I would have gladly throttled him. My nerves were shot and he wasn't helping one bit.

He started off again. "Come on," he called over his shoulder.

"Where are we going?" I puffed.

"To catch a thief," he replied enigmatically.

WE MOTORED back into town in silence. D'Almeida seemed preoccupied. My head was still sore from its recent intimate contact and my mind was numb from all the mental exercise. We pulled up at the office after forty-five minutes.

D'Almeida leapt out. "Wait here," he instructed.

I got out onto the five-foot way to stretch my legs. I longed for a smoke, but a quick search through my pockets only turned up a loose button, a couple of one-cent coins and some lint.

The whole affair was incomprehensible. I ran through the facts in my mind. Fact: Russell had been seen going to the house in the morning. Why? Either he had some business there or he had gone to see Iskandar. Fact: Russell had disappeared, but his clothes — soaked in blood — had been found in the house. Unless he had a habit of running around the jungle stark naked, it seemed inescapable that something had happened to him. Fact: Iskandar had been found in the house with a bloody *parang* and in the same room as a bag of money that Russell had been carrying. Conclusion, he had met Russell some time that morning. But why should Russell bring the money to the house? What business of his was so urgent that he would carry such a large sum of money into the ulu? It seemed likelier that Russell's business was with Iskandar. But what was that business? What had become of the Strachan chickens? Where were the antiques that the house was supposed to be bursting with? And how did Jefferies and the inscrutable incompetent Dr Soong fit in?

My head had begun to throb unmercifully by now, but a theory was beginning to form in my mind. Suppose, just suppose, that Iskandar and Russell were in league together. Suppose some of the stuff in the house was really valuable. Breach of trust — it's not unknown. Sell the antiques and keep the money. No one need ever know. Then they had a falling out and Iskandar killed Russell. Or maybe he got greedy when he saw all that money. The more I thought about it, the more attractive the theory grew. Of course Alec Russell was a scoundrel. No doubt about it. Cheating his own wife in connivance with a servant.

A dishevelled Malay in a dirty sarong was pawing at the Rolls. "Here you!" I yelled. "Get away! Go on! Beat it!"

He shuffled up to me and started whimpering. His claw-like hands gripped the lapels of my coat. "Stop that!" I thrust him away.

"Where are your manners young man? Haven't you any of the milk of human kindness in you?"

I was struck speechless. "Mr d'Almeida?" I queried weakly.

"Of course it's me," said the Malay. "Get in the car."

I started to climb into the driver's seat.

"No, no," ejaculated d'Almeida impatiently, "Use your head. How would it look, you driving me? Sit in the back, *tuan*."

Sheepishly I got out. He held the back door open for me with exaggerated deference.

D'Almeida took the wheel and drove off across Anderson Bridge and past the Municipal Buildings. I took the opportunity to expound my theory to d'Almeida. He listened and nodded. "Hmmm," he hummed noncommittally. He still seemed distracted. I subsided.

At length I plucked up the courage to speak again. "Where are we going?" I asked.

"Where would you most likely find stolen goods?" he shot back.

"I can't think..." I began.

He cut me short. "That's the trouble with you young fellows. You should practise more often."

A short drive brought us to one of the less salubrious parts of town. The streets were narrow and festooned with washing, like bunting hung out for the King's birthday. A foul-smelling canal ran parallel to the road.

D'Almeida stopped the car next to a rubbish tip reeking of rotting fruit and other unutterable stenches. He gestured to a side lane. It teemed with humanity like flies on a dung-heap.

"Thieves' market," he said laconically.

He hopped out of the car with surprising agility and disappeared into the throng.

Left to myself, I fell to musing. The day's events had been truly memorable. Not only had I suddenly been reunited with a lost love, but also I had been precipitated in the midst of a murder mystery, zipping around Singapore town with the legendary Clarence d'Almeida, who even now was hot on the trail of the killer. Who needs fiction?

I glanced idly around me. The tide of life swirled around the car, vibrant, pulsing, frenetic. Before me paraded a cross-section of all the coloured races of the Empire. As I watched this intercourse of nations it came to me that here was the heart of the city, the lifeblood that coursed through its veins. A mere mile away were the manicured lawns and glossy tinsel of white Singapore. But this was the reality.

I looked around me. The *tuans* might fool themselves that they were the driving force. A cursory glance around the teeming streets would belie that notion. The faces were alive, purposeful; one could imagine the fortunes that were made from nothing, the castles built from straw. So different from the languid, effete atmosphere of "civilised" society.

Yet paradoxically the attitude of the whites towards the Asiatics was one of patronising condescension. They lived in a cloud-cuckoo-land of racial superiority, oblivious to the fact that the real prosperity of the Colony was built on the sweat of these nameless faceless throngs. That the Inspector — Wyndham-Smythe, I later discovered his name was — considered himself to be in charge. To him d'Almeida — cocoa-brown d'Almeida — was a curiosity, like a talking dog or performing horse, not to be taken seriously. Yet d'Almeida it was who was doing the job. He was in there, mixing, looking, asking. No white man could hope to do that. D'Almeida would get information in a few hours that a white man would take days, perhaps weeks, to wheedle out.

My head ached and I was irritable. Inspector Wyndham-Smythe had gotten under my skin. His arrogance made me boil. I had spent the better part of my life in England, and was a King's Chinese through and through, like the rest of the Baba community. The climate in England might be rotten, but as a rule the Britons I met were decent chaps. Somewhere beyond the Suez Canal, things changed. A man might be perfectly civil and friendly in Cambridge or Croydon, but in Calcutta or Colombo he was a *sahib*, entrusted with the task of civilising the benighted natives. It was no different in the Settlements and the Malay States; the white *tuans* lorded it over the teeming masses. Here the *orang puteh* was on top of the pile. Even the lowliest white clerk in the great trading houses considered himself to be socially superior to mere Asiatics, no matter how respectable, intelligent or high-born. On this gulf, they were told, the Raj and the Pax Britannia depended. In retrospect, I realise that the arrogance and pomposity were born of self-doubt; a young District Officer placed over an area the size of an English county with thousands of non-English-speaking natives under him often retreated into bluster to maintain his authority. It didn't help that many of them were complete mediocrities; the really first-class chaps stayed in London to run the Empire.

I had by now worked myself up into quite a lather of indignation at the injustice of it all. I hadn't quite crossed the mental border into sedition when my profound reflections were interrupted by the return of d'Almeida. He was hot and sweaty, but there was the unmistakable gleam of triumph in his eyes. Under his arm he bore a package wrapped in newspaper. I glanced at my watch. He had been gone just over an hour.

D'Almeida tossed the packet into the back seat. "Take a look at this," he said, climbing back into the driver's seat.

I undid the strings. It was a jewel box, ornately decorated and somewhat dated in style. I lifted the lid. It played a few bars of some hackneyed sugar-sweet tune — Offenbach, I think it was. There were several compartments and trays. All were empty. I examined the cover. Incised into the metal of the inner face of the lid was an inscription. I squinted to make it out.

"Here, use this," said d'Almeida, handing me a piece of charcoal.

I rubbed the charcoal on the inscription. "To my dearest sister Emily," I read aloud, "with love from J.S. Malacca, 1906."

"If you've lost anything, it's a pretty good bet that sooner or later it will turn up there." He jerked his thumb in the direction of the teeming street.

"But how did you find this?" I asked d'Almeida wonderingly. "Don't tell me you knew exactly where to look."

D'Almeida gave a short laugh. "I really should keep you guessing. A good magician never explains his tricks."

I must have looked really crestfallen, because he laughed again and continued, "A little commonsense will take you along way, my lad. It's simple once you know the explanation. I was at Miss Strachan's house several times after her death. A few curios stuck in my memory. So I went hunting through the stalls to see if I could find any of them. And sure enough, here's one."

I gazed at d'Almeida admiringly. The public only saw the cool, efficient lawyer. To them he was nothing but a talented talking machine. But that day I was privileged to see the first-class mind at work. He really looked as if he was enjoying himself immensely.

It then occurred to me that all this fitted very nicely with my surmises. Alec Russell and Iskandar had conspired to sell the household effects. Here was confirmation.

"Doesn't this support my hypothesis?" I remarked, feeling somewhat pleased with myself. "Is it very valuable?"

"No, not very," replied d'Almeida. "Only worth a few dollars."

"I don't suppose you found out who sold this to the hawker in the first place."

"As a matter of fact I did. It was a white man. With a large moustache."

I was puzzled. This didn't fit.

"Jefferies?" I ventured.

"Perhaps," remarked d'Almeida noncommittally. Then he burst into activity again.

"Come, we have another visit to pay."

The engine roared to life, and I was thrown back against the seat as we zoomed off.

"I don't suppose," I called above the din, "that you're going to tell me where we're off to?"

WE DROVE back into town again. Crossing the river once more, we threaded our way through the narrow streets along its banks until we reached a whitewashed building overlooking a quay. I read the name; Masterson & Co., Ship Chandlers.

"Isn't this where Russell works... worked," I queried.

D'Almeida nodded. "Go in and ask for him," he instructed, "I'll be right behind you."

I glanced at him quizzically. "We know he isn't in," I said.

D'Almeida frowned. "I know that. But humour me. Keep asking for him until I tell you to stop."

Obediently, I got out of the car and walked in. The premises were open-fronted like most of the shops and offices along the quay. It was cool and dark. A Chinese clerk sat at a desk. I glanced at my watch. After five. All the Europeans would long since have departed to down their *stengahs* at their clubs.

"Hello," I called, "I've come to see Mr Russell."

The clerk at the desk looked up at me with a puzzled expression on his face. To him, an English-speaking Chinese was a novelty. He said nothing. I pressed him again.

He answered reluctantly. "Mr Lussell no here."

"Has he gone home then?" I persisted.

The clerk looked even more puzzled. "Mr Lussell no work here."

It was my turn to be puzzled. "What do you mean, no work here. Are you saying he's gone home?"

The clerk was getting irritated. "No, Mr Lussell no work here already. Long time no work. You talk to boss."

I felt that this was a good suggestion. "All right, let me speak to the boss."

"Boss no here."

Heavens above, I thought to myself, here we go again. "You mean boss no work here already?"

The clerk seemed flustered. "Boss no here. Boss here tomollow. You come back tomollow." He got up and began to shoo me out.

I was getting peeved. "Now hold on. Will Alec Russell be in tomorrow or not?"

"You talk to boss. You talk to boss."

I was rescued by d'Almeida, who suddenly materialised at my side. "Right," he said, "let's go."

Leaving one rather annoyed clerk at the door, we piled into the car and drove off.

"One more call and then we're done," remarked d'Almeida. "You won't mind working after hours?" I signified my assent.

To my surprise d'Almeida drove right back to the office.

"Wait here," he commanded and disappeared up the back stairs.

He was back in ten minutes, in his proper guise. He gestured towards the wheel. I climbed into the front seat and took it.

He got in next to me. "His Majesty's prison, if you please."

I glanced at him out of the corner of my eye. There was the ghost of a smile on his lips.

THE GREAT gloomy edifice that was the prison loomed over us. Across the road were the grounds of the General Hospital looking tranquil and park-like. But His Majesty's Prison brooded greyly and sombrely at the edge of town. They shot the 1915 mutineers outside its walls. The bullet holes were still there. It was not a pleasant place. I don't think His Majesty would have been happy there.

As we passed through the gates they clanged shut behind us with a disquieting finality. I waited in the car while d'Almeida had a quick word with the Governor. They all knew him here. He was out in a moment. A doleful Sikh warder led us down the melancholy corridors.

"Are we going to see Iskandar?" I asked under my breath. D'Almeida nodded.

"How did you manage that? We're not representing him."

"I lied," replied d'Almeida shortly.

We stopped in front of a heavy iron door. The warder opened it with much clanking and rattling. The door creaked as he drew it open. I'm sure they do that deliberately; it creates such a dramatic atmosphere. Iskandar was lying on a bare steel bed in the corner.

"Oy, *bangun*," growled the warder, "lawyer *datang*."

Iskandar looked at d'Almeida with surly eyes. Then he noticed me. He cast me a homicidal glance that would have felled an elephant at fifty paces.

"Hello Mr Iskandar," began d'Almeida pleasantly, "we're here to represent you."

A look of puzzlement crept into his eyes, but still he said nothing.

D'Almeida turned to me. "Would you please ask the warder for a cup of coffee. Black, no sugar and make sure it's hot."

By now I knew better than to question him. I left him alone in the cell and sauntered down the corridor.

When I returned with the coffee, d'Almeida was sitting on the table staring at Iskandar. Iskandar was sitting on the bed staring at d'Almeida. For all I knew they might have been at it since I left. The warder let me into the cell again. d'Almeida took the cup from me. He stood up and began to pace. Iskandar watched him sulkily. He still hadn't said a word.

D'Almeida spoke. "You know you could hang," he said nonchalantly, as if this were some trifling inconvenience.

He held the coffee cup in one hand as he spoke. He had the habit of waving the cup to emphasise his words.

"A man comes up to a deserted house, carrying two hundred dollars. The man later disappears. You are found in possession of the house and the money. The man's wife appears. What do you do? Do you pretend that nothing has happened, like a rational being? No, according to my young friend here, you make a murderous attack on them."

D'Almeida paused and took a sip.

"But were you actually trying to attack them?" he said softly.

He moved up close to Iskandar, so that he was looming over him.

"Or were you trying to escape before you were recognised?"

He raised his voice suddenly "You called Mrs Russell 'Madeline'. How did you know who she was? You supposedly hadn't met her. How did you, a servant, know her Christian name? Totally inexplicable unless..."

Here d'Almeida threw his arms out in an extravagant gesture. The coffee sloshed out of his cup onto Iskandar's arm. He gave a yelp of pain and surprise. D'Almeida's hand darted out and caught Iskandar's arm. He wiped it on the bed clothes before the latter recovered from the shock. The sheet was stained with brown. But the arm was that curious off-grey pink colour that we call white.

"...unless you already knew her, Alec," concluded d'Almeida quietly.

The whole episode had taken only a second. My mind was still reeling. He turned to me. "Dennis Chiang, Alec Russell. Alec Russell, my associate Dennis Chiang," he said conversationally, introducing us.

I was struck dumb. d'Almeida was speaking again. "The game's up Alec," he said tranquilly, "you might as well come clean."

Iskandar — or Alec — had his head between his hands.

"All right, all right," he said, with a stifled groan, "you win." He looked up and his face was drawn. "I am Alec Russell. How did you find out? Does Madeline know?"

D'Almeida shook his head. "The only people who know are in this room."

"How did you find out?" repeated Russell.

"You're not the only one who can impersonate a Malay, you

know. You'll have to do better than that if you want to get away with it. It's the little things that will give you away. Iskandar – Alexander – Alec. Not very original. Never choose an alias related to your own name. I asked myself, isn't Iskandar rather a grand name for a *jaga*. A few other things. Like using lard to cook your satay. What self-respecting Malay would use the fat of a pig? And the fact that your clothes hadn't a tear on them. If someone had been slashed to death, you'd expect a rent or two wouldn't you? And your knowing Madeline's name. Little things."

I could contain myself no longer. "But the *parang*. He attacked us. How about that?"

"You thought he was attacking you." said d'Almeida, "A natural conclusion under the circumstances. But if he was intent on killing you, he would have raised the *parang* like this..." d'Almeida crooked his arm above his head. "...instead of holding it in front of him like you described." He turned to Russell. "You were trying to get out before Madeline realised who you were, weren't you?" Russell nodded.

My head was whirling. "But... but the blood?" I asked weakly.

"Unless I miss my guess, that's chicken blood."

Again Russell nodded.

"Why?" I asked, completely mystified. "Why this whole elaborate rigmarole? And what about Madeline?"

D'Almeida looked straight at Russell. "You lost your job didn't you. Six months ago. Shortly after Miss Strachan died."

I looked at d'Almeida with wonder. He answered my unspoken question.

"I peeked at the staff ledger at Masterson's while you were having your tête-à-tête with the clerk." He turned again to Russell. "You couldn't bring yourself to tell your wife, am I right?"

"Yes, yes," answered Russell in a strained voice, "you seem to know it all."

"But why the fancy dress?" I persisted. "Why didn't you just get another job?"

Russell rounded on me with vehemence. "Do you think that jobs for an *orang puteh* grow on trees like coconuts? You think you can just sit around and wait for one to drop into your lap." His voice was bitter. "God knows I tried. But no one had anything. No one! I tried selling things in the streets. But some pompous ass of a Police Inspector rounded me up and gave me a lecture on the white man's burden. 'Not done for a *tuan* to go flogging stuff on the five-foot-way. What will the natives think? Can't let down the side.' Silly old goat!"

"So you went native," remarked d'Almeida quietly.

"So I went native. I have, shall we say, a talent for impersonation. Not perfect, as you say, but still a talent. And I can cook."

"Aunt Emily's chickens!" I exclaimed.

"Yes," answered Russell sardonically, "Aunt Emily's chickens. That's what gave me the idea in the first place. Hundreds of the fat little buggers pecking around. I only did a couple at first, just to tide me over until I got a job. But things didn't improve. And the money was good. You'd be surprised how much a street hawker can turn over each day. I used to cycle down to Raffles Place every tiffin time. I'd be sold out within an hour."

"Where did Jefferies come in?" I asked curiously.

"Jefferies? What's that old buffoon got to do with it?" Russell replied with surprise.

"He was selling your aunt's possessions on the sly."

D'Almeida broke in. "I think that I may have misled you. A white man with a moustache sold Miss Strachan's possessions. But I think it is clear that Mr Russell here is an accomplished actor."

I was flabbergasted. So I was right after all.

"You cheating bastard," I exclaimed, "robbing Madeline blind behind her back."

"Not robbing," he rejoined with some heat. "I thought of it as... as a temporary loan. Besides, it's as much mine as hers," he replied rather defensively.

"To think that you almost got away with it," I said angrily.

"Almost," interposed d'Almeida. "Tell us what happened."

"Almost," repeated Russell. He sighed. "I suppose that I got over-confident towards the end. Today was to have been the last day. I've got a job in Colombo. We're leaving at the end of next month. Besides, Madeline will be of age soon, and the trust money becomes hers. I was going to tell her. Honestly. I'd have paid back every cent to her. She'd have understood."

"I drove up to the house after I'd collected the workers' salary. That's what I usually do. I have to do the cooking early to catch the tiffin crowd. I was in a hurry. Normally I'd change first, but this get-up takes a long time to put on. So I worked in my suit. I'd got the last four chickens ready. The blood was in a basin. You put it out in the sun to gel. I was careless. I tripped and splashed myself. So I changed into my Iskandar suit. I was cleaning up in the room when you came in. God, the shock I had. My only thought was to get out quick. That's when you bolted the door on me. I really panicked. So I chopped up the floor and got out through there. And I'd have got away too if you hadn't got such a hard head." He rubbed his head at the memory.

"Why didn't you tell the police?" I asked.

"How could I? I was out cold. When I woke up I was here already. Besides, they can't hang me. They've got no proof that I've committed murder. I know my rights. They can't make me say anything."

"There is such a thing as theft," remarked d'Almeida evenly. "Dishonest misappropriation of someone else's property. You could be put away a long time."

"Look," said Russell desperately, "I didn't mean to steal anything. I just couldn't tell Madeline that I'd lost my job. It was only for a few months. I'd have paid her back. Every cent. Plus interest. Please, do what you like with me but don't tell Madeline." His eyes were pleading.

"Well," said d'Almeida, "I think we can get you off. But Mrs Russell must be told." He stared steadily at Russell. Russell nodded woodenly.

"There is just one other thing," continued d'Almeida, "I'm afraid I... ah... misrepresented our position to get in here. I presume that you would like to retain us to represent you?"

Russell nodded again. "Good," remarked d'Almeida, "I'd like your instructions in writing, if you please. And not a word to the Bar Committee."

There's little else to tell. In due course Alec Russell alias Iskandar was hauled up before the Police Courts to be committed to stand trial in the High Court for murder. It wasn't a full dress trial of course. That would come later, complete with judge and wig and jury and press, but only if the Police Magistrate found that there was a case to go to trial. D'Almeida's tactics were simple; say nothing. Let the prosecution put up a case.

The prosecutor was none other than our good friend Inspector Wyndham-Smythe. Wyndham-Smythe tried valiantly to spin a web of circumstantial evidence around Iskandar, but d'Almeida fenced skilfully, pointing out how each apparently damning piece of evidence was in reality but a mirage. And when d'Almeida boxed the good Inspector into a corner by getting him to admit that the lab report identified the bloodstains on the murder weapon and on Alec Russell's clothes to be non-human, the Police Magistrate had no choice but to discharge the prisoner. The prosecution had failed to show a *prima facie* case he ruled, banging down the gavel. You could hear the gnashing of Wyndham-Smythe's teeth from the other end of the courtroom. We left him swearing to high heaven that he would see justice done.

Unfortunately for Inspector Wyndham-Smythe, Alec Russell reappeared out of the jungle that very day. Iskandar for his part, disappeared, never to be seen again. The press had a field day. But Russell obstinately refused to answer any questions. The police gave it up as a bad job. Russell and Madeline left on the first boat to Colombo.

I NEVER saw her again. That is, not until today's paper.

She makes a lovely widow.

I wonder if she still remembers me.

THE WIDOWS' TALE

THERE IS a Chinese saying that wealth only lasts three generations. It has been my misfortune to be four generations removed from the fount of wealth. My father's grandfather came to the Straits Settlements shortly after Raffles had conned the Sultan of Johore into ceding Singapore to the British. Great-grandfather did a little of this and a little of that, but his big break came when he was appointed gambier and opium farmer — he didn't grow the stuff, just imported it and collected the taxes for the British. Anyway, a couple of years as the honourable East India Company's tax collector provided him the capital to buy a small coastal vessel, and the rest, as they say, is history.

Unlike most of his countrymen, he didn't go home to China when he made his pile. It is the ambition of every Chinese coolie to become a *towkay* and go back to the ancestral village to put up a grand mansion and generally swank around. Great-grandfather didn't. He stayed in the Straits, married and founded a family. My suspicion is that he couldn't go back — the southern Chinese are notoriously rebellious, and I think that Great-grandfather may have trodden on the pigtails of some mandarins. Anyway, whatever the reason may have been, we became Babas — Straits Chinese, born and bred in the Settlements, and owing allegiance to the British Crown. We were the King's Chinese, British subjects, whose loyalty was beyond question. During the Great War, Eu Tong Sen even bought a tank for the war effort out of his own money, and the battleship HMS *Malaya* was paid for to a large extent by the contributions of the Baba community of Malaya and the Straits Settlements.

Grandfather carried on the family trading business, but decided that his two sons should be brought up as gentlemen. So it came to pass that my uncle and my father both attended the Anglo-Chinese School and in due course became lawyers. I have very little recollection of my parents, who died when I was two. In my mind's eye they appear as shadows flitting at the edge of memory. My uncle took me into his house as a son; he himself had three daughters by his first wife. After the third, he stopped trying for a male heir, and as fate had provided him with an orphaned nephew (complete with the right surname), he felt that he had done his bit for the continuance of the family.

My uncle's first wife is also a dim memory, for she too died shortly after I became part of my uncle's household. Uncle married again, to a vivacious young woman ten years his junior. To me, she was Mak; she provided me with the warmth and love that my distant and rather Victorian uncle could not provide. I never felt anything less than a son towards her, and she treated me and her stepdaughters as her own children. Uncle tried again for a son of his own, but after two more daughters he gave it up as a bad job and resigned himself to the fact that the survival of the Chiang line rested on my bony shoulders.

Uncle determined that I should be brought up as a proper English gentleman. So it was that I was forcibly wrenched from my sun-filled childhood at the age of twelve and packed off to an English boarding school in the dank and dismal Fens. Over this episode I draw a veil; suffice to say that until I experienced a Japanese prison camp I always considered Fenton Abbey to be the hardest of penal institutions. I never saw my uncle again; he died just before I went up to Cambridge. I was fortunate in that my uncle as executor of my father's estate had established a trust fund that paid for my education and subsistence. Mak was left to fend for her and the five girls on what was left of the family fortune.

After spending half my life abroad, I finally came back to Singapore, a stranger in my home and homeland. Fortunately, Mr d'Almeida felt warmly enough about my late father to take me in sight unseen. No doubt Mak also worked on him quietly behind the scenes. She could, when she got going, be as inexorable as a steamroller; but he was too much of a gentleman to resent a mother's importunity. Getting a place in chambers so quickly was a bit of luck. Though my trust fund saw me through school and university, there was precious little left by the time I graduated; certainly not enough for a family of seven, two servants and a dog to live on.

Uncle was brought up as a gentleman, and in those days this signified more than just a sign on a lavatory door. He had little time for financial affairs. He sold land when he needed a little extra spending money. Legal practice to him was the interlude between breakfast at the Turf Club and tea and tennis at the Recreation Club. By the time I got home, the residue of my uncle's estate consisted of a few shares, an anaemic bank account and the family mansion — a crumbling warren thrown up at the turn of the century by a rubber baron, given as a wedding present by Grandfather (who got it cheap when the baron went bust).

The slide into genteel poverty was a common enough phenomenon among the Babas. Sometimes it was precipitated by a spendthrift wastrel son (a Baba black sheep, one might say). More often than not, the transition was so gradual as to be unnoticeable. One simply woke up one day to the realisation that one was poor. The three Settlements were full of old widows living among the faded remnants of bygone opulence. Such was the case with the Khoo widows, who lived down the hill from us.

KHOO GUAN KIM was a second-generation Baba whose father had struck it rich in rubber and tin. Khoo himself was more interested in the racetrack and probably wouldn't have recognised a rubber tree even if he had walked into one in broad daylight. The Great Depression wiped him out, and he died shortly thereafter.

Khoo was unusual among the Babas in having two wives. A British judge had declared that the Chinese were inherently polygamous, and it was not uncommon among the non-Baba Chinese (China gerk or, more politely Sinkhek, as we called them) for a successful businessman to have several wives — they accumulated wives like they collected Rolls-Royces or objets d'art. As soon as they were rich enough, they sent back to China for a bride. The richer they were, the more they could afford.

But among the Babas monogamy was generally the rule, or at best, sequential matrimony if one had the opportunity (which was rare, as Nonyas generally outlived their husbands). The Baba bridegroom would not think of getting a China bride except as a last resort. The ideal was a Nonya from one of the old established families.

Nonyas were in short supply, so the bride's family had much more influence than normal among the Chinese. In fact, in a reversal of the usual Chinese custom, the groom went to live with the bride's family.

However, Mr Khoo had gone beyond the usual hunting grounds and his two wives were Peranakan Chinese from the Dutch East Indies. I think that they may have been distantly related. The story was that Khoo was offered them as a job lot and thought that the bargain was too good to miss.

Anyway, he set them up on separate floors of a terrace house in Buckley Road, the elder one on top and the younger one at the bottom. While their lord and master was alive, there was an armed truce between the two, breaking out sporadically into guerrilla warfare. It was only when Khoo died that open hostilities commenced. Like all Chinese, Baba or Sinkhek, he refused to contemplate the fact of his own mortality. Thus, when he finally snuffed it, there was no will. Sorting out an intestate's estate is complicated enough when the beneficiaries are friendly; when there's money around and two hostile claimants, the whole business turns labyrinthine. The same judge who decided that the Chinese were inherently polygamous also decided that all widows were equal (a notion unknown to Chinese law). This baleful precedent had been firmly established in the law reports since the end of the last century, and with the certitude that the law was on her side, neither of the Khoo widows would defer to the other on the question of letters of administration. The dispute dragged on and on for over half a decade, while the estate over which they wrangled dwindled away.

The two ladies were generally too refined to indulge in shouting matches or physical attacks. Warfare was psychological for the most part. Wife No 1 (I can't remember her real name; we just referred to her as Mrs Khoo Besar) would get a sudden urge to tango just when Wife No 2 (Mrs Khoo Kechik) was about to sleep. In these old terrace houses, with their wooden floors, it sounded like a stampede of brontosauri. Kechik would respond by shaving Besar's cactuses bald. Besar would get her own back by hanging out her washing to dry right over Kechik's. And so it went on for years and years. The courts opened a special file for the complaints and private summonses of the Khoo widows.

I got involved because d'Almeida & d'Almeida represented Mrs Khoo Kechik in the matter of the estate. Actually, I was precipitated into the affair by a sudden escalation in hostilities. Mrs Khoo Besar had hung out her best *kebaya* to dry, draped on a bamboo pole projecting from her upstairs veranda in the normal fashion. Mrs Khoo Kechik had chosen that very day to offer prayers to the soul of their dear departed husband. She lit giant three-foot joss sticks, right under Besar's washing. Her upstairs neighbour was incensed. They had words. Words led to blows, and blows led to the Police Courts.

Cuthbert d'Almeida appeared on Kechik's behalf at the hearing of the private summons. Besar had taken out a summons against Kechik for criminal assault and Kechik had retaliated in kind. The Magistrate, a fresh-faced product of some minor provincial university, was clearly out of his depth when confronted by these two genteel old ladies who kept darting venomous glances at each other. He had a thick dossier in front of him, and seemed hardly to know where to begin. Evidently each Mrs Khoo had recited the entire life history of the other, with particulars of every iniquity, in her complaint. Having heard submissions by counsel for both parties, he decided that Mrs Khoo Kechik was more to blame in this instance and bound her over to keep the peace. The cross-summons was dismissed. The smirk on Besar's face was most unladylike. No doubt they kept score.

Outside the court, Cuthbert explained to Kechik her precise situation.

"Well, Madam, I'm afraid that you are going to have to be civil to the other Mrs Khoo, whatever the provocation. The Magistrate has been very indulgent under the circumstances, and I fear that any further trouble may lead him to fine you. If you cannot pay, he would have no alternative but to incarcerate you."

He mopped his glistening brow with a gigantic square of cotton. "We have finally got the High Court to order an equitable distribution of the estate *in specie*, and my learned friend Mr Lim and myself will be submitting a list of items belonging to the late lamented Mr Khoo to the judge next week. I anticipate that the matter will be disposed of finally within a fortnight, and I must emphasise that any further fracas will be detrimental to your interests."

A look of puzzlement crossed the brow of his client. I stepped into the breach, translating Cuthbert's peroration into Baba Malay.

"Bibik, you must not fight with the other Mrs Khoo again. Otherwise you may go to jail. The judge will divide your husband's goods next week. You will get half and she will get the other half." Kechik nodded comprehendingly.

Cuthbert beamed and sponged off another half pint of sweat. "Excellent, excellent, I am glad that you appreciate the situation. I am confident that the outcome will be satisfactory to both parties. Now, if you will excuse me, I must be off to my next appointment. Mr Chiang here will escort you to your abode."

He turned to me and I signified my assent. With a slight bow to Kechik, he waddled off hurriedly into the crowd like the White Rabbit on his way to the Queen of Hearts's tea party.

Normally, I would have walked or taken a trolley bus. However, I didn't feel that it would be appropriate with Kechik in tow. She had the look of a lady, if you know what I mean. She wasn't big — in contrast to the other Mrs Khoo, who was of Wagnerian proportions. On the contrary, it looked as if the next strong wind would carry her off.

Like all Nonyas she was carefully dressed in the usual *sarong kebaya*. The *kerosang* that fastened the front of her *kebaya* was not particularly ornate or expensive, unlike the baubles that bedecked the wives of many of the *towkays*. There were no rings or bangles or diamond brooches. She had, nevertheless, an air of gentleness and gentility. One would never have guessed that she had once throttled her upstairs neighbour's chickens with her bare hands.

I hailed a cab and we bundled ourselves in. Halfway down North Bridge Road I suddenly remembered that I hadn't had time to cash a cheque. I put my hand surreptitiously into my pocket. The only things I could feel were the customary ball of lint and a few square-shaped one-cent coins. I leaned over to Kechik.

"Bibik, I hope you do not mind if we drop in at my place for a short while. It is not far from your house. I must get a few things."

She nodded, gently fanning herself with her fan and sniffing occasionally at a knot tied in her handkerchief, which she had doused with eau-de-cologne. I gave quick instructions to the cab driver.

Ten minutes later we pulled up under the porch of the family mansion. I bounded out, leaving Kechik in the cab. Taking the steps two at a time, I nearly collided into Mak, who was arranging orchids from the garden in a vase in the entrance foyer.

"Ayoh, why are you running around the house? Have you eaten?"

This last part was the standard greeting among the Chinese, Baba or Sinkhek. It probably reflects some racial memory of famine and deprivation over millennia. If Mak had her way, I would have been eating from sunrise to sunset.

I gave her a quick peck on the cheek. "Yes, Mak, I had tiffin in the office. I must get money to pay the taxi driver. Mrs Khoo is waiting for me."

With that, I hurried up the stairs to my room.

"Mrs Khoo? What Mrs Khoo?" Mak shot after me as I disappeared up the landing. She went to the door. With an impatient clicking of her tongue, she sailed down the steps to the taxi.

Having retrieved my spare stash of cash from under the *almeirah*, I galloped down the stairs and out the door, just in time to see the taxi disappearing through the garden gate. Mak and Kechik were just proceeding to the door.

Mak shook her head at me disapprovingly. "Why are you like that? You should ask Mrs Khoo in."

To Kechik she said, "Please excuse my Boy, Tachi. He may be a lawyer but he is a *gobblock*." She wagged her finger at me in admonishment.

"He went to England, you know, to Cambridge," she added with motherly pride.

The two ladies glided through the foyer and along the corridor out onto the back veranda. I hung around irresolutely, and then followed them.

Mak turned to me and whispered, "Boy, call Ah Sum to bring tea."

Obediently I set off in search of Ah Sum, who as usual was pottering around behind the house in the kitchen garden.

Ah Sum was our *amah* and had been with us since a time beyond the memory of living man (or at any rate, beyond the memory of me and my cousins). She was in fact Grandfather's servant and had joined his household as a girl of twelve, just before Queen Victoria's Golden Jubilee. All her life she wore the standard white blouse and black pants of her calling. She doted on us children, and while the other servants dropped away one by one, she stayed on. There is no more faithful creature in the world than an old black-and-white *amah*.

Despite what must have been nearly a half century in the Straits, Ah Sum had contrived to pick up neither English nor Malay. Since I had no ability to speak any Chinese dialect whatever, our conversations generally were a pantomime of monosyllables and mime. However, she had been with us so long that she readily understood what I wanted.

I returned to find Mak, Kechik and my cousin June seated around the marble-topped table in the veranda. June was the youngest daughter of Uncle's first wife. My uncle was a whimsical man. He had given his first daughter the conventional name of Gek Neo; but his subsequent children were called May and June. He continued the series with Mak — her daughters were Julie and Augusta respectively. It's just as well that he didn't have sons; Julius and Augustus are terrible names to inflict on small boys.

Kechik was telling Mak the story of her life. From the way the two Nonyas spoke one might have concluded that they had been friends all their lives, instead of having just met that very day. This is the way with Nonyas; there are so few of them that they feel a sense of sisterhood. Nothing gets them going more than a tale of woe regarding the shenanigans of their menfolk.

Kechik was just explaining that Khoo, though otherwise quite a good husband (as far as husbands go), couldn't provide her with a child. Khoo had an eye for the horses, but fortunately not one for the ladies. Ah, how hard life was! Still, she was thankful for small blessings, she had her health and her house. Unfortunately, there was that *perumpuan sial* upstairs, who made life a trial. The iniquities of that woman! A long catalogue of sins followed. Mak listened sympathetically, clicking her tongue every now and then in commiseration.

I insinuated myself into an empty chair next to June, who was lapping it all up — much better than the radio. The next time she met her friends, she would have a whole lot of news for them. One made one's own amusements in a sleepy town like Singapore, and disinterring long-buried skeletons was always guaranteed to command a rapt audience.

The tea came, together with Mak's *sireh* box. The two ladies helped themselves to the betel nut paste and lime, while June and I poured ourselves a cup of tea.

Kechik had just finished explaining that the estate had been tied up since her husband's death because of the lawyers, and darted me a reproachful glance, as if I had personally conspired for the last six years to keep her from her rightful inheritance. Mak and June turned to me too, and I felt compelled to defend my profession.

"It's not as easy as it seems. Normally, when there are two widows and no children each would get half. The problem is that neither of the widows wants to let the other handle the estate alone, and obviously they won't handle it together. So we have to be careful to be fair to both parties. Anyway, the estate was a mess, or so I've been told. It's taken this long just to sort out what Mr Khoo owned and who his debtors and creditors are. The other Mrs Khoo's lawyer is a very suspicious man and has queried everything we've proposed. But the good news is that we've just got a court order to divide the residue of the estate *in specie*, so things should be settled soon."

"*In specie?*" queried June with a quizzical look. "You mean that one Mrs Khoo takes the dogs and the other one takes the cats?"

"No, silly," I answered, "I mean that we divide up the estate 50-50, each widow taking half of the goods. This way we don't have to sell the stuff. Mr Lim and Cuthbert will be going through whatever remains and making a list. The judge will then have a look at it and give his approval for the distribution."

"How will he decide?" asked June.

"I heard that he'll pronounce a Solomonic judgement and cut the baby in half. Whatever's on the top floor goes to Mrs Khoo number one and whatever's on the bottom floor goes to Mrs Khoo number two. Heaven knows, we've considered every other alternative to divide the estate equitably; this is the only one left."

Mak had been tutored by American missionaries in her youth (an unusual state of affairs for a Nonya) and understood English quite well though she preferred not to speak it. Kechik, however, was completely lost during the exchange between June and me. She looked at me interrogatively. Explaining legal concepts in simple

English is hard enough, but translating them into the Baba patois was completely beyond my ability. However, I did my best.

"The judge will divide your husband's goods next week, Bibik. Mr Cuthbert and Mr Lim will write down what is in the house, and you will get what is in your part of the house and the other Mrs Khoo will take what is in her part."

At this Kechik became agitated. "Not fair, not fair," she said, dabbing at her eyes with her handkerchief.

The other Mrs Khoo (a pox on her) would be sure to take advantage, she said. She lived in the upper part of the house, which was bigger, and therefore had more of Khoo's things. Their dear husband's body wasn't even cold yet when that woman started moving things to her part of the house. She took the most valuable items. She would hide them for certain before the list was made, if she hadn't sold them already.

Kechik paused to blow her nose, and then continued with renewed vim and vigour. All her life the other Mrs Khoo had bullied her. She might be younger, but that didn't give the other one the right to lord it over her. While her dear husband was alive, he made sure that she was treated properly. She was the husband's favourite, but when he died (evil day!) that Shaitan showed her true character. That woman had even taken the expensive Chinese vase that her husband had given to her. It was the most valuable thing left, but beyond the money it was a gift from the dear departed to her personally. Now the *perempuan sial* would get it, because it was in her part of the house.

Mak patted her on her shoulder and muttered a few comforting words.

"My boy here will make sure that you are treated fairly."

I nodded in agreement.

Kechik composed herself, thanked Mak for her kind hospitality and invited her to drop by at her place. A few more pleasantries were exchanged, and then Kechik indicated that she had to go.

I hurried out to dispatch Dollah the gardener to flag down a rickshaw.

The rickshaw took a good half hour to procure, as Dollah had to trot all the way down to the main road to get one. Eventually, the transportation was arranged, and Kechik rose to leave.

As we ushered Kechik down the front steps, June said to me, "I will take her back if you want. I have nothing on this afternoon and she has offered to show me her orchids."

"Would you really? I'd be ever so grateful. I've a pile of work at the office."

"No trouble at all." June and Kechik got into the rickshaw, which was pulled by a bronzed coolie with a wide straw hat. They clattered over the gravel and out onto the road which led downhill back towards town.

After a quick goodbye hug, I set off to catch the trolley bus back to the office.

The sun was past its zenith, but the air was as hot as if it had come straight out of a baker's oven. Fortunately, the road ran downhill from our house, but even so it was uncomfortable work.

I glanced to my left as I toiled sweatily downwards. In those days the domain around Government House was open to all and sundry. The cool tree-lined paths beckoned me. Deciding that Cuthbert and Mr d'Almeida wouldn't mind if I took an extra half-hour to get back, I left the road and strolled through the impressive wrought-iron gates.

The path meandered past the *sepoys* guarding the drive that led up to the porch of Government House. That was where His Excellency the Governor of the Straits Settlements and High Commissioner to the Malay States (referred to universally as "H.E.") held court. I turned right onto the avenue of stately rain trees and after a brisk walk in the delicious shade reached the main road, where the trolley buses clattered their way along the middle of the street.

I got to the bus stop just in time to see my bus pull out. With a running jump I hurled myself onto the footboard of the departing bus, elbowed my way into the centre through a scrum of sweaty humanity, and hung onto the strap while the bus rattled back into town. By the time I got back to the office I felt like a freshly-baked bread roll.

I didn't get home until late that night. The fireflies were already twinkling among the mangosteen trees when I finally tottered through the garden gate. I let myself in, trying not to wake anyone; we retired early as a general rule, as there were no night-time distractions to stay up for. Besides, electricity wasn't free and it cost a pretty penny to light up the whole mansion.

Thinking only of a shower and my bed, I dragged myself up the stairs. To my surprise, I bumped into June at the top of the stairs, clad in her pyjamas.

"Every word was true you know," she said, without preliminaries. That was just like June. No consideration for the weary. No "Hello cousin, would you like a drink" or anything of the sort. Bang, straight to the point.

"What? What was true?" I asked tiredly.

"Everything that Mrs Khoo told us. I went to her place — she has the nicest orchids, you know — it is just as she says. Small, but very nice, you know. But the upstairs is much bigger. And there are a lot more things upstairs."

"And how would you know?" I rejoined irritatedly. "You've never been. It's all hearsay."

"Ha! You just hear what I say. I saw with my own eyes. Piles and piles of things."

"Really?" I asked, my curiosity piqued. "You can't have been upstairs. Not with the other Mrs Khoo there. She would have grilled your liver for supper."

"We went when she was out. Mrs Khoo has a key."

I was lost for a moment. "Mrs Khoo has a key? Downstairs Mrs Khoo or upstairs Mrs Khoo?"

"Your Mrs Khoo of course, *gobblock*. She has a key to the upstairs. She let me in and showed me around upstairs Mrs Khoo's flat. I saw old Khoo's vase, the one he gave to your Mrs Khoo."

My head was beginning to spin a little by now. Too many Khoos in the plot. "Wait, wait, you've lost me. Call them Besar and Kechik like we do. Start again."

She folded her arms and started again, speaking slowly as if instructing a retarded child.

"Okay, your Mrs Khoo — Kechik — has got a key to the other Mrs Khoo — Besar's — flat. Got that? Good. She — Kechik — let me in to have a look at the flat. It is really true what she said. There is a lot more things in the upstairs flat. Kechik has hardly anything. Well, not hardly, but not as much. And there is the vase. It is an antique. Very valuable. Only one of its kind in the world. She — Besar — keeps it in an *almeirah* right in the hall. She does not even display it. She is a real dog in the kennel."

"You mean manger," I corrected.

"Kennel, manger, whatever. Anyway, she took the vase out of spite. She knows that old man Khoo gave it to Kechik. She does not even want to show it off. She hides it away in that dusty old *almeirah*. It rightly belongs to Kechik."

"Hold on a sec. How did Kechik get a key to Besar's flat?"

"She has had it for years and years. She said that she had it made when old man Khoo was alive. She used to creep up and spy on them when Khoo was upstairs with the other Mrs Khoo."

I rolled my eyes heavenward.

"Don't look so like that, okay. I would have done the same —

not that I will marry a man who already has a wife, but you know what I mean. Anyway, she once... she once..."

Here June dissolved into a fit of giggles. After choking for a minute, she continued. "She once went upstairs and put icing sugar into Besar's *bedak sejok*, her face powder. Besar had ants crawling all over her face in the night and did not know why." She collapsed into a chair, with tears streaming.

I put on my stern face. "You really shouldn't go around with Mrs Khoo trespassing on other people's property."

June collected herself. "Hey, don't you use that big brother tone with me. I am older than you, okay."

She had me there, though actually the age difference was only a matter of months. She grabbed my arm. "Come, I have got something to show you."

She pulled me into her room, which she normally shared with May. May was away spending the night with friends; Mak was scandalously lax with the girls, so the neighbours used to say. They would never get married, or at best would end up with the dregs of society. The old Nonyas clicked their tongues, but the girls had fun regardless.

On the washstand next to her bed stood an object draped with an old curtain. With the air of a conjurer, June stepped up to the object and whipped away the cover. It was a vase. A Chinese vase. A large, expensive-looking Chinese vase.

I BLINKED in the dim light of the single bulb. "You've got a vase," I said, somewhat redundantly.

June nodded.

"*Where* did you get that vase?" I queried, with an uncomfortable sensation of impending doom.

"From Mrs Khoo — I mean Besar's — flat. We took it with us

when we left. Mrs Khoo asked me to keep it for her."

"Kechik asked you to keep it for her," I repeated slowly, trying to grasp the enormity of the crime.

June nodded again.

The tiredness had left me entirely. "You've got to put it back, right away and no arguments," I said sternly.

June started to remonstrate, but I didn't give her the chance. "You really have no idea, absolutely no idea, of the seriousness of what you've done. You entered Mrs Khoo Besar's flat without her permission and filched a valuable vase. At the very least it's criminal trespass. It could be housebreaking. And theft. Kechik was just today bound over to keep the peace. She could be locked up for years. And you'd be there to keep her company as an accomplice. Didn't they teach you anything in Sunday School about honesty and all that?"

"But it is hers," said June defiantly, though with a little edge of trepidation.

"Of course it isn't hers. Not till the judge says so. Does she have a receipt? A deed of gift? Any proof beyond her word that her old man gave it to her?"

June shook her head.

"So how are we going to convince a Magistrate that she was taking her own property? No, you have to put it back. At once. Tonight."

"I cannot," said June.

"Why in heaven's name not?" I expostulated.

"Because young ladies should not go wandering around town at night. Besides, Mrs Khoo Besar is back in her flat. Anyway I have already changed into my pyjamas."

I threw my hands up in exasperation.

"I'll come with you, okay. Change into something quick. We've got to get the thing back into the flat before Besar notices that it's missing. If she makes a police report and they quiz Kechik, she'll tell them that you have it and then we've all had it. Mr d'Almeida will turf me out so fast my feet won't touch the ground as I whizz through the door."

June had sobered somewhat by now. I wrapped the vase back up in the curtain. She was standing around irresolutely.

"Go on, get changed!" I hissed.

"Can't," she said shortly, "you are in my room."

I let out a low growl of pure frustration and left with the vase. Ten minutes later we were sneaking out the kitchen door into the night.

I remember quite distinctly that it was a beautiful night. There's something about embarking upon a housebreaking expedition that etches things vividly on one's memory. The day had been cloudless and the night was crystal clear. Orion glimmered starkly against the black vault of the sky, the three stars of his belt pointing clearly the way to our destination. I would have enjoyed the walk immensely, had it not been for the looming prospect of being disbarred before I had even been called to the Bar.

Silently we made our way through the silent streets. Though it was not yet nine, the place was empty. The pulse of the city was to be found in the teeming warrens of Chinatown, not out here in the suburbs. We passed hardly a soul.

Stealing past the silent gardens, we eventually reached the Khoo residence. It was a modest double-storeyed terrace house, one room broad and with no front garden. The entrance to the bottom flat opened directly onto the five-foot way while a flight of stairs to the side, barred by a collapsible iron gate, led upstairs to the other flat. On either side were similar terraces.

Old man Khoo himself had lived elsewhere, in a grand mansion with a large garden out on Grove Road. There he threw lavish parties for his business and gambling cronies. Khoo's mah-jong parties were legendary. We discovered when settling the estate that the mansion was rented, along with the car. The only real property he owned was this little pokey terrace house. Things must have been going pretty poorly for some time before the Great Depression gave the coup de grace to his fortune.

The doors and windows of both flats were shuttered, and no light showed through the chinks. I paused.

"I suppose we'd better get the key," I said to June doubtfully.

She nodded but made no move.

"Well, go on," I urged.

"Me? You knock on the door and get the key," she responded. "I'm not going to make a noise at this time of the night and wake all the neighbours."

Taking a deep breath, I rapped tentatively on the wooden front door of Kechik's flat. The sound reverberated through the still night like the roll of drums. A dog barked at the sudden noise. I was about to try again when June put her hand on mine.

"No use. I just remembered. Mrs Khoo said that she sleeps with cotton wool in her ears, because upstairs Mrs Khoo always makes a terrible noise at bedtime. She drags the furniture around or stamps on the floorboards or something."

I bit my lower lip. "That's done it then. I can't hammer on the door loudly enough to wake her. What shall we do?"

"We could go home," suggested June tentatively.

I shook my head vigorously. "No we can't, and you know it. Tomorrow morning Besar is going to miss this vase and then all hell will break loose. Let's try the back."

I crept furtively round the block with June trailing behind me. She carried the vase, wrapped in its curtain. It was shaped somewhat like an urn, with handles on the side sticking out like ears. Wrapped up, it resembled a decapitated head. We must have had the look of a pair of grave robbers after a successful night out.

A narrow alley separated the block of terraces from their neighbours behind. Rats scampered in the open drains that lined the alley, making little scurrying sounds that were greatly magnified to my keyed-up senses. At the back of each terrace house was a narrow-walled garden, blocked off from the alley by a high brick wall with a small wooden door. These houses had only one bathroom and a toilet out back, and access to these facilities for the top flats was provided by a spiral stone staircase.

I indicated the staircase to June. "Let's see if we can get in that way," I whispered.

"I will stay here if you do not mind," said June. "I am not dressed properly to go around climbing."

Those were the days before girls had won the privilege of looking like boys, so June wore her ordinary going-out clothes. Only Gek Neo habitually wore the *sarong kebaya*; my other cousins usually dressed in Western style, which was generally quite unsuited to the climate but was considered the height of chic. I cast my eye up and down June. She wore a frock and flat-heeled shoes; not ideal for shinning up drainpipes and such, but acceptable for a run-of-the-mill burglary.

"You'll do," I whispered. "You have to come with me to show me where to put the dratted thing."

She was about to protest but I held up my hand to pre-empt any remonstration.

Fervently praying that I had counted the right number of houses, I pushed gently on the door that I guessed led into the Khoos' back garden. It opened squeakily and we crept in. Along one side wall was the toilet and bathroom. Along the other side was ranged a collection of carefully tended pots, abloom with orchids. The scent of jasmine caught my nostrils.

We climbed the spiral staircase noiselessly. It led to another collapsible iron gate, but the door behind it was open. After the heat of the day, Besar must have left the door open to let in the cool night air, just shutting the gate. I pulled at it gingerly. It slipped aside with a metallic rasp. We squeezed through the gap and found ourselves in the kitchen.

Picking our way carefully across, I was terrified lest we dislodge a pot or pan or *kwali*. The kitchen wasn't very big, and when Besar was in it I could imagine that not much room for manoeuvre was left over. However, we got through without mishap. The floor was stone-flagged here, and we tiptoed across without a sound.

A dark passageway led from the kitchen to the living room, past what I took to be the bedrooms. The entire flat was in darkness. The first step I took caused an audible clop on the polished wooden floor of the passageway. "Shoes off," I whispered urgently to June. Leaving our shoes in the kitchen, we tiptoed down the passageway.

There were two doors leading off the passageway. The first was shut, but the second was ajar. I peeped in cautiously. On a bed under a mosquito net lay a recumbent dark form, shaped rather like a deflated barrage balloon. Soft rhythmical snores emanated from it.

"She's asleep," I whispered, putting my finger to my lips. We slid silently past the door, gliding on the polished wood.

The living room was quite large, crammed full of furniture and bric-a-brac, the flotsam of a lifetime of indiscriminate collecting. The furniture was rosewood in the Chinese style, carved with blossoms and phoenixes and inlaid with mother-of-pearl. A marble-topped table stood in the centre of the room on a Persian carpet. On various side tables lay an assortment of clocks, vases, urns, boxes and objects of indeterminate utility. A grandfather clock stood by the main door. On the walls hung family pictures, dozens of them, in wooden frames. The rows of unsmiling faces glared glassily at us. Against the wall next to the passageway was the altar, bare now except for two large brass candlesticks. A large framed photo of a Chinese man in coat and tie occupied the centre, surrounded by spirit tablets carved with incomprehensible characters.

"Where's the *almeirah*?" I asked June softly.

She indicated a large cupboard by the door. I moved over to it silently as an owl and opened the door. The musty smell of stale air assailed my nose. Evidently Kechik was right about Besar not caring about the vase. I took the wrapped vase from June and placed it carefully in the almeirah. We both let out our breath, which we had been unconsciously holding.

I suppose that after our successful escapade we were both careless. Whatever it was, disaster overtook us with unlooked-for suddenness. As we made our way back down the passage, June's silk-clad foot lost traction, precipitating her on her rump with a thump. The sound was like the crack of doom, magnified in the silence. She stifled a cry while I froze completely, visions of the Day of Judgement flashing through my brain. I wondered whether breaking into a house to replace things carried the same penalty as breaking in to take things out.

For what seemed an eternity we kept our position as if turned to stone. No reaction. Cautiously, I peered into Besar's room. The blimp was still on the bed, a dark bulk under the mosquito net. She was evidently a very sound sleeper; either that, or Kechik wasn't the only one who slept with cotton wool in her ears to block out the sound of her neighbour's nightly rituals. I helped June back onto her feet and we made our way back to the kitchen.

We fled down the stairs and out into the alley without a word. June was rubbing her bottom.

"My backside will be black and blue because of you," she said to me reprovingly.

"Good," I responded unsympathetically, "Consider it divine retribution. Saved me the trouble of spanking you myself."

We made our way home in silence. I threw myself onto my bed without bothering to shower and tried to get some sleep. I must say that I didn't have a restful night. For some reason, my mind kept trying to remember what the proper term was for being struck off the Roll. I suppose if they had taken away my wig, the proper term would have been "dis-tressed", but somehow it didn't sound right. I fell into a fitful slumber, dreaming of the Bar Committee pursuing me with barber's shears. When I finally awoke it was way past sunrise.

THE FOLLOWING DAY was a Saturday and the house was full when I got down to breakfast.

Everyone was in on Saturday. Mak had already eaten, as was her custom; she got up at 5:30 every morning. The girls were scattered around the house. Gek Neo was helping Mak with the household chores.

Of all the girls, Gek Neo had the most conventional upbringing as a Nonya. May was a nurse. June had managed to secure a cushy position as a companion to a rich and lonely old lady. It wasn't usual at the time for a young Nonya to go out to work, and this liberalism caused a lot of raised eyebrows. However, poverty has an extraordinarily emancipating effect on women. The girls enjoyed the opportunity to get out into the world and earn their keep. Their contemporaries were still immured behind closed curtains, learning to be good housekeepers and waiting to be married off to some suitable boy. Mak was quite open-minded about the whole thing, having been filled with subversive notions about women's suffrage and the like by her missionary teachers in her youth.

After a quick bite and gulp of coffee, I dashed off in search of June. I found her in the veranda, reading a 'penny dreadful' by some forgettable writer.

"Right-ho, old girl, we're off to visit Kechik. Come on, time to get dressed."

"What?" she responded rather crossly. "What for? We put the thing back. My backside is still sore."

I hauled her to her feet. "We have to explain to Kechik why you haven't got the vase. And I have to make it absolutely clear to her that she has to behave. You don't want to see her behind bars do you?"

June got up reluctantly and slouched upstairs to get ready.

The two younger girls, Julie and Augusta, were busy harvesting rambutans from the trees in the garden under the supervision of Dollah, the old gardener. He had long since ceased to protest that young ladies shouldn't be out in the hot sun. Dollah was another old retainer, who had been with my Uncle since his marriage to his first wife. Like Ah Sum, Dollah was a fixture around the house, absolutely loyal and devoted to the girls. His own children were the companions of my youth, playing marbles and catching spiders together. They had all married and gone back to their *kampong*. Dollah himself stayed with us, living in a small one-roomed shed at the bottom of the garden.

June reappeared shortly, and we set off downhill once again towards the Khoo house. A light breeze was blowing and the day was slightly overcast, which made walking less tiresome than normal. Taxis were hard to come by in our part of town, and of course the trolley buses were only to be found in the busy roads of the town centre. Unless one had the good fortune to catch a rickshaw dropping off a passenger, walking was the only way to get around.

In daylight, the row of terrace houses looked much more pleasant. The pastel-coloured fronts were sun-bleached, but the whole area was well-tended and generally clean.

There was a group of boys playing a noisy game of football on the road, and several old gentlemen could be seen conversing animatedly on stools under a banyan tree at the end of the street.

Kechik's door was open, with the collapsible gate pulled shut. I rapped politely on the door. Kechik appeared and invited us in. If she was surprised at our unannounced visit, she did not show it. She led us into the living room and offered us a seat.

"Have you eaten?" she asked politely.

We assured her that we had, but she insisted that we should try some *kueh* that she had just made. Off she bustled to the kitchen, while we made ourselves comfortable in a couple of overstuffed armchairs.

Kechik's flat was indeed smaller than Besar's. It was, however, equally cluttered. It seemed as if old man Khoo's entire life had been spent accumulating an ill-matched assortment of knick-knacks. To my surprise, there was also an altar against the far wall of the room. I saw the same photograph that I had seen in Besar's flat. Even in death, Khoo was shared by his two widows. Kechik's altar was bare however; evidently Besar had managed to get her hands on all the ancestral tablets. In front of the photo was a bronze joss-stick holder, piled with ash. In the middle were the stumps of used joss-sticks, one still smouldering with a pleasant sweetish smoke.

As I cast my eye around the room, I caught sight of a wrapped object in the corner. The wrapper was a piece of cloth, with an unsettlingly familiar pattern. With a grim sense of foreboding, I approached the object and gingerly lifted the hem of the cloth. I dropped it immediately and turned to June.

"It's back."

"What's back?" she asked.

"The vase. That," I said pointing tremblingly, "it's come back."

June came over and unwrapped the vase. No question about it. It was the same one. The ugly ears and convoluted pattern of flowers and other assorted herbage was unmistakable. Why anyone would buy such a thing, much less treasure it, was beyond me. As far as I was concerned, the world of art was undiminished when they stopped making the things.

While I was recovering my senses, Kechik glided in with a tray of coffee and *kueh*. As she poured the coffee, I cleared my throat and asked, "Bibik, where did you get that vase?"

She looked at me directly. "That vase? It is mine. I took it from upstairs."

I stared at June. She stared back at me. Kechik went on pouring coffee nonchalantly.

"When did you take the vase, Bibik?"

She put down the coffee pot. "I took it last night. I was awakened by a loud noise from upstairs. Looking out my window, I saw a strange thing. Two people — a man and a girl — were in my back garden. They came down from upstairs. So I went up to see. I found the vase in the *almeirah*. It is mine, so I took it."

She passed round the coffee cups and offered us each a piece of *kueh* in a perfectly normal fashion, as if a confession of larceny was an everyday occurrence for her.

I drew my breath. June glared at me. Kechik sipped her coffee genteelly and inquired about Mak.

"Bibik, I'm sorry, but the vase must go back. You cannot keep it."

Kechik raised her eyebrows.

I went on, "What you have done is not right. You cannot go into people's houses and take things. You might get into trouble with the police."

Kechik looked at me with a level gaze. "The vase is mine. She has no right to it. My husband gave it to me."

"I know your husband gave it to you, but you must leave it where it is. If the upstairs Mrs Khoo finds it is gone, she will call the police. The police will look for it here. When they find it, you will go to jail. Please give it back."

Kechik's lips tightened. "They will not find it."

"You cannot hide it, they have bloodhounds, they will find it," I continued desperately. "Think of yourself. Think of your husband's memory."

I was making absolutely no impression. Her mouth grew tighter. Then I had an inspiration.

"Think of my *adek* here. She will also be in trouble because you gave her the vase. If she has a police record, no one will marry her."

June was just about to protest at being referred to as my younger sister, but I hushed her with a glance.

Kechik seemed to waver. Nothing is more calamitous to a Nonya than having an unmarried daughter. I pressed my advantage.

"Mak will be so upset. She will not know where to hide her face. All the neighbours will talk."

Kechik capitulated. "All right. Take the vase. Do what you must." She looked away from me.

"Thank you, Bibik. Mak will be very grateful that you have saved her daughter's face."

Gulping down my coffee, I grabbed the vase. With a perfunctory goodbye, I bolted from the room with the infamous object under my arm before Kechik could change her mind. June followed me hurriedly, apologising profusely to Kechik for my rudeness.

Out on the street, she grabbed my arm. "Why didn't you just leave it? You upset her so much. There were tears in her eyes. It is her vase. It was a love-gift from her husband. It is all she has of him. Leave it with her. The other one does not value it. She took it from Mrs Khoo — Kechik — for spite."

I was still walking fast and June was trotting along trying to keep up.

"I've already explained. If it's found in her possession, she'll go to jail. You think she's such a sweet old lady. There's a history of complaints from Besar to the Police Courts, files of summonses.

She was just bound over to keep the peace. She can't prove the gift. It's her word against Besar's. She broke into the upstairs flat and took a valuable object. Something like this can't be overlooked by the magistrate. He'd have to send her to prison. Jail would kill her. Do you want that?"

June subsided. We walked along in silence.

"Do you want me to go with you tonight?" she asked quietly.

"No," I answered shortly, "you've done enough."

Seeing her crestfallen look, I softened my tone. "It's all right, it's not your fault this time. I'll take it to the office. It'll be safe there."

THE EUROPEAN commercial heart of Singapore ceased to beat on weekends. Battery Road and Raffles Place were deserted. The only persons I saw as I made my way to the office were the bearded Sikh *jagas* stretched out on their *charpoys* in front of several boarded-up shops.

I let myself in with my pass-key and climbed the dim stairs to the pupils' room. My mind was clogged with the problem. We were lucky the first time not to have been caught. A second nocturnal expedition? — that would really be mocking the Fates. I wasn't keen on pushing my luck. Yet I had to get the thing back to its place before Cuthbert and Mr Lim did their inventory on Monday.

So engrossed was I in my thoughts that I bumped into a small figure who was standing quietly in the musty dim half-light of the firm's library, intently scanning the shelves for some learned tome. I jumped at this unexpected apparition and nearly dropped the vase.

"Working on weekends, Chiang? I commend your industry."

"Mr d'Almeida," I stammered, "I didn't expect you to be in."

"Evidently not." He returned to his search.

I stood there in embarrassed silence, relegated to the status of the furniture and fittings. He picked a book from the shelf and began to read it, his finger skimming down the lines as he sought the relevant passage. Plucking up my courage, I broke in on his musings.

"Er... Mr d'Almeida." He peered at me over his glasses.

"May I trouble you on a personal problem? Well, not exactly a personal problem... more like a professional problem with personal aspects."

He shut the book and replaced it carefully on the shelf. "Come into my office," he invited.

Ensconced in one of the large leather armchairs in d'Almeida's spacious office, I poured out the whole tale to him. He listened attentively, but did not interrupt me. When I was done, he got up, went over to the desk where I had placed the vase and unwrapped it. He examined it carefully from all angles for a while, picked it up, looked at the inscription on the base and then replaced it without a word.

"How much do you think it's worth?" he suddenly shot at me.

"Ah... um," I responded inadequately, "several thousand dollars?"

He raised his eyebrows at me.

"Perhaps over $10,000," I ventured again, feeling a complete chump.

"It's an antique, the only one of its kind. Mrs Khoo says it's very valuable," I added lamely.

He looked at the vase carefully again.

"Come," he said suddenly and strode out of the office.

I followed him obediently downstairs and out onto the road.

He motioned me to take the driver's seat of his car. "Drive to Chinatown. I'll direct you."

Chinatown was as usual a teeming mass of humanity. We threaded our way through the heedless throngs, honking constantly.

Not that anyone paid the least bit attention. Life followed different currents here, quite different from White Singapore or the languid *kampongs* along the coast. Every soul here seemed to be bent on some quest. The rickshaw pullers, the coolies, the street hawkers, the shopkeepers — each chasing a personal dream of prosperity. Chinatown never stopped, not on Sunday, not on holidays. I myself seldom visited this part of town. To me it was a completely foreign land.

At d'Almeida's direction, I turned off the bustling street into a quieter side-road. The rows of terrace houses were so close to one another that the washing hanging from the upper verandas almost touched in the middle of the road. The five-foot way ran under the overhanging verandas, shaded from the sun. Dark caverns opened up onto the pavement, the fronts of shops selling the wares of a thousand lands and islands, an aromatic assortment of medicines, spices, fruits and sundries. The noise of the city's life was muted here, a subliminal rumble in the background.

We pulled up in front of a nondescript shop front. Carefully parking the car so that the dripping washing above did not wet the paintwork, I got out and nearly stepped right into the open drain beside the road. Brown cockroaches scurried into the cracks that lined the side. An indescribable pong assailed my nose. There was no room for another vehicle to squeeze past us, but cars were a comparative rarity in that part of town and traffic wardens an as-yet-unknown hazard.

D'Almeida had hopped out of the car and was walking briskly along. I trotted after him. He turned abruptly into a narrow doorway and climbed a dim flight of stairs to the upper floor of a shophouse. We entered without knocking.

The room we entered was in semi-darkness, the only light coming from the full-length windows overlooking the road. Like other typical terrace houses, this one was one room wide. In the inner recesses very little sunlight intruded. The place was piled high with porcelain of all varieties — household gods, plates, cups, saucers and *kamchengs*. On the shelves were row upon row of vases, painted with an assortment of garish designs.

A wizened gnome appeared out of the gloom. "Mr d'Almeida," he greeted in a rasping voice. He held out a bony hand. "Long time not see you here."

"Mr Yong," replied d'Almeida, grasping the proffered hand. "It has been a long time. I trust you are well?"

The gnome nodded and grinned. His teeth were broken and stained brown with tobacco juice. He reeked faintly of smoke. "I am well, I am well. Have you eaten? Will you have tea?"

D'Almeida accepted and seated himself on a wooden stool at the side of the room. I did likewise. The gnome disappeared into the back. He returned shortly, carrying a round tray with three small Chinese tea cups and a porcelain teapot. This set was beautifully painted, with a delicate pattern of flowers on the translucent rose-pink of the porcelain. He poured out the steaming liquid and lifted his tea cup in salutation.

"You have come for more snuff bottles? I have some nice ones, just come today."

"No, Mr Yong," replied d'Almeida, sipping his tea, "today I come on business, not for pleasure. I need your help to locate a certain piece of china."

Briefly he described my vase, emphasising the ear-like handles. The gnome nodded and disappeared without a word. He was back in five minutes, carrying a vase.

"Like this?" he asked.

I stared. It was an exact replica of the thing. "Where'd you get that?" I blurted out.

D'Almeida took the vase from Yong and turned it over.

"It's quite common," he explained, examining the base. He

handed it to me. I took it by the handles and stared at it.

"How much?" asked d'Almeida.

"For you, Mr d'Almeida, I give a very special price. Only hundred and fifty dollar."

I almost dropped the dratted object. One hundred and fifty dollars! For this I had risked my neck and my career. D'Almeida stared impassively at the vase. He shook his head slowly. "No, I think not. All it is worth is a hundred."

Yong shook his head vigorously, "No, no for such a thing, hundred is too little. You good customer. For you, hundred forty."

"Hundred and ten," countered d'Almeida.

"Mr d'Almeida, I give you best price — hundred forty dollar. Already I make no profit."

D'Almeida got up to leave. "Thank you for the tea, Mr Yong. Perhaps I shall have a look at the snuff bottles some other time." He beckoned me to follow. Reluctantly I put the vase down and got up.

We were halfway through the door when Yong called out. "Okay, I give you best price, hundred thirty."

D'Almeida stopped. He turned deliberately. "One twenty-five."

"Ai-yah, you are a hard man Mr d'Almeida. I have children. How can I take one twenty-five? One hundred thirty, and I give you snuff bottle."

D'Almeida nodded and reached for his wallet. He counted out the notes. Yong beamed his nicotine smile and went back in to wrap up the vase.

ON THE way back to the office, d'Almeida unwrapped the packet and took out the snuff bottle. "Yes," he said, "a very nice specimen. It will fit well in my collection."

I was bursting to ask questions and could stand it no more. "Mr d'Almeida?"

He was holding the bottle up to the sunlight. "Yes, what is it?"

"The vase. How is it that you could find another so like it? Mrs Khoo told us it was one of a kind, an antique. And very valuable."

D'Almeida chuckled. "My dear boy, someone has been having you on. Or more likely, someone has been having her on. Yes, such a vase would be valuable — if it was genuine."

I creased my brow in puzzlement. d'Almeida continued, "It's not a Chinese vase. It's a German — or more precisely, Saxon — interpretation of a Chinese motif. By Meissen. An original would be worth something."

We pulled up at the office and I switched the engine off. He handed me the vase. "Yes," he continued, "an original Meissen would be worth owning. But you know, the locals are very enterprising. When they discovered that the *orang puteh* and the nouveaux riches were willing to pay handsome sums for such things, they took to making them here. These come from the Dutch East Indies, somewhere outside Batavia. Not perfect copies, but the collectors here can't really tell the difference. They'll buy anything, as long as they're told it's valuable."

He took the vase from me and turned it over. "See here," he said, pointing to an inscription. It was an 'X' with the date '1789' under it. "A dead giveaway. That should be a pair of crossed swords. The craftsmen don't bother with little details like this." He handed the thing back to me.

"What should I do with it?" I asked plaintively.

D'Almeida raised his eyebrows. "My dear Chiang. There are two widows. You now have two vases. Surely it is not beyond your wit to engineer a satisfactory solution to the problem?" With that he strode back up the stairs to resume his interrupted researches.

THAT EVENING, June and I returned the original vase to Kechik. She beamed at us and wished us long life for the good turn we had done her. It was obvious that her happiness went beyond merely being one up on Besar. I felt that burglary did have some small compensations. As for Besar's vase, I managed to wrangle myself onto the valuation team with Cuthbert. While he and Mr Lim were in the other room, I sneaked the vase back into its rightful place. Besar never noticed the difference.

In due course the judge made the order dividing the estate, and that was that. It would be nice to record that everyone lived happily ever after; I suppose the Khoo widows did, after a fashion. Neither could move out, so they remained neighbours. The firm received a steady stream of fees from the regular visits to the Police Courts, where their dossier continued to grow. Age however soon mellowed them — or more likely sapped their energy.

Besar eventually died in the early 'fifties. Kechik survived her only by a month or so. I suppose that the spice went out of life once her rival left. Or maybe she couldn't bear the thought of that *perumpuan sial* monopolising their husband in the afterlife.

A PRINCE AMONG MEN

IN MY TIME I've tried murder and I've tried rape. But the most trying of trials I've always found to be are family affairs. I never looked forward to them when I was on the bench. There's almost always something intractably bitter about a family quarrel that ends up in court. The ones I hate the most are those involving custody of children. The Solomonic practice of cutting babies in half is impractical (apart from being unspeakably messy), so the judge must make a decision and hope to God that he has done the right thing. Give me a hardened murderer any day; it's less strain on the nerves. My initiation into the intricacies of the family court came very early in my career. I'll never forget her.

SHE WAS a princess. Well, actually, not quite; to be precise, she married a prince. She was in fact a flower girl in Covent Garden. Not one of your common or garden barrow-girls though; she worked in a flower shop and could, as they say, speak posh. It would have been unthinkable in her mother's day; but in those enlightened 'thirties, middle-class morality ceased to be scandalised by the sight of a single girl making her own way in the world. One fine summer's day along came a dusky oriental gentleman who claimed to be a prince in his country. The flower girl was flattered and not a little awed. He took her to the Proms. They strolled through Hyde Park. They ate in the little back alleys of the great metropolis. After a couple of months, they consummated their grand passion. A daughter was born; a lusty, healthy creature. Like so many other crosses between oriental and occidental, the little girl inherited the best features of her father and mother. She was beautiful. The prince was so pleased that he actually proposed marriage. They were later married at the registry office in Hammersmith.

The prince and the flower girl lived in wedded bliss for nearly a year. Then the day came when he said that he must return to his country. He had come to London to do the Bar Finals, but he found the racetrack more congenial. He attempted the exam seven times. On the eighth go his examiners let him pass, no doubt worn down by his persistence. He cabled the good news home. His father the Maharajah was overwhelmed. No one in the royal family had ever achieved such academic distinction. There was feasting and merry-making in the streets. The old Maharajah was so impressed that he recalled his son. What had seemed a complete waste of money now turned out to be a glittering investment. He would be raised to the rank of Tengku Mahkota, crown prince no less.

He had to return. Duty calls and all that. He would take the baby first. The sight of his granddaughter would melt the Maharajah's heart and they would live in bliss. He promised to send for her. She took the news quite stoically. A nurse came to fetch the child from her. She saw them off at the docks, moist-eyed. You know the rest of the story. For the first few months letters came regularly, proclaiming his undying love. Then the letters stopped, though her bank account still was credited at decent intervals. After a year, the money stopped as well. She wrote imploringly to him. Back came a curt note from the Royal Chancellery. His Royal Highness was busy with official duties, he did not have time to answer importunate letters from impecunious flower girls and would she please stop bothering him. The missive was sealed with an impressive ornate wax seal. A cheque for five hundred pounds was enclosed.

She took the note to the Colonial Office. By making a most un-English scene in the building foyer she managed to get to see the Assistant Deputy Undersecretary of State. The man was impeccably polite. He tut-tutted reprovingly at the right places in her story. But, he said, spreading his well-manicured hands in a gesture of hopelessness, His Majesty's government could do nothing. The Native States were foreign countries and not British territory, unlike the Crown Colony of the Straits Settlements. Though he had a British Resident to advise him, the Maharajah was a sovereign prince. On his island domain, he was the unchallenged lord. His son was Tengku Mahkota and outside British jurisdiction. The Assistant Deputy Undersecretary of State commiserated as he showed her the door. There was nothing to be done he said but to put it all down to experience and start afresh.

They reckoned without her determination. She cashed her cheque and bought a one-way ticket on the next P&O steamer to the East. Six weeks later I met her in Mr d'Almeida's office.

THE SUMMONS from on-high was brought to me by Moraiss, the chief clerk. Moraiss had been with the firm from a time whereof the memory of man runneth not to the contrary. He had all the animation of a year-old corpse. I always thought that Moraiss would have been right at home in Tutankhamun's tomb. "Come," he said laconically and shuffled off. I shuffled off behind him.

I always did like d'Almeida's room, with its musty-sweet smell of old paper and overstuffed leather furniture. D'Almeida was pacing up and down as was his wont. He beckoned me in.

"Ah, Chiang, I'd like you to meet Miss Earnshaw. Miss Earnshaw, my assistant, Dennis Chiang."

The lady in the armchair nodded her head politely. She couldn't have been more than twenty-two or twenty-three. Not really pretty, but pleasant enough. She didn't have a really upper class look. More solid middle class, one would have concluded by her dress and bearing. She extended her hand, which I took with due formality.

"Miss Earnshaw has come to the Straits to find out if she's still married," said d'Almeida.

Seeing my puzzled look, he explained the circumstances. At the end of his rapid-fire resume he barked out, "Right, young man, the law."

"Er... um," I began, still trying to digest the story.

D'Almeida had this unsettling habit of behaving like a Tripos examiner and shooting out legal questions at the drop of a hat. I feverishly dredged my memory to recover the proper principles from the ooze of half-remembered textbooks.

"Ah, well, er...," I temporised, trying not to look like a complete fool, "capacity to marry is governed by the law of the subject's domicile, while formalities are governed by the law of the place of celebration."

"Yes, yes," said d'Almeida impatiently, "we know that. We have a marriage certificate issued by the Registry at Hammersmith. Is she married now?"

"Er..., that would depend on whether she's been divorced," I answered rather lamely.

To my surprise, that turned out to be the right answer.

"Right!" exclaimed d'Almeida, "and how do we find out?"

"We check the Registry?" I ventured hopefully.

D'Almeida snorted. "Use your head, man. The husband's a Mohammedan. He doesn't have to get a civil divorce. He can get rid of his wife by *talaq*. In any case, the man's the son of a sovereign prince. D'you think that his divorce would be recorded in the Colony?"

"Then how can we find out?" I asked, rather pathetically.

D'Almeida snorted again. "You ask the man," he said, "I happen to know that His Highness Tengku Ibrahim Iskandar Shah is in town with his whole *caravanserai*. He's staying up at the Istana on the east coast. Go up there and ask the man."

D'Almeida addressed the lady. "Miss Earnshaw, as I told you, there is nothing to be done if he has in fact divorced you. A Mohammedan does not have to go through the tiresome ritual that others must. He can divorce his wife merely by pronouncing a *talaq*. No reasons need be given. I very much fear that your husband has already done so. But you have a good chance of getting your daughter back and getting some maintenance from him."

She nodded comprehendingly. "I'm not really interested in the money," she said. "My daughter is what I came for." There was a fierce glint in her eyes.

"Well," said d'Almeida, "I leave you in good hands. Chiang is one of my most capable assistants and he will handle the matter for you."

He shot me a side-long glance and motioned me to go. I sidled towards the door hastily, glad not to have been set another *viva voce* examination.

"Mr d'Almeida," the lady interrupted unexpectedly, "I'd like to go along."

D'Almeida raised his eyebrows. "If you like, Miss, but it may be unpleasant."

"Mr d'Almeida, nothing that he does to me is going to be as unpleasant as what I shall do to him if he does not give me back my daughter."

D'Almeida smiled and motioned her to the door, bowing slightly as he handed her through to me.

THE DRIVE down to the east coast was pleasant as always. We sped down Grove Road, lined with coconut palms and the mansions of the rich Babas, past the Swimming Club and the Seaview Hotel. Well, perhaps "sped" is a little exaggeration. I had managed to scrape up enough to buy a small car. It was at an awkward age; old enough for the *kampong* kids to run alongside hooting derisively, but not yet old enough to be an antique.

I tried to make light conversation. "Your first time in the East, Miss Earnshaw?" I ventured, realising as I did so how silly a question it was.

"Kate's good enough for the likes of me," she answered shortly.

"Where are you staying, er... Kate?"

"At the YWCA."

I struggled manfully for a few minutes more. Her answers were civil, succinct and to the point. I gave it up as a bad job. We progressed in silence.

At last we reached the gates of the Istana, a massive Edwardian pile at the end of a long drive. The old Maharajah's Anglophile tendencies showed plainly in the architecture of the place. The architecture was nothing if not eclectic. It looked like a cross between an English stately home and a mosque, with part of the Brighton Pavilion thrown in. The long stately European façade was incongruously crowned with minarets. The whole ensemble was painted pale pink. It was in the style that one local architect dubbed "Anglo-Marzipan".

We nosed through the massive over-wrought iron gates down the path. The impressive double doors were flanked by royal-yellow silk umbrellas. A minion in native livery salaamed as we alighted and ushered us into the receiving hall.

The hall was just as impressive as the façade. It was tiled in checkerboard fashion with black and white marble. A wide double staircase flung itself flamboyantly from the ground floor to the mezzanine floor. White plaster Grecian urns in the classical style adorned niches along the walls. In contrast, the doors leading from the reception hall were ornately carved wood, with fretwork screens at the top, gracefully curved in the Middle Eastern style. The whole place reeked opulence. It was obviously the fantasy of a man with more dollars than sense.

Another more gorgeously dressed flunkey appeared. In halting English he asked our business. I presented my card and requested an audience with His Highness the Tengku Mahkota. The flunkey withdrew bowing.

We were shown into a small drawing room in a short while. The furniture and decorations were distinctly European, with little evidence of any oriental influence. It was a room that could have fitted nicely into any English country house. I chose myself a plushly upholstered armchair. Kate sat primly on a high-backed sofa. As we had long since run out of small talk, we sat in a somewhat uncomfortable silence. Half an hour passed. No sign of hide or hair of the man. I began to examine the contents of the bookcases on the walls. There was quite a collection — Ovid, Livy, Sophocles, Plato, Cicero, along with classic novels and anthologies of poets. Very impressive. Funnily enough, when I picked up a volume it had a crisp smooth feel of newness, as if it had never been opened. There was no sign of scuffing or even a dog-ear on any page. Not a crease marred the elegant leather binding. I placed the book back reverently.

Another half hour dragged itself by.

Kate spoke. "How long are we going to wait?" Her voice was tinged with impatience.

"Well, these oriental potentates don't have the same sense of time as we do. I suppose we'll give him a few more minutes."

"I think we should look for him," she declared decisively, marching to the door.

Before I could stop her she was through the door and striding purposefully across the hall and up the staircase. Snapping the volume I was holding shut, I hurried after her.

I caught up with her at the top of the stairs.

"We can't go traipsing round the place like this," I remonstrated.

"Why ever not?" she retorted.

I mumbled lamely about trespass and a man's home being his castle but she took no notice.

She began trying the doors that lined the long corridor leading off from the mezzanine floor. Most of them were locked. A few opened into rooms, bare for the most part, some strewn with rugs and cushions. There didn't seem to be anyone about.

The tenth door we tried led into a largish room with shuttered windows. The shutters were open and the noonday sun streamed in. It was bare except for a few woven mats on the floor. Suspended by a rope from the ceiling was a sarong. A largish Malay lady was sitting on the mats gently rocking the sarong and crooning softly. She stopped abruptly when we appeared, startled by the sudden irruption.

"Lucy!" exclaimed Kate. She rushed to the sarong and scooped a sleepy-eyed baby out. The child whimpered a little, and then clasped her chubby arms around Kate.

Personally, I was surprised that the child could recognise Kate after so long, but there must be something in this mother-child bonding business that the shrinks are always talking about. Kate was making idiotic gurgly-goo noises, which the child obviously understood going by its expression. The *amah*, who had initially drawn up her vast bulk menacingly, melted and simpered at this touching reunion.

We stood round in a small circle. Now that I could see her closely, Lucy was indeed a beautiful child. She had large brown eyes with long lashes and the rolls of baby fat that surrounded her cheeks and arms made her look like a little white bolster. The *amah* was beaming benevolently and Kate continued babbling in a soft voice, cradling the child in her arms. She would have stood there all day spouting infantile gobbledygook if the door hadn't slammed open suddenly.

"What are you doing here!" thundered the apparition. I stepped forward to explain. "Who the devil are you?" he barked. Then he saw Kate and the child. "You! I thought you were in London."

I gathered that I was in the presence of the proud father.

He was dressed in a white linen European suit, complete with patent leather shoes to match his black slicked-back hair. A thin wraith of a moustache crowned his upper lip. I guessed that he was in his late thirties. He spoke with a clipped upper-upper English accent, the product of some expensive public school. I had met several such specimens when I was in London. They were all over the Inns of Court, trying to out-English the English. To hear one speak made my back hair prickle. I always had an irrational urge to pull the blighter's tongue out, tie a granny knot in it and stuff it up his nose.

"I've come for my child, Abraham" said Kate fiercely, "and you're not having her."

"Your child?! My dear lady, you have no right to that child, none at all. Put her down at once."

Kate's eyes blazed and she clasped Lucy tighter. The child, bewildered by all the commotion, instinctively clung closer to her mother. The Malay *amah* had retreated to a corner of the room, quivering like a mountainous agar-agar.

Abraham moved menacingly closer. "Put her down I say!"

I interposed myself between them. "Your Highness," I said, though the title stuck in my throat, "I represent your wife in this matter. I trust that we can discuss this like civilised people."

"And who the devil are you?" he demanded again angrily.

I proffered my card, which he snatched from my hand.

He read it and snorted. "If you think that I'm going to be intimidated by a solicitor, you're very much mistaken. I'm a barrister myself. You're not on British territory here. This is my house and my land and I am the law here."

"I beg to differ, Your Highness," I answered, trying to keep my temper. "As long as you're in the Colony you're subject to British law. Your wife has rights, which you as a barrister should be well aware of."

"Don't lecture me on the law, young man," he answered condescendingly. "This woman is not my wife."

"Your divorce won't stand up in court," I bluffed.

"Divorce!" he snorted, "who said anything about divorce. She's never been my wife."

I was slightly taken aback at this and shot a quick glance at Kate. She wore a puzzled look. I pulled out the marriage certificate from my briefcase. "Are you saying that this marriage certificate is a forgery?"

"Hah! A worthless piece of paper. If you knew anything of the law, you'd know that I am not subject to the law of England. My father the Maharajah is a sovereign prince, bound in treaty to the British Empire. My country is a sovereign state. A prince of the blood has no capacity to marry without the Maharajah's express consent. Even you must know that such a so-called marriage is null and void."

He had me there. From what little I remembered of the law, he seemed to be right. I was saved from the embarrassment of having to answer by the arrival of a cohort of minions in response to some unheard signal.

"For the last time, put the child down," said Abraham menacingly.

The minions advanced; Kate and I retreated towards the window. I decided that a tactical withdrawal was in order.

"I think you'd better let them have Lucy back, Kate," I whispered.

The minions advanced another step. Lucy started to cry.

"Look," I pleaded, "if you don't give Lucy back, they'll take her from you by force. They'll say that you trespassed and took the child without consent. You might never see your daughter again."

This dire threat seemed to sink in. Kate wavered, though she could not bring herself to surrender the child. Ibrahim barked an order. The *amah*, perspiration beading her forehead, waddled over and took Lucy from Kate's unresisting grasp. Lucy was still wailing. Kate had an agonised look on her face.

"I'll have the law on you, I will!" she threatened.

"The law!" Abraham laughed unpleasantly. "Ask your lawyer friend what sovereign immunity means." The minions took us by the arms and marched us to the door. "Now get out!" commanded Ibrahim.

The last thing I heard were Lucy's pathetic cries mingled with the wails of the *amah* and the slap of leather on flesh.

THE DRIVE back to town was even more uncomfortable than the drive out. Kate was wrapped in a cloud of black rage. I was uncomfortably aware of not having exactly covered myself in glory. We pulled up at the YWCA and Kate started to get out.

"Miss Earnshaw... Kate, I'm sorry about what happened, but we'll soon put it right."

"Not your fault," she replied curtly.

"Will you be all right?" I asked.

She glared directly at me. There was fire in her eyes. "I can take care of meself," she answered. She turned to go.

"Kate, wait." She stopped and turned round. "Look, I feel absolutely rotten about the whole business. I don't think it's right that you should have to stay by yourself here. My mother's got a big house with loads of room. Would you like to stay there?"

She hesitated. I pressed on. "It's not charity. I know what it's like to be a stranger in a big town. Mother would be ever so glad for the company. It'd be a treat for her to have a guest, and you'd be safe."

I blurted out the last without meaning to. At the back of my mind had been the haunting thought that Abraham might not be above some rough play. A young girl alone in a port town. Any number of things might happen.

Kate reflected for a while, and then smiled at me. It was the first smile that I'd had from her. She was quite attractive really.

"Thank you," she said. "Are you sure it'll be all right with your mother?"

"Absolutely no trouble. I'll help you with your things."

It took only a little while to sort out her things. For a lady who had come half a world away from home she had very little, only a trunk and a couple of boxes. I loaded them into my jalopy and we drove off with a rattle and wheeze.

At that time of the day only Mak was home. The younger girls were in school and the older ones at work. If she was surprised to see me escort a young Englishwoman up the stairs, she didn't show it. Actually, I think she might have harboured some hopes that Kate had a relationship with me. Since my return from England Mak had been working overtime to get me hitched. She would of course have preferred some nice Nonya girl from an old family, but a white woman would do at a pinch. Anyway, I disillusioned her quickly when I introduced Kate. After explaining the situation, Mak was completely sympathetic. She took over Kate and bustled off. Knowing that Kate was in good hands, I drove straight back to the office.

D'Almeida was at his desk when I returned. He peered at me over the rim of his spectacles. "I take it that the interview was not satisfactory?"

"No, not very." I felt completely drained and flung myself down on the sofa. D'Almeida got up and came over.

"Did you find out if he's divorced her?"

I nodded. "He didn't say anything about a divorce. In fact he claims that they were never married properly. Something to do with the law of his country. He can't get married without his father's consent."

Briefly, I narrated the morning's events to d'Almeida. He took off his spectacles and started polishing them absently as he paced the floor.

"Is he right about this sovereign immunity business?" I asked at length.

D'Almeida started. "What? Oh, yes, to a degree. The Native States are technically foreign territory, though we in the Colony often forget that. His father the Maharajah can't be sued in our courts, that's certain. Whether he's covered by the same immunity is a point that hasn't yet been decided. He thinks he is; I think not. But the point is that there is an even chance that he has immunity."

D'Almeida was pacing again. He continued talking, more to himself than to me. "If we bring an action for custody of the child, he will almost certainly take the point on immunity. If we lose the point, that will be that. If we win the point, he might spirit the child back to his country. Once she's there, we won't be able to touch her." He stopped, put on his spectacles and rounded on me. "So what's the answer?"

I had been with d'Almeida long enough to know that he had the answer. "We go to court and sue him?" I ventured.

"No, no, of course not! We can't go to court. He must go to court and sue us. The moment he sues, he forfeits whatever immunity he has. We must force him into court."

"And how are we going to do that?"

"Simple," said d'Almeida, his eyes twinkling, "we must kidnap the child."

I HAD in my youth always dreamed of tooling around town one day in a chauffeured Rolls. Somehow, though, I never thought it would be this way. We were heading back towards the Istana in d'Almeida's antique Rolls. It was two days since my unfortunate interview with the Tengku Mahkota. D'Almeida had news that the fellow would be attending a garden party at Government House. He immediately contacted Kate and got together a party of his own.

I was in the back of the car, looking smart in a dark suit and clutching an impressive leather briefcase. I had a fake moustache under my nose and plain-glass spectacles perched on top of it. When I spoke, it felt like two amorous caterpillars doing a mating dance in my nostrils. My fellow pupil Ralph Smallwood sat next to me, resplendent in white *tutup* jacket, trousers, shoes, gloves and solar *topi*. He had a monocle scrunched up in his right eye and a walrus moustache, the very caricature of an Imperial official. Kate was in the front passengers seat, dressed in a nurse's uniform that she had scrounged off one of the inmates of the YWCA. D'Almeida himself was driving. He was a real sight. He had obtained in some way a court attendant's uniform. Decked out in this and in a red silk cummerbund and velvet *songkok*, he looked most magnificent as a driver. From the bonnet, a heraldic pennant fluttered. It was actually an old college pennant of mine. As it was liberally spangled with lions passant and fleurs de lys, it looked most impressive when pressed into service as a flag.

It was all d'Almeida's idea as usual. Since my first adventure with him, I had come to realise that he enjoyed these little charades. They evidently lent a little excitement to his life.

Ralph was with us to ensure an entree into the Istana. In the Colony, white was right and two Wongs most certainly did not make a white. Ralph's grandmother was Chinese, though this wasn't noticeable at a casual glance. Of course, he could never get into the Singapore Club or the Tanglin Club because of this, the nigger in the woodpile as they so eloquently put it. But looking White certainly had its advantages. For one thing, salesgirls were so much more attentive. D'Almeida, on the other hand, was quite clearly coloured; a sort of warm cocoa colour. In fact, in chambers we had the whole spectrum, from Ralph who could pass off quite easily as a *tuan*, all the way to George Singham, who when he grinned on a dark night disappeared completely, leaving his smile hanging like the Cheshire Cat's.

We pulled up in front of the Istana. "Are you sure this'll work?" I asked *sotto voce*. "What if they recognise us?"

"All Chinamen and *orang puteh* look alike. They won't recognise you," d'Almeida replied evenly as he held the door open for Ralph.

We dismounted regally and swept into the reception hall. We were met by the major-domo, who had evidently been summoned by the doorkeeper.

"We have come for the child," Ralph announced in his most pompous tones. Evidently, the sight of him in full regalia had quite taken away the major-domo's precarious command of the language, for he only stared blankly. D'Almeida intervened, explaining the situation in faultless Malay.

The major-domo shook his head vigorously.

"Is there some problem?" Ralph demanded testily, in his best *tuan besar* manner.

He motioned imperiously to me, and I withdrew a massive manila envelope from the briefcase that I carried and presented it to the major-domo. He took it gingerly, as if he were afraid that it would bite. He opened it and unfolded the letter within. It was written on the Tengku Mahkota's notepaper, with his seal unmistakably at the bottom. At the sight of this missive, the major-domo's reluctance evaporated and he summoned a guard with a hand clap. He invited us into one of the adjoining reception rooms, but I thought that the white man's dignity would be better upheld if we stood around haughtily in the reception hall. I whispered hurriedly to Ralph, who nodded slightly and stayed put.

A minute later the *amah* appeared at the top of the stairs, palpitating visibly as she hurried down. Lucy was in her arms. I looked out of the corner of my eye at Kate, but she remained impassive. The *amah* approached us with downcast eyes. There were red welts on her arms. Ralph motioned regally towards Kate. D'Almeida interpreted into Malay. The *amah* handed Lucy over to Kate.

As she did so she looked up. For one brief moment she hesitated. Sweat began to form on my forehead. The guards each carried a ceremonial *kris*. Personally, I thought the wavy blades looked uncomfortably sharp.

The seconds stretched out eternally as Kate and the *amah* looked straight into one another's eyes. Then, abruptly, the *amah* let go of Lucy and retreated hurriedly back up the stairs. I let out my breath, which I had been unconsciously holding. We withdrew amid many bowings and scrapings, which Ralph returned with a condescending nod of the head.

SPEEDING BACK to the city, mother and child were the picture of perfect bliss. Ralph had sunk back in the seat, his monocle dangling from its string. His *topi* was askew and his moustache hung limply. He was completely stupefied. I divested myself of my moustache and undid my tie.

"Never again," I swore. "I'm sure the *amah* recognised Kate. Heaven only knows why she let Lucy go. Anyway, where did you get that letter? Did you forge it?"

D'Almeida allowed himself a ghost of a smile. "No, it's genuine. It's from Abraham himself. The letter he sent to Miss Earnshaw."

I sank back into the seat. "God, what a risk. We could have been skewered."

"No, the risk was minimal. You must have faith in a trained servant's instinct to obey. I was counting on the fact that none of the staff could read English. I was right. But they could recognise the Tengku Mahkota's seal and signature. I merely suggested that it was a royal command. The man's training did the rest. That and his natural awe of the *orang puteh*. You both did well. The very spitting image of a *tuan besar* and his faithful minion."

We basked in the unexpected compliment. It wasn't often that d'Almeida praised us.

Then an uncomfortable thought struck me. "He'll know it was us."

D'Almeida nodded. "Indubitably. And unless I miss my guess, we shall soon have the pleasure of His Royal Highness' company. I think that you had better leave the YWCA, Miss Earnshaw. Would you care to spend the next few nights at my place?"

"Thank you, Mr d'Almeida, but Dennis has been kind enough to let me stay with his family. We'll be quite fine."

D'Almeida nodded. "Excellent. I know you are in good hands."

I was still uncomfortable. "What will the Bar Committee say if they find out?"

"The Bar Committee is the least of our worries," replied d'Almeida soberly.

THAT EVENING after dinner I drove over to return Kate's nurse's outfit to the YWCA. The place was abuzz with activity when I got there, like an ant's nest disturbed by a careless foot. Apparently, hooligans had broken in during the day when everyone was out. They had tied up the porter and terrorised the staff. They ransacked several of the rooms. No one knew exactly what they were after, for they had left without taking anything. The police were scouring the grounds for clues. I didn't wait to hear more. I pushed my old banger to its limits speeding back home.

I screeched to a halt in front of the door with a shower of gravel. Two heads popped out of the upstairs veranda windows to see what all the commotion was about.

"Where's Kate?" I yelled to Julie and Augusta.

"Behind the house," replied Julie. "What's the matter?"

Without answering, I dashed into the house and out onto the back veranda.

I found Kate there, together with all the rest of my cousins. Baby Lucy was holding court, sitting in the centre like a little teddy bear with her chubby legs outstretched, playing with some shiny glass marbles. There is something about babies that renders the average female absolutely dotty. The girls were standing around in a simpering mess, cooing and making other incomprehensible gurgly noises.

I cut in abruptly. "Kate, did you leave a forwarding address at the YWCA?"

"What?" she asked, looking up from Lucy, who was monopolising her attention.

"A forwarding address. Did you tell anyone in the YWCA where you were going?"

"Yes," she replied, with a puzzled tone. "I gave them your firm's address. They'll send anything that comes for me on to the firm. Is anything the matter?"

I heaved a sigh of relief. "Thank God for that."

By now the girls had gone quiet, looking at me with a mixture of irritation and apprehension. I sat down in an unoccupied chair and started to explain gravely.

"I don't want to alarm anyone, but the YWCA was broken into this afternoon. Some thugs went through the place." There was a collective gasp of consternation. "The police don't know who did it or why, but I'm pretty sure it was Abraham's people."

"That'll be just like him," Kate said, "He thinks that the rules don't apply to him."

"Anyway, just as a precaution, I'd like everyone to get indoors. Shut the windows and bolt the doors. I don't think he knows where Lucy and Kate are, but we'd better take no chances. We might have visitors in the night."

The group broke up in a flurry. I went down to the bottom of the garden to fetch old Dollah the gardener. When I got back to the main house, I found preparations for the siege well in hand. Mak had taken the news calmly when the girls broke it to her. She had told Ah Sum to sleep in the living room that night rather than out back in the servants' quarters. Dollah would spend the night in the kitchen. He had brought along his trusty parang. The house was a fairly large rectangular structure, with verandas all around. The doors were bolted and the dozen french windows leading out onto the verandas were locked. Only the upstairs windows remained open to let in some air, otherwise we would all have been cooked by the heat.

I surveyed the house with some apprehension. It wasn't built to resist an assault of any sort. Architects in the tropics designed houses to let air in, not keep intruders out. A determined monkey with a screwdriver could have forced his way in. I had a nasty feeling that we were dealing with more than just monkeys. A quick rummage through the attic produced only a few rusty knives. Tying one onto a stake, I fashioned a makeshift lance. Mak had hustled the girls off to bed. She had taken over Lucy, with Gek Neo's help (this was a golden opportunity to train Gek Neo in the art of baby-minding, and Mak wasn't about to let it slip).

After a quick patrol around the grounds with Dollah, I retired to the upstairs veranda. This protruded out from the front of the house, creating a porch over the entrance. It was glassed in with windows to form a small room. Seating myself in an easy-chair, I settled down to wait. The twittering from the girls' rooms gradually ceased. The moon came up after a while, bathing the garden in a blue-white glow. Only the crickets disturbed the silence with their soothing song. Occasionally, I heard the metallic "toc-toc" of the nightjars as they flitted through the dark. Sometime, unnoticed and without volition, I drifted from consciousness to sleep.

I awoke with a start, my consciousness jolted by the realisation that I wasn't alone. A white figure stood close by. I fumbled frantically for my lance.

"Shh, it's only me," whispered a voice. I subsided with relief. "Are you all right? I couldn't sleep," said Kate.

"What time is it?" I mumbled, struggling to wake myself.

"2:30. Sorry I woke you."

Kate was there, barefoot and in her nightdress. She slid silently into a chair.

She had thawed out somewhat in the last couple of days. After the arrival of Lucy she was positively animated. The girls were about her age, and they hit it off well. She hadn't been in the Colony long enough to become a *memsahib*. Out here, even a flower girl put on the airs of a duchess when dealing with the natives. Polite society would have been shocked by the thought of a single white woman consorting with the locals in such a way. But in Kate's case, she had well and truly crossed the colour bar. She had put herself beyond the pale and there was no turning back.

"How's Lucy?" I asked, making polite conversation.

"Sleeping like a baby. Your mother's wonderful. I have so much to thank you all for."

"No need for thanks," I mumbled, a trifle embarrassed. We sat for a while in silence.

"You know, I can't really blame him," said Kate at length.

"Who?"

"Abraham. Or Ibrahim, which is his proper name. Lucy meant a lot to him."

"Did you love him?" I asked.

"Me? Yes... No... I'm not sure." She gazed out the window. "It was different in London. He was different." She paused, as if searching for the words. "He was... more of a gentleman, like. He treated me all right."

I kept silent.

"Things, they're different here. I feel it," she continued. "Mr d'Almeida, he's a real gent, like the gents back home. But, you know, it's not the same. I saw what you and Ralph did when you were play-acting. Is it like that all over?"

I nodded. "Yes, the rules change out here. Even now, when we're supposed to be so enlightened. You judge us by your mores and your standards and find us wanting."

"Me?" asked Kate with some surprise.

I hastily clarified. "No, no, not you personally. I meant the white *tuans*. You're not like them."

Kate nodded slowly. "Poor Abraham. He wanted so much to

be one of them. But they won't have him. I suppose he's going back to what he was before."

I pondered that for a while. Poor Abraham indeed. I suppose I could understand a little of his feelings. But somehow I found it hard to pity the fellow. The uncomfortable prospect of being disembowelled by a wavy *kris* at the hands of his retainers had a somewhat drying effect on the milk of human kindness.

My sympathies actually lay with Kate. Like a lightning rod, she seemed to be the focus of his frustration and resentment. He was not a person to be trifled with. He might have been a gent in London, but out here he was the archetypal oriental despot, who cared little for ordinary mortals.

Obviously, Kate couldn't stay in the Colony. Even if Abraham's homicidal minions could be restrained, she would have been a pariah among her own people. Though we hadn't discussed it, I was sure that she couldn't go back to London either. We drifted back into silence. Daylight crept up slowly upon us.

D'ALMEIDA was already at his desk when I reached the office. I brought Kate with me, as he had instructed over the telephone. I briefly explained the incident at the YWCA. He didn't seem surprised at my news.

"I received an early call from him," d'Almeida informed me. "He wants to meet Kate. He should be here any minute now."

I moved to the door. D'Almeida beckoned me back. "No, I want you here. Sit in the corner, please."

At that moment, Moraiss entered to announce the arrival of Tengku Ibrahim and Inspector Fergusson.

The Tengku entered first, looking like a tropical storm seeking an unsuspecting village to burst over. "What have you done with my child?" he thundered at Kate.

"Tengku Ibrahim, I presume?" inquired d'Almeida evenly.

The man ignored him. "Inspector, arrest this woman. She's guilty of kidnapping."

"Tengku Ibrahim, we can do this in one of two ways. We can be civilised and sit down and have a cup of tea. Or I can have you shown off the premises and charged with a breach of the peace. Which is it to be?"

Ibrahim's eyes blazed. He had never in his life been spoken to in such a fashion. D'Almeida drew himself up to full height and stared directly back. Ibrahim dropped his gaze.

"Won't you sit down?" invited d'Almeida. Ibrahim and the Inspector did so. "And now, what can I do for you gentlemen?"

Ibrahim opened his mouth to speak, but the Inspector hurriedly broke in. "This here gentleman has made a very serious charge against your client, sir. A very serious charge indeed. I must ask a few questions."

"Be my guest, Inspector," replied d'Almeida.

The Inspector turned to Kate. "Well, Miss, did you or did you not forcibly abduct one two-year-old infant, known as Lucy Abraham, from the custody of her father, one Tengku Ibrahim Iskandar Shah?"

"If you are asking me whether I took my daughter, the answer is yes," replied Kate.

Ibrahim exploded. "There you are! She admits it. Arrest her, man."

The Inspector looked distinctly uncomfortable. "You realise, Miss, that kidnapping is a very serious crime. Very serious indeed."

D'Almeida broke in. "Inspector, since when has it been a crime for a mother to regain custody of her child? Miss Earnshaw is the child's natural mother. She is — or was — married to Tengku Ibrahim. I have here a notarised copy of a marriage certificate issued by the Registry at Hammersmith, London. You will note the date and the names of the parties. The man referred to as Abraham Alexander is Tengku Ibrahim."

The inspector turned to Ibrahim. "Is this all true, sir?"

Ibrahim's customary bluster seemed to have deserted him momentarily. "Well, yes. I mean, no. She's not my wife. The marriage isn't valid."

"You have a court order declaring the marriage void, I presume," inquired d'Almeida.

"Well, no. Hang it all, man, she broke into my house and kidnapped my child."

"When you say 'broke in', are you saying that Miss Earnshaw forced her way into your house past your staff and took the child?"

"No, but..."

"Are you saying that your staff were coerced by threats to give up the child?"

"No, but..."

"Are you denying that she is the mother?"

"No, damnation..."

"Have you an order of court granting sole custody of the child to you?"

"Damn you! You know jolly well I don't. I won't be cross-examined by you. I want justice and I want my child back."

The Inspector stood up and pocketed his notebook. "I'm sorry to have wasted your time Mr d'Almeida."

Ibrahim blazed again. "What! Aren't you going to do anything about this disgraceful woman?"

The Inspector heaved a sigh. "Nothing to be done, sir. She's the mother. You've admitted that yourself. A case for the courts. Good morning to you, gentlemen, Miss." He touched the peak of his cap in salutation. "I'll see myself out."

"Damn you, d'Almeida!" hissed Ibrahim. "I'll report you to

the Bar Committee!"

"For what?" responded d'Almeida placidly. "Surely you don't think that I or my assistants had anything to do with this?"

Ibrahim clenched his fists. "I'll see you in court!" He left in a cloud of fire and brimstone.

"What are my chances, Mr d'Almeida?" asked Kate when our guests had gone.

"Better than they were before, Miss," said d'Almeida, quietly polishing his spectacles, "much, much better."

IBRAHIM was as good as his word. Within the day we were served with his papers seeking a declaration that his marriage was void and asking for custody of Lucy. I was in d'Almeida's room discussing another matter when Moraiss brought the papers in.

D'Almeida looked at them quickly and then threw them over to me. "Have a look at these. Are they in order?"

I glanced quickly through them. "He's representing himself."

"Good for him," responded d'Almeida. "I want you with me when we go in." He walked over to the bookcases along the wall and pulled out a heavy tome. "Meanwhile, you have some homework to do."

I glanced at my watch in trepidation.

D'Almeida understood my gesture and said, "Don't worry about your family. I've sent Smallwood and Singham over to stand guard. But I don't think anything will happen. He's obviously decided to do things the legal way, so I'm fairly certain that we'll have no trouble before the hearing."

D'Almeida proved to be right. Either Ibrahim didn't know where Kate and Lucy were, or he had decided to let the majestic apparatus of British law take its course. Whatever the reason, we were spared any nocturnal visitations.

Ralph and George took turns to do sentry duty at my place, just as a precaution, but their presence on that score proved superfluous. However, they livened up our social evenings no end. Actually, the girls had the time of their lives, what with the baby and two jolly bachelors around the place. Our neighbours began to shun the mansion as a house of ill-repute.

The case was fixed for hearing in the chambers of Mr Justice Gibson. It came on within a week, which was a record. There are compensations in being a prince. Gibson was a brown wrinkled walnut of a man, dried out by a lifetime in the tropical sun. He was due to go back to England on retirement in a few months. No doubt the Chief Justice thought that he should keep busy in the meantime.

On the appointed day, we appeared at the Supreme Court in full fancy dress. The interior was pleasantly cool after the scorching heat of the day. Across the road the new Supreme Court building was slowly and majestically rising on the site of the old Hotel de l'Europe. Some people were nostalgic about the Europe, but personally I preferred the new building. For one thing I would never have got past the doorman at the old Europe.

Gibson's court was on the first floor. Ibrahim was there before us, decked out in full regalia. I must admit that he certainly looked the part. He stared at us coolly, barely deigning to acknowledge our presence. We were ushered into the Judge's chambers by his clerk. The Judge was there, looking rather shrunken behind his large desk. After the customary formalities, Ibrahim launched his case. The Judge listened impassively to the torrent of words. At length he spoke.

"I have read the affidavits, gentlemen, and subject to what you may have to say, Mr d'Almeida, I am minded to grant the application."

Ibrahim beamed. D'Almeida bowed. "As your lordship pleases.

We have no objection to the granting of the declaration that the putative marriage between my learned friend and my client is void."

Ibrahim stared at d'Almeida suspiciously. The Judge scribbled laboriously. "An order in terms of the application then," he said.

"However, my lord," interjected d'Almeida, "before your lordship makes the custody order, may I point out that the child is illegitimate."

Justice Gibson stopped writing abruptly and looked up. "Illegitimate, Mr d'Almeida?"

"Your lordship will note from the birth certificate displayed with my client's affidavit that the child was born before my learned friend's marriage to my client. In the normal turn of events, she would have been legitimated by her parents' subsequent marriage, but as your lordship has declared that the marriage is void...." d'Almeida left the sentence unfinished to let the Judge draw the conclusion.

"Umm, yes, indeed," mused the Judge.

D'Almeida continued smoothly. "As your lordship is well aware, custody of an illegitimate child is vested with the natural mother. The cases that my learned friend has cited to your lordship are regrettably not in point, as they deal with legitimate children. May I direct your lordship's attention to this passage in *Rayden*, where the principle is quite clearly set out."

I pushed a heavy black book over to the Judge, who took it and read at length.

Ibrahim was fidgeting uncomfortably. At last the Judge spoke. "Well, Mr d'Almeida, I see that you are quite correct. Mr Ibrahim, have you anything to say?"

"Ah, well, your lordship, I submit that the cases that I have brought up determine the point," he argued lamely.

Justice Gibson made an impatient noise. "Mr d'Almeida has

already pointed out that those cases deal with legitimate children. Have you anything else?"

Ibrahim fidgeted again. "With your lordship's permission, I withdraw my application to declare the marriage void."

D'Almeida interjected again smoothly. "With due respect to my learned friend, I cannot see how that would make a difference. He has given evidence in his affidavit that by the law of his domicile a prince of the blood may not marry without the express permission of the Maharajah. May I bring your lordship's attention to this passage in *Dicey*, which I think states the position quite clearly. Capacity to marry is governed by the law of the subject's domicile. Where a party has no capacity by that law, the marriage is void. I see no reason to doubt the veracity of my learned friend's evidence as to his capacity."

I pushed over another weighty tome which the Judge again mused over.

"Well," said the Judge, "the law seems clear enough. I grant the application for a declaration. Custody to remain with the mother." With that he rose and swept out.

Outside the court Ibrahim stopped us. "You think you have won," he snarled. "I warn you, do not cross me again." He stormed off.

On the way back to our office I congratulated d'Almeida on a famous victory. He brushed my congratulations aside.

"I fear that we have made a bad enemy, my boy," he said. "There is still a final act before the curtain falls."

He walked silently for some time. Suddenly, just as we were about to reach the office, he stopped. "I think that I shall have a party tonight. I'll need you at my place. Come early. I'll expect you at 6:30. Don't worry about Miss Earnshaw and the baby. I'll make arrangements for them."

He strode up the stairs rapidly, leaving me wrapped in puzzlement.

D'ALMEIDA lived in a large, rambling double-storey bungalow on the outskirts of town. It had an acre of grounds and backed onto a wooded hill. On either side were similar mansions, the occupants of which read like a Who's Who in the Colony. He had a retired Judge on one side and a Chinese millionaire on the other. I putt-putted up the driveway in my car at the appointed time. D'Almeida himself came to greet me at the door.

"Thank you for coming. I wouldn't normally trouble you, but it's the servants' night off," he explained. "I have some other guests already inside."

Night was already falling and the air was filled with the soothing "creek-creeking" of the crickets. Large luminous moths flew in and out, circling the lights. Kate was there, with Lucy. D'Almeida had had them fetched from my place shortly after the hearing. He led us to an enormous dining room, where dinner had been spread for two.

"You'll excuse me if I don't join you," he said. He took me aside and quietly to me, "I'd like you to keep an eye out for intruders."

"Do you expect any?" I asked.

He shrugged noncommitally. "I would not be surprised. Look after Miss Earnshaw and the child. I must see to my guests. Pull the bell-cord if you hear anything. On no account fall asleep." With that he left us.

Kate said very little during dinner. She seemed preoccupied. She had lapsed again into her monosyllabic mood, so after a while we ate in silence. After dinner we cleared away the dishes and retired to the library. Kate put Lucy to bed, and we both settled down to read.

With the tension of the day and the stress of the past week, I was feeling pretty tired. The sound of the crickets drifted in from the open windows. It was a cool night, and a soft breeze was blowing. Kate was dozing in her chair. Very soon I was nodding too.

I woke with a start. Kate was still asleep. It was 11:15. No sign of d'Almeida. I was just about to return to my book when I heard the floorboards above me creak. I knew that it was the spare bedroom, where Lucy was asleep. Cursing myself for my dereliction of duty, I cast around for a weapon. Nothing. In the end I armed myself with a volume of Shakespeare's collected works, a tome that had always floored me in school.

Cautiously, I crept upstairs. The house was in darkness. There was no sign of d'Almeida or of any other guests. I supposed that they had all left. My every step seemed to find a creaky floorboard. At last, I reached the guest bedroom. I stole in quietly, Shakespeare poised aloft.

The next thing I knew, an iron hand grasped my wrist and an arm was around my throat. I elbowed the man's stomach with my other arm and the grip loosened. Swinging around, I felt the impact of a blunt object on the side of my head. I yelled. Lucy woke and started to yell too. The intruder threw me to the side of the room. Another intruder ran to the cot and grabbed the child. Weakly, I tried to stop them. They brushed past me and thundered down the stairs.

Kate had been aroused by the commotion and came to the library door just in time to see the two black-garbed intruders rushing out the front door. With a despairing wail she flung herself after them. The door slammed in her face. She tried to open it. It wouldn't budge. Evidently, the intruders had jammed it with something or other.

I ran onto the second-floor veranda and switched on the lights. The two black figures were racing across the lawn, Lucy being held like a bundle in the arms of the bigger one. I looked around the veranda. D'Almeida grew orchids there. I picked up a piece of broken brick and hurled it at the running figures. By luck or divine guidance it struck the smaller man on the back of the knee. He fell with a groan. The big man stopped and turned, hesitating. I leapt off the veranda onto the ground, falling heavily. Picking myself up, I hobbled across the grass. The big man was there ahead of me. He had put Lucy down. In his hands he held a wicked looking *kris*. I halted abruptly.

The big man advanced. I picked up a stone from the driveway. At that moment I realised how David must have felt when confronted with Goliath. The man was large. With his face obscured by a handkerchief, he looked like a huge ape. Obviously, he hadn't evolved much from his pithecanthropoid ancestors. I licked my lips nervously.

Lights blazed suddenly from the house. The pithecanthropus flung up his arms, dazzled. Figures ran out from the main door onto the grass. One was carrying a gun. He pointed it straight at my adversary, who promptly turned and ran. Kate and another man ran over to Lucy, who lay whimpering on the damp grass. The others grabbed the fallen intruder, who was still lying on the lawn.

D'Almeida came up to me. "Are you hurt, lad?" he demanded.

"No," I replied testily, "not unless you consider a fractured skull and a broken ankle a hurt. How did they know Lucy and Kate were here?"

"I mentioned to the court peon that Miss Earnshaw and Lucy would be staying with me," replied d'Almeida. "He must have tipped off Ibrahim's men, as I expected. I imagine that we were followed from the office when we came here."

"You could have warned me," I said reproachfully.

"I did," he replied. "I said to pull the bell-cord if you saw anything. Why didn't you?"

"Forgot in the excitement," I admitted sheepishly.

"Well, no harm done," he said, with masterly understatement. "Come, let's see our bag. Unless I miss my guess, these will be Ibrahim's minions."

We strode over to where the smaller intruder was being held. He was rubbing his leg. To my astonishment, I saw that it was Ibrahim himself.

"Well, well," said d'Almeida, "this is better than I thought. I suppose you didn't trust anyone else?"

"You can't hold me," hissed Ibrahim through clenched teeth, "I have immunity."

"On the contrary, Your Highness, we are holding you. Excuse my manners, I haven't introduced you." D'Almeida gestured towards the men holding Ibrahim. "Tengku Ibrahim, may I present Mr Tan Choon Guan JP, and Subedar-Major Baldev Singh Bahadur. The gentleman over there with Miss Earnshaw and Lucy is Sir James Allen, formerly one of His Majesty's Judges. Gentlemen, may I present Tengku Ibrahim Iskandar Shah."

I was taken slightly aback by the number of luminaries surrounding me.

D'Almeida continued, "We were having our usual neighbourly poker game in my attic when you interrupted. I am not sure how the authorities will view your rather rude intrusion into our little circle."

Ibrahim fell silent. I sat down heavily.

D'Almeida came over and put his hand on my shoulder. "You did well." I looked over to Kate, who was cradling Lucy and whispering soothing words. She turned and gave me a wan smile.

THE AUTHORITIES were in a quandary. To prosecute would have caused an almighty stink and led to all sorts of complications with Ibrahim's State. As it was, the old Maharajah was flirting with the Dutch, and public humiliation of his son was the last thing likely to endear the Empire to him. His little island kingdom might have been a pestilential mudhole, but it was a pestilential mudhole floating in a sea of oil. The Colonial Office would not have been amused. To let Ibrahim off was out of the question, given the standing of the persons who had caught him in the act. Eventually a compromise was reached. D'Almeida generously agreed not to press charges, and Tengku Ibrahim quietly left the Colony. He would have stayed, but I suspect that the old Maharajah pulled him out quickly to avoid a scandal.

As for Lucy and Kate, d'Almeida thought it advisable that she should get out of the Colony as soon as possible. Even if Ibrahim himself took no further retaliatory action, one could never be sure that his followers might not take it into their heads to avenge his humiliation. In any case, Kate was irredeemably beyond the pale as far as white society in the Colony was concerned. Her liaison was widely known in the close confines of colonial society, and a single mother with an illegitimate daughter would hardly find life congenial here. Nor would little Lucy have had much of a future; she would always be tarred with the brush of her mixed ancestry.

In the end, Mak's American missionary friends arranged passage to San Francisco, where she was to put up with a friendly couple until she could get her life back in order. In that great melting pot, Lucy would have a chance. Kate wanted to give d'Almeida what was left of her five hundred pounds, but he refused.

"Keep it for the child," he said.

I'll skip over the tearful scenes when they left us. The girls were inconsolable over the loss of the baby. I don't recall that they made that much fuss when I left.

I took them down to Clifford Pier myself. The cavernous hall was crowded with wellwishers seeing off friends and family. Sampans bobbed like leaves in a stream, packed with baggage and humanity, bumping gratingly against the sides of the pier as they jostled for space. Here and there among the throng of black and brown boats gleamed spotless white launches from the passenger ships moored offshore. There was a steady chain of tongkangs ferrying cargo from the freighters anchored out in the harbour to the godowns lining the Singapore River.

We reached the head of the steps leading down to the launch that was to take Kate to her ship. There was an awkward silence. Kate took my outstretched hand in an embarrassed way, as if uncertain what to do.

"Goodbye and good luck Kate," I said; one would have liked to make a better speech, but the words did not come.

"Goodbye and thanks again," said Kate, with downcast eyes.

Lucy fretted in her arms. She started to walk down the steps, eyes fixed on the slippery stones. Then she stopped, turned around and came back up. Without a word, she put her free arm around my neck and gave me a quick peck on the cheek. Lucy curled her podgy arms around me too and squeezed. It must have caused a stir, but I didn't notice.

Then they were gone, running to get aboard their launch before the crew cast off. The little white speck dwindled until it was lost to view in the bustle of the harbour.

EVELYN

I DISCOVERED early in life that one of the secrets of a good practice is to look the part. You don't have to be brilliant to be successful. Clients generally can't tell a good lawyer from a bad lawyer; a grave expression and grey hair are always an asset. It doesn't matter if when you open your mouth you put your foot right in it, as long as it is done with decorum and dignity. You can always blame the Judge later. We had a perfect example right in the firm.

Though Clarence and Cuthbert d'Almeida ran the firm, there was in fact a third partner. Simon Da Silva was the third man. He owed his position to the fact that some time in the distant past the d'Almeidas had had a spot of financial bother and were bailed out by Simon's father. As a result, old man Da Silva owned a third of the firm. When the old man passed on, Simon was taken on in his place. No doubt the d'Almeidas did it out of gratitude to the father and to repay the debt of honour. Either that or they had a collective breakdown of common sense.

Simon was in his late thirties when I joined the firm. He was a fine figure of a man, with chiselled features and prematurely grey hair, which actually enhanced his appearance. He looked every inch a lawyer. He even sounded like a lawyer. However, after a short acquaintance one came to the conclusion that that wonderful head only existed to keep his ears apart. Simon, in short, was a simpleton. What was worse, he didn't realise it.

Simon was generally too self-absorbed to be deliberately offensive. He rather fancied himself to be a hotshot lawyer, and we pupils played our little part in keeping up the charade. He was actually quite a pleasant fellow, once one got used to the fact that he was a twit. A little flattery always worked wonders. The trick was to agree wholeheartedly with everything he proposed, no matter how egregious, and then do something else entirely. We didn't take him seriously. He didn't seem to mind. The d'Almeida brothers were always around if we needed any serious guidance.

The d'Almeidas had over the years developed the ability to manage Simon into a fine art. He never ever did a case alone. One or the other of the brothers was always around, in an advisory capacity. Simon was good at one thing. He was a society person, and knew practically everyone worth knowing in the Colony. And he had a wonderful bedside manner with clients. They always went away reassured. Mr d'Almeida generally was too impatient and mercurial for a client to be totally at ease with him, especially when they were not being totally candid. Cuthbert, for all his talents, had the look of a buffoon. But Simon... Simon was cool, urbane and suave. With his impressive leonine mane and polished voice, he was the very embodiment of the successful advocate. It mattered not one jot to clients that he had no measurable IQ. He sounded right and fitted the part perfectly, and that was what mattered. And so the partnership flourished, with Simon pulling in the clients and the d'Almeidas doing the work.

One fateful day after Christmas, however, both brothers were called away to Penang on the occasion of a relative's passing. Penang was a good day's journey away, by train or by boat. They left Simon in charge of the shop, no doubt saying a prayer that nothing would crop up in the meantime. It was a slack period anyway — the limbo week between Christmas and the beginning of the new year. No one in town was in the mood for work. People had partied themselves into a stupor on Christmas and Boxing Day, and were taking a deep breath before plunging into the new round of New Year's parties. We pupils were left to our own devices.

Simon had come late to fatherhood and had taken to it with enormous enthusiasm. He had stacks of baby photos and insisted on showing them to everyone several times a day. We were also treated to blow-by-blow accounts of Junior's development. Every burp, belch and babble was faithfully chronicled and recited to whichever poor soul happened to be handy. On the day after the d'Almeidas' departure, George came stumbling into the pupils' room, seeking sanctuary from the incessant pater-patter of little feats.

"Something's got to be done about that man," moaned George. "One more tale about Junior's dietary habits and I shall puke."

Ralph and I commiserated. For some reason unknown to us — but for which we were profoundly grateful nonetheless — Simon had formed the impression that George was particularly interested in children. Perhaps it was because of his wonderful performance with little Lucy. Uncle George was always pulling faces and giving horsie rides and telling funny stories. Whatever the reason may have been, George was the preferred victim whenever the latest bulletin on Junior's development was issued. If he was around, both Ralph and I were safe. We took to moving about the office in his company whenever Simon was on the prowl — the principle was not unlike that of a lightning rod.

George did not reciprocate Simon's interest. He was just as quick as Clarence d'Almeida, and a lot more impatient. He was in fact related to the d'Almeidas. His mother was a cousin of Clarence and Cuthbert, and he had obviously inherited the smart genes from the d'Almeida clan. Looking at him, however, one would not immediately have guessed at the relationship, for George was ebony-dark from his father's side. He was obsessively touchy about the relationship. When Ralph had teasingly mentioned his "Uncle Clarence" one fine day before we got to know him so well, George had immediately detonated. After picking ourselves up out of the rubble, we were very careful from then on not to allude to the relationship at all. George wasn't one to suffer fools gladly. I'm surprised that he managed to keep his temper with Simon, whose egregiousness sometimes drove even Ralph — the embodiment of patience — to distraction.

"Here," said Ralph, flinging over a copy of the latest Agatha Christie mystery, "bury your beak in that." Normally, we were much more discreet when the d'Almeidas were around. The casual visitor would find us deeply engrossed in some monumental tome by Rayden or Dicey or Chitty. Of course, the contents were something else. Ralph had purchased a set of old out-of-date textbooks at a pittance and had hollowed them out with painstaking care. Each massive volume neatly took one copy of the latest Christie or Dorothy Sayers pot-boiler. Nowhere in the Colony was there to be found a set of more diligent pupils. With the d'Almeidas out of the way, however, discretion was thrown to the wind. Moraiss the chief clerk would shuffle in and out casting dark disapproving glances at us, but who cared for Moraiss?

Just as George was settling himself, Simon strode in without so much as a preliminary knock to announce himself. There was a flurry of shuffling as the incriminating evidence was quickly hidden.

"More news about the kid?" asked George sweetly as he hurriedly swept his book into the drawer.

"I do wish you wouldn't refer to him as a kid. His name is

Aloysius. A kid is the young of a goat," said Simon.

"Precisely," muttered George under his breath.

"Pardon?" asked Simon, arching his eyebrows.

"Oh, I was just saying how I admire how precise you are in your use of the language," responded George smoothly. Simon simpered at the compliment. Ralph and I could only marvel at George's sang froid.

"Yes, indeed," continued Simon, "precision in language is always a tremendous asset to an advocate. One must know exactly what word to use on any particular occasion. A misplaced mot here or there can be devastating to a client's case. You young gentlemen will doubtless pick up the nuances as you progress in your careers. And I am always at your disposal should you require advice. Feel free. My door is always open."

He turned to leave. We opened our drawers halfway, in anticipation of his departure. Then he stopped.

"Oh yes," he said, "I was forgetting what I came for. Do any of you know any newspapermen?"

"Newspapermen?" queried George. "I know the paper-wallah on the street corner if that's any use. Always buy my papers from him on the way to work."

"No, no, not that sort of newspaperman," responded Simon. "I need a reporter at a newspaper with a good local circulation. Or better still an editor."

"Well, I know the assistant editor of the *Free Press*," chipped in Ralph. "He's quite a sociable bloke if you'd like to meet him."

"Yes, just the ticket. If you'd be so kind as to make the arrangements, we can have a *stengah* at the Recreation Club after work. Say, five o'clock?"

"Right-ho, five o'clock it is," replied Ralph, pencilling the appointment onto his cuff "What shall I tell him you want to meet him for? Business? Or are you just expanding your circle of friends?"

"Business. You see, I've just received this telegram." Simon turned conspiratorial. "I suppose there's no harm letting you lot in on the secret. It came this morning. From Colombo."

Simon unfolded the telegram. It was couched in the usual telegramese, but the gist basically was this. One William Jayasiri, a gentleman of some considerable fortune in Colombo, feeling the cold breath of mortality upon his neck, had expressed the wish to see his lost grandchild Evelyn once more before he died. Evelyn was the child of William Jayasiri's only son Herbert, who had married a woman from the Straits Settlements during the Great War. When Herbert died at Megiddo, the mother had taken Evelyn back to the Straits Settlements after a quarrel with the old man. This was in November 1918. Nothing more had been heard from them since. Old man Jayasiri was now at death's door and was holding on in the hope of seeing his only grandchild for the last time. His fortune would of course go to Evelyn. Jayasiri held d'Almeida in high esteem and bade him find the child. D'Almeida's correspondent stressed that time was of the essence as the old man might go at any moment.

"Well," said Simon, "so there it is. Now of course we can't wait for Clarence to get back, in the light of the urgency of the matter. I shall handle it, as the senior man around here."

George looked doubtful. "Don't you think you ought to cable Mr d'Almeida at least?"

"No, no, my boy," answered Simon, "Why should we trouble the man in his hour of grief. As I said, I shall handle it. I have a foolproof plan. That is why I require the assistance of a newspaperman."

He paused dramatically. We looked expectantly at him. "I shall leak the story to the newspapers. They will publish it and by tomorrow evening Evelyn Jayasiri will be standing here in this office." He ended with a note of triumph.

George looked at Ralph. Ralph looked at me. I looked at George.

"Don't you think that the response to such a story might be, er, a trifle enthusiastic," said George tentatively.

"Enthusiastic?" asked Simon, his eyebrows raised.

"Well, Evelyn has been missing since 1918. She's now around twenty. The old man hasn't seen her since she was a baby. Every gold digger in town will want to have a go at getting the fortune. How will you tell the real Evelyn from the fakes?"

Simon's brow clouded. "No, no, there will be no problem. I shallcross-examine her minutely to establish her bona fides."

He brightened at the thought of his prowess as an advocate. "Yes, I shall break any fake by cross-examination. It's a foolproof plan."

He turned back to Ralph as he left, "Don't forget now, have your newspaperman at the club this evening."

He disappeared through the door, repeating "foolproof."

George muttered, "Yes, more proof of your foolishness."

Simon's hearing was extremely acute and his head popped back in. "Pardon?"

"Oh, nothing," said George, smiling beatifically, "just repeating that it sounds foolproof." Simon nodded and left.

George turned to us. "Well, chaps, I fear we're going to be in for a long day. Mark my words, every prospector from Klondike to Ballarat will be outside that door tomorrow. It'll be up to us to sort the gold from the dross."

Simon's tea with Ralph's friend went well. They hit it off wonderfully and parted with mutual promises to have tiffin together sometime soon. The story was splashed on the front page of the *Free Press* morning edition: "Colombo millionaire seeks long-lost granddaughter." Full details of the story were carried, with a photo of Simon. I must say he was extremely photogenic. The paper ended by stating that the firm of d'Almeida & d'Almeida had been entrusted with the search and that the rightful claimant should present herself there promptly.

When we got back from tiffin, there was a queue four-abreast snaking halfway down Battery Road.

Moraiss was waiting for us at the head of the stairs. "He wants to see you," he intoned in sepulchral tones, jerking a finger in the direction of Simon's room. We dutifully trooped off in a file.

Simon was not his usual self when we got in. While not exactly dishevelled, he wasn't entirely hevelled either, as Bertie Wooster might have put it. His tie was ever so slightly off-centre and a couple of stray strands marred the perfection of his hairstyle.

"Ah, there you are," he greeted us, rising as we entered. "It, ah, seems as if we, ah, have a trifle more applicants than I anticipated."

George glanced at Ralph and me smugly. "Ballarat and Klondike," he whispered.

"Pardon?" said Simon.

"I said we should smell out the rats and tell them to take a hike," responded George smoothly.

"Ah, yes, precisely. Exactly what I was going to suggest, though not in quite such graphic terms." He paused. "Ah, have you any suggestions how we might proceed?"

"Well," said George, "I noticed quite a number of Chinese in the queue and even a couple of *orang puteh*. I suggest we get rid of those for a start."

"Yes, excellent. Exactly what I was going to suggest myself."

"Then we can shoo off those who are obviously too old. Anyone with wrinkled skin and false teeth is out, for instance."

"Yes, yes, absolutely. Get rid of the old ones, what. That should thin the crowd." Simon was looking a little happier now.

"And then you can interview the rest. With your brilliant cross-examination you should be able to pick out the real Evelyn Jayasiri in no time at all."

Simon looked a little doubtful, but he nodded his head. "Yes, I think that's how we should proceed." He rummaged in his drawer for a folder. "I'll question them about... about...." He trailed off.

"About their life in Ceylon," suggested George, "and about old man Jayasiri and poor Herbert."

"Yes, exactly. About their life in Ceylon. And Jayasiri and Herbert."

He paused. His brow furrowed. Obviously a thought was trying to burrow its way to the surface. It finally broke through.

"But will she remember? She was only a baby then. A baby would hardly know, would she? But then again, I know that babies can be awfully smart. Take Aloysius, for example. Why just the other day he..."

George hurriedly broke in. "That's precisely the point. Anyone who tells you a detailed tale is obviously a fraud. Evelyn was only a baby. She wouldn't remember anything. Aloysius is after all unique."

Simon beamed. "Yes, he is. As I was telling you, just the other day..."

We beat a hasty retreat, with George at the head. "Got to get started," he called over his shoulder.

After the great culling, we were left with about twenty winsome maidens who looked about the right age and race. All professed to be Evelyn. One wanted to show me her birth marks, but I protested that I was still on duty and disappeared back into the throng.

We got them organised finally, and they trooped in one by one to be interviewed by Simon. We sat in to listen to their tales; and what a cornucopia of fairy stories we got. Everyone had a distinct recollection of dear old granddad, how nice he was, how he'd bounce them up and down, what a lovely place Colombo was. George started taking down notes, to be used in his great unfinished novel, he said.

By eight o'clock it was all over. The street was deserted and we were utterly spent. Simon was looking dejected. No one had fitted the bill. He packed up in silence, dispiritedly stuffing papers into his briefcase. Ralph had left by then, pleading an important engagement. George and I went through the office locking up the windows. Simon slipped out without saying goodbye.

"C'mon," said George as I crashed the folding metal gate shut, "let's get a drink at the Club." I nodded.

We were only a few yards down the road when a large dark woman waddled up to us. She was clad in a greasy sari, and rolls of fat bulged under the folds. Her mouth was stained red with the juice of betel nuts. She clutched at my sleeve. Instinctively I drew it away.

"You want Evelyn Jayasiri," she said, almost belligerently. She spoke with a strong Tamil accent, evidently unused to speaking English.

We stopped. George answered her, "Yes, we're looking for Evelyn Jayasiri. Do you know where she is?"

"I know. You come." She turned her attention to George and pulled at his sleeve. He hesitated. She clicked her tongue impatiently. "Come."

"Come where?" asked George. "Is it far?"

"Serangoon. She is there. Come."

"Serangoon? Walk to Serangoon at this time of the night? You must be joking. Let go of me. Go on, let go." He shook himself free. "Besides, how do you know Evelyn? Have you any proof?"

The woman stopped. She fumbled in the folds of her sari. When she withdrew her hand, there was a shiny trinket in it. It was a gold bangle, of the sort they put on babies' legs. She held it out to us. I took it.

"Look behind," she said.

I held it up to the light of the street lamp. Incised in fine strokes underneath was the name Evelyn. I passed it on to George, who squinted at it. We drew back a little to consider the evidence.

"Well," I said softly, "what do you think?"

"I don't know," he said. "The name on the bangle fits, but then there must be a thousand and one Evelyns in the Settlements." He looked at the woman. She stood there looking back at us, arms folded across her ample breast. George turned to her.

"Where did you get this?"

"It belong to Evelyn. Her grandfather give it. Come, I take you."

"Wait a moment. How do you know her?"

"She is my daughter," said the woman shortly.

WE WERE struck dumb momentarily by this information. Certainly, the woman before us hardly fitted my conception of what Evelyn's mother should have been. I had pictured her as young, engaging — perhaps even pretty. But then, that was twenty years ago. A war widow would not have had an easy time. Hard work, a squalling child, penury. All these things take a toll. The creature before us looked work-worn and coarse. She was fat, but not with prosperity. She looked like she had gone completely to seed, given up totally on her appearance. Her dark skin had a sickly hue, and her eyes were tinged with yellow. A faint, stale smell clung to her, compounded of alcohol and spices.

While we stood there deliberating, a familiar shadow fell between us. We turned to see Simon at the gate of the office, fumbling for his keys. He noticed us at the same time.

"What, you fellows still here? Left my papers in the office," he volunteered by way of explanation.

I crossed over to him. "Mr Da Silva, there's been a development. This lady here," I said, jerking my thumb at the woman, "claims to know where Evelyn Jayasiri is."

Simon's face brightened up immediately. "I knew it," he said triumphantly, "I knew we would find her."

"The evidence is a little equivocal," I said, trying to bring him back to earth. "She has a bangle with the inscription 'Evelyn' on it. She claims to be the mother. George and I are a little doubtful..."

"No, no I'm sure that it's her," he cut in. "I have a feeling, you know, a nose for this kind of thing. I can tell by looking at someone whether they're telling the truth. She has a truthful face."

He crossed over to the woman. "My dear lady," he gushed, clasping her hand, "how delighted I am to meet you. I understand that you can take us to Evelyn."

The woman started back a little at Simon's effusive greeting. However, he was patting her hand reassuringly, and she concluded that he meant no harm.

"You come with me?" she queried. "I take you to Evelyn."

"But of course, madam, of course. Come, let's take my car. Is it far from here?"

"Serangoon. We go to Serangoon."

"Yes, of course. Lead the way madam. My car is at your disposal." He took her arm and guided her towards his parked car. George and I dutifully followed.

A short drive took us to our destination. Crossing the Rochor Canal, we passed into a different world. In contrast to Raffles Place, which was abandoned to the stray dogs and the *jagas* after hours, Serangoon was still pulsating. It was a different life from Chinatown. The varied hues of the Indian Empire milled about here, from the rugged leather brown of the Northwest Frontier to the rich ebony of the Tamil south. The night was perfumed with spices and the scent of frangipani. I found it a trifle overwhelming, this olfactory assault by a thousand different smells. However, as I got used to it I found the mixture to be strangely pleasant and addictive.

We turned off on one of the side streets. The scents of Little India were masked here by the stench of the nearby canal. Our guide indicated that we should stop in front of a ramshackle hut. We got out. The hut itself was made simply out of rough-hewn planks. It had a zinc roof and unglazed windows. A gap-toothed fence separated it from the street. The woman motioned us to the door.

Stepping into the hut, our noses were assailed by the stench. The woman fumbled in a corner and lit a kerosene lamp. By the orange glow of the lamp we discerned a scene of total chaos. My first thought was that someone had discovered the heiress within and had kidnapped her. On closer examination, however, it was evident that the jumble was natural. Cardboard boxes of all descriptions were piled along the walls. Old kettles, flatirons and tin cans littered the floor. In one corner was a cascade of old newspapers. The place was unfurnished except for two plain wooden chairs and a table, covered with linoleum of a nondescript pattern, so faded now as to be barely visible. There were blankets and cloths heaped in piles. An iron bedstead stood in the corner. The smell of rancid food and unwashed humanity pervaded the atmosphere.

"Where's Evelyn?" asked George in muffled tones, his nose buried in his handkerchief.

Simon, to his credit, did not show in the least that he was disturbed. He repeated the question in less antagonistic tones. "Now, madam, if you would be so kind as to introduce us to Evelyn Jayasiri."

The woman indicated what I had taken to be a bundle thrown haphazardly on the bedstead. I squinted my eyes. It was a person, covered with a dirty blanket.

Simon lost a little of his composure. "Ah, you mean that is she?"

Our guide nodded. She prodded the bundle, from which a low moan emerged. A dirty, unkempt head raised itself. The girl had jet-black hair, uncombed and unoiled. Her eyes were dull as she tried to focus on us. When she realised that she was in the presence of strangers, she recoiled and drew the grubby blanket up to her chin, staring at us with frightened eyes. A series of guttural sounds emanated from her throat.

"She is Evelyn. She cannot speak. She is dumb and deaf," explained the woman.

Simon was obviously crestfallen. This unwashed apparition evidently did not fit his conception of the long-lost heiress. "Well, ah, madam...you understand I must have proof." He darted a sceptical glance at the girl. "The fortune is a considerable one, and I must be absolutely sure that this girl is Evelyn Jayasiri."

Without a word, the woman retreated into the gloomy depths of the hut, rummaging under the newspapers and cloths. She emerged with a case, evidently a small cabin trunk of leather, much worn. Wordlessly she handed it to Simon. George and I pressed close to get a glimpse.

Simon fingered the cover of the case. It was embossed with a faint name. Simon screwed up his eyes to make out the writing in the dim glow of the kerosene lamp.

"Here, try this," said George, pushing a pencil and paper over to Simon.

"Ah...what should I do with these?" asked Simon bewildered.

"Let me have that," said George impatiently.

He took the case from Simon, set it on the table after having swept the jumble off onto the floor. Placing the paper over the incised words, he started shading with his pencil. A name took shape. Jayasiri.

George tried to open the case. "It's locked," he said.

The woman produced a small brass key. George put it in the

keyhole and turned it. It clicked and he lifted the lid gingerly.

Inside was an assortment of items, packed tightly together. George extracted a brass photo frame first. There was a photograph of a handsome young man in uniform, attended by what was evidently his valet. Written on it was the inscription, "To my only love and mother of my child, Herbert." Next came another photograph, this time of a group of soldiers. On the back was written: "Hong Kong & Singapore Mountain Battery, Palestine, 1918." A packet of letters followed, tied with a silk ribbon. George handed these to Simon, who extracted them one by one and read them. He passed them on to me. They proved to be love letters, written in a small neat hand, from Herbert Jayasiri to his wife, whom he consistently addressed in the most affectionate terms. I felt uneasy at reading such personal correspondence, embarrassed to be intruding into a private world. Folded baby clothes were unpacked, and right at the bottom of the case was a creased, faded piece of official paper. Simon unfolded it. The ink had faded badly, but we could just about make out the writing. It was a birth certificate, issued at Colombo on 9 April 1918, for Evelyn Jayasiri. Simon placed it carefully back and turned to the woman.

"Well, madam...ah, Mrs Jayasiri...I think that you have made your case. I am satisfied that this girl is Evelyn. I shall cable Colombo tomorrow and arrangements will be made to put you in contact with your father-in-law."

The woman nodded.

"I bid you goodnight." Simon bowed and shook her hand gravely.

As we were leaving, he suddenly turned and asked, "As a matter of curiosity, how did you locate us?"

"I collect newspapers and I read," said Evelyn's mother, indicating the mess piled against the wall. "I read in the *Free Press* that you look for Evelyn. So I come."

Simon beamed. "Excellent, just as I intended." He strode jauntily to the parked car, humming merrily. "A foolproof plan," he repeated, "foolproof."

Simon gave us a lift back home. George was strangely withdrawn during the journey.

THE NEXT MORNING, I got in to the office a little later than usual as the d'Almeidas were still out of town. Simon was already in, dictating telegrams to announce his success. He was utterly pleased that his grand plan had so clearly succeed. He had been totally vindicated in his confidence. Deep down, I think that Simon may have had some inkling of his inadequacies, and a success like this did no end of good in boosting his self-image. He went humming around the office, and even forbore to bore us with the usual bulletin on Aloysius's latest antics.

George rumbled in a few minutes after. He flung his briefcase down on the desk and said, "I don't like it."

"What?" I asked innocently.

"This whole business with Evelyn. I don't like it. It doesn't add up."

"Oh come now," I replied, "don't be peeved just because Simon is right for once in his life. Think of it as beginner's luck."

"No, this hasn't anything to do with Simon," he responded moodily. "The whole business has been bothering me all night." He started to pace. Evidently d'Almeida's mannerisms were contagious. George sucked the end of his pencil.

"Let's review the facts. One, Herbert Jayasiri was obviously an educated man — his letters show that. Two, he's obviously rich, and besotted with his wife. Three, his father is clearly not the sort to let his son marry any old body. Now consider exhibit A, the woman who claims to be Evelyn's mother. She's not educated.

She's not charming or witty or cultured. What would a man like Herbert see in a creature like that? Would old man Jayasiri let his only son and heir marry her?"

"Well, love is blind, as they say," I remarked.

"Blind?! Hah! Love would have had to be dumb and deaf too, as well as possess a defective sense of smell."

"You're not being kind at all. She may not have been like that twenty years ago. Poverty can do terrible things you know. As for the old man, he evidently didn't get on with his daughter-in-law. Don't forget, Herbert was barely cold in his grave when he drove her and the child from his door."

George stopped pacing. "I'm going to get to the bottom of this." He turned abruptly, grabbed his jacket off the rack and started for the door. "You coming?"

"Coming? Where to? During office hours?"

"I'm going to trace a ship. C'mon, Simon won't miss us. We'll just leave word that we've gone to sit in on a trial."

He scribbled a quick note on a piece of paper for Ralph to pass on to Simon, and galloped down the stairs. Hastily grabbing my own coat, I trotted after him.

"Trace a ship?" I huffed when I caught up with him, "What ship? Where?"

George was striding purposefully along, his long legs propelling him a yard at a time. He stopped abruptly and I almost collided into him.

"Did you notice the label on the trunk yesterday?"

I had some vague recollection of the thing, so I nodded, saving my breath for the next sprint.

"I read it carefully while Simon was fooling around with the baby clothes. SS *Dongala*."

"Okay, so we know that they were on the *Dongala*. So what does that prove?"

"Nothing yet. But I'll eat my hat and yours too if they were on the *Dongala*. I don't believe that that woman is Evelyn's mother and I don't believe that that pathetic creature is Evelyn."

"So how did she get hold of the birth certificate? And the letters? And the baby clothes and the picture of Herbert?"

George sucked his lip. "I don't know. But I'm going to find out. And you can help me. We need your car."

"All right," I answered doubtfully, not at all sure that we weren't off on a wild goose chase. "Where to?"

"Harbour Board," replied George laconically.

KEPPEL HARBOUR was a good half-hour's drive from town. The lifeblood of Singapore flowed through the harbour. For a place of such importance, security was surprisingly lax. The dark clouds of war had yet to form over the Straits, and we breezed past the security guard at the gate with a friendly wave of the hand and a merry toot of the horn. George directed me through the maze of docks and godowns. His father had worked for the Harbour Board, and it was evident that George was thoroughly familiar with the place.

I stopped the car where he indicated, and he disappeared into a nondescript brick building. Lolling in the driver's seat, I idly watched the busy scene, savouring the luxury of indolence amidst the toiling masses. Work did not stop here, not for Christmas or New Year. The gangs of sun-roasted stevedores threaded their way up and down the gangplanks of the moored freighters, like streams of ants carrying scraps of food from a picnic. Lorries trundled along, piled high with boxes, bundles and bags. Crates of merchandise were stacked along the quayside like giant wooden building bricks. The sun speckled the water of the harbour with a million points of light. In the background loomed Pulau Blakang Mati, the Isle Behind Which Lies Death. It was a pirate's cove when Raffles landed, and it is said that the beach was covered with skulls. The military was now in charge, and we were reassured that the heavy guns of Fort Siloso and Labrador made us the Gibraltar of the East.

My ruminations were interrupted by the return of George, who plumped himself into the front passenger seat and motioned me to go. Obediently, I started the car and under his guidance we arrived shortly in front of what seemed to be a small warehouse. George leapt out.

"C'mon, journey's end. Let's get cracking."

He said a few words to the porter at the door and showed a piece of paper. The porter unlocked the door, and we passed into the gloomy interior. The place was dark after the glare of the morning sun, and pleasantly cool. It smelt of mildew and moths. The whole building was filled with shelves, piled practically to the ceiling with boxes and files.

"What are we looking for?" I queried.

"Somewhere in this lot," said George, gesturing with his hand at the stacks, "is the passenger manifest of the SS *Dongala* for December 1918. That's what we're looking for."

My heart sank. George evidently had a massive masochistic streak. There were literally thousands of boxes.

"You're joking," I said, "it'll take us till next Christmas."

"Not if we use our heads, my son," he replied. "You must think like a bureaucrat. All the records from one year are likely to be together, simply because that's the easiest way to store them. Everything's in here somewhere, and I'm betting that the deeper we dig the further back in history we go. So you start over there, and I'll start over here." He pulled the nearest box out from the shelf, opened it and picked up a file. "Aha," he said, "not far back enough. Only 1931."

I shuffled moodily over to a stack at the far end. "I hope this is worth it. The things I do for friendship."

George stopped. He came over to me. "Look, Dennis, I'm not doing this just to spite Simon. He's an irritating so-and-so, but definitely not worth this much trouble. I'm doing it for justice. I don't think that woman is Evelyn's mother. Do you?"

"I'm keeping an open mind," I replied.

"All right, fair enough. But just say, for the sake of argument, that she isn't. The girl's a deaf-mute and doesn't look overburdened with brains. Old man Jayasiri is going to pop off any moment, and he's going to leave everything to this so-called Evelyn. If she is the heiress, then good luck and long life to her; but if she's a fraud, I'm not letting that Black Widow get her claws on the money. Are you with me or not?"

I nodded. He was right. If the woman was trying to get her greasy paws on Jayasiri's money by passing her daughter off as Evelyn, I couldn't just sit back and let her. Simon was completely convinced that he had found Evelyn and wouldn't even consider probing a little further. As far as he was concerned, the birth certificate and the personal items were absolute proof. With a deep sigh, I got down to work.

Archaeologists have the most mind-numbing job in the world, sifting grain by grain through the garbage of dead civilisations. That afternoon, I had a taste of an archaeologist's life. At least Howard Carter had found a tomb. All I found were the mummified remains of ancient arachnids, and enough dust to rebury Troy.

Stained with sweat, with my tummy protesting at its enforced abstinence, I was just about to drag another box off the shelf when George exclaimed, "Eureka!"

"You reek quite a bit yourself too," I responded testily, coming over to join him. "What have you got?"

"Nothing more than the passenger manifest of one SS *Dongala*, dated December 1918," said George triumphantly, waving a tattered file at me. "Ah, ah, no snatching," he said, holding it high up beyond my grasp.

We brought it over to a table near the window, and pored eagerly over the yellowed pages. They were brittle, and the ink had faded to a light brown. Eagerly, we squinted at the neat cursive handwriting.

George ran his finger down the list. "Died, buried at sea, died, buried at sea, died, buried at sea. What the devil were they carrying? Typhoid Mary?"

"Close enough," I said, pointing to a notation in the margin. "Influenza. I think there was an influenza pandemic at the end of the war. Carried off millions."

George wasn't listening. His attention was fixed on the list. "Look here," he said, "no one got off at Singapore. They were in quarantine for two weeks, and then they went on to Batavia."

"So you're right. But what about the trunk?"

George sucked his upper lip. "There's no Jayasiri listed as a passenger. But then again, the mother may have been travelling under her maiden name. Lots of women with children. A couple with one child. Wait, here's something — Louise D'Sequeira, one infant, died, buried at sea."

"Could that be them?" I asked, straining to read the faint text.

"No," said George, with a tinge of disappointment, "look here — the baby was a boy. Also died and was buried at sea." His finger went down the list. "Aha!" he exclaimed, "here it is. One Malathi Devaraj, accompanied by an infant girl, left the ship at Penang. That must be them. No one else fits the bill. They're all families or single women."

"Hold on a sec," I said, struggling with my doubts, "this doesn't prove anything, you know. This Devaraj female might just be our

Black Widow. We didn't even get her name. She could have gotten off at Penang to escape that floating funeral parlour, taken a train to Singapore and collected her things here."

George nodded. "That's an extremely possible hypothesis, my dear Watson."

"I'd say it's a damned probable hypothesis. Why would she abandon her luggage to that woman otherwise? Face it, George, whether we like it or not the evidence does seem to be in favour of the Black Widow."

"Not so fast," returned George equably, "there is just one thing that was missing."

"What?"

"Her husband died in the war, right?"

"Right."

"That makes her a war widow, right?"

I nodded, but not out of comprehension. I couldn't see what he was driving at.

"War widows get pensions. I didn't see the pension book in the trunk, did you?"

"No, but that doesn't mean she hasn't got it."

"True, but the pension book would have been proof positive of her relationship with Herbert Jayasiri — more so than the photos and the letters. She didn't produce it."

"So what does that mean?" I asked.

"It means, my son," responded George, "that we have another call to make."

I DON'T know why they're called civil servants. The ones we met that day were far from civil, and not very servile to boot. We had driven directly from the harbour to the centre of town, where we had spent the last three hours buried in the bowels of colonial officialdom. On the face of it, our task was easy compared to the one we had just completed. All we had to do was trace one war widow.

Singapore was the commercial and political centre of the Straits Settlements, a miscellaneous collection of disparate properties collected by the British like unwanted Christmas presents and lumped together as a Colony for lack of any other logical geographical entity to tack them onto. Deep in the caverns of Empress Place, there had to be one department that kept records of payments to war widows. The trick of course was to locate that department.

We had spent the afternoon being bounced back and forth between surly secretaries and cantankerous clerks. Now, as the hands of the clock in the tower of the Victoria Memorial Hall drew inexorably towards five, a kind of eerie calm had descended upon the offices. Life was suspended in anticipation of the moment of release. We took the opportunity to collapse on one of the hard wooden benches put out to discourage the public from lingering too long.

I was totally shot, and leaned my head back against the bare wall. George, in contrast, was still fidgety.

"Give it up, George," I urged, closing my eyes and trying to still the drumming in my head. "There's always tomorrow."

"No!" he said fiercely. "Tomorrow's New Year's Eve, and then the weekend comes. Simon's already sent his telegram to Colombo. There's no knowing how long the old man will last, and if he makes his will over the weekend and pops off, SHE will get the loot."

I could see that this was getting to be a personal matter for George. Like his English namesake, he had an inner urge to slay dragons. This particular dragon seemed to have taken hold of him and he was clearly determined to master it or perish in the attempt. I had the uncomfortable feeling that he expected me to perish along with him.

"Be reasonable. It's five o'clock. Everyone's leaving. We're not going to get anything today."

Reluctantly, he saw reason. We got up to join the throng streaming out of the government buildings. Just as we were about to pass through the door, George suddenly let out a hoot.

"Hey! Hey! Malik!" he yelled.

A bronzed man in spotless white shirt and khaki trousers turned round. There was a moment of non-recognition, and then he flashed us a blinding white grin.

"George Singham! It is you! *Apa khabar?*"

"Good, good," said George, embracing the man. "Malik, let me introduce you to my friend Dennis Chiang."

I took the outstretched hand and shook it warmly.

"Dennis, this is my good friend Malik. We grew up in the same *kampong*. What are you doing now Malik?" he inquired.

"Long time no see, George. I am clerk here, in Revenue Section. I work here for three years already. So why are you here?" asked Malik.

"I came to find out about a war widow," said George.

Malik's brow furrowed in puzzlement. Briefly George explained our errand.

Malik placed his hand on George's arm and said, "You wait. Maybe I can find out for you. What is the name?"

George wrote Herbert's name down on a scrap of paper. Malik took it from him and disappeared down the corridor. Five minutes stretched to ten, and then to an hour. We paced up and down wordlessly. The building had long since emptied. A peon came along to chase us away, but George bought him off with twenty cents. I had just about made my mind up to leave when Malik returned, his trademark grin flashing in the gloom.

He handed a piece of paper over to George, who devoured its

contents eagerly. "Malik, you are a miracle worker. *Terima kasih* a thousand times."

"*Sama-sama*," responded Malik deprecatingly, "I do it for you, my friend."

We parted, having extracted from Malik a promise to dine with us at George's place the following week.

George handed the paper over to me. Herbert Jayasiri's widow had been collecting her pension without fail every month since January 1919. Her address was on record. It was in Penang.

George grinned fiercely in triumph. "That's it. That must be Malathi Devaraj."

"All right," I conceded, "you were right all along. Simon's going to be awfully upset that his foolproof plan only proved that he was a fool."

"Right, let's get going," commanded George.

"What, again? What for? You've got your proof. The Black Widow isn't Herbert's wife. What more do you need?" I was tired, hungry and my head felt as if some infernal blacksmith was forging thunderbolts inside it. George was not at that moment at the top of my list of persons most likely to be mentioned in my will.

"We've got to locate Evelyn quick," George responded, "before old man Jayasiri does something irrevocable. If we don't find her tomorrow, it might be too late to stop him leaving everything to that fraud."

I sighed. I was in it to the bitter end. "Okay, where to now?"

"To the railway station Jeeves, and don't spare the horses."

IT WAS dark by the time we got to the railway station, a grey granite block with four giant lily-white statues tacked onto the front. What they were supposed to represent I never discovered. The pigeons however were doubtless overjoyed to have such large targets to practice on. The interior of the station was cavernous, soulless and practically empty. It smelt vaguely of bird droppings.

I hurried off to call Mak to tell her not to keep dinner while George inquired after trains to Penang. To tell the truth, I wasn't entirely unhappy at the prospect of leaving for Penang. Since I got back from England, Mak had been assiduously combing the local population for a suitable Nonya in order to get me hitched. I had a vague suspicion that there might be a New Year's surprise waiting for me back home — my cousin May had tipped me off that dinner with a young lady and her parents had been arranged.

As I anticipated, Mak was adamant that I should come home that night for dinner. However, as she had not specifically told me beforehand that there would be guests, she couldn't rightly complain about me running off at short notice, especially as the matter concerned my work. Promising that I would meet her guests some other time (with fingers crossed behind my back), I pleaded that I had a train to catch and hurriedly blew her a peck on the check over the receiver. I rang off with relief.

The telephone was still warm when George grabbed my arm. He waved two tickets in my face. "Got 'em," he remarked triumphantly, "Come on, the train's waiting."

"What, now?" I bleated pathetically. "Don't we eat first?"

"No time!" he shot back. "The express leaves at 7:11. There isn't another until tomorrow. Come on!"

With that he was striding purposefully towards the platform. I followed him, pausing only to buy a couple of packets of *kachang puteh* from a vendor squatting at the gate.

We settled ourselves in the third-class compartment. "Settled" is perhaps not quite the right word. The benches were plain wood, with wooden backs. Not a creature comfort in sight. When H.E. the Governor made his stately progress down the Peninsula by train, he had the latest in luxury, a real air-conditioned carriage.

For us ordinary mortals in third class, a small fan distributed hot air around the coach, whirring like a demented bumblebee. Fortunately, the night was cool and we pushed all the windows down to let in the breeze.

We had the carriage to ourselves. I looked around vainly for some sign of refreshment. No buffet car. A quick visit to the facilities revealed that they too were somewhat spartan. Basically, there was a hole in the bottom of the carriage, over which one squatted and did what one had to do. No wonder the grass grew so luxuriantly along the track bed.

When I got back, I found George stretched out on one of the hard benches, blissfully snoring. After a quick dinner of dry *kachang puteh* I decided to join him. The rhythmic "clack-clack" of the wheels proved strangely hypnotic. Using my coat as a pillow, I lay flat and watched the dark silhouettes of trees flash by the windows. Occasionally we passed a yellow firefly-glow that betrayed a squatter hut perched beside the track. Time soon lost all meaning, and I drifted from consciousness to slumber without realising it.

The cold grey light of dawn found us at Butterworth. The ferry ride across to Penang Island was uneventful, and we got in just as Georgetown was waking. Dishevelled as we were, George was all for starting. But this time I put my foot right down. We repaired to a nearby coffee shop to get a bowl of porridge and a mug of black coffee. George could survive on sheer nervous energy, but I preferred my meals regular, hot and generally large.

Fortified with sustenance, I was ready to face a new day of hunt-the-heiress. We determined that the first thing to do was to get in touch with Mr d'Almeida. He and Cuthbert were staying at the E&O, as was their wont.

Hailing a passing rickshaw, we clattered our way through the busy streets of the town. Georgetown, like Singapore, was mainly

Chinese. Families squatted by the roadside taking their breakfast. The washing hung like coloured bunting from poles stuck out of the crowded terraces. An occasional car honked its way through the crowd, nosing carefully past heedless pedestrians.

It didn't take us long to get to the hotel. By sheer good luck, we found that the porter knew d'Almeida well and was able to tell us exactly where he had gone. Disdaining the usual hotel breakfast, d'Almeida had gotten up at the crack of dawn to seek out his favourite stall along Gurney Drive. Our muscular rickshaw-wallah was soon between the traces again, trotting steadily along Northam Road past the seafront mansions of the *towkays*.

We stopped at a collection of ramshackle stalls clustered under a large banyan tree. The sea air was bracing, and the smell of cooking pervaded the atmosphere. Vendors were hawking their wares, from fish fresh out of the water to sweets of all descriptions. We paid off the rickshaw with our last few dollars and plunged into the crowd in search of d'Almeida.

We found him at last, sitting on a high wooden stool sans coat and tie, sipping coffee from his saucer. He looked just like any other retired civil servant out for his morning constitutional. If he was surprised to see us, he certainly didn't show it. He invited us to have a cup of coffee with him, as if it was the most natural thing in the world for two truant pupils to turn up unannounced in Penang at eight o'clock in the morning. We gratefully accepted his offer, and George explained the circumstances animatedly.

D'Almeida listened gravely, not interrupting. After George's recital was over, he asked, "And now, Mr Singham, what do you propose that we do?"

"Well sir," replied George, "I say that we should go and find Evelyn, and then cable the good news to Colombo."

"You needn't have rushed, you know," said d'Almeida evenly. "Even if William Jayasiri dies over the weekend, his fortune would only go to the real Evelyn. If there is proof that the claimant is an impostor, the money would not be disbursed."

George's face sank. "However, as you have done such a good job tracing Mr Jayasiri's heir, I think we should do as you suggest."

George's face lit up again. D'Almeida paid for the coffees, and we threaded our way past the stalls back to the road.

It wasn't easy to get a taxi, but we finally caught a stray that had wandered out of the centre of Georgetown. The address that we had for Herbert Jayasiri's widow was in Ayer Itam, a small village a few miles away. A half-hour ride through fruit and rubber smallholdings brought us to our destination.

Ayer Itam was just a cluster of buildings along the road, thrown together absent-mindedly without a thought for town planning. Its crowning glory was the imposing Buddhist temple that towered above the village. A few languid souls wandered around, meandering with apparent aimlessness along the road.

We located the address easily enough, in one of the side streets of the village. It was a simple house in a row of terrace houses, with doors opening directly onto the five-foot way. George knocked on the door. The woman who opened it looked about forty, with fine features and jet-black hair tinged with white. She wore a simple sari, faded but clean, patched discreetly in places.

"Mrs Jayasiri?" said George politely. "We represent Mr William Jayasiri of Colombo. We've come about Evelyn."

The woman dropped at out feet in a dead faint.

FOR ONE moment we were frozen by her unexpected reaction. Then George recovered, and with my help carried the woman into the house. This was simply furnished, with cane furniture and linoleum on the floor. We settled her on a settee, where she recovered slowly.

"Sorry... I'm so sorry," she said, "It was the shock." Then a look of trepidation crossed her face. "You aren't the police?"

"No, madam," said George soothingly, "We're solicitors. We've been asked by William Jayasiri to locate Evelyn. Mr Jayasiri is dying, and would like to find Evelyn before he dies. He's going to leave her everything."

"How... how did you find us?" she asked uncertainly.

"Through the Pensions Office," replied George. "They had a record of your late husband. We found out that you'd been collecting a war widow's pension and this was the address they gave us. You are Malathi Devaraj, aren't you?"

She nodded mutely. "So many years. After so many years...." she muttered, almost to herself.

"May we see Evelyn? We'd like to meet her and tell her the news about her grandfather."

Madam Devaraj was about to reply, when a young woman entered the front room. She looked about twenty, with the same fine features and dark skin as her mother. Her hair was a lustrous ebony, plaited in a long tail that hung almost to her waist. She too was dressed in a sari, the folds of which clung to her lithe figure.

"Mother," she cried in alarm, "are you all right? Who are these men? Have they hurt you?"

"I am all right, child. This is Mr... Mr..."

"Singham," said George smoothly. "And you must be Evelyn."

Before anyone could answer, d'Almeida interposed quietly. "No, I think not. And I think that you are not Herbert Jayasiri's widow, madam."

Soft as d'Almeida's voice was, his interjection made us jump. We had forgotten his presence in the excitement. George was struck speechless. The young girl looked at d'Almeida in amazement.

"I am Evelyn Jayasiri," she said hotly. "I have proof if you want.

You may see my school certificate. I do not know who you are sir, but I know who I am and who my mother is."

D'Almeida turned to the mother. "Am I right, madam?" he asked evenly.

We all turned to her. She nodded slowly, her eyes downcast. There were tears in them.

"Mother..." began Evelyn, anxiety and confusion playing on her face.

Her mother motioned to her to sit. She dabbed at her eyes, and addressed d'Almeida, "You are correct, sir. I am not Herbert Jayasiri's widow, and my daughter is not his daughter."

D'Almeida nodded. "Perhaps you would be so kind as to explain."

George and I collapsed onto a handy sofa. Evelyn was sitting next to her mother, looking completely bewildered. Only d'Almeida seemed in complete possession of himself.

"I... I am Malathi Devaraj," she began hesitantly, "and Evelyn is my daughter. But I was not the wife of Herbert Jayasiri, and Evelyn is not his daughter. My husband..."

She choked a little. "My husband is there," she said, indicating a small framed photograph on a side table.

I looked at the photograph. I had seen that face somewhere before. Then it hit me. "Herbert's valet!" I exclaimed. "He was in the photo that we saw."

Madam Devaraj nodded. "Yes, he was Herbert Jayasiri's manservant." She turned to d'Almeida. "How did you discover that Evelyn was not his daughter?"

"Because," said d'Almeida slowly, "Evelyn Jayasiri was a boy."

We were absolutely flabbergasted by this pronouncement. George was sitting there open-mouthed, gulping like a goldfish. D'Almeida continued in an even tone.

"Let me explain. My two capable assistants here have done an excellent job tracking you down and with their help I think that I can piece some of the story together.

"I have known William Jayasiri for many, many years now. We became good friends when I worked in Colombo, oh, forty years ago. He had just returned from Egypt. William had been an assistant to Sir Evelyn Baring, the British agent and consul-general, for a long time. He was very loyal and thoroughly devoted to his employers. When his family converted to Christianity, he insisted on naming his son after Sir Herbert Kitchener, the Sirdar. And when Herbert had a son, William wanted to have him christened after Sir Evelyn Baring, his old master. Sir Evelyn — or Lord Cromer, to give him his proper title — condescended to allow them to name the child after him.

"Herbert lived in the Straits for a quite few years, looking after the family business. I knew him well. He married secretly and without his father's consent. He never introduced me to his bride. I suppose he was afraid that I would tell his father. All was forgiven when the baby was born. The family went back to Colombo. As I said, William melted when he knew he had a grandchild. Herbert went off to war while his wife and child stayed with William. When Herbert died, William was devastated. He was not a man to show his feelings openly, but Herbert meant everything to him. He must have quarrelled with his daughter-in-law. She left him, taking the baby with her. He never told me the details. After this he retreated into himself, and we lost touch. I take it that she found her way to the Straits with the baby, on the SS *Dongala*."

Malathi Devaraj spoke softly, "No, they never reached the Straits." She paused, her faced contorted with the pain of recollection. "Louise and I were... friends. I was the wife of Naidu, Mister Herbert's manservant. When Louise married Mister Herbert, I became her companion. We became close. She confided in me.

"When Evelyn was born, we thought that all would be well. Old Master William did not know of Louise until Mr Herbert married her. He was very angry when he found out. He wanted to disinherit Herbert. But when the boy was born, all changed. Master called for Herbert to return to Colombo. My husband and I, we went with them. I had my own baby." She indicated the girl Evelyn. "We were like family to Mr Herbert and Louise.

"Then one day Mr Herbert went to war. There was an artillery battery from Singapore in Palestine. Mr Herbert wanted to join his friends. My husband would not leave his side. He went as his servant, without a uniform. Master would not say goodbye to his son. He was angry that Mr Herbert should go when he did not have to. Life was difficult when they left. Master was very angry still. He was angry with Louise. He said that she should have stopped his son from going.

"Then one morning the... the telegram...." She broke down completely. We sat around abashed, at a loss how to comfort her. After a few moments, she recovered herself. "I'm so sorry. I did not think that the memory would still hurt so much. The telegram came. Mr Herbert had died of fever, in Palestine. My husband tended him to the last. Then he too died, of the same fever.

"The old Master took the news very badly. He locked himself in his room for days. Louise and I, we only had each other, and the babies. When the Master finally came out, he was changed, old. He shouted at everyone. He threw things. We could not live with him. He would have hurt Louise. One night we left.

"Louise worked at the hospital, day and night, tending the sick and the wounded. She became sick herself. I saw her slowly fading. I told her we must go back home. She had a brother in Singapore. She agreed at last. We got passage on the SS *Dongala*.

"It was crowded, families and children, women. Many were sick. We lived cramped together. Louise and I were lucky. We got a cabin to ourselves. But she was sick, and so was her boy. When the boy died, she gave up. She called me in the day after they buried the baby. I could see that the end had come. 'Lathi,' she said to me, 'you are my only friend. I have nothing to give but this.' She gave me her widows' pension book. It had her name and that of her boy, Evelyn. She said to me, 'take it. Put your finger print there. No one will know. You can collect the pension every month. I will not need it. I go to be with my husband and my child.' I refused at first. But she was persuasive. My husband died also, with Mr Herbert. He would not leave his master. But he was not a soldier, so I got no pension. Louise said to me, 'take it, if not for yourself, then for the sake of the baby.' So I took it. She died that same hour. We buried her in the Bay of Bengal. I came here, to Penang. I knew no one. We have lived here since. The neighbours know me as Louise Jayasiri, and my daughter is Evelyn Jayasiri."

There was silence. At last d'Almeida said, "Well, madam, I am sorry that we have disturbed you. We will take our leave now." He rose to go.

"But... but you will not inform the police?" said Madam Devaraj.

D'Almeida shook his head. "Herbert is dead, and so is his son. You keep his name alive, and his memory. Should I gainsay what his widow has done? Come, gentlemen."

He bowed graciously to her and started for the door. We dutifully followed. He stopped. "By the way, what became of Louise's cabin trunk?"

"Trunk?" replied Malathi Devaraj, with a confused look. Her brow creased. "I took nothing but my own things. Louise's goods were sent back to Singapore, to her brother. I do not know what happened to them."

"Was the brother married?"

"No, I do not think so. He was living with a woman when I knew him, ah... what is her name... yes, Letchumi. Why? Is it important?"

"No," replied d'Almeida, "Not important. I bid you good day, madam."

We travelled back to the E&O in silence. George looked extremely crestfallen. After the excitement of the last two days, the denouement had completely drained him.

As we stepped into the lobby, d'Almeida turned to George. "Excellent detective work, Mr Singham. I trust that you gentlemen will be spending the New Year's weekend here? Perhaps you will require an advance on your salaries." He gave a wad of bills to George and strode up the stairs before we could thank him. George brightened up considerably. We spent a very pleasant weekend in Georgetown that New Year's.

D'Almeida cabled his news to Colombo. William Jayasiri died that very weekend. As for the Black Widow, she did in fact turn out to be Letchumi — Louise Jayasiri's brother's mistress. She refused to admit it, and continued to claim for years after that some sharp lawyers had cheated her daughter out of her rightful fortune.

SIMON TOOK the news rather well on the whole, and did not bear George a grudge. However, the episode finally convinced him that the law was not his true vocation. He left the firm and joined the *Free Press* as its social editor, and an excellent gossipmonger he proved to be. He remained on good terms with the d'Almeidas, and would pop in once in a while to chat. On the last occasion, years later, he brought Aloysius, who was then a strapping youngster of ten. George, who had grown older and mellower, complimented Simon on his son.

"Oh yes, he's a fine lad. He gets his looks from his mother, you know. But his brains," said Simon, beaming with fatherly pride, "he gets his brains from me."

THE ADVOCATE'S DEVIL

"I NEED you to devil for me."

The request came like a bolt out of the blue. I was quietly
rummaging through the library, looking for something to read
that would not instantly send me into a state of terminal boredom,
when Mr d'Almeida materialised at my side.

"Don't look so shocked, young man," he continued, "I'm not
asking you to put your eternal soul in jeopardy. Come into my
office."

I trotted along dutifully. He motioned me to one of his
overstuffed leather armchairs and took his place behind the
enormous desk.

"I have a case upcountry — a small matter that I'm doing as a
favour for a friend. It's not complicated, just a private summons for
criminal trespass. The Magistrate has asked the parties to attend
on him in chambers to see if the matter can be amicably resolved
without a full hearing. Unfortunately, the case that I am presently
engaged in has gone into overtime. I fear that I shall not be able to
get away. Therefore I need someone to devil for me — to appear
before the Magistrate in my place."

He pushed a plain manila folder across the desk to me.
The sunlight was streaming in from the windows behind him,
surrounding his chair with a glowing nimbus. Mephistopheles

must have looked somewhat like that when he made his deal with Faust. Except perhaps for the spectacles.

"Not a difficult case," d'Almeida went on. "The accused is one Abdul Samad, a houseboy on the Bergenholm Estate. Or, I should say, a former houseboy. He allegedly was caught in the house after his dismissal intent on stealing things, according to the complainant. That is his former employer, a Mr Owen Evans, manager of the Bergenholm Estate.

"Samad says that he was treated like a slave and incarcerated against his will. He managed to escape with the help of some wellwishers, and returned to get his things. According to him, Evans is a petty tyrant and slave driver. He denies that he intended to take anything that did not belong to him.

"Evans has taken out a private summons against Samad for criminal trespass. We are defending him. The matter will be heard on Monday, or to be more precise, the magistrate has asked us to attend on him on Monday. I need you there as I shall most likely be delayed by my present matter."

I took the folder with a little apprehension. Thus far in my career I had been merely following the d'Almeidas or Simon around the courts. Here I was, being asked to fly solo. I wasn't sure I was ready. True enough, I'd seen a lot of good barristers in action, especially when I was at the Inns in London. I'd even taken part in a moot. But going it alone, for real.... A little knot of anxiety formed in the pit of my stomach.

"There's no need to be overly concerned," said d'Almeida, as if reading my thoughts. "I doubt that the matter will proceed to a hearing. The magistrate is a solid man — Andrew Richards. He's been here fifteen years and knows the people. He'll be scrupulously fair and even-handed as he twists Evans's arms to get him to withdraw the summons. No one wants the heart of darkness laid bare publicly, least of all the big plantation companies. All you have to do is to watch out for Samad's interests — make sure he gets a fair deal in the settlement. No giving up of wage arrears or any of that sort of thing.

"You'll have to spend the weekend there. I've arranged for you to stay with my old friend Conrad Davis at his place. The train leaves tonight at 9:30. Go home and pack now. Your tickets are in the folder. Get off at Parit Lambong. Someone will be there to fetch you."

D'Almeida turned his attention to another file on his desk. I took the hint and rose to leave.

"By the way, Chiang," he called to me as I got to the door, "the village is called Gua Langsuir. I hope you're not superstitious."

My brow was furrowed as I returned to my room, which I now shared with George. Ralph had been taken over by Cuthbert, who had installed him in an oversized closet next to his office. George, in his usual style, contrived to do as little as possible, while giving the impression of activity. He had a stack of law reports piled on his desk and a writing pad in front of him. Closer examination would have revealed that he was composing yet another poem to his current lady-love.

"What rhymes with Joan?" he asked, pensively chewing his pencil. "Groan? Moan? Loan? Not very promising, I must say. I need something beautiful, something poetical, something to move her soul. At any rate, something to move her over to my place this weekend."

"What's a *langsuir*?" I inquired, breaking into his romantic reverie.

"A langsu-what?"

"*Langsuir*. D'Almeida has asked me to devil for him upcountry. The place is called Gua Langsuir. He asked if I was superstitious. So what's a *langsuir*?"

George shook his head. "Not a clue."

"It is an evil spirit," intoned a sepulchral voice from right behind me. I jumped. It was Moraiss, the chief clerk. Moraiss had the habit of gliding noiselessly in and out like a wraith, bearing files and other missives from on-high. I hadn't noticed him come in. "A banshee. It is a place of ill omen." He glided out again.

"So there you are, my son," said George, "you're being sent to the Banshee's Cave. What better source of information could you ask for than our resident ghoul, Mr Moraiss?"

"I wish he wouldn't do that," I responded. "My heart nearly dropped out. Here, pass me a pad and a couple of pencils, will you? I've got to rush." I stuffed the folder into my briefcase and rummaged around for my things. George tossed over a writing pad.

"Happy hunting. Better you than me, I always say. Take a big stake and don't forget the garlic," said George as a parting shot. "Or does that only work in Transylvania? Maybe *belachan* will do the trick."

THE TRAIN journey was pleasant enough, just a single stop at KL for a bit of early-early breakfast, then a short hop across the platform to the local train. After rattling along for a couple of hours I was at Parit Lambong. There wasn't much to see of the place, just a platform and a stationmaster's office. The jungle pressed in from all sides. It wasn't difficult for my contact to identify me. No one else was barmy enough to get off in the middle of the *ulu*. He was a thin, dark Malay, who introduced himself as Awang. He took my suitcase and piled it into the back of an old lorry.

Our conveyance had obviously seen better days. Doubtless, it had been sent there to die in peace. On close examination, I deduced that it had been a Ford of some sort in an earlier life. However, it was so patched and mended with all sorts of parts of indeterminate provenance that it was hard to characterise it as any particular model of lorry. Awang climbed into the driver's seat, and I consigned myself to the mercy of that mongrel monstrosity, saying a little prayer for protection.

The road to Gua Langsuir climbed steadily upwards, towards the grey-green peaks of the Main Range. Awang was uncommunicative, and I wasn't in the mood for small talk myself. I settled back in my seat and took in the sights. The sun had risen, burnishing the top of the range with red and gold. As we rose, the air got noticeably fresher and cooler. The road clung to the slopes of the foothills, snaking back and forth like a giant python. The hillsides were covered with a dark-green fleece of jungle, still patched here and there with mist.

For the most part, we followed the course of a stream. Occasionally, a waterfall spurted off a cliff and tumbled over the mossy stones to join the stream. We splashed across a couple of little rivulets. Rounding a bend, I was dazzled by the flash of a million yellow wings, swirling like leaves in an autumn wind. I gazed fascinated. I had never seen so many butterflies congregated in one place before. Afterwards, when I described my encounter to d'Almeida, he told me that I was privileged. Once in a long while the feeding would be good and the population of Common Grass Yellows would boom. For a brief time, a fortnight maybe, they would throng the little moist spots, swirling up in drifts when disturbed by a passing vehicle.

We left the butterfly dance behind soon enough. The lorry began to labour as the gradient got steeper. We had parted company with the stream and were climbing up the slope of a mountain. From the jungle below, I could hear the echoing hoots of the siamangs as they swung from tree to tree. A couple of hornbills darted across the treetops, honking like impatient drivers in a traffic jam. Here and there a vivid splash of fire-orange betrayed the presence of an African Tulip tree. Civilisation seemed far away, and I felt the better for it. There was a freshness in the air, a sense of liberation.

We rounded a final bend and there it was, spread below us — the Bergenholm Estate. It nestled in a little valley set amid the peaks of the Main Range. A stream — the one we had followed for much of our journey — issued from a col between the mountains. Just where the stream emerged from the jungle lay a village of several dozen houses. Bergenholm had chosen well for his estate, ill-omened though the name of the nearby village might be.

The Bergenholm Estate was a tea plantation. Tucked up in the highlands, it covered acres and acres. It wasn't as well known as, say, the Boh Tea estates, but evidently it was profitable enough to keep going, even after the Great Depression. Labour was cheap and the estate manager was lord over a fiefdom complete with serfs. Right in the middle of the fields of green lay a neat white bungalow. It was a two-storey building, square in shape, with an enclosed veranda on the first floor forming a porch over the driveway. A cluster of buildings at the rear comprised the servants' quarters. The journey had taken the better part of the morning. The sun was almost at its zenith as we started our descent into the valley.

We drove right past the entrance of the estate and into the village. Awang brought the lorry to a halt in front of a single-storey bungalow, the only one in the village as far as I could see. A gravel path flanked with bougainvillea and hibiscus shrubs led from the road to the veranda. As I pulled my luggage from the lorry, a lean, tanned man came towards me.

"Hello," he said, extending a leathery arm, "you must be Dennis Chiang. Davis is the name, Conrad Davis. Clarence said to expect you. Welcome. Come in and make yourself at home."

He was of indeterminate age, with grey hair flecked with

strands of black. His skin was honey-brown, the sun having long ago burnt off the whiteness. Laugh-lines crinkled the corners of his eyes. He wore a trim moustache and a pipe protruded from the side of his mouth. I grasped his hand. He had a firm, business-like grip. I guessed that he might have been d'Almeida's age, but he had the build and grip of a much younger man.

"Thanks, Mr Davis," I responded, lugging my luggage down the path. I had packed every criminal law book I could get my hands on, and dearly regretted the decision now.

"Conrad. Call me Conrad, everyone does. Here, let me give you a hand."

Without allowing me to protest, he took my bag in one sinewy paw and placed the other on my shoulder, steering me up the steps into the veranda.

"Tiffin's not till one o'clock, so you've time to freshen up a bit, what. Come and have a drink first."

A houseboy appeared and took my things from Conrad. He led me through the house and to the back veranda. There was a glass-topped table there and four peacock-backed rattan chairs. Two were occupied, judging from the smoke rising from them.

"Gentlemen," said Conrad, "our last guest has arrived."

The occupant of one chair got up, cigarette in hand. He was Malay, fortyish, quite obviously cultured and sophisticated.

"Idris," he said with a smile and an extended hand, "I'm pleased to make your acquaintance."

I took his hand and shook it, introducing myself. Conrad motioned me to the chair opposite Idris. It was only when I had seated myself that the occupant of the other chair spoke:

"Well, Mr Chiang, I trust you had a pleasant trip."

My jaw dropped with what must have been an audible clang.

"Mr d'Almeida! But...but how did you get here?"

D'Almeida's eyes twinkled. His back had been towards me as

I came in, so the surprise was complete.

"You know, I really should stop explaining my little conjurer's tricks to you. It so happens that my case was settled this morning. Raja Idris was kind enough to give me a lift in that," he said, gesturing to the open field at the back of the bungalow. There, a startling signal-red against the green backdrop, stood a neat little Tiger Moth.

"I thought I'd join you up here. I've never flown in a biplane before. The trip was most exhilarating."

I whistled in admiration. "She's a beauty."

"Yes, she is rather," responded Idris with pride. "Shipped her over from England and put her together myself."

I gazed at the Tiger Moth in fascination, eyeing the sleek lines. I've always had a weakness for aeroplanes.

Idris saw my lean and hungry look and said, "Would you like to come for a spin?"

"Really? May I?" I answered, trying not to sound too much like an overeager schoolboy.

Idris beckoned and I followed. D'Almeida and Conrad came too. Idris climbed into the back cockpit and I got in the front. He passed over a flying helmet and goggles. Conrad spun the propeller and the engine burst into life with a throaty roar. The chocks were pulled away and we began to taxi down the grassy field. We pulled up sharply and did a couple of slow barrel rolls that sent the blood sloshing into my brain. Opening my eyes, I half expected to see the Red Baron and his Flying Circus circling us for the kill. Idris put the little aeroplane through its paces. He was a superb pilot. He slid into an Immelmann Turn, diving down at a stomach-wrenching speed and then pulling up and banking at the same time, until the little Moth hung on the edge of a stall.

From the height I could see the lie of the land much better. The little stream issued from the mountainside and meandered its way past the village of Gua Langsuir until it was lost in the distant jungle. Here and there along its reaches I could see small clearings and stilted houses. These I surmised must belong to the Senoi, jungle-dwelling aborigines who inhabited the mountains that ran down the spine of Malaya. I hadn't realised how deep into the *ulu* we had gone. The jungle surrounded the little village and the estate, cutting them off entirely from the rest of the universe. Civilisation was somewhere over there, beyond the beyond, below the emerald horizon.

Idris leaned over and tapped my shoulder. He pointed downwards. We were right over the estate. Waggling his wings, he banked sharply and swooped down like a falcon. He pulled up seconds before we hit the ground and buzzed the estate. A group of tea-pickers waiting patiently near the coolie lines dissolved into a mass of fleeing mites. Idris pulled the aeroplane round in a tight circle and did another strafing run practically at bush-top height. I could see the startled white face of the houseboy with his mouth agape as we swept past the bungalow. My face must have been equally white. I was holding onto the sides of the cockpit until my fingers hurt. By the time we landed my hands were numb.

Idris brought the Tiger Moth to a halt right next to d'Almeida. "Enjoy the flight?" he asked me as he unbuckled his flying helmet. I was too shaken to do more than nod my head. He chuckled heartily. I hauled myself out of my cockpit unsteadily.

My feet had barely touched the ground when a large saloon car roared down the road and screeched to a halt opposite us.

A red-faced man erupted from the interior. "What the devil d'you think you're up too?" he yelled. "This isn't bloody Farnborough! Scaring the willies off the bloody natives!"

Conrad intervened. "No need to get upset, Owen. It was just a bit of harmless fun."

"That's *Mr* Evans to you," he shouted. "Harmless bit of fun!

The whole bloody useless lot of 'em has buggered off. Now I won't get a decent day's work out of them. I'll have the law on you, you and your bloody lot of wogs and chinks."

He trailed off into incoherence, evidently having run out of epithets for the likes of us. I'd never before seen a man foam at the mouth. If there was any rabies in the village, I could guess where the dogs had got it.

"Calm down, Evans. He didn't do any harm. Your chaps will be back."

"Back? Back you say?? It's part of your plot isn't it? Trying to get the rest of my workers as well. That thieving dog Samad isn't enough for you is it? Well, I'll see you in court and then I'll see you in hell." His chest heaved with the effort. "Or maybe we should have it out here and now. Come on, let's settle this right here."

He started to pull off his shirt, revealing a brawny hairy chest that wouldn't have shamed a gorilla. Puffed up with rage, he seemed twice the size of Conrad. He started to advance menacingly on us.

"Owen! Stop it at once!" A cold voice cut through the air.

Evans hesitated. A thin woman emerged from the car. She was well dressed — too well for the place and the occasion. Her face was lined with thin wrinkles that the layers of rouge and mascara camouflaged but did not entirely hide. Evans stopped. He glared at us.

"We are leaving now, Owen," said the woman imperiously.

Reluctantly, he stepped back. Still glaring at us, Evans got back into the car. "You just wait. I'll see you in hell," he growled. The syce started the motor and the car began to move off.

Conrad nodded in the direction of the woman. "Good day, Cynthia," he called.

"Good day, Conrad," she responded coolly.

I was watching Evans' face. It turned crimson — not just pink, but a bloodshot lobster-crimson. Evidently he would have liked to stop the car there and then, but the woman overruled him. They disappeared up the road in a cloud of dust and brimstone.

An embarrassed silence had descended on our group. D'Almeida broke it. "I take it that we have just made the acquaintance of the complainant?"

Conrad nodded.

"And I suppose that she was the banshee I've heard so much about," I added facetiously, trying to ease the strain. Conrad stared at me. I shrank back red-faced.

"Don't joke in public about such things," said Conrad quietly. He started back to his bungalow. "You come from a big city, where these are grandmother stories told to frighten little children. Here, people believe them." He waved his hand around. "Look at that. It hasn't changed since the dawn of creation. The people here have been living side by side with the jungle for generations, Malay and Senoi both. There are creatures and powers in there that we know nothing about. To you a *langsuir* is a creature of myth and fantasy. To them it is a living reality and a terror."

Idris broke in. "Come now Conrad, surely you don't believe in *hantu-hantu*?"

"I believe in many things, some seen and some unseen," replied Conrad slowly. "I've lived here since before the Great War, and I've seen things that many others may dismiss with scorn. I don't say that the *langsuir* and pontianak are real, but I know that the village folk believe that they are. It does no good to joke about it. Not in public."

"I apologies for my people," said Idris. "They are backward in many things. But modernity will come, and the old ways will change. Modern science will light the way. You, of all people, should set a good example. Do not encourage them in their superstitions."

"Call them superstitions if you will, but I have seen a *pawang* in action. There are some things that science cannot explain."

Idris made a dismissive noise. "Hah! No good Muslim should believe in these jungle medicine men. One day soon we will have proper roads, and schools and electric light. Then the *langsuir* and the *pawang* can go back to the jungle where they belong."

"Why do they call this place Gua Langsuir?" I broke in. "Surely there must be some reason. Or is it lost in the mists of time?"

Idris smiled. "No, the origin of the name isn't lost. In fact, it's quite recent. One of my ancestors, three generations ago, was chief here. The village was called Jelabu then. He discovered a curious yellow metal in the stream. When word got around, strangers came from afar to collect this gold. The villagers, fearing an invasion, changed the name of the village to Gua Langsuir and the mountain they called Gunong Malang, the mountain of ill-fortune. They hunted the newcomers with blowpipes. Luckily for them, the yellow metal turned out to be iron pyrite — fool's gold. This isn't another Raub, and there's no goldmine in those hills. So they were left in peace. But they kept the name, just in case."

"So there isn't a *langsuir*?"

"I've never seen one, and I've lived here all my life. Except for the time I spent in Europe. Are you disappointed?"

"Idris, you're a better Englishman than me," interjected Conrad quietly. "I've lived here longer than you, and I'm not ready to dismiss the *hantu-hantu* just like that."

"And you, Clarence?" asked Idris, turning to d'Almeida.

D'Almeida was walking slowly, his hands clasped behind his back. He spoke deliberately and clearly. "There is no evidence that the *hantu-hantu* exist," he said evenly, "but absence of evidence is not evidence of absence."

Idris laughed heartily. "Spoken like a true lawyer." He clapped me on the shoulder. "Well, young man, *langsuir* or no *langsuir*, we live here in peace, forgotten by the world. But that will change, that will change. We will drag my people into the twentieth century, and friend Conrad together with them whether he likes it or not."

We had reached the bungalow by now. "And who was the lady then?" I inquired, anxious to change the subject. "Is she Evans' wife? She seems rather grand for an uncouth bastard like him."

Conrad furrowed his brow, and whispered softly as if to himself:

> *"Her lips were red, her looks were free.*
> *"Her locks were yellow as gold.*
> *"Her skin was white as leprosy.*
> *"The nightmare death-in-life was she.*
> *"Who thicks man's blood with cold."*

"Pardon?" I said.

"Oh, nothing," responded Conrad. "Just a little bit of Coleridge. It often pops into my mind when I think of Cynthia." He went over to a cabinet and extracted four brown bottles. "Have a beer? Sorry it's not cold. There's only one ice-box in the whole town, and that's in Bergenholm. They have their own generator." He passed them round. I accepted mine gratefully. Conrad lowered his sinewy frame into a chair.

"You're right on both counts," said Conrad, "Cynthia is Evans's wife and a bit of a *grande dame*. It's her second marriage, you know. Her first husband was manager of a big trading company in India. She was the daughter of a baronet or something of the sort. The marriage didn't last long. Her husband — poor blighter — broke his neck playing polo. When she married Evans, he was up and coming. But drink and the devil got to him, and he had to leave India. I heard that he killed someone. So they banished him out here, where he can drink himself to death quietly."

"He seemed a trifle possessive about her," I remarked.

Conrad smiled seriously. "Yes, he's like that. Thinks that the whole world's after his wife. It doesn't help that she thinks she's too good for him, and he believes it. It drives him mad. When they first came, I went out of my way to make them at home. We even became good friends. But Cynthia... well, let's just say that she has certain needs, and I'm the only white man for miles. She can be quite passionate in her own cold way. She made... advances. I'm too old for that sort of thing. But Owen got insanely jealous even though there was nothing between us. So I stopped visiting. But he still thinks I'm out to steal his wife from him."

"Only when he is drunk," contributed Idris, "which is all the time. I can't say I altogether blame him. She tortures him with her silent reproaches. Those cold eyes, that superior disdain. A man can live with a shrew, but with an iceberg...?" He shrugged his shoulders and took a deep draught of his warm beer.

"It's quite pathetic actually," continued Conrad. "he just sits there in his study, brooding. With only a monkey for company."

"Monkey?"

"Yes," replied Idris, "he picked up a sick monkey in jungle when he first came and nursed it back to health. He calls it Sabbaruddin. It's a stupid, ungrateful beast. Snarls at every visitor I'm told. It bites even the hand that feeds it. But it's his only friend. It tickles his fancy that something needs him. He's reached the point where the company of a mangy beast is better than being alone with his wife."

"Why doesn't she just leave?" I asked.

"And live in penury in England? Not she," answered Idris scornfully. "In India she was a *burra memsahib*. Can she be a great lady in England? Here, she is queen. She says, come, the servants come. She says go, they go. She wants a lackey, she has a lackey. She wants a lover, she takes a lover."

Conrad shook his head. "You shouldn't go around spreading rumours like that," he said quietly.

"Rumours? My friend, the whole village knows of her boys.

She takes one, sucks him dry and throws away the husk. Only her husband does not see — or does not want to see. He thinks that you want his wife. He guards her from you like a tiger guarding its meat. That is funny, really funny. And behind his back, what does she do?" Idris chuckled.

"Even if it's true, it does no good to speak of it openly," answered Conrad. "There is a time to speak and a time to keep silent."

"To protect a lady's honour," said Idris, "even when she has none. Conrad, you are a rare gentleman." He raised his bottle in a toast. "Out of respect for you, my friend, I keep silent."

"I suppose you'll want to meet Samad now?" asked Conrad.

I looked over to d'Almeida. "Mr d'Almeida, will you be taking over the case?" I ventured.

"No, I think not, young man. I'm sure that you can handle it."

This was precisely the answer that I feared. It was bad enough that this would be my first time in court. No matter how well one prepares, there is always that nagging apprehension that one will make an almighty ass of oneself. I had had the small comfort that my debut would take place in a distant court among strangers. If I fumbled, no one would have known about it — at least no one that really mattered to me. But now here was my boss, looking over my shoulder, on my very first solo appearance. It was not a comforting thought.

"Thank you," I mumbled, not very convincingly.

Conrad sent a houseboy to fetch Samad. I got out my legal notepad.

"I suppose you'd better fill me in on the details," I began doubtfully, looking at d'Almeida for support. He remained impassive. Conrad however smiled encouragingly.

"Well, it's a long story, but I'll keep it short. Samad's the son of my cook. I've known him since he was born. When Evans came, two years ago now, I recommended him as a houseboy. He's a good lad. A bit slow up here," said Conrad, tapping his skull, "but a good lad. I taught him to read and write a little English. Things were all right for a while. I visited the house regularly, and he seemed happy enough. After my, ah, unfortunate experience with Cynthia, I stopped visiting. I heard that things got bad soon after that. Evans started to drink more than ever. I tried to talk to him, but he wouldn't listen to me.

"About three months ago, things came to a head. Evans beat Samad and locked him in the servants' quarters. Said he had been pinching the silver. Samad broke out and came here. I let him stay. Evans accused me of poaching his staff. He threatened to burn my house down unless I handed Samad over. Of course I refused. It wasn't pleasant." Conrad stopped and got up to fetch another drink from the cabinet.

Idris took the opportunity to add his contribution. "He was one of *her* boys," he whispered, winking at me.

Conrad appeared not to have heard. He continued, "I don't know what possessed Samad to go back, but he did. One night, after I'd gone to bed. Evans caught him in the house. Accused him of coming back to steal more things. Threatened to shoot him there and then. The other servants came and got me. I had the dickens of a time trying to calm him down. If it wasn't for Cynthia, I do believe he would have killed Samad on the spot. She told him to let Samad go. I brought him back here."

At that moment, Conrad's houseboy returned with a slim youth whom I took to be Samad. He salaamed to the company and stood quietly next to Conrad. I cleared my throat nervously and asked him to describe how he had come to be in Evans' service. Samad looked at Conrad, who nodded to him. He answered briefly, in a low voice, speaking so softly that I could hardly hear him. I persisted with a few more questions about his background.

"Why did Evans dismiss you?" I asked.

There was a short silence, then it seemed as though a dam had burst. I was unprepared for the torrent of words that spilled forth. Samad became quite animated. A whole litany of ills unfolded, verbal abuse, curses, beatings, little petty annoyances. Apparently, Evans kept the staff terrified. He had, they said, an evil eye and the monkey he kept was his familiar. They would all have left but for the fear of his curse. The final straw came when Evans locked Samad up and left him without food or water, falsely accusing him of stealing the silver. The others were too frightened to help him. But Samad had broken out, and returned to his father and to the protection of *tuan* Davis.

"Why did you go back?"

Samad fell silent again. I repeated my question. Conrad prompted him. He answered reluctantly, with downcast eyes, speaking this time in a dialect that I did not understand. "He says he went back to fetch his *barang-barang*," translated Conrad.

This struck me as rather lame. "He went back to get his things? What sort of things? Valuables?" I asked, hardly able to keep the skepticism out of my voice. I looked hard at him. He refused to raise his eyes.

"I go to get my *barang-barang*," replied Samad stubbornly.

I shook my head. "You expect the Magistrate to believe that you went back just to get your things? After all the abuse? Do you seriously think he'll believe you? You could go to jail. Have you thought about that?"

Samad remained sullen.

Conrad intervened. "These gentlemen have come a long way to help you. You must tell them all."

Silence. He continued staring down, as if the cracks in the floorboards were matters of all-absorbing interest.

D'Almeida's quiet voice broke in, "Did you go back to see her?"

Samad started at the voice. He turned to face d'Almeida, who fixed him with a level gaze. He stared back for a few moments. Then he nodded slowly. "I go back for *mem*."

I looked at d'Almeida expectantly. He however merely motioned for me to carry on. I hate it when my train of thought is derailed. I wasn't prepared for this new line. Trying furiously not to appear discomfited, I asked directly and somewhat aggressively, "Why did you go back for *mem*?"

Samad stared at me. His eyes narrowed. Suddenly, he became voluble again. "He treat her bad. He will pay. Tonight he will die."

"Die? What do you mean, he will die? You can't be serious," I responded, somewhat taken aback by this sudden prospect of homicide.

"He will die," replied Samad stubbornly. "I send a *hantu* to take his life. You cannot stop it. He will die."

Conrad broke in. He spoke quickly in Samad's dialect. Samad answered easily enough, his face impassive as though invoking malignant spirits to kill unpopular bosses was a run-of-the-mill matter. Conrad turned to us.

"Well, he's got it fixed in his head that a *hantu* will deliver us from Evans some time this evening. He's quite open about it. Apparently, the local *pawang* will be holding a ceremony at seven in the village."

"He's not going to assist the fates in their task by any chance?" I asked.

"Not directly," answered Conrad. "He says that the *pawang* will use him as the medium for invocation of the *hantu*. We're all invited to the party."

"Superstitious nonsense!" interjected Idris. "I suppose it's that scoundrel Usman up to his old tricks again. We should go and unmask this charlatan."

I looked at d'Almeida, who seemed deep in thought.

"I suppose we'd better go along and keep an eye on things," I said uncertainly. "Meanwhile, it may be best that Samad should stay here. We don't want him getting up to any mischief."

Conrad nodded. "Yes, I'll tell him to stick around until it's time. Do you want to ask him anything else?" Frankly, after his last revelation, I couldn't think of anything but the impending séance. All my careful reading about defences to criminal trespass had evaporated. I shook my head dumbly. Conrad dismissed Samad, impressing upon him the necessity to stay with us until the time came. He agreed and disappeared on noiseless feet.

Evening came without much of a transition. The bright sunshine of the morning had disappeared shortly after lunch, and a solid grey bank of cloud covered the valley. When the sun sank behind the mountains, the gloom only deepened a shade. At 6:45 we turned out to make our way to the village. Idris and Conrad lighted the way with kerosene lamps. Samad walked silently ahead of them. True to his word, he had made no attempt to leave the house before the appointed time.

The track was muddy from the afternoon's rain, and we picked our way among the puddles. The trees formed a jagged silhouette on the black bulk of Gunong Malang, the mountain of ill-fortune. The mountain itself stood dark against the glowering sky, tinged at the edges with the red of the dying day. I saw a cloud of specks emerge suddenly from the mountainside. It looked at this distance like a swarm of bees. I strained my eyes, trying to identify them.

"Bats," said d'Almeida shortly, materialising at my side, "*Pteropus vampyrus*."

"Vampires?" I asked with some surprise.

"No, flying foxes," he replied, "fruit eaters. They always come out at dusk. I am told that they make a fine dish."

We walked slowly along as I digested this information. The wind was chilly, and I shivered a little. All around us the jungle loomed darkly. I could imagine the villagers huddled around the weak glow of their cooking fires, surrounded by the brooding trees. It was no wonder that the old superstitions died hard in these remote settlements. Hemmed in by the ancient forest, one realised that humanity was an upstart interloper. As Conrad said, there were powers and creatures in there that were already old when our anthropoid ancestors forsook the trees.

We reached the meeting house at length. It was a simple wooden structure with an *attap* roof, open at the sides. A large brass gong hung at the farther end, above a small dais. The hall was lighted by burning lamps, evidently fueled with coconut oil from the smell. A curious crowd of onlookers had gathered. They made way for us respectfully. We stood at the front of the crowd just before the dais, where a woven coconut-fibre mat was spread. Looking around, I noticed several men clad in loin cloths and holding long bamboo poles. Clearly word of the séance had percolated to the jungle settlements as well. I nudged Idris, pointing to the strangers.

"Are those your people too?" I asked.

He shook his head. "No, they come from further up the valley, near the mountain."

"What are the fishing poles for?"

"Those aren't fishing poles. They're blowpipes. They use them for hunting still. A skilled hunter can put a dart through a squirrel's eye at a hundred yards."

I gazed fascinated. This was the first time that I had had any contact with the Senoi. It seemed unreal to me that in the age of the aeroplane one should come face to face with Neolithic hunter-gatherers.

Conrad interrupted us. "Here they come."

A pair of brawny Malays had entered the meeting hall. Despite the chill they were bare-bodied, each wearing only a simple checkered sarong. They proceeded to lay out an assortment of things in the centre of the mat: bowls of white and saffron rice, betel nuts, containers with different liquids, a small brazier filled with charcoal.

"Which one's the *pawang*?" I asked.

Conrad shook his head. "I don't see him. I suppose he'll turn up when everything's ready."

Samad was ushered up. He sat cross-legged on the mat, his face impassive. I wondered whether anyone had bothered to tell Evans of his impending doom. The two attendants took their positions on either side of Samad. We waited. The crowd buzzed with whispered conversation, their voices hushed.

A sudden silence descended on the throng, as if the angel of death had swept by. There was a stir at the farther end of the hall and the crowd parted. I watched eagerly for the entrance of the great and terrible wizard.

I was disappointed. The man who entered was small of stature and wrinkled like a raisin. He wore a plain cloth headdress, a faded shirt and a simple sarong. No feathers, war-paint, wand or staff. Then he looked directly at me. I shuddered involuntarily. He had the deepest, most piercing gaze that I have ever seen, then or after. I felt that he was boring into my soul, laying it bare. The face was not gentle, but had a fierce, predatory look. The surrounding crowd was absolutely silent. For a moment I felt as if his entire malevolent attention was focused on me. Then he turned and the feeling evaporated. I released my breath, which I had been holding involuntarily.

I sneaked a look at the others beside me. They seemed unaffected. Idris stood there with his arms folded, frowning at the proceedings. D'Almeida watched with detached interest, observing points of anthropological interest, no doubt making mental notes for future reference.

Conrad leaned over to me and whispered, "Quite a fellow, eh?"

I nodded wordlessly. This fellow gave me the creeps. I had met *bomohs* before. Every *kampong* had its resident medicine man, who could whip up a cure for everything from laryngitis to lovesickness. But this man here was no *bomoh*, no kindly dabbler in folk-magic. He was a witch-doctor, a shaman, and a conjurer of demons who consorted with dark forces. I heartily wished that I had not come.

The séance began. The *pawang* lighted the brazier, and sprinkled a handful of powder on it. It flashed briefly, producing a cloud of pungent white smoke. He began chanting, rocking from side to side rhythmically, waving his hands hypnotically over the hot coals. One of the attendants stood up and produced a white cockerel from a gunny sack. It must have been drugged, for it made no sound, staring glassily at its captor. The *pawang* produced a knife, and with a quick sideways stroke slit its throat. The blood trickled into a bowl at his feet.

He beckoned to Samad. I could see beads of sweat on Samad's forehead as he stood up. He seemed a trifle unsteady on his feet. Slowly he approached the *pawang*, who was still chanting and waving his hands. His eyes however were firmly fixed on Samad. He took Samad's hand and nicked the thumb with his knife, squeezing the blood into the bowl, mixing it in. With his fingers he smeared the mixture on Samad's brow and cheeks. He took Samad's hands in his own, guiding them over the brazier, waving hypnotically back and forth.

Samad too began to chant, repeating monotonously the syllables that he did not understand. The two attendants joined in, quickening the tempo. The pawang let go of Samad's hands. He closed his eyes and began to rock faster, swaying back and forth, too and fro. Abruptly he opened his eyes and stared around. The crowd shrank back before his gaze. He began to snarl, a mewling alley cat sound at first, but gradually building up in tone and timbre to a throaty growl. He began to crawl on all fours around the mat, his body sinuous and almost feline in its movements, sniffing and growling. Samad's eyes were wide with fear, but he continued to chant and wave.

"What's happening?" I whispered urgently to Conrad.

"The tiger-spirit has got him. He's possessed."

The *pawang* stood up. He started to spin. Round and round he went, snarling, hissing, his eyes glazed. Round and round, faster and faster, spinning like a dervish. I watched with rapt attention as the chanting built up to a crescendo.

The gong sounded suddenly, reverberating in the still night. I don't know about the others, but I could swear that my heart stopped dead. The *pawang* screamed, an unearthly screeching sound that pierced the dark. Then he collapsed. The chanting ceased. He lay on the mat, unmoving. There was froth at the edges of his mouth. The crowd stared wide-eyed, not daring to move. We stood for an eternity, frozen by the spectacle. My skin was clammy with sweat and I could feel my heart straining to burst my chest. One of the attendants picked the *pawang* up and put a cup to his lips. He opened his eyes slowly. He seemed dazed and uncertain of his surroundings. Samad was pale and his hands were trembling.

Slowly the crowd began to melt away at the edges. Conrad took Samad's arm and led him gently away. The man walked like one unconscious. He stumbled. I held his other arm to steady him. It was cold, and covered with sweat. Outside the meeting house, the chill night air cleared my head. The nameless fear that had gripped me inside left me. Above, the clouds had parted and the moon broke through, bathing the scene with a pale glow.

"Well," said Conrad to me, "how did you find it?"

"It was... interesting," I replied, trying to keep my voice from shaking.

"A rather intense experience, isn't it," remarked Conrad drily.

"A load of superstitious nonsense," snorted Idris contemptuously. "I should have that charlatan Usman locked up. Only the feeble-minded would believe that he has conjured up a *hantu* to kill Evans. The only spirits you will find in Bergenholm are in his whisky bottles. Why, I tell you, this very minute he is sitting in his study, with his evil-eyed monkey, drinking himself to death. And good luck to him too. I wager..."

Idris's observations were cut short by a commotion among the crowd. A figure pushed his way through and made for Conrad. It was one of the houseboys.

"*Tuan*," he panted, "*mem* say to come quick. *Tuan* Evans is locked in his room. He does not answer. She think something has happened to him."

For a moment we stood there dumbly. Conrad and Idris exchanged glances. Then Conrad began to run. We followed him, with the crowd at our back.

THE TRACK seemed much longer running back. I was panting by the time I reached Conrad's bungalow. Evans's black Chevrolet was there. Conrad was already in the front seat. I piled in the back, together with Idris and d'Almeida. The car roared off, jerking me back into the seat, my arm in Idris's stomach.

Bergenholm was ablaze with lights when we pulled up under the front porch. The house was a large square building with a veranda all round the ground floor. Most of the windows were shuttered. Mrs Evans stood at the front door, pale in the glow of the harsh electric lights.

Conrad bounded up the stairs two at a time. To my surprise, Cynthia Evans went up to him and buried her head in his shoulder.

"Oh Conrad, it's good of you to come so quickly. I've been so alarmed. I heard a scream from Owen's study. I tried the door but it's bolted. He doesn't answer. I don't know what to do."

Conrad patted her on the back, soothing her. "It's all right, Cynthia. Stay here. We'll have a look."

Conrad led the way through the reception room and down the passage to the back of the bungalow. Evans's study was at the rear right-hand corner of the building, directly facing the jungle.

Conrad banged on the door. "Owen! Are you there? Are you all right?"

No answer. Conrad turned to the syce, who had followed us.

"Have you an axe or something to break the door in?" he asked in Malay.

The man disappeared, returning shortly with a couple of *changkuls* and a *parang*. Samad was with him. Conrad took the *parang* and began hacking at the door. There wasn't a keyhole; it had been bolted from within. After a dozen hefty strokes with the *parang*, we started on the splintered wood with the *changkuls*. Then, putting our shoulders to the door, we heaved with all our might. The door gave way with a mighty crack.

The room was in darkness, save for a dim pool of light cast by a table-lamp on the large desk in the far corner. Ghostly moonbeams shone on the floor through the gaps in the shutters. The smell of alcohol was pervasive. Our ears were assaulted by a shrill screeching. Someone found the light switch and flicked it on. The harsh light of the naked electric bulb was dazzling at first.

The room was cluttered with bric-a-brac. On a perch by the desk was a chained macaque, jumping up and down and chittering furiously. Its ugly simian face was contorted with rage. This I surmised was Sabbaruddin. It was certainly the least attractive pet that I had ever seen, squint-eyed and unkempt.

My attention was wrenched away from the beast by a gasp from Cynthia Evans, who had followed us into the room. Evans was sprawled on the floor by the desk. His eyes were wide open, staring as if in horror. His mouth was agape. But what riveted our attention was his neck. Highlighted clearly by the overhead lights were two small red punctures, set close together. Like the mark of fangs.

Conrad turned the body over gingerly. There were no wounds, no blood on the floor or furniture.

"Dead?" inquired Idris.

"As a doorknob," replied Conrad. "He's still warm. It must have happened not long ago."

Samad raised his arms upwards and intoned what I surmised to be a prayer of gratitude. I felt a frisson down my spine.

D'Almeida stepped over to the body. "When did you last see him, Mrs Evans?"

Cynthia Evans was white-faced but dry-eyed. Conrad was next to her, with his arm around her shoulder. She had a handkerchief in her hands, which she was unconsciously twisting. She answered in a low mechanical voice, "Just after five o'clock. We had tea in the upstairs veranda. Then he came down and bolted himself in his study as usual." She frowned. "I don't believe we've been introduced," she said a trifle coolly.

"Clarence d'Almeida," said Conrad, "one of the best lawyers in His Majesty's dominions."

D'Almeida made a small bow. Cynthia Evans inclined her head, but made no attempt to shake hands. She didn't deign to acknowledge my presence at all. As for Idris, he might have been part of the furniture for all the attention she paid him.

"Well, Clarence," continued Conrad, "what's the next move? I suppose we'd better call the police and the D.O.?"

D'Almeida nodded. "Perhaps Mrs Evans would answer a few questions?" he asked.

Cynthia Evans stiffened. "Are you connected with the police, Mr d'Almeida?" she inquired, her voice laced with disdain.

"Not at all, Madam," he replied evenly, "but it may assist their investigations if we have a statement prepared for them when they get here. It will spare you the undoubted pain of being questioned at length by the police."

She hesitated a moment, then said, "Very well, Mr d'Almeida. Ask your questions."

D'Almeida motioned to me to take notes. I went over to the desk to look for pen and paper. Evans must have been sitting there when he died. The chair was overturned, and a practically empty bottle of whisky lay on its side on the desk. Sabbaruddin was still making a racket. Seen up close it was even less attractive than before. Evidently Evans did not believe in grooming his companion.

Cynthia had begun her story. She had left Evans after tea. He had locked himself in his study as was his custom. About 7:15 she had heard a distant gong. Then there was a scream from Evans's study. She had called him repeatedly, but there was no response. Fearing the worse, she had summoned the syce from the garage and sent him off to find Conrad.

D'Almeida looked around the room. "Is there any other way to get in?"

Cynthia shook her head. D'Almeida went to the windows and tested the shutters. They were the usual louvred sort, with gaps between the louvres to let the air circulate. He poked his fingers between the gaps and tried to pull out the slats. One moved a little creating a gap, but nowhere large enough for anything larger than a mouse to enter. Or a bat. D'Almeida pushed hard at them. The shutters remained firmly closed, bolted from within. He unbolted and opened them. The cool night air flooded in, dissipating the smell of whisky. The air seemed to have a soothing effect on the monkey too, for he subsided into a irritable murmur. D'Almeida poked his head out. The veranda was empty. Two hundred yards away, the jungle began.

"Would you be good enough to switch on the outside lights?" d'Almeida asked. Nimbly, he climbed out the window onto the veranda. He examined the floor closely, then went over to the railing and had a look around. We craned our necks out the windows watching him. He climbed back in.

"Well, Madam," he said, dusting off his suit, "I think that we should move your late husband to a cool room. The police will not be here until tomorrow, even if we can get in touch with them immediately."

Cynthia strode off mechanically, stiff upper lip to the fore, to arrange for the disposal of the remains of her husband.

"Shouldn't we leave things as they are?" asked Conrad doubtfully.

"Normally, yes," replied d'Almeida, "but the local police aren't equipped to examine the *locus delicti*. By the time a detective comes up from KL the body will smell somewhat."

Conrad nodded. "What shall we do with him?" he asked, indicating Samad, who was standing quietly looking at the body.

Samad looked up. "I go with the police," he said in a calm tone, "The *hantu* has killed him. I called the *hantu*. It is my deed. I am ready for my punishment."

"Perhaps you should send him home," suggested d'Almeida. "I don't think he will run away." Conrad spoke quickly to Samad, who nodded and left.

"Well, I'm speechless, friend Conrad, absolutely speechless," remarked Idris after Samad had gone. "I do not know what to believe any more."

Conrad looked grave. "A bad business, this. Evans may have been a bounder, but to go in that way.... I suppose it's got to go to the Coroner. Though heaven knows what he'll make of it. Murdered by a vampire." He shook his head.

A couple of stalwart fellows arrived to take the body away. Their faces betrayed their fear. They kept darting looks at the open window, into the black night beyond. They heaved the body away unceremoniously. Conrad went over to the monkey and started to undo the chain.

"What are you doing?" asked d'Almeida.

"Letting the poor beast go," said Conrad. "There's no point keeping him, now that his master's gone."

"Ah, but there is a point," said d'Almeida quietly. "He's our only witness."

BOTH CONRAD and Idris stared at d'Almeida as if he had suddenly sprouted two heads. I was used to my boss by now, and such pronouncements no longer evoked any astonishment.

"You're not serious, Clarence," said Conrad.

"Ah, but I am. Deadly serious." D'Almeida began to circle the room, polishing his spectacles as he did so. "Look at the situation. We have a dead man in a locked room. The windows are shut, the door bolted from within. No man can get in or out. How was it done?" Here he paused and turned to me, wagging his spectacles, "What would your Mrs Christie and Miss Sayers say to that, eh?"

I reddened. Evidently our efforts at hiding our extra-curricular reading were not as effective as we had thought.

"I admit it's a real nutcracker," said Conrad, "but how can the monkey help? He can't speak."

"My dear Conrad, there are ways," replied d'Almeida. "I have, shall we say, a little talent for unearthing information. I propose to hold a séance of my own tomorrow night, in this very room, at the very time of Evans' death. This little fellow shall be the centre of the proceedings. We must keep him well until then. It would be unfortunate if something were to happen to him."

He turned to Idris. "I assume that there is a market nearby where I can get a few things?"

"Yes," replied Idris doubtfully, "within reason. But for this sort of mumbo-jumbo, I'm not sure. What do you need? Bats' blood and crocodile tears?"

"No, nothing out of the ordinary. Just a bit of rice and some incense. A few spices. And a couple of bamboo poles."

Conrad and Idris exchanged glances. Evidently they had never seen this side of their old friend's character.

"Are you absolutely sure you know what you're doing?" asked Conrad a trifle doubtfully.

"Perfectly sure," said d'Almeida, "Now, gentlemen, I propose that we retire for the night. We have a big day ahead of us. By this time tomorrow evening everything should be clear. Mr Chiang, if you would be so good, perhaps you would take custody of the monkey."

I didn't relish the prospect, but obeyed anyway. The rotten little beggar tried to bite me as I undid his chain, but a sharp swat with a rolled up newspaper got him to toe the line. We sallied forth in a procession, with me and Sabbaruddin bringing up the rear.

Cynthia Evans met us in the front hall. Conrad explained quickly what d'Almeida intended. "It's for the best," I heard Conrad say in a low voice, "the matter's got to be settled."

Cynthia looked very skeptical. Her face was pale but she kept her ice-cold composure. "He's going to make the monkey talk?" she asked.

"I'm not entirely sure, but Clarence knows his business. Leave it to him. I'm certain that it'll turn out right."

"I don't want a whole crowd of... of Asiatics wandering around my house. It isn't right. I won't have it, poking their noses where they don't belong, playing policeman."

Conrad held her shoulders and looked her straight in the eyes. "We've got to co-operate," he said, "the natives need to be reassured. The houseboys won't go anywhere near the room. The plantation workers may not turn up. Let Clarence do his stuff. I don't think anything will come of it, but it will help to calm the natives. The alternative is the police, and you know what they're like around here."

She bit her lower lip. "Well, if you say so. But only in that one room. Nowhere else. They're absolutely not going to go wandering around the house."

"I promise," replied Conrad soothingly. "I'll speak to Clarence." He put his hand on her shoulder. "You'll be all right? I mean, financially? Now that Owen's gone... I've got a little bit put away, you know."

Cynthia nuzzled against Conrad's hand momentarily. "No, I'll be all right. The company pays a generous pension to widows, and there's an insurance policy. But it's marvelous of you to ask."

She looked at him meltingly for a brief instant. Conrad seemed embarrassed. He cleared his throat and moved off. Cynthia reverted to ice as we passed, not deigning even to wish us good night.

A crowd had collected outside the house. They stood silently, carrying burning torches and kerosene lamps, waiting expectantly as we emerged. Samad was there, squatting at the head of the steps.

"I think you should address your people, Idris," said d'Almeida.

"What on earth shall I say?" responded Idris, with a shake of his head.

"Tell them that Evans has been killed, and that I will find the truth tomorrow. I shall hold a séance, at the time of Evans' death, in the very same room. The monkey will help me. Keep them calm. Tell them to go home."

Idris nodded. He proceeded to the top step. The low buzz of conversation ceased. Idris began speaking in the dialect of the town. A murmur ran through the crowd when he pointed to Sabbaruddin, who was nonchalantly grooming himself. He bade them to be patient and to return home. As soon as he stopped speaking the buzz began again, more intensively than ever. We passed through the throng, Samad at the side of Conrad. Anxious faces peered at us from all sides. Someone put out his hand to touch the monkey, but a snarl from him dissuaded the attempt. We walked the whole way back to Conrad's bungalow, trailed by the silent crowd.

I DID not have a restful night. For one thing, I was kept awake by an intermittent simian serenade from Sabbaruddin, from whom a burst of chittering broke out every now and then. During the intermissions, I drifted into a broken doze, haunted by visions of bats and other dark creatures. It was a relief when the first rays of the sun peeked over the rim of the mountain.

I breakfasted alone, if one excludes the monkey. Idris had returned to his house and Conrad had left early to fetch the police and the doctor. The servants eyed the monkey suspiciously as they brought me my tea and toast. Sabbaruddin had calmed down, probably through exhaustion. I fed him a papaya, which he took with a snap and a baring of teeth.

D'Almeida returned from his habitual walk around 7:30. He appeared on the veranda with a mug of coffee. "If you have breakfasted, Chiang, I would be obliged if you would accompany me to the market."

"Mr d'Almeida," I ventured, "are you seriously going to hold a séance?"

"Absolutely," he answered in an even tone, "this is the only way to catch the murderer."

I must have looked more perplexed than usual, for he then went on. "I believe firmly that we have a very clever murderer in our midst. You are the only one I can trust in this village. It is absolutely imperative that you protect the monkey. He is the key to this business."

"You're going to interrogate him?"

D'Almeida made an impatient noise. "Of course not. He cannot speak. But others believe that he can be made to divulge the true manner of the killing. They will try to kill the animal. Be alert. On no account let the monkey escape." With a last sip he finished his coffee and started off down the stairs.

The day was bright and dry and the morning air pleasantly fresh. A few minutes' brisk walk took us to the market. It was held on a patch of open ground along the stream. Evidently Gua Langsuir was the metropolis of the surrounding highland area, for amongst the crowd were not a few scantily-clad Senoi from the mountains, the women bare-breasted and the children naked. Some traders had also come from the lowlands and hawked a variety of cloths, trinkets and gadgets.

We wandered among the stalls, trailed by two houseboys. D'Almeida picked up all manner of things, from parched rice to spices to bamboo poles. These were dutifully carried by our escorts. Sabbaruddin ambled along at the end of his chain, munching a banana, pausing only occasionally to snarl at the passers-by. Word of the coming séance had evidently spread around the town, for everywhere we went curious faces peered at us and the crowd parted as we approached like the Red Sea before Moses.

A pack of ragged urchins hovered on our flanks. Suddenly d'Almeida stopped. He beckoned to the littlest one, a small boy encrusted with grime and dressed only in a tattered shirt. The adults drew back, but the child stood transfixed. D'Almeida approached him slowly. The boy gazed fixedly at him, sucking one finger. D'Almeida put out his hand with a flourish produced a square one-cent coin from behind the boy's ear. The crowd gasped. D'Almeida offered the coin to the boy, who reach out a grimy paw hesitantly. Then he took it and darted away. D'Almeida turned to the next child, who squealed with delight when another one-cent coin materialised out of his hair. Soon d'Almeida was producing coins out of thin air for the whole ragamuffin band. When the last had gone, he turned nonchalantly and resumed his shopping. A ring of awed faces surrounded us.

He turned to me and said in a low voice, "I hope you have some small change. I seem to have used up my supply." I nodded and made a mental note never to play cards with my boss for money.

When we were done, d'Almeida led the way back. To my surprise, he did not choose the path we came by, but made a detour along a side street. We were quite a procession and evoked a fair amount of interest. The village children and a pack of mangy dogs hung around our flanks, watching our passing with curiosity. As we passed by a particular house, d'Almeida stopped and ostentatiously came to pet Sabbaruddin. The little monster was taken aback at this unexpected favour, and was evidently too astonished to protest as d'Almeida picked him up. Crooning softly, he fed Sabbaruddin a ripe banana. From the depths of the house I saw a pair of eyes peering out at the proceedings. With a shock I recognised their owner — Usman, the *pawang*.

In the bright sunlight of the morning the nameless fears of the night had faded. But the sight of Usman resurrected the memory of the *pawang's* séance and the look on Evans's face. Those two red punctures on his neck.... I shook myself. D'Almeida handed Sabbaruddin back to me and we made our way back to Conrad's bungalow. I looked back at Usman's house. The cold eyes were still following us. Daylight had not lessened the malevolence of his gaze.

When we got back, d'Almeida stopped in front the gate and said to me, "I have a few matters to attend to. I will be gone for possibly the whole day. I must impress on you the seriousness of the matter. Do not go outdoors. Keep the monkey safe."

I nodded. D'Almeida put his hand on my shoulder. "Take care, my boy," he said and left.

Conrad's bungalow was a single-storey edifice, but raised on pillars in the usual local style. The floors were wooden and there were no locks on the doors. The windows looked out on the jungle on three sides. I decided that the best strategy was to bolt myself into my room and wait for d'Almeida to return. I contrived a little perch for Sabbaruddin in my room out of a clothes-horse. Making sure that the monkey was securely fastened, I went down the stairs at the back of the house to the kitchen to secure supplies for the siege. I armed myself with a chopper and a large loaf of bread. A small tin of sardines was also procured from the larder. Two bottles of water completed my load.

On my way back up, I suddenly recalled that I needed a tin-opener. I turned abruptly in mid-stride. To my utter astonishment, I bumped into someone. He was a burly chap, with a handkerchief over his face. In his hands he held a length of rope. A moment later and it would have been round my neck. In my shock, I dropped one of the bottles of water, which promptly shattered. This was my salvation, for the glass shards cut the intruder's bare feet, causing him to flinch momentarily. I threw the tin of sardines, which bounced off his head with a satisfactory thud. Pushing with all my might, I shoved him back down the stairs. As he tumbled, I called out at the top of my voice. The houseboys came running down the passage. But my assailant was on his feet, hobbling off towards the jungle. The houseboys made a half-hearted attempt to follow him but gave it up the moment he reached the shrubbery.

I ran back to my room. A familiar high-pitched scream greeted me. Relieved, I sank down into the easy chair. I was up in a moment. Quickly gathering the remainder of my supplies from the corridor, I dashed back into the room and bolted the door and window.

There was no fan in the room, and the atmosphere soon became stuffy. This was in a way a blessing, for Sabbaruddin became drowsy and I was spared his incessant screeching and chittering. There wasn't a lot to do. To my intense regret, I had forgotten to bring something light to read. All I had to keep me company was *Mallal on Criminal Procedure* and a pile of similar dreary tomes.

It was a struggle to keep awake. Reading hardly helped, and not reading wasn't much better.

Around one o'clock there was a knock on the door and someone inquired whether I would be coming out for lunch. I sent him away curtly. There was no one I could trust. The long day dragged on towards evening.

IT WAS a relief to hear d'Almeida's voice at the door. I opened up and gratefully gulped in the cool air.

"Come," said d'Almeida shortly, "and bring the monkey."

I handed the beast over to d'Almeida and made a quick dash to the lavatory. When I returned, I briefed him on my little adventure. He nodded, but made no comment.

We walked over to Bergenholm, laden with various articles. Unlike the previous day, the evening was warm and light. Curious eyes peeked out from behind curtains. I was itching to know what he had been doing all day. However, he remained lost in thought and uncommunicative as was his wont. We were met at the door by a houseboy, who relieved us of our burden. Sabbaruddin was uncharacteristically subdued.

Conrad, Idris and Cynthia Evans were gathered in the sitting room. She nodded curtly as d'Almeida entered.

"So you're really going through with this, Clarence?" asked Conrad doubtfully.

D'Almeida nodded. "Is everything prepared?" he asked.

"Yes," replied Idris, "I have instructed the villagers to remain in their houses while you conduct the séance. They will not stir."

"I hope you know what you're doing," repeated Conrad.

Idris gave d'Almeida a thumbs-up and an encouraging grin. Cynthia Evans fidgeted uneasily on the sofa, staring steadfastly at the wall.

"What's happened to Samad?" I asked Idris quietly.

"The police and the doctor came early this afternoon. He confessed to the murder, and they have taken him away."

"And the doctor?"

"He can't give an opinion until he's done the autopsy. He is a man of science. He will not be taken in by this mumbo-jumbo."

D'Almeida's keen ears caught that. "Mumbo-jumbo to you, my dear Idris, but a deadly serious business to some. Deadly serious."

"I realise that, Clarence," replied Idris. To my surprise he produced a revolver, spun the cylinder and checked the chambers. "I, at any rate, will be ready, whether it be man or beast or spawn of Shaitan that we face."

"Good. Be prepared. Come quickly if we call. Well, gentlemen, we will meet in approximately two hours' time," said d'Almeida. "Come, Mr Chiang, we must get ready."

I tugged a dispirited Sabbaruddin into Evans' study. The battered door had been replaced. The windows were shut. The heat in that closed box of a room was oppressive.

Having secured the monkey to his perch, I went over to open

the windows to let some cool air in. D'Almeida stopped me. "Leave them shut," he said.

He unpacked his things. There was a length of bamboo, a collection of bricks, a primus stove, a kerosene lamp, rice, some spices I could not identify and a plucked chicken. With a knife, d'Almeida opened up a section of bamboo. He built two piles of bricks and suspended the bamboo between them, placing the primus stove beneath. He filled the hollow section with water and placed the rice in it. I could restrain my curiosity no longer.

"Mr d'Almeida," I ventured, "what are you doing?"

"Cooking our dinner," he replied calmly.

"Cooking our what?" I ejaculated.

He turned from his preparations. "My dear young man," he said, "we are going to have to wait a little time for our murderer to appear. I propose not to waste time while doing so. Since I must brew up something, it might as well be dinner. You can make yourself useful by sitting there, under the windows. Watch carefully for anything unusual."

I subsided. I knew better than to expect explanations. D'Almeida delighted in his little conjuring tricks, even with an audience of one. I just wished that I knew exactly what to expect, man, bat or demon. I glanced at my watch — 6:45. Half an hour to go. The sun had already sunk below the rim of the mountain as I gazed through the gaps in the shutters. The valley nestled in sinister twilight. The room was dark now except for the flicker of the stove and the steady glow of the kerosene lamp.

Presently d'Almeida's preparations were done. He fetched Sabbaruddin from his perch, on which the monkey had been sitting somnolently. He placed the beast in front of the stove, tethered to a chair. I remarked that Sabbaruddin seemed very well-behaved.

"Gripe water," said d'Almeida shortly.

"Pardon?"

"I fed him a whole bottle of gripe water. It contains a little opium. As you see, it has a marvelously soothing effect."

D'Almeida settled himself down, sitting cross-legged on the floor opposite the monkey. "Now, Chiang, if you would be so good as to conceal yourself under the windows. Watch carefully. Our lives may depend on it."

I needed no second bidding. I scrunched up in the corner under the windows, armed with a stout walking stick that I found in the study. D'Almeida cast an eye over to my position and nodded with approval. It was just before seven o'clock by my watch.

D'Almeida produced a battered leather-bound volume from his bag, flipped it open, and by the light of the lamp he began to read in a deep, sonorous voice. Every now and then he struck an upturned brass spittoon, like a gong. I strained to hear what he was saying. At last I made it out. It was Latin. The man was reading out loud from Caesar's *The Gallic War*!

The steady drone of his voice muttering the familiar syllables brought back memories of Fenton Abbey and Mr Slaughter, my Latin master. It soon had the usual effect on me. I began to nod.

I don't know how long I drifted on the boundary of consciousness. It might have been seconds or minutes. Mr Slaughter had a very effective method of securing one's attention. He would pad up quietly, still reading, to the victim. Then like a bolt from Jupiter he would bang his cane on the desk right in front. The effect was electrifying. Those subjected to this treatment remained palpitating wrecks for the rest of the day. In my drowsy haze I could almost see Mr Slaughter's cane hanging in mid-air before me.

With a shock I suddenly realised that the cane was real! A narrow bamboo rod was being inserted slowly through the chinks in the shutters. "Watch out!" I cried, striking the pole with my walking stick. There was a soft "phut!" and something struck d'Almeida's spittoon with a clang.

D'Almeida was on his feet. "Open the window! Get him before he can reload!"

I unbolted the window and thrust it open forcefully. There was a thud and a cry of pain. I leapt out the window onto the veranda, nearly twisting my ankle. A dark figure had just clambered over the railings and was sprinting for the jungle, holding one hand to his head and carrying a blowpipe in the other. Heedlessly, I vaulted the railing and ran after him. He was small and a good runner.

"He's going to get away," I thought grimly to myself and willed myself to run faster.

The figure reached the fringe of the jungle. The outside lights blazed on, bathing the compound in a yellow glow. In the glare, I saw that it was Usman, the *pawang*. He spun round to face me, face contorted with an evil rage. Before I had time to think, the blowpipe was at his lips, aimed directly at me. I skidded to a halt, not twenty feet away. I should have ducked or weaved, but at the moment my mind was blank and my limbs were frozen. With a look of malevolent triumph he puffed up his cheeks to blow. I braced myself for the dart. Suddenly, there was a bang and Usman threw up his arms with a cry. I heard a soft whizz as the dart skimmed past my ear. I turned round. Idris was framed in the light, a smoking revolver in his hand. Shakily, I waved to him. He waved back, giving a thumbs-up sign.

WE GATHERED again in the study. The fire was out and the monkey gone. Usman's body had been removed. He wasn't dead yet, but it was touch and go whether he would survive the night. His blowpipe and darts lay on the table.

"So, it was Usman all along," said Idris, "I always knew that he was a bad sort. Not to be trusted at all."

"How was it done?" asked Conrad as he picked up the blowpipe, fingering it curiously.

"With this," answered d'Almeida, producing a bowl with a small puddle of liquid at the bottom. We all stared at it. Idris put a probing finger in, but d'Almeida hurriedly snatched the bowl away.

"I would not touch it if I were you," he said. "It's a deadly poison. A little scratch is enough to kill a grown man, as poor Evans discovered."

"But how did Usman kill Evans?" asked Conrad. "The room was shut from inside. If he used the blowpipe, we'd have found the dart."

"Ah, but he did use the blowpipe," replied d'Almeida. "That liquid is what is left of the dart. He fired it at me. Fortunately, my young friend spoiled his aim. It was ice — frozen poison, shaped into a two-pointed dart." D'Almeida moved over to Evans' chair and sat down. "From the window, it's quite easy to hit a man sitting in this chair. Usman, I take it, is a Senoi and quite an expert with the blowpipe. One shot to the neck, two puncture marks. The man would be dead in minutes. The evidence would melt away."

"An almost perfect crime," commented Idris. "I hope he survives, so that the hangman will have his due."

"That may yet come," said d'Almeida quietly, leaning back. "Usman was only the agent. The instigator remains at large."

There was a startled intake of breath. D'Almeida placed his elbows on the table, his fingers touching. "Let me tell you my conjecture, and perhaps you would let me know what you think of it. When I saw Evans, I knew that it could not have been the *langsuir* that did the deed. The vampire bat is unknown to Malay culture. The bloodsucking demon vampire is the invention of an Englishman, Mr Bram Stoker. It has entered popular culture through the cinema, for which we can thank Mr Bela Lugosi.

Usman would never have thought of such a thing himself. Someone must have put him up to it. Someone familiar with English literature or American cinema."

"That's a pretty serious matter, Clarence," said Conrad. "Are you accusing someone in particular?"

D'Almeida looked around the room steadily. His eyes rested on Cynthia Evans. "You almost got away with it, Mrs Evans. You would have but for the superstitions of Usman. The monkey was the only witness. He believed that I could make the monkey talk. So he had to get rid of me or the monkey."

Cynthia Evans flushed. Her eyes blazed. "Preposterous! How dare you accuse me! In my own house." She turned to Conrad beseechingly. "Conrad, surely you aren't going to let this... this... man... accuse me of this horrible crime." She placed her arm on his and looked him in the eyes.

Conrad appeared flustered. "Well, see here, Clarence, I mean, you can't jolly well go around accusing Cynthia of murder. I mean, not without proof. How's she supposed to have done it?"

"Consider, my friends, how the deed was done," went on d'Almeida serenely. "We were all at the séance. Usman was there. So he would appear to have a cast-iron alibi. If the deed took place when Mrs Evans said it did."

We turned to Cynthia Evans. Her lips were pursed and her hands clenched. D'Almeida continued.

"No one else heard Evans cry out. The servants were conveniently out of the way. As far as I can reconstruct the crime, Usman came before seven, while we were all gathering for the séance. Evans was bolted in his study. Usman poked his blowpipe through the shutters and shot the dart into Evans's neck. After killing Evans, he came to the hall and began his performance. I spent the day exploring the paths around the bungalow. There's one path directly from here to the village hall. It's only a matter of fifteen minutes at a good trot. Time enough for Usman to get back and put on his act. A real masterpiece, I may say. After last night's doings, his reputation would have spread across the mountains and beyond."

D'Almeida gazed steadfastly at Cynthia Evans. "My guess is that the gong was the cue. When you heard it, you went through your little charade and sent the driver for us, isn't that so?"

Her hands were clenched, but she said nothing. D'Almeida carried on placidly.

"You were the one who put the idea of the *hantu* into poor Samad's head. He's completely devoted to you. He'd do anything to protect you from that beast of a husband. You suggested that he go to Usman. The lad was completely taken in, wasn't he? A perfect victim. He was convinced that he had conjured up the *hantu*. He would have gladly gone to the gallows believing it, and all for your sake. Come Mrs Evans, the game is up. Usman won't go alone to the hangman. He'll take you with him."

Cynthia's eyes blazed. "You haven't any proof, you horrible little man. The word of a jungle-wallah! What judge would take his word against that of a white woman? You can't prove a thing."

"Ah, but I can," responded d'Almeida quietly. "Usman used a frozen poison dart. No one in the valley has a refrigerator. No one but you. I'd be curious to see what's in it now. A forensic scientist may be able to lift some very interesting prints."

Conrad looked stricken. "Cynthia, why? In heaven's name, why did you do it?" he asked plaintively.

"Why, Conrad? You ask me why!" She laughed mirthlessly. "You've gone native. You'd never understand what it's like to be trapped in a hell-hole like this. To be shackled to a drunken sot. To face a living death day after day after day. I hate it! I hate this place and the jungle and the plantation and the natives! The devil take all of them!" The icy composure was gone. She spat the words out with vehemence.

Then abruptly she took a deep breath and composed herself, drawing herself up with hauteur.

"So, Mr D'Almeida," she said coldly, "I congratulate you on your powers of deduction. You have been very clever. But you shall not have me."

Before we could stop her, she seized one of the darts from the table. Conrad lunged forward. Too late! She scratched herself on the arm, a deep laceration. The blood flowed red onto the floor.

"I will see you in hell," she gasped out, staggering against the desk. As she did so, she flung the dart right at d'Almeida.

I reacted instinctively, throwing myself across the desk. I felt a sharp pain as the dart pierced my shoulder. I plucked it out. Stupidly I looked down at it in my hand. Then the room dissolved into formless shapes and everything went black.

NURSE'S ORDERS

THE SENSATION was not so much of waking, but of emergence.... I felt myself moving without volition towards a bright light. Slowly as my vision cleared I made out a ring of faces, haloed by the warm glow of sunlight. My first thought as I awoke was that I must be in heaven. My second thought was that if this is heaven, what is my boss doing here? D'Almeida's face was there right in front of me. I shook my head. I felt a soft hand was patting my brow and a familiar voice was speaking.

"Boy, can you hear me? Are you all right?"

"Yes, Mak, I can hear you," I responded. My voice was hoarse and the words slurred.

Mak took my hand in hers and pressed it. "Thank God," she repeated several times, in a voice choked with emotion.

My eyes were open but I could scarcely focus. The light was blinding, and I had a headache to end all headaches. I closed my eyes again. The small room was filled with flowers. Somehow, as if to compensate for my blurred vision, my sense of smell was heightened. I detected the faint pleasant aroma of jasmine and camellia.

A nurse materialised and took my temperature. She helped me up to a sitting position. I felt groggy and retched a little. My shoulder hurt as I tried to move my arm. An excited babble broke out as I sat up.

"How long have I been here?" I asked.

D'Almeida answered. "I'm glad to see you're well, my boy. We were very concerned. You've been unconscious for two days now."

My fuddled brain strove to make sense of the information. I ventured to open my eyes again. The light hurt less this time. The mental fog ebbed and the memory of that last evening came back slowly.

"What happened...?" I asked hesitantly. "What became of Cynthia Evans?"

"I regret to say that Mrs Evans is dead," answered d'Almeida in a serious tone. "She took most of the poison in her system when she scratched herself. You would have been dead too but for that. There wasn't enough poison left on the dart to kill you outright. You owe your life to Conrad and Idris. Conrad cut the wound and sucked out the blood. Idris flew you back here in his little aircraft, at night. If it wasn't for them you might be dead."

"I must thank them... I owe them my life," I said, striving to get up. The effort was too much. I lay back down heavily.

"Later, my boy, you can thank them later," said d'Almeida. "But I must thank you. You saved my life."

I flushed a little. "No need for thanks," I mumbled. I hardly knew what to say.

D'Almeida went on, "I shall not forget. In the meantime, the important thing is for you to get well. I am glad to see you conscious again. Now that I am assured that you will recover, I will leave you to rest."

He turned to Mak, "Do not hesitate to call if you should require anything, my dear lady. Good day." He bowed to her, gave me a reassuring pat on the shoulder and left.

The girls were all gathered at the foot of the bed. They were in awe of d'Almeida, but the moment he was through the door they started chattering away. I could hardly make out who was asking what.

Mak hushed them. "Enough! You all 'cheep, cheep' like birds. Boy is tired now. Let him rest." She shooed them out of the room but they promised to be quiet and settled themselves around my bed, whispering and giggling.

Mak insisted that I should drink some chicken soup that she had cooked. I wasn't quite ready to talk yet and my head was still heavy. The soup was delicious and brought some vigour to my bones.

"Your Mr d'Almeida is very good," she said. "He was here all day yesterday, and the day before. He is good to you like he was to your uncle and father. He is paying for you to stay in hospital. He says you do not have to go back to work until you are really well. You must work hard for him."

I nodded dumbly, sipping the hot liquid slowly.

"When he told me you were in hospital I nearly died," she continued. "His friend, that Malay man... I forget his name... he flew you back from upcountry. They drove you here to the hospital at night. You were so white, *puchat sa-kali*. I thought you were dead," She wiped her eyes. "The doctors and nurses have been so good. And your cousin May has been with you all the time, even on her off-duty time."

She gabbled on, and I was content to drink my soup and listen, soaking in the soothing tones of a well-loved voice.

After a few minutes, the nurse returned in order to clear the room of visitors. Mak however resisted stubbornly, and the nurse relented, leaving me to Mak's care. She smiled at me reassuringly, holding my hand. I gave a weak smile back, and then drifted off again into sleep.

IT TOOK me a couple of days to find my feet again. Whatever the poison was, it was powerful stuff. I heard that the Senoi hunted elephants with it. Modern science had yet to make its acquaintance properly. As a consequence, I was an object of some curiosity to the local scientific community, which turned up in the form of a couple of aged physicians specialising in toxicology. They prodded and poked me, but I drew the line when they suggested that I should donate a couple of pints of blood in the interests of medical research. They went away downcast, but were somewhat cheered by the fact that I was to be kept under observation for a few days more to see what other exotic symptoms might develop. Nothing would have pleased them more than if I had turned yellow with green spots.

D'Almeida was very generous. Not only did he pay for my hospital stay, he also continued to pay my salary over to Mak, which was a welcome relief. I got indefinite leave from work.

After the first day, I received a steady stream of visitors. Apart from Mak and my cousins, almost all the office staff dropped by either individually or in groups. I was touched by the genuine solicitude they showed for my welfare. I was in particular surprised by the attitude of Ralph, who came regularly after work. Ralph was not a man of many words. He'd update me on what was going on in the world and then would sit quietly in the sole chair while my cousin May did her nursing. May had more or less taken over my case. She had swapped her regular shift for the night shift in my ward, especially to look after me she said. I was moved by all this care and concern.

I had a room to myself, located in a bigger ward. My room possessed the luxury of a ceiling fan. The whitewashed walls separating me from the others reached only three-quarters of the way to the ceiling, letting in the sounds of the outside. Nevertheless they provided some welcome privacy. In the main ward the patients lay in long rows, one next to another. Of privacy there was none. At visiting time the place resembled a bazaar. Children scampered in and out the side doors, which lined one wall and opened out onto a long veranda-like corridor, beyond which was a small lawn with frangipani trees. Wives of all hues came bearing tiffin carriers reeking of curries and spices and other delicacies.

After feeding time in the evening the babble of Babel subsided and a hush descended. All visitors departed. The silence was punctuated by the occasional cough or wheeze and by the regular padding of the night nurse's feet. Sleep generally eluded me those first few nights in the hospital. Whether it was the strange surroundings or the unfamiliar smells or the unaccustomed sounds, I found it impossible to drift off. For the first three nights I put up with it, tossing and turning or lying on my back watching the languid circling of the ceiling fan until sleep finally stole over me in the small hours of the morning. The fourth night I could stand it no more. I got out of bed and poked my head round the door.

There was no sign of anyone. I sauntered out of my room. In front of me was the nurses' room, but as far as I could see no one was in it. May must have left on some little errand of mercy. To my right the long rows of beds stretched out along the ward. The doors to the corridor were shut. It was stiflingly warm. The ceiling fans creaked rhythmically as they swirled the air around the room. To my left was the main entrance to the ward. I tried it. It wasn't locked. I pushed the double doors open gingerly and emerged into a dim passageway. There was that usual hospital smell, concocted of equal parts of antiseptic, disinfectant and medicine. I decided to go for a walk to stretch my limbs.

I hadn't gone ten yards when I heard an urgent pattering of feet behind me. I turned. It was May.

"What are you doing?" she asked in a loud whisper.

"I got tired of lying down," I replied. "I'm going for a walk."

"A walk? In your condition?" She took my arm and firmly led me back to my bed. I went unresistingly. I have a policy never to argue with a nurse, especially one with the power to jab me full of holes in sensitive bits of my anatomy.

"I'm feeling perfectly all right now," I said as May tucked me back into bed. "I can't stay cooped up here all the time. I'll go bananas."

May stopped fussing about the sheets. She looked at me. "You really feel all right?"

"Absolutely."

"No more pain? Dizziness? Nausea?"

I shook my head vehemently. "Not a bit."

She looked thoughtful. "I heard Dr Maxwell say that you seemed quite well," she said.

My heart leapt. A chance for release!

"But," she continued, "they must keep you here for another week at least to make sure that there are no side-effects."

My face must have fallen a mile, for she said quickly, "Don't look like that, it is for your own good."

A black depression began to settle over me. At least one more week....

"Maybe I can help you a bit," said May slowly, "And you can help me."

"Help you?" I looked at her. She was blushing.

"You know about Ralph...about Ralph and me?" she said hesitantly.

"Ralph? Ralph and you? What about Ralph and you?" I asked in puzzlement.

"Ralph says he wants to know me better," she replied, with her eyes downcast. "We... we like each other."

This revelation almost knocked me over. The idea that Ralph, of all people, should fancy a girl took my breath away. Ralph was quiet and bookish and totally uninterested in the opposite sex as far as we knew. While George had a never-ending stream of girlfriends, Ralph lived only for his books. That was why I got all the female clients — George couldn't be trusted with them and Ralph wasn't keen. To be told out of the blue that Ralph liked my cousin May — May, who spent her youth climbing trees and frolicking in the mud with me — that took my breath away. I scratched my head.

"When did this all happen?"

"When he was at our place looking after baby Lucy. We... we talked and became friendly."

I nodded. Actually I was quite pleased. Ralph was a decent sort, and would fit in nicely in our little circle. "Does Mak know?"

"No!" exclaimed May, her eyes wide. "Mak would never allow it. She will never consent to let Ralph come to the house to see me. The neighbours will talk."

I nodded again. It was true that the neighbours would talk and shake their heads. For a young man to come calling was unknown in our society. Young girls were not courted; they were hitched to some suitable suitor by their parents. I knew Mak had a lot of non-traditional ideas, but I wasn't sure that her tolerance of new-fangled notions extended this far.

"How can I help?" I asked sympathetically.

May smiled tentatively. "Are you sure you feel fine?"

"Perfect."

"Good. I... I would like you to change places with Ralph."

I creased my brow. "Pardon? Change places? What do you mean change places?"

"Ralph comes every evening now," said May patiently. "We just want a little more time together. If you could let him wear your pyjamas and lie in the bed, we can talk for a few minutes more before he must leave."

"And me? What do I do?" I wasn't sure that I quite liked the idea of sitting around naked while they had a pleasant tête-à-tête.

"You can go for a walk. My friend Siew Chin will look after you. She is a nurse also. She will help us."

"I'm not sure..." I mused.

Tears started welling in May's eyes. If there's one thing I can't stand, it's when a girl turns on the waterworks.

I capitulated. "Oh, all right."

May clapped her hands and gave me a delighted hug. "Oh, thank you, thank you." She tucked me in and gave me a little peck on the forehead.

I sank back in my pillow. For some reason, that night I fell asleep with no trouble.

THE NEXT DAY a new doctor appeared at my bedside. He didn't bother to introduce himself. His hair was grey and his clothes rumpled. He had a craggy, weather-beaten face that pointed to a life in the tropics. I guessed that he might be fiftyish. He took my chart, peered at it over the rim of his spectacles and twitched his moustache occasionally.

"The stuff they're giving you isn't any good you know."

I was taken aback by the sudden utterance. "Er...ah?" I responded.

The doctor whipped off his spectacles and stared at me. "You speakee English? *Chakap Inggeris?*"

I was stung. I replied in my best BBC voice, "Yes, well, just a bit. Picked it up at Cambridge, you know."

It was the doctor's turn to be startled. He harrumphed and replaced his spectacles. "Ah... well, yes, good."

"Could you please repeat what you said?" I asked ever so politely.

He regained his composure. "Yes. The stuff they're giving you. No good. Won't do you any harm mind you, but won't cure whatever it is you've got."

I raised my eyebrows interrogatively. "Dr Maxwell said..."

He waved his hand dismissively. "Yes, yes, Dr Maxwell. A good man, good man. But a bit behind the times, what? Hasn't been keeping up with the literature. You've got..." He paused and peered at my charts again. "Ha, interesting. Poisoning by substance unknown. Shot with a poison dart." He whipped off his spectacles again and waved them at me. "I know these native poisons. Deadly stuff. One day you're right as rain. Next day... gone." He made a throat-cutting gesture.

I was getting vaguely disturbed. The doctor continued.

"Yes, the stuff they're feeding you won't do the job."

"What do you suggest, doctor?" I inquired. Obviously he was building up to something.

"What you need, lad, is a couple of doses of the new wonder drug. Penicillium. Guaranteed to cure most anything."

I nodded. "It sounds good," I said cautiously. "Where can I get some?"

"Not in this hospital. But I have a supplier who's bringing over a batch for shipment to Sydney. He can let me have a box. I can let you have a couple of weeks' worth. But it's not cheap, not cheap at all."

"How much?"

"Oh, $10–12 a go. Say, $150 for the whole course."

I pondered. $150 was a lot of money. D'Almeida might be generous, but I wasn't sure that I wouldn't be stretching his generosity by asking for this new drug. "Can I think about it?"

"Well, yes, but don't take your time." He flipped my charts closed and hung them on the bedframe. "If you don't want it, there are others that do. I'll be back tomorrow. You can tell me then." With that he swept out of the room.

This news unsettled me somewhat. I was in truth feeling perfectly fine until then. I had recovered my appetite. George, never one to put a fine point on things, commented that I was slurping at the trough like a famished hog. The initial dizziness had gone and the light no longer hurt my eyes. I had full faith in Dr Maxwell, who was a man of considerable charm and oozed competence. But to be told out of the blue that there might be a chance of fatal side-effects.... I decided to tackle May on the point when I next saw her.

She breezed in at the start of the evening shift with a spring in her step and a tune on her tongue. I realised that it wasn't joy at my speedy recovery that lightened her spirits. It pleased me somehow to see her happy; Ralph was a decent sort, and they would make a good couple. However, I had more serious things on my mind.

"There was a new doctor in here today," I began.

"Hmm?" she responded, her mind obviously on other things as she bustled around the room.

"An oldish sort of fellow, grey hair and rumpled coat. Is he helping Dr Maxwell?"

May paused and furrowed her brow. "A new doctor?"

"Yes, he offered me some sort of new wonder drug. Penny-something-or-other at $150 for the lot. He says it'll cure whatever I've got. Otherwise there might be... side-effects."

May shook her head. "Dr Maxwell is still your doctor. He has been called away for a few days, but he told me that you are completely fine. He wanted to discharge you, but the toxicologists have asked to keep you under observation for a few more days. Since Mr d'Almeida is willing to pay, we will keep you here, okay?"

"But this doctor...?"

"I think you must mean Dr Hill," she replied. "I do not know what wonder drug he has offered to you. I am not sure he should do that. Better to stick to the prescribed medication."

I subsided. She was right of course. His hard sell tactics didn't exactly inspire confidence. He sounded like a snake-oil salesman, but there's something about a white lab coat and stethoscope that lends authority to one's pronouncements. Anyway, I had full confidence in Dr Maxwell, or so I told myself. Besides, I couldn't very well ask d'Almeida to cough up $150 for some unproven pill on the off-chance that it might work. I put the matter of the wonder drug out of my head.

Ralph came in at 6:15. May beamed at him and he smiled back. She left to do her round of the ward. He shuffled sheepishly around to my bedside.

"It's awfully good of you to help, old man," he said, hanging his head bashfully like a schoolboy.

"Don't mention it. May's a sweet kid. Happy to help."

There was an awkward silence. He cleared his throat and looked at the fan. I looked at the fan too. He switched his gaze to the floor. I decided that I had to take the initiative. "Well, how shall we proceed?"

He cleared his throat again. "I... er... think I have to change into your pyjamas."

I nodded. "And I suppose I should get into your clothes. Right, let's get started."

Ralph shook his head. "Er... no. May said that you should wear these." He produced a white shirt and a pair of khaki trousers from a paper bag. I stared at them. A hospital attendant's uniform!

May came back in. "I'm not wearing a peon's suit," I expostulated. "If I can't wear my clothes, then at least let me have a lab coat. I've always fancied being a doctor."

"Please don't give trouble, Denny," replied May. "You cannot wear your own clothes or Ralph's. People will see you and chase you away after visiting hours. And you cannot dress like a doctor. We know all the doctors in this hospital. You will be questioned and then we will be in trouble. Dressed like a peon, no one will think twice about you. And when you walk around with Siew

Chin they will not think it strange."

I was inclined to argue, but at that moment a new nurse stepped in. She literally took my breath away and my protest died unheard. She had a delicate, symmetrical face and piercing dark eyes. Her lustrous ebony hair was done up in a bun. May introduced her.

"Denny, this is Siew Chin. She is my friend. She will take care of you while Ralph is here."

She smiled a little and held out her hand. "How do you do?" she asked in a pleasant lilting voice.

I took her hand gently and shook it. "Very well thank you, especially now you're here."

She giggled and averted her glance. Evidently there were some compensations in helping out.

I turned to May, "All right, I'll get changed if you'd leave us."

She beamed at me and left with Siew Chin. In a couple of minutes Ralph was comfortably tucked into my bed, with my cousin fussing over him. I followed Siew Chin out into the corridor.

We wandered around the hospital talking in low voices about trivial things. It was pleasant making light conversation with a pretty girl. After the intensity of my experience upcountry, this was a tonic for the soul. Siew Chin was reserved but not in an unfriendly matter. Evidently she was not entirely at home speaking English, though she spoke competently with a pleasant lilt. I surmised that she was Chinese-educated. Her father was a rich businessman in Ipoh. She had come down to Singapore along with her mother when she was young. Reading between the lines, I suspected that Siew Chin was the daughter of a discarded wife. The *towkay* must have banished his wife to Singapore when she failed to produce a son. It was a common enough story. He was probably living a merry existence with his present favourite wife. I didn't ask, and she didn't volunteer any information.

No one gave us a second glance as we walked along the endless corridors, me pushing an empty trolley. The place seemed chronically understaffed. We met a few nurses but no doctors. The corridors were mostly empty, lit by anaemic light blubs hung spider-like from thin wires. Siew Chin was off duty so there was no need to visit any of the wards. In any case that would have aroused suspicion, since the appearance of a new peon would inevitably have drawn questions from the nursing staff and the other peons.

After about an hour we wandered back to my room. Ralph was lying propped up on my pillows, wearing my pyjamas and looking as strong and healthy as a bull. May was standing next to him holding a sheaf of papers. In one hand she held a thermometer. Presumably she intended to shove this into his mouth if anyone turned up to ask questions. Till then I hadn't realised the depths of deviousness that existed in my cousin. They seemed not quite pleased to see us, but Ralph emerged from the bedclothes without protest. We changed clothes quickly while the two girls modestly averted their eyes, as if they hadn't seen everything before.

Ralph pressed May's hand to take his leave, with an embarrassed expression plastered all over his face. Evidently he wasn't quite sure whether a kiss or a hug would be in order. In the end he just squeezed her hand like squashing a sponge, muttered something indistinct and exited through the door. Siew Chin went with him to fend off any curious bystanders. May looked entirely contented. She tucked me back into bed in a distracted way. Then she gave me a quick hug.

"Thank you," she said softly and went back to her station outside. I lay back for a while looking at the fan, then dozed off suddenly.

SO THE NEXT few days passed. Every morning my pair of tame toxicologists appeared, peered and disappeared. To their obvious disappointment I showed no sign of turning blue, green or any other interesting colour. Moreover, I displayed a disgustingly healthy appetite and seemed to all observers to have made a complete recovery. Dr Hill did not put in an appearance again in my room. Evidently he had concluded that I was not a likely prospect.

As I didn't much feel like lying down all day, I wandered around the ward and the hospital. The day nurse had remonstrated at first but gave up trying to confine me to bed after catching me literally climbing the wall. Actually I was trying to slap a particularly distracting mosquito, but the sight of me balanced precariously on my chair stretching to reach the top of the wall must have convinced her that I had reached the end of my tether. She made no further objection to my peregrinations as long as I didn't disturb anyone else.

I was given pretty much a free run of the place and got to know the layout of the hospital quite well. There was a European wing: quiet, spotless and sparsely occupied. Then there were the Asiatic wards: noisy, bustling and constantly full. The staff seemed to be in perpetual motion, the few doctors and nurses buzzing from bed to bed like bees collecting pollen.

I saw Dr Hill several times in the Asiatic wards. He seemed to be the one European doctor who was in constant attendance. I soon discerned a pattern to his activity. He was mostly to be found in the single rooms. As a long-staying guest I kept my room and consequently our ward was exempt from Dr Hill's attentions. But in the other wards there was a constant turnover of patients. If a new patient was admitted to the single rooms, it was a good bet that Dr Hill would be there shortly. I assumed that he was flogging his wonder drug to the inmates. Once or twice I saw envelopes change hands. I pictured them stuffed with notes. Hill seemed to have quite a decent little side practice going. Judging from the rapidity with which the patients changed it must have been effective stuff that he was feeding them — either that or he was killing them off at a breathtaking rate.

Wandering around the corridors quickly lost its appeal. Conversation with the other patients was limited since most of them could only manage a few halting sentences in English. The nurses and doctors were too busy to pay much attention to me, and after the first few days they accepted me as part of the furnishings.

I looked forward to the evenings — not only because of Siew Chin but also as a welcome relief to the tedium of hospital life. I had long since read every pulp novel I owned from cover to cover and back again. In any case, the wards began to have a depressing effect on me. Too often there was a little commotion, with nurses and peons rushing in followed by a doctor. Usually, the excitement abated fairly soon; after a short interval a peon would unobtrusively push a draped trolley out of the ward. I had thought that I was fairly hardened to death, especially after my own experience. But after the first two or three I began to get morbid thoughts about mortality. Dr Hill's warning about my possible sudden demise kept returning. I tried to put it out of my mind but didn't quite succeed. However, for an hour or so in the evening these dark forebodings were held at bay. I wandered around the hospital with Siew Chin while May and Ralph had they little private time together. We talked of many things, of shoes and ships and sealing wax... trivial, domestic things of no great moment. It was a relief.

Then, one afternoon, completely out of the blue, came the bad news. May appeared at my bedside. She was almost in tears. She carried my file in her hand. I sat bolt upright in bed and laid aside my newspaper.

"You are being discharged! You're completely well!" she announced accusingly

I didn't know what to say. "I'm sorry," I mumbled.

"Here!" she said, thrusting the file at me, "The toxicologists say that they cannot find anything wrong with you. They have recommended your immediate discharge."

She wiped away a tear. May evidently wasn't overjoyed by my return to health. She and Ralph were getting on so well. She reproached me with her looks for being so inconsiderate as to make a total recovery so soon.

"Well, well," I said, somewhat nonplussed by this development.

Of course I was relieved to receive a clean bill of health. But at the same time I was concerned that I wouldn't have the chance to see Siew Chin again. Nurses lived a very cloistered life in the hostel. Visitors — especially male visitors — were not welcome. I fingered the file thoughtfully.

"Could I delay the discharge till tomorrow?" I asked.

May had composed herself. "Until tomorrow?"

"Yes," I went on, "it would give you and Ralph time to make other arrangements." And me too, I thought to myself.

May brightened up. "Yes," she nodded, "I think that it can be done."

Any reprieve was better than nothing. She left in a happier frame of mind.

That evening I was somewhat surprised to find that Siew Chin turned up in mufti. Instead of her usual starched nurse's uniform she was wearing a fetching flowered *samfoo*. Her hair was done up in two braids. She had two paper bags with her.

"I have an errand," she said. "I must go to Chinatown. Do you mind coming with me?"

I did not mind at all. "Might I ask where we're going?" I ventured.

"To a medicine shop," Siew Chin responded. "I have to give these things to the man there. It may take us a little time to walk there and return. I hope that it is all right with you."

I nodded my assent. Evidently May and Ralph wanted an extended session together. I was quite happy to oblige them. It was a good forty-five minutes' walk to Chinatown at the very least.

We passed along the empty corridors and out along the road. The night was clear and a light breeze blew. I didn't know what to do with my hands. If it had been Madeline Strachan, I would have offered her my arm. That didn't seem the right thing to do with Siew Chin. Somehow Western courting rituals appeared totally inappropriate. In the end I solved my problem by carrying her paper bags.

We wandered along in silence. The road was lined with frangipani trees. The fragrance was subtle and pleasant, but in the dark the spindly branches had the look of fingers reaching into the night. The tree of ghost fingers the Malays called them. It was good to be out of the hospital with its stale antiseptic smell. I breathed deeply.

"Can I ask you a question?" said Siew Chin at length.

"By all means," I responded.

"Are you Chinese?" She looked at me curiously, as if I were some strange laboratory specimen.

I was somewhat taken aback by the question. "Yes, I suppose so," I replied.

"But you do not speak Chinese at all."

"No, not a word. Never had a chance to learn. We're Babas. May must have told you. My father was born here, and his father and his father's father before him."

"How strange," she said thoughtfully, considering this odd phenomenon. The concept of a non-Chinese-speaking Chinese was evidently a contradiction in terms to her.

"Do you feel nothing for China then?"

"Feel? What do you mean, feel?" I asked.

"For example, when the Japanese invaded China and killed our people and bombed our cities, did you not feel outrage? Have you no emotion about that? Do you not feel a sense of patriotism?"

To tell the truth, I found it hard to feel patriotic about a motherland that I never knew, sundered as we were by a chasm four generations and an ocean wide. However, I decided that it wasn't wise to be quite so blunt.

"Well, of course I'm outraged at the atrocities," I answered truthfully. "The Japs haven't any right to invade China, any more than the Italians have a right to be in Abyssinia. The things I read in the papers about the capture of Nanking — it's terrible. Any civilised person would be revolted."

Siew Chin nodded. We continued in silence for a while. I found it maddening that I could read nothing from her expression. Did she agree with me? Did she despise the fact that I wasn't a Chinese patriot? Her face was inscrutable. It disquieted me, not knowing whether I had risen or sunk in her estimation.

We had reached the bright lights now. The five-foot way was crowded with people, bustling around on their little errands. No one paid the least attention to us.

"I want to ask a favour," said Siew Chin suddenly, touching my arm.

"Sure, anything," I replied, encouraged by the touch.

"I know that you are a good man," she said slowly (that's nice, I thought to myself) "and a scholar." She paused. We had come to a halt. The tide of humanity eddied around us. She took me by the elbow and led me to a quieter corner under a garish cinema poster.

"I...we need your help," she continued, looking earnestly into my eyes.

"There is a group of us — a few, only a dozen. We are pledged to help our comrades in China in their heroic struggle against the Japanese. We collect things — money, medicine, things to send back."

I nodded my head reflexively, though I didn't quite see what she was leading up to.

Her voice dropped, "The corrupt Chiang Kai-shek regime does not approve of us. The fat landlords would rather see the motherland subjugated than give up their privileges."

Her vehemence startled me. I had never seen this side of her before.

"They have told the British that we are subversives, that we desire to undermine the white man's rule. We are being observed by the police. My comrades fear that some of us will be arrested. We may need a lawyer — a good lawyer."

She stopped. She took my hand in hers. "Will you help us?"

"Yes, of course," I blurted out without thinking. That's the trouble with me; faced with a pretty face my mouth is often in fourth gear before my brain is engaged.

I was rewarded with a dazzling smile. "Thank you," she said simply. We resumed walking.

As we walked the enormity of what I had agreed to began to sink in. I hadn't even been called to the Bar yet, and here I was pledged to defend a potentially subversive group against prosecution by the colonial authorities. I didn't even know what they were up to, whether they were bomb-chucking anarchists or whatever.

"These, er, comrades of yours," I ventured hesitantly, "they're not violent are they? No guns or bombs or anything of the sort?"

She giggled. "No, no, we are not violent at all. I told you. We only collect things." She darted a glance at the paper bags I was carrying. "Things for our brave comrades back home fighting the Japanese pigs."

I glanced down at the bags. They weren't heavy but they were full. It felt like boxes of some sort. "Will you tell me what's in these?" I asked.

"Medicines," she replied lightly, "just medicines. And medical supplies."

I forbore to ask where she got them or whether they had been fully paid for.

"Here," she said, "we must turn into the next lane. The shop is not far."

The lane was narrow and flanked by open drains. Rats scampered merrily in the shadows. I smelled the medicine shop before I saw it. Like most of the other shops it opened directly onto the five-foot way. A pleasant herby smell emanated from it. There was a wooden glass-topped counter running the length of the shop. Behind, reaching up to the ceiling, were rows upon rows of drawers.

Siew Chin took the paper bags from me and handed them over to a bespectacled man behind the counter. He glanced at me only once, impassively, and then began a conversation in Hokkien with her.

I glanced around the shop. Under the glass were all manner of roots, seeds, leaves and other assorted horticultural remnants. To me they looked like the sweepings of a pigeon loft. A couple of velvet-covered antlers nestled in one corner. In a jar were oddly-shaped roots that I took to be ginseng.

Siew Chin finished her business with the medicine shop man and motioned me to leave. Relieved of my paper bags, I faced the old problem of what to do with my hands again. I stuffed them into my pockets and followed her out.

We hadn't gone two paces when she suddenly seized my arm. "Quickly! We must hide! Get back into the shop."

At first I thought that she had spotted the Sikh policeman at the end of the lane and was hiding from him. Then I saw a white man slouching along the road in the half-light. I recognised him immediately. It was Dr Hill! I ducked back into the shop with Siew Chin. There was no place to hide in that brightly-lit space. In any case, Hill gave us no time to disappear. He came into the shop practically on our heels. I hunched over the counter staring fixedly at a voluptuous ginseng root, fervently praying that he wouldn't recognise me. Siew Chin stood right next to me, touching my shoulder. She was trembling slightly.

But Hill showed no sign of recognising us. I breathed a prayer of thanks that he was one of those white men who couldn't tell one Asiatic face from another. Besides, from the sound of his voice he appeared to be well and truly sloshed. I could smell the alcohol on his breath. He could have sterilised a hypodermic needle at ten paces.

"Here," he bellowed, "here's your stuff. And don't be so stingy this time, you miserable bugger." He banged a package wrapped in brown paper roughly onto the counter and shoved it over to the shopkeeper.

The shopkeeper looked at Hill impassively. He exchanged a quick glance with us, as if to say that this was only to be expected of a white man. He took the package and quietly undid the string that held it together. He examined the contents with an exaggerated deliberation. Quietly he withdrew a wad of notes from a secret drawer and counted them out one by one. Hill stared at them and scowled.

"Only sixty! They're worth twice that price you thieving Chink!"

The shopkeeper answered in an even tone, "You are welcome to have your goods back if you wish, Mr Smith." He stared directly into Hill's bloodshot eyes. The light glinted off his rimless glasses.

Hill dropped his gaze. He growled, swore inaudibly under his breath and grabbed the notes. He lurched out into the night still grumbling.

I exhaled loudly. Siew Chin went over to the counter and asked a question which I did not understand. The shopkeeper opened Hill's bundle for Siew Chin to examine. There was a largish box, packed full of bottles of different sizes and shapes. Siew Chin held them up one by one to the light.

"Quinine, insulin, morphine," she said. "I do not recognise these others." She placed the bottles back carefully.

We left the medicine shop, carefully looking around to make sure that Hill was gone. We took a different road back to the hospital.

"So," I said unguardedly, "Hill's been stealing medicines too."

Siew Chin darted a sharp look at me. "Too?" she asked with arched eyebrows.

"Ah...I mean...uh," I stammered, "I'm sorry."

"You think that I have been stealing medicines?"

I had a sinking feeling in the pit of my stomach. She stared at me for what seemed an eternity. I hung my head. I felt my ears turn red. Then, all of a sudden, she giggled.

"Stop," she said, "you look just like a little boy."

I breathed again. "I'm really sorry," I said, "I didn't mean to imply..."

She shook her head. "No, you are quite right to suspect me. But it is not true. We do not steal medicines. I buy them at the hospital pharmacy. They have a special price for nurses. I get aspirins and cough syrup cheaply. And I take cotton wool and bandages that no one wants any more. The small pieces that are of no further use. Yes, I suppose I do steal those."

We walked along in silence for a while as I sought to remove my foot from my mouth. Luckily she didn't seem to hold it against me.

"Strange about Dr Hill," she said, almost to herself. "Why would he sell medicines? Surely he does not need the money." We mused on the subject for a while and then passed to other things. Hill was forgotten. We chatted pleasantly as we strolled. Without realising it, we were back at the hospital. We walked along the darkened corridors back to the ward. At the door of the ward I paused and took her hand.

"When will I see you again?" I asked. She blushed a little and looked down. I had just screwed up my courage to give her a little peck on the cheek when all hell broke loose.

IT BEGAN with a sudden scream, which ended on a strangled note. I heard the clatter of a body falling onto the floor. Siew Chin was through the ward door in a flash. May was just ahead of her. Ralph, still clad in my pyjamas, was at the door of my room blinking like an owl caught in the light. In the ward the patients were all up. The two nurses headed to a bed in the centre of the left row, the occupant of which was thrashing around on the floor. I followed, though what I could do I didn't know. The man seemed to be having a fit of some sort. The three of us held him down. He struggled for a while, then went limp. We dragged him back onto the bed.

All of a sudden I was aware of a figure at my side.

"What's going on here?" a voice demanded. It was slightly slurred, and I could smell alcohol.

"The patient seems to have had a seizure, Dr Hill," replied May.

Hill nodded, produced a syringe from his medical bag and injected the patient. He stood over the recumbent form, taking the man's pulse with every appearance of competence. He turned to me. I tried to shrink back into the shadows.

"You!" he barked.

I stared at him wordlessly, my head bowed.

"Yes, you boy," he growled testily, "clean up this mess. And get that damned broken glass off the floor." There was no spark of recognition in his face.

I nodded with relief and fetched a broom from the corner cupboard.

He seemed to notice Siew Chin for the first time. "And who are you?" he asked, though not as roughly.

"Nurse Lim," responded Siew Chin quietly. Her face was pale.

"Well, Nurse Lim, help Nurse... Nurse what's-your-name here to settle the patient." Hill's talent for recognising faces was matched by his ability to recall names.

The commotion had subsided and the other patients were quietly bedding down, grumbling about their interrupted sleep. Hill headed to the door with May alongside, explaining the treatment to be given to the patient. He stopped abruptly in mid-stride as he passed my room door. Ralph, the great gawping twit, was standing in the doorway watching the proceedings, mesmerised like a half-witted owl.

"Who the hell are you?" demanded Hill. "You're not a patient here!" He might not have been able to tell one Asiatic from another but a white face was quite something else. No self-respecting European would have been caught dead in the Asiatic ward — or to be more precise, would have had to be dead to have been caught in the Asiatic ward.

Ralph was mumbling something incoherent and backing into the room. May had gone completely pale. She looked like she was about to faint.

Hill rounded on her. "What's the meaning of this, nurse? Who's this fellow? How did he get here." May was on the verge of tears as she struggled to answer.

Ralph gallantly stepped into the breach. "It's not her fault. I'm a... a friend. It was my idea to... to..."

He hesitated. Siew Chin was staring at him with pleading eyes. It would be all over with her too if Ralph spilled the beans. But he rose to the occasion. "I took over this empty bed when my friend was discharged. The nurse didn't know anything. It's not her fault."

Hill's eyes narrowed. "You just took over the empty bed. Without her knowing. To have a good snooze I suppose," he snorted. "What d'you take me for? Get dressed!" he commanded, "then the pair of you see me in my office."

RALPH AND MAY returned ashen-faced from their interview with Hill. Siew Chin and I were waiting in my room. I had not changed back into my pyjamas and was still dressed as an attendant. We waited silently for them to speak. May lost her control and began to weep. Ralph put his arm around her.

"I'm afraid I've made rather a mess of things," said Ralph. Judging from the state that May was in, I surmised that that was an understatement.

"What happened?"

"Well, I started off by telling him that I was a lawyer," explained Ralph, "and that May belonged to one of the oldest Baba families in the Colony. You know, to assure him of our good intentions, that everything was all above board and all that. That she was a lady and I'm a gentleman and nothing passed between us. I thought that I'd appeal to his sense of honour and fair play."

I rolled my eyes upward. Ralph obviously lived in a different century. I resolved firmly to wean him off the Jane Austens when this sorry business was over.

"I take it that it didn't work?"

Ralph shook his head glumly. "No, not a bit. His eyes lit up when he heard the bit about defending a lady's honour. He went on and on about immorality and the shenanigans today's generation got up to. And..."

"And...?"

"And then he said that he'd give us a chance."

"Give you a chance? But that's good!" For one fleeting moment I thought that I might have misjudged the old bugger.

"Provided we help him out. He wants money," said Ralph softly.

"Otherwise he will go to Matron and have May dismissed."

Ralph stopped abruptly. He began to get agitated. His face was white. He kept clenching and unclenching his fists. I'd never seen quite so upset before. It was clear that some titanic oath was striving to burst forth. I waited for the eruption.

"Blast the man!" exclaimed Ralph.

I let my breath out and sighed inwardly. Being cursed by Ralph was not unlike being flagellated with a wet noodle. Having got *that* off his chest, he proceeded with a little less agitation.

"Nothing happened between us, nothing. The blighter knows it. But he's going to put it about that he caught us in bed together... that she's a woman of loose morals. Unless we pay him."

I really didn't know what to say. The threat of being sacked wasn't the worst thing for May. It was being caught alone with a man in such a situation that was the more serious matter. Back in England one would have made light of the whole thing. Ralph would have been the butt of some ribald jokes and May would have been teased by her girlfriends and that would have been that. But here, in our social milieu, things were different. May would be dishonoured and the family disgraced. A scandal like this would make her unmarriageable. There would be no hope of a good match with an eligible bachelor from an established Baba family. Mak would be devastated. She would never be able to hold her head up in society. Publish and be damned wasn't an option. It would be May who would be damned.

"How much does he want?" I asked.

"$500 to start with," responded Ralph.

"$500!" I ejaculated. "Where are we going to get that kind of money?"

"To start with," said Ralph bitterly. "The bugger has debts, he says. We're supposed to 'help' him. In return he keeps his slimy mouth shut. Oh, he made it quite clear what he was getting at.

You pay up and I'll shut up. But it's only the start. Once he gets his claws in he'll keep squeezing and squeezing and..."

Siew Chin patted May's hand. "I have some money saved," she offered, "only a few hundred dollars. But you can have that."

May smiled through her tears, shaking her head.

"No, Siew Chin, we can't take your money," I answered on May's behalf. "It's our problem, we'll find a solution."

Ralph took my hand and pumped it. "Thanks old man, I knew we could depend on you. But I'm damned if I can think of a way out of this."

"There is one way," I said slowly. They all looked at me expectantly.

"You could marry May." I looked at Ralph meaningly.

"I'd do it in a flash if May would have me," said Ralph with feeling. May blushed. "But it wouldn't stop that blighter Hill from telling what he saw. May would be kicked out and there'd still be a scandal. Besides, your mother would never agree."

"Mak would not know where to hide her face," said May almost inaudibly. "Even if we were to marry, she would be disgraced. I could not face her." She buried her face in her hands.

I patted her consolingly on the shoulder. "Don't worry," I said comfortingly, "we'll think of something."

Ralph took her hand and squeezed it. She smiled at him. He smiled back. The gawkiness was gone. Well, that's one problem solved, I thought to myself glumly. Ralph could be counted on to do the right thing — even if it meant elopement and exile.

IT SEEMED rather pointless to spend the rest of the night in the hospital. All the paperwork had in fact been done that very day and I was free to go. We just packed up and moved out of the ward. Siew Chin very kindly agreed to take over the rest of May's shift.

The poor kid wasn't in any shape to continue. She went off to the nurses' lounge to rest. It occurred to me that I might perhaps keep her company, but Siew Chin advised against it. There were enough complications already without having to explain the appearance of a new peon. Ralph offered to put me up for the night.

Needless to say, neither of us had a restful night. The problem kept me tossing and turning until the *kampong* cocks crowed. Ralph's red-eyed appearance at breakfast testified to a similarly disturbed sleep.

"Any suggestions about what to do with Hill?" he asked, moodily nibbling at his *kaya* bread.

I shook my head glumly. It ached as if some of the brackets holding my brain steady had come loose. "I think we ought to ask Mr d'Almeida," I replied slowly.

Ralph's eyes widened. "Mr d'Almeida?! You must be joking. Mr d'Almeida will sling us out on our backsides!" Ralph still held d'Almeida in awe. As far as he was concerned, one did not disturb The Oracle for trifles.

"Three reasons," I responded, resting my fevered brow on my hands, "one, I have the mother of all headaches, and one more thought is going to blow my brain all over your nice clean kitchen floor. Two, d'Almeida owes me his life, so he'll at least listen before he slings us out on our backsides. Three, I don't have $500. You don't have $500. We couldn't raise $500 even if we sold our bodies to medical science for experiments. Where else are we going to get that much money?"

Ralph saw the inexorable logic of what I was saying but he still hung back.

I fired my last shot. "Anyway, whether we pay or not, Hill may still tell all. It's better that d'Almeida hears it from us rather than from that slimy bastard."

Ralph nodded. "All right," he said reluctantly, "but Mr

d'Almeida...." He voice trailed off on a worshipful note, as if he had just invoked The Deity.

For once we were at the office bright and early. Moraiss gave us the evil eye. As far as he was concerned, pupils who got in early must have been up to no good. We collared d'Almeida when he arrived at nine on the dot. He ushered us into his room gravely. Ralph was inclined to be tongue-tied and stammered a lot. In the end I took over the narration and told the whole sorry tale from beginning to end, omitting nothing, including the corroborative fact that I'd personally seen Hill flogging stolen medicines in Chinatown. D'Almeida listened gravely and without comment. At the end of the story, he put the tips of his fingers together and closed his eyes. We waited expectantly. Nothing happened for some minutes. He could have fallen asleep for all we knew. At length, I could wait no longer. I cleared my throat.

"Er... Mr d'Almeida?"

"Yes?" he responded without opening his eyes.

"I was wondering... we were wondering, that is... er, what should we do next?"

He opened his eyes and fixed us both with a basilisk stare. "What do *you* propose to do next?"

"Ah... well," I temporised, looking to Ralph for support. None was forthcoming. He sat there with his mouth agape like a trophy trout mounted on a wall.

"We thought... that is, we hoped that you could, er, perhaps, advance us some money. We'd pay it back, every cent, out of our salaries."

Still fixing us with his unblinking gaze he asked, "How much?"

I swallowed hard. I knew that he had said that he owed me his life, but I wasn't sure that his gratitude would extend to parting with large sums of cash. Nevertheless, I had to try.

"$500," I said simply.

He didn't even blink. "Very well, it can be arranged. I shall write a chit for Moraiss. He will arrange payment and terms of repayment."

I looked at Ralph. Ralph looked back at me. D'Almeida looked at both of us.

"Was there anything else, gentlemen?"

We shook our heads in unison. Mumbling our thanks somewhat incoherently, we bolted out of his room. Back in the pupils' room we collapsed into our chairs.

"Well, that wasn't so bad," I said doubtfully.

I felt vaguely discontented. It was true that we had got the $500 from d'Almeida and painlessly at that, but I had expected more. Not money, but in terms of sage advice. I had by now come to expect that d'Almeida would pull the proverbial rabbit out of the hat every time, and the fact that he had not suggested any solution to our problem disconcerted me. Ralph, on the other hand, had expected at the least to be masticated into little chunks and expectorated. To have emerged from the holy of holies with our skins intact and with money to boot was a signal victory as far as he was concerned.

"What now?" he asked.

What now, indeed. I racked my brains. My head was still heavy.

"I suppose you may as well pay the bastard," I replied.

Ralph nodded. "I suppose so," he said heavily, "but I doubt that we've heard the last of him."

I concurred. Paying Hill would merely whet his appetite. We had to find some way to put paid to him. If only I could get my hands on some of that poison that Cynthia Evans had used.... I shook my head violently. I was drifting into the realms of fantasy. It's all right for mystery writers to bump off characters with gay abandon, but that isn't the way things work in the real world.

"If only we had something on him...."

"Something on him," echoed Ralph, "some dark secret that he wants to keep dark."

We both looked up at the same instant.

"Drugs!" I exclaimed, "Stolen drugs!"

Blackmailing the blackmailer. It had a certain attraction. Galvanised by the prospect of getting the goods on Hill, we began to discuss the matter feverishly.

"Catch him in the act!" said Ralph excitedly. "We lie in wait for him to swipe the stuff and then nab him with the goods."

I shook my head. "No good. Where does he get the stuff? We don't know. We'd have to shadow him all the time. Anyway, he can give any number of reasons for taking medicines out of the store or wherever." I tried to think despite my throbbing head.

"What about waiting at the medicine shop for him to turn up with the goods?" suggested Ralph a tad more soberly.

"Still no good," I replied reluctantly. "For one thing, it isn't a crime to sell medicines and there's no proof that he hasn't actually paid for them."

"What do we do then?" asked Ralph peevishly.

My head was throbbing. "I don't know," I replied. "I suppose we could break into his office."

"And do what?"

"Look for evidence," I responded. "Maybe he has records or chits or something incriminating."

Ralph looked doubtfully at me. It's always so easy in crime thrillers. The criminal invariably leaves a trail, a clue, something to hang himself with. But when you're actually planning to catch a crook, it isn't quite so straightforward. Ralph began to demur.

"Have you any better ideas?" I asked, a bit shortly.

Ralph shook his head. I didn't have any better ideas either. We eventually agreed that while Ralph was keeping Hill busy with the money, I would break into his office and snoop around. On that note we parted.

That evening found me back in the hospital, pushing my trolley around with Siew Chin as I had done for the past week. May had told Mak some tall tale about me being moved to another ward for special tests so that she wouldn't be worried to find me gone. Out of curiosity I looked in on my old bed. It was occupied. A frail old Malay gentlemen with a straggling beard was lying there, apparently comatose. I didn't disturb him.

Ralph had arranged to meet Hill at nine o'clock at some deserted corner of the hospital. I would do my rounds until I saw him leave his office and then break in. Siew Chin was game. She didn't seem to mind being an accomplice to criminal trespass. We decided it would be better to keep May out of it. She carried on her duties as night nurse, though clearly her heart wasn't in it.

The time dragged. I must have pushed that trolley halfway down the road to Mandalay. We hardly spoke. It would have been too distracting if we'd carried on in the normal way. I had keyed myself up for the sortie, and it wouldn't have done to have missed my cue. Hill showed no sign of leaving. He didn't seem to be in too much of a hurry to get his paws on the money.

About 9:15 the door finally opened and Hill emerged, red-eyed and evidently sloshed to the gills. With the amount of alcohol in him he must have been impervious to even the most virulent of germs. He meandered along the corridor in generally the right direction.

Quickly I parked my trolley in a dark corner and hurried to his door. It was locked. Fortunately the lock was an uncomplicated device. It was the work of a moment to get it open. One does not spend six years in an English public school without developing some useful skills, especially if one wants to be fed properly. I tiptoed in. Siew Chin was behind me.

"Time for you to go," I said quietly.

"What? Why? But I want to help," she remonstrated.

"Because it wouldn't do for you to get caught. Besides I need someone to keep a lookout for me."

I propelled her gently out the door. "Whistle or something if someone comes along." I closed the door firmly behind her and locked it.

The office was a mess. There were papers all over the desk. The place smelt of formaldehyde. I had no idea what Hill might be using formaldehyde for, but I suspected that it was just to cover up the smell of the alcohol. Where to start? I couldn't put on the light for fear of being noticed. A pale glow from the corridor lights filtered in through the frosted glass pane of the door. By the light of a pocket torch, I started sifting through the mess.

There were a lot of bills, a sheaf of chits from his club and the remains of racing tickets. Not a pretty picture, but far from incriminating. The drawers of the desk were unlocked. I opened each. More of the same and a couple of bottles of whiskey. I began to despair of finding anything that might help us. Somehow, I didn't think that he was the type to keep records of his nefarious activities. If anything, he seemed to be an opportunist, pouncing on the prospects that the tide of chance swept his way.

Behind the desk was a curtained alcove that I assumed was the examination area. I drew back the curtain. The alcove contained a spartan examination bench, a sink and a work table. Bottles of various sizes littered the work table, mostly partly filled. There was a collection of phials in the corner, together with a cardboard carton. I picked one up. It was labeled "penicillium" in scrawly handwriting. A bottle full of clear liquid stood at the side, together with a funnel. A jar of white powder, half empty, lay open next to the other things. Curiosity overcame me. So this was the wonder drug! I put a drop from one of the phials on the tip of my finger and tasted it. It was slightly sweetish. Turning to the powder, I was revolted to find a dead fly in it. I gingerly removed the thing from the jar and dabbed my finger in it. It had the feel of talcum powder. I cautiously put my finger to my tongue. I may be no doctor, but I do know my way around a pantry. The stuff was icing sugar, no doubt about it.

I was just about to search the drawers of the work table when I heard a strange whistling sort of noise from outside the door. It sounded like a kettle coming to the boil. I couldn't imagine what it could be. Then suddenly I realised what it was. Siew Chin was trying to warn me, but she couldn't whistle properly! In a panic I considered bolting through the window. No good. The louvres had transverse bars. I looked frantically around. No other door. The sound of footsteps outside was distinct now. A key rattled in the lock. I considered briefly hiding under the desk, but there was no modesty board to shield me. In desperation I retreated to the treatment nook and drew the curtains.

Hill entered, followed by a second person. I heard him cough, a nasty dry hacking cough. I heard Hill's footsteps draw near and cringed, trying to squeeze myself into the back of the alcove. However, he didn't draw the curtains. Instead, I heard him unlock a cupboard and open it.

"Here," he said, "two dozen doses of penicillium. All ready and packed for you."

The second man spoke. His voice was weak, and from the accent I surmised that he was Malay. "It will cure me, you are sure?"

I sneaked a peek through the curtain. It was the old man who had taken my bed. Hill had wasted no time in swooping on the new arrival.

"A 100 per cent guaranteed," said Hill. "Now, my dear Tunku, we agreed on $240. You pay me and I'll let you have the medicine."

"Let me take now," said the old man.

Hill made an impatient sound, but when he spoke he was conciliatory, as if to an idiot child. "No, you don't have to take it now. We do it the way I told you. You have the bottle? Good. You pour the medicine they give you into the bottle. When you give me the bottle, I give you one dose. Understand?"

"Let me take!" repeated the old man querulously, "I have pain now! Let me drink one!"

"No," said Hill firmly, "First dose tomorrow. After you give me the bottle."

"I pay you $50," wheedled the old man. "I pay you now if you let me drink one. To stop pain."

He fumbled in the folds of his sarong and produced a fifty dollar bill.

Hill's back was to me, but I could imagine his face. His fingers twitched. "Very well," he said after the briefest of pauses, "$50 it is. But don't expect instant miracles."

He opened the box and extracted a phial. The old man took it greedily, shoving the balled up note into Hill's waiting paw. "I drink this? It cure me?"

"Yes, yes, just like that. Go on, since you wanted it." A trace of impatience coloured Hill's tone. He was having a bit of trouble keeping his temper, but he didn't want to offend an obvious sucker — and a rich one at that.

The old man squinted at the phial in the light. He placed a drop of liquid on the tip of his finger and smelt it. I thought this was most peculiar. Hill evidently thought so too. "What the hell are you doing?" he asked testily.

The old man took a sip. He wiped his mouth. "Sugar water, I'd wager," he said in perfect English. I stared. He had straightened up. I knew that voice.

"Who the hell are you?!" demanded Hill.

"My apologies for not properly introducing myself, Dr Hill," he responded. "My name is d'Almeida. Clarence d'Almeida, Justice of the Peace."

For a moment Hill stood as if petrified. Then he growled, "Give me that!" and lurched forward. D'Almeida deftly stepped aside and put the desk between himself and the doctor. "Give me that!!" repeated Hill menacingly, his voice rising half an octave.

"Violence will do you no good, Dr Hill," said d'Almeida calmly. It made as much impact as raindrops on a rhinoceros' hide. Hill was still advancing, trying to corner d'Almeida. They slowly circled the table. I thought I had better make an appearance.

Seldom have I ever made a more theatrical entrance. I whipped the curtain aside and yelled "Stop!" Hill jumped. D'Almeida, to his credit, merely raised an eyebrow, as if he had expected me all along.

"Ah, Mr Chiang," he said with considerable sang froid as I stepped to his side, "thank you for joining us." To Hill he said gravely, "Allow me to present my associate, Mr Chiang."

Hill's face betrayed his confusion. "Who... how...?" he stammered. All of a sudden the bluster was gone. He fumbled his way to his chair and collapsed into it.

"The game's up, Dr Hill," said d'Almeida evenly. "It's time to close down your practice."

The alcohol-induced rage was gone. Seen up close, Hill seemed a lot older than I remembered. His face was positively haggard. It was a pitiful face, had I the heart to pity him.

"Are you the police?" he asked. He produced a cheroot and lit it. His hand was trembling.

"No," replied d'Almeida, "not the police. Let us say, a concerned individual."

"What do you want?" demanded Hill. "Money?" He laughed bitterly. "I haven't any."

"Not money, Dr Hill. Just your promise that you will cease your activities."

Hill's eyebrows arched. "Just that? Nothing else?" He smiled crookedly. "All right, I promise. There, is that enough?"

"In writing, if you please. I shall dictate the text," responded d'Almeida. Hill looked as if he was about to remonstrate, but then seemed to change his mind. Heavily he took a pen and began to write according to d'Almeida's instruction. He proffered the finished confession to d'Almeida. I took it and handed it over. It was in an illegible scrawl, but d'Almeida seemed satisfied with it.

"What next?"

"Nothing," replied d'Almeida, "as long as you do not misbehave. Dr Maxwell has suspected for some time, but had no proof. I shall give your note to him. He has authorised me to say that if you give no further trouble, your pension is secure."

Hill nodded. D'Almeida handed the phial to me. He motioned to me to pick up the carton of phoney drugs. Hill watched us listlessly. We turned to leave. As we reached the door, d'Almeida paused.

"There is one other thing. A small matter about a nurse and a young man."

Hill started. Evidently he hadn't expected d'Almeida to be quite so well informed about his activities.

"Leave them alone, Dr Hill. I trust that nothing further will be heard of the matter." He fingered Hill's confession meaningfully. Hill nodded again. We left him slumped in his chair.

Once outside d'Almeida said to me, "Well, my boy, I am in your debt again. I had not anticipated that Dr Hill might become violent."

I coughed to disguise my embarrassment. "How did you know I was there?" I queried.

"I notice a certain young lady still lurking in the shadows," he said with a ghost of a smile, nodding in Siew Chin's direction.

She emerged shamefacedly. "You have not introduced me to your friend," he said to me. I made the introductions. He shook her hand gravely and inclined his head in salutation. Siew Chin, her face completely scarlet, did a sort of half-curtsey.

"This charming young lady was making the most peculiar noise — a sort of hissing sound," d'Almeida continued. "Hill did not notice anything, but I saw her and your trolley. I surmised from what you had told me earlier of your... ah... nocturnal excursions that you were in the vicinity."

"But how did you know I was in the room?"

D'Almeida's eyes twinkled. "My dear Mr Chiang, one should always remember when peeking through curtains that one's nose protrudes somewhat from one's face. And reflects light unless camouflaged."

I felt my ears redden.

We walked along a little way. "What are you going to do with Hill?" I asked.

"Nothing, as I promised, so long as he behaves. He only has a few months more before he retires. Dr Maxwell has long suspected that he was up to something, but there was never any proof. The patients who recovered from his treatment are all convinced that he cured them, while those who did not recover are in no position to testify."

"You mean that some patients recovered, even though he fed them sugar water?" I asked with some surprise.

"Certainly. The majority of them in fact. Do not underestimate the power of faith. I believe they call it the placebo effect. And in case you are curious, I did a little checking. There is no such thing as penicillium. Sugar water and faith did the trick."

"Does Dr Maxwell know, er, everything?" I asked.

D'Almeida smiled a little. "About Hill, yes. I told him everything that you and Smallwood told me. We arranged this little charade to flush Hill out. About the other matters, I did not think it necessary to inform him."

I felt Siew Chin breathe a sigh of relief. So did I.

"Now, if you would be so kind," continued d'Almeida, "I have some things in my room that need to be collected. It is the same one you were in. I must talk to Dr Maxwell." With a small bow to Siew Chin, he strode off.

IT WAS with considerably lighter hearts that we collected both May and Ralph. Ralph was still waiting patiently at the appointed place for Hill to turn up. It was lucky that Hill was greedy. He'd gone for 'Tunku' first, no doubt confident that Ralph would hang around. As things turned out, we saved ourselves $500. We were a jolly party as we returned to my familiar old room, May draped on Ralph's arm.

The chatter died on our lips as we entered the room. Sitting quietly on a chair next to the empty bed was Mak.

"Mak!" I exclaimed, "what are you doing here?"

She looked at me accusingly. "I telephoned the hospital. They said that you had gone home. I became worried and came here. What have you been doing? And who is that man with May?"

It was very awkward. I glanced at May and cleared my throat to speak. But Ralph got in first.

"Bibik," he said in Malay, "I want to marry May. I ask your permission."

I stared at Ralph. The lingua franca of the Colony was bazaar Malay, but in Ralph's mouth it was more accurately designated bizarre Malay. The pronunciation might have been odd, but there was no mistaking either his meaning or his sincerity.

"You want to marry May?" repeated Mak with a confused look.

Ralph's limited Malay ran out and he reverted to English. "Yes, I want to marry May. I love her. I want her to be my wife if you will agree. I promise that I will be a good husband. Your daughter will want for nothing."

Mak looked at May. May looked back, pleading with her eyes. No one spoke. An eternity passed.

"Will May be happy?" asked Mak.

"Yes!" answered both of them together.

Mak sighed. She took out her handkerchief and dabbed the corners of her eyes. "If May is happy, then I am happy to. You have my permission."

I let out my breath, which I had been holding. Siew Chin squeezed my arm and I squeezed her hand back. May gave Mak a big hug, then turned to Ralph. He hesitated a moment and then put his arms around her and embraced. It was the perfect end to all our troubles.

Then in walked Matron.

"Nurse Chiang! What is the meaning of this?!"

I turned to Ralph. "Ralph, you great *gobblock*," I said, "the next time you're alone with May, do us all a big favour and *lock the bloody door!*"

THE RED CELL

THERE COMES a time in every lawyer's life when he is called upon to win his spurs on the field of battle. Mine came not long after I was called to the Bar. The d'Almeidas had decided to keep all three pupils. During my convalescence a new partner had joined the firm. Raja Aziz was the half-brother of Raja Idris — same father, different mother. He was in his late thirties, educated in England and just lately returned to the Straits. George became Aziz's assistant while Ralph was allocated to Cuthbert. D'Almeida decided to keep me as his personal devil. He decided that I should get some experience in advocacy as soon as possible.

To ease me in gently, I was assigned the simplest, most uncomplicated matter available. It was an open and shut case — a tug had collided in good weather with a dumb barge. We represented the owners of the barge. On the other side was a grizzled lawyer named K. Muthuraman. Muthuraman held himself out as a barrister and rather fancied that he was good at it. There was nothing he liked better than the sound of his own voice. He would stand in front of Judge and jury, hands clutching his robe, declaiming in flowing phrases like Olivier in *Hamlet*. We called him The Yeti because he was such an abominable showman.

Most other lawyers would have settled the case. Muthuraman, however, never knew when to give up and had bills to pay besides.

So it was that I made my maiden appearance before Mr Justice Sloan. Sloan was a good Judge. He had been a lieutenant on a destroyer during the Great War. He knew his stuff, especially when it came to ships. Muthuraman, on the other hand, would have been hard put to tell one end of a boat from the other — not that it deterred him in the least.

Muthuraman's closing speech went on and on. He kept referring to the "right side of the boat," the "left side of the boat," the "back side of the boat." Mr Justice Sloan began to fidget. His nautical soul was perturbed by this display of landlubberly inexactitude. At last he could stand it no longer. After Muthuraman had referred for the fourth time to "the front side of the boat" in as many sentences, Sloan felt he had to intervene.

"Bow, Mr Muthuraman," said the learned Judge without looking up from his notes.

Muthuraman paused in mid-gesture. A look of puzzlement crossed his face. "My lord?" he queried.

"Bow, Mr Muthuraman," repeated Mr Justice Sloan evenly.

Muthuraman shrugged his shoulders. "As your lordship pleases," he said, and made a deep theatrical bow from the waist.

Mr Justice Sloan sighed deeply. He put down his pencil. He took off his glasses. He stared at Muthuraman, who was still bent over.

"Mr Muthuraman," said Mr Justice Sloan with infinite patience, "the front side of a ship is called the bow."

Muthuraman gurgled and straightened up. He swallowed hard. He muttered, "Much obliged to your lordship."

The Judge's clerk nearly died of suppressed laughter.

Muthuraman tried manfully to salvage his speech, but it was obvious that the wind was gone from his sails. Shortly thereafter his case foundered totally and was lost with all hands. I was not called upon to reply.

WE HAD our traditional post-baptismal binge in the pupils' room, now suitably rechristened the Assistants' Lounge as befitted our enhanced status. We were halfway through a week's wages worth of refreshments when Moraiss appeared.

"Ah, my dear Moraiss," called out George jovially, "come and join the festivities. Dennis here has returned gloriously from the field of battle with drums beating and colours flying. Pull up a pew and tuck in."

Moraiss showed no inclination to thaw, however.

"Client," he said succinctly staring directly at me, "asking to see you."

I was taken aback and nearly choked on a curry puff.

"A client!" said George. "A living, breathing client. My dear chap, news of your fame has spread! The dizzy heights of the Privy Council beckon you."

I chucked a bun at him, wiped the crumbs off my mouth and hurried off after Moraiss.

"Are you sure he wants me?" I asked to Moraiss's receding back.

"Yes," he replied, conveying with that one syllable his opinion that anyone who wanted me also wanted to have his head examined.

It was a new experience to have a client all to myself, and I entered the reception room with some trepidation.

The client turned out to be a white man in a faintly rumpled white suit. He held a panama hat in one hand and offered me the other as I entered.

"You Dennis Chiang?" he asked straight off in an unmistakable American accent.

"Yes," I acknowledged, taking the proffered hand, "and you are Mr...?"

"Rouse. Bill Rouse. Call me Bill." He squeezed my hand hard, pumped it up and down a couple of times like a car jack and then relinquished it.

"Mind if I smoke?" Without waiting for my answer he produced a packet of clove cigarettes and lit up.

"Right... er... Mr Rouse, and how can I be of assistance?" I inquired, discreetly nursing my mangled paw.

"I'll come straight to the point," he said, waving his *kretek* at me. "Friends of mine are in trouble. Got mixed up with the law. They need a lawyer. Seems we got a mutual acquaintance, as they say. Girl by the name of Siew Chin. Nice kid. Speaks highly of you. So will you take the job?"

I was a trifle overwhelmed by this unexpected referral.

"Ah...yes, of course, but could you give me some details?"

"Easy enough. They're a bunch of hot-headed kids. Took it on themselves to picket a factory. They don't hold with capitalism and capitalists. The owner didn't take too kindly to that, especially when they started calling him names. He called the cops. They're being charged with..." he reached into his pocket and produced a crumpled piece of paper, from which he read out loud: "riotous and disorderly behaviour in a public place or place of public resort contrary to Section Twenty of the Minor Offences Ordinance."

"Right," I said, "that seems quite straightforward. I presume they will be tried before a Magistrate. Any indication of when?"

He looked at his wristwatch. "At three o'clock this afternoon. You've just got time to get there. My car is downstairs."

Without waiting for my answer, he jammed his panama back on his head and went for the door.

"C'mon," he said waving to me.

I would have protested, but he gave me no time. He took me by the arm and propelled me downstairs to his car.

Fifteen breathless minutes later we were at the Police Courts. Rouse was voluble and in that time told me his entire life story. He was a special correspondent for *The Newark Sapphire*, a newspaper of small circulation but with intellectual pretensions. He had been in Spain lately, covering the Civil War with the International Brigades. He had watched Franco's Nationalists march to the sea and witnessed the decimation of the Republicans. With the virtual destruction of the Abraham Lincoln Battalion on the Ebro he had thought it high time to make himself scarce. Now he was out East, sniffing around as he said for "human interest stories."

Rouse had a very direct style of driving, much like his style of speaking. He was a Euclidean driver — as far as he was concerned the shortest distance between two points was a straight line, and woe betide any pedestrian, cyclist or motorist who got in his way. At the end of our little trip I felt that my face had frozen in a permanent grimace.

I had barely half an hour to make the acquaintance of my clients. We found them congregated just outside the magistrate's court. There were about a dozen of them, all Chinese and all young. The only one I recognised was Siew Chin, who gave me a delighted smile when I appeared. A thin young man about my age materialised by her side and glowered at me. His complexion was darkish, evidence of a life in the sun. His arms, though thin, were thickly veined. Like the others, he wore his shirt open to display a thin singlet.

"Comrade Bill, we are so pleased that you have come. And that you have brought our friend Dennis," said Siew Chin warmly.

Rouse waved his hand dismissively. "Promised I'd be here, and here I am."

He turned to me. "There are your clients. Go and do your stuff."

I was about to tell him that "my stuff" required a modicum of preparation, but Siew Chin took me by the arm.

"Come and meet my friends."

She brought me to the dark young man. "Dennis, this is Comrade Chen. He is our leader."

I extended my hand. Comrade Chen frowned even more deeply. He seemed somewhat reluctant to greet me. Siew Chin raised her eyebrows interrogatively. He took my hand and gave it a perfunctory shake without saying a word. She went round the group, naming names that I promptly forgot. There were in all three girls and eleven young men. Some smiled shyly at me. Most were impassive. With the exception of Chen all looked a little nervous.

I cleared my throat. "Well, Mr Rouse has explained your problem. But I haven't had time to do any research. I'll have to ask for an adjournment."

"No need," said Siew Chin brightly. "We are all guilty."

"Well," I said slowly, "even if you admit the facts, there might be a legal loophole, or at least some mitigating factor. If you're just going to plead guilty and take your lumps you really don't need a lawyer."

At this point Comrade Chen intervened. "He is right. We do not need a lawyer. We will get no justice from this corrupt imperialist court."

I was surprised by his command of English. Evidently there was more to Comrade Chen than met the eye. He turned to the others and started to harangue them in Chinese. There were some murmurs and nodding of heads. Siew Chin broke in. She spoke quickly and earnestly. An agreement was reached. Chen seemed reluctant to contradict her, but it was evident from his face that he wasn't happy.

Siew Chin turned to me. "Comrade Chen wanted us to keep silent as a protest against the injustice. But I said that if we do we will be sent to jail. Is that not so?"

"Yes, possibly," I responded, "but it's more likely that..."

She interrupted me. "Yes, so I said that we will do the cause no good if we are in jail. I told them that you are a good lawyer, and that you will get us off because our cause is just. They have agreed," she concluded with a bright smile.

I had the feeling that my day was going to be all highs and lows with no in-betweens. The euphoria of having won my very first case was going to be immediately counterbalanced by the indignity of losing this one, and in front of Siew Chin as well. I was a little flattered at her simple faith in me. Nevertheless, I didn't relish the task of trying to persuade the magistrate to let them off when Chen at least was bent on martyrdom.

Any thought I might have had of exploring the matter further was banished when the usher came out and shooed us into the courtroom. The defendants were arrayed in the dock and I was swept forward to the counsels' table. Rouse sat at the back of the court, near the door. I was seriously contemplating making a bolt for it when the Magistrate entered. We all rose and my spirits immediately rose too. It was Bernie Higgins.

Bernie and I were friends from university. We had been in the same college. He had gone up two years before me and had a set of rooms in the same court. His father and grandfather had both been civil servants in the Straits. Bernie's academic record was undistinguished, but even so he had been inducted into the ranks of the "heaven-born" and became a member of the Malayan Civil Service. Here he was, sitting in judgment on my case — a piece of unlooked-for good fortune.

As far as colonial powers go, the British were pretty benign. They were at that time in the process of being embarrassed out of India by Gandhi and his followers. Bernie belonged to the school of apologetic colonialists and openly admired Gandhi. He and I spent countless hours debating the morality of colonialism, with me defending the Empire as a force for good while he listed the evils of imperialism. He really believed that the colonial peoples had a right to be free and that the British should quit India. He even went so far to say that colonial peoples had a right to fight for freedom; something that would have gotten me thrown into jail for sedition had I uttered such sentiments. A good Fabian and anti-imperialist was Bernie Higgins.

He spoke. "You appear for the defendants, Mr Chiang?" He gazed at me seriously, not deigning to acknowledge our acquaintance.

"Indeed, your Honour," I replied equally gravely, with a little bow. Justice had to be seen to be done, and it wouldn't have looked good to have been on chummy terms with the Magistrate.

The charge was read. "The accused plead guilty, your Honour," I interposed as soon as this was done. "But I would like say in mitigation that what they did was done out of a sense of misplaced altruism. They were merely giving vent to their opposition to the exploitation and oppression of others. They have themselves no direct interest in the dispute save perhaps a feeling of solidarity with the workers. You might say that they were merely struggling for justice, without violence. Not unlike Gandhi."

Bernie regarded me gravely. He thought for a few moments.

"Very well, Mr Chiang," he said, "I find the accused guilty. However, in view of the mitigating circumstances I grant a conditional discharge."

We settled the terms of the discharge quickly and he banged the gavel and rose. The accused seemed to be totally unaware that they were free. For a moment they stood there in a bunch, like a flock of sheep in a pen. Then when it dawned on them that they could go, smiles broke out all round.

At this point Chen called out. "I have a statement!" he shouted at the Magistrate's retreating back. "I denounce the so-called justice system. It..."

Fortunately, the usher had opened the dock and Chen was swept out in the rush before he could finish. Bernie showed no sign of having heard anything. I saw Rouse in the back tuck away a notebook.

Outside the courtroom I was solemnly thanked by my clients, who shook my hand one by one before trooping out of the building. All except Chen, who darted me a venomous look as he brushed past.

Siew Chin came last, beaming brightly. She took my arm and said, "I knew that you could do it."

From the corner of my eye I noted Chen's look change from venomous to positively homicidal.

Rouse sauntered out of the courtroom casually.

"Well," he said, "you really did your stuff. Didn't think anyone would get them off. How much do I owe you?"

I was taken aback. "Owe me?"

"Yeah," he responded. "I never knew a lawyer who worked for free. What did this little shindig cost?" He pulled out a wad of banknotes.

"Comrade Bill has kindly agreed to pay for our defence," explained Siew Chin. "He has been a great encouragement to us."

I was completely stumped. I had never given a thought to such mundane matters as billing. I had always taken for granted that there was some elf in the bowels of our chambers who dutifully took care of such things.

"Can I send you a bill?" I asked weakly.

"Yeah, that's okay," replied Rouse. "You got my address." He lit up another of the foul *kretek* cigarettes. "Don't go overcharging me now, you hear," he said, waving the burnt-out match at me.

"Dennis would not do that," said Siew Chin.

We walked out of the courthouse together. Chen was waiting. Siew Chin gave me her hand to shake. "We have a cell meeting next week on Friday evening. Six o'clock. I will send you the address. Will you come?"

"Yes, of course," I said, surprised but pleased at the invitation.

Chen took her by the arm and led her away. She waved gaily at me. I waved my palm back.

MORAISS was waiting for me when I got back. "He wants you," said he laconically.

I stumbled into d'Almeida's room. "Ah, Mr Chiang," he said, "so good of you to join us."

I mumbled my apologies. "Sorry, I had a case at the Police Courts."

D'Almeida raised an eyebrow but did not comment. Instead he turned to a man who was sitting in one of his armchairs.

"This is my assistant, Dennis Chiang," he said. "Mr Chiang will be helping me in the case."

The man in the chair peered round the wing and nodded to me. I positioned myself discreetly in a corner and whipped out a notebook.

D'Almeida leaned back in his chair, his eyes half-closed and his arms on the table with the fingertips touching.

"Allow me to summarise, Mr Alfonso, and do please correct me if I am wrong. You are a minority shareholder in Sawah Nipah Plantations Limited. The majority shareholder is Dr Alcantra, your sister's husband."

"Late sister," interjected Alfonso. He was a small balding man, and the large armchair almost completely enveloped him.

"Yes, quite, late sister," continued d'Almeida unperturbed. "You believe that Dr Alcantra has been diverting corporate contracts and assets to another company that he controls, Alnilam Properties. You have informed the board of Sawah Nipah of your suspicions but they have declined to take any action."

"Totally spineless, the whole lot of them!" ejaculated Alfonso with surprising heat.

Spineless, I scribbled in my notebook, my thoughts on the forthcoming meeting with Siew Chin on Friday next.

D'Almeida continued his exposition without any apparent irritation. "You have also reported the matter to the police and written to the Attorney-General. But now Dr Alcantra has served you with a writ alleging defamation and obtained an injunction against you."

"Absolutely correct and succinctly put, my dear Mr d'Almeida," said Alfonso. "This Alcantra is an absolute rogue, a rapscallion of the lowest order."

Rogue and rapscallion, I noted, still far away in spirit.

"That may be, Mr Alfonso," replied d'Almeida, "but the law courts are not closed to rogues. I take it that you do admit to circulating the offending letter?"

"Yes, absolutely. To every single shareholder, banker and accountant connected with that scoundrel's companies."

D'Almeida nodded. "You admit publication of the defamatory statements. Your only defence is justification."

Alfonso looked blank. D'Almeida explained, "You rely entirely on the defence that the statements you made are true."

"Yes, absolutely," affirmed Alfonso, vigorously nodding.

"Can you prove it?"

"I know for a fact that Alcantra is robbing the company. He has overreached himself with his latest outrage. He has procured the sale of a valuable piece of land to Alnilam Properties. The Royal Navy has acquired the land and will pay a handsome compensation to Alnilam. Money that in all good conscience belongs to Sawah Nipah! I have taken the liberty of writing down the details."

He handed a sheet of paper to d'Almeida, who peered at it intently.

"An old factory in Sembawang," said d'Almeida, half to himself. "This must be for the Naval Base."

Alfonso nodded. "Yes, precisely. My information is that the Navy is paying twice the going price in order to obtain vacant possession at short notice. That scoundrel Alcantra knew about the impending acquisition beforehand and procured the so-called sale of the land to Alnilam Properties."

D'Almeida looked steadily at him. "But you have not answered my question, my dear Mr Alfonso. Can you prove any of this?"

There was a pregnant pause. Alfonso replied slowly, "Well, not with pieces of paper. But the truth is on my side."

"Indeed it may be, Mr Alfonso," said d'Almeida, "but the court is not concerned primarily with truth. It is concerned with proof."

Alfonso seemed taken aback by this pronouncement. "Mr d'Almeida, I am a British subject. Are you saying that I will not receive justice in a British court?"

"Mr Alfonso," said d'Almeida patiently, "you will receive impeccable justice from the court, in accordance with the law. But the law cannot function without proof of facts. No matter what a Judge's personal inclinations may be, he is bound to apply the law to the facts as they are determined according to the rules of evidence. There are many things that are true that cannot be proven in a court of law — because the evidence is lacking."

"I have a witness. An unimpeachable source within the company."

"Well and good," responded d'Almeida, "but will your source testify?"

Alfonso bit his lower lip. "I fear not, Mr d'Almeida. My confidant has informed me of the state of affairs only under the strictest vow of confidentiality. He fears for his job, you see. He has a young family dependant upon him and cannot afford to be dismissed."

"There we have the nub of the problem, Mr Alfonso. You allege that Dr Alcantra has diverted contracts and assets from Sawah Nipah to his own company. He denies this. You have circulated a letter to many people repeating those allegations. On the face of it, this is defamation. The law now requires you to prove your allegations or withdraw them."

"Withdraw them! But they are true, every word!"

"I do not doubt that, Mr Alfonso," responded d'Almeida, "but the court must have the proof."

Alfonso shook his head ruefully. "I must confess that I am dismayed and disappointed, my dear Mr d'Almeida. I had supposed that I would receive vindication from the courts. That scoundrel Alcantra is using this baseless defamation suit to silence me. And the courts will abet him. I had expected more of British justice. It is checkmate."

"Not quite checkmate, Mr Alfonso," said d'Almeida, "Your king may be under threat, but the game is not yet lost. The best defence is to go on the offensive."

Alfonso raised his eyebrows. "The offensive, Mr d'Almeida? How so?"

"By suing Dr Alcantra for breach of his fiduciary duties as a director of Alnilam Properties. He has taken property that belongs to the company. You may sue to get it back."

"It was my understanding that such a suit could only be instituted with the authority of the board of directors and in the name of the company," said Alfonso slowly. "This is why I confronted the board with evidence of Alcantra's wrongdoing."

"Quite correct, in the normal case. However, the law is not quite such an ass as one assumes it to be. In exceptional cases, where the board is unwilling or unable to commence litigation on behalf of the company, a shareholder may do so."

D'Almeida spoke deliberately, weighing each word. "I will not pretend that this is an easy case. The risk of losing is high. The financial burden of litigation would have to be borne by you. The fruits of victory will go to the company. But this is your only chance to bring Alcantra to justice."

"How does this affect the defamation suit against me?"

"If we succeed," replied d'Almeida, stressing the 'if,' "we will have unearthed enough material to support a plea of justification. But I do not think it will go that far. I expect that Dr Alcantra will settle his defamation suit against you in return for an acceptable compromise on your suit. If we win."

Alfonso stroked his moustache distractedly for a few moments. At length he spoke, "You feel that this is the only hope?"

D'Almeida nodded.

There was another pause. Alfonso seemed to be considering the matter very carefully. Finally, he rose.

"Mr d'Almeida, I feel strongly enough about this matter that I am willing to underwrite the cost of the litigation. It may be quixotic I know, but I cannot let Alcantra get away with daylight robbery. I place myself in your hands. Do what you must."

"Rest assured, my dear Mr Alfonso, you shall have my personal attention to this matter," said d'Almeida, escorting him to the door.

"You are most kind," rejoined Alfonso, tipping his hat to d'Almeida and to me. D'Almeida responded with an inclination of the head. As soon as the door was shut, d'Almeida rounded on me.

"Well, my dear Chiang, it appears that we shall have our work cut out. I shall need all available materials on the Rule in *Foss vs Harbottle*."

I tried desperately to recall the case. "E ... Foss and Bluebottle? And the citation would be...?"

"Harbottle, lad, Harbottle. Some time in the 1840s. I shall be in the Supreme Court library." He breezed out the door. A moment later he reappeared. "And by the way, congratulations on your case." Then he was gone.

THE REST of that week and the next are a blur in my memory. Besides the mountain of research that d'Almeida plumped on my lap for the Alfonso matter, Ralph suddenly had to take time off to attend to personal affairs. I was called upon to step into the breach as Aziz's junior. The case was straightforward but time-consuming.

I became practically a resident in the corridors of the Supreme Court. It was there that I bumped into Rouse again. To be more precise, I smelt his *kretek* cigarettes before actually catching sight of him. He saw me simultaneously.

"Well, if it ain't my old pal Dennis," he said jocularly, putting his arm around my shoulder. "What's up with you, son?"

I was at that moment harassed to the point of distraction. Somehow his jocularity put me on edge. "Er...hello," I grunted noncommittally.

"Anything new? Got some interesting cases?"

"No, not at the moment," I replied, eager to be away.

"Didn't think so, but you can't blame me for asking. See you." He waved dismissively and turned to disappear back into the throng of litigants.

For some reason that stung me. Though I had affected a becoming modesty when people congratulated me on my double debut in court, in truth I was thoroughly pleased with myself. Rouse's easy assumption that I wouldn't have anything worth reporting pricked my vanity.

"Well if you must know, I've got a case involving the acquisition of an old factory up in Sembawang by the Navy. Very interesting point of law."

Rouse turned back. "Navy, huh? An old factory? Are they closing it down?"

"Well, yes, I suppose so," I replied hesitantly. I hadn't really thought about it.

He stroked his chin. "Sounds like it might be interesting. Any names?"

I hesitated. A doubt about the propriety of discussing my forthcoming case with a reporter began to niggle at the edges of my conscience. But Rouse stood there with his eye cocked cynically on me. I felt I had to back up my claim.

"Yes, well, it's owned by a company called Alnilam Properties. But I can't really discuss it. And I hope you'll keep this in confidence."

"Yeah, sure," he said and started to walk off.

I watched his retreating back, cursing my big mouth and comforting myself with the thought that I hadn't really told him anything. Then I was swept off in the whirl with Aziz and promptly forgot about Alfonso, Alnilam and Rouse.

By Friday evening I was totally drained of life force. I only wanted to crawl back to my lair and hibernate. But I had promised to attend, and the prospect of seeing Siew Chin again reanimated me somewhat. Besides, I was curious about this cell of hers.

I made my way to the appointed address, following the Singapore River upstream along Boat Quay. The godowns never failed to fascinate me. Deep in their cavernous recesses lurked a faceless army of compradors and clerks, unobtrusively oiling the wheels of the commerce that was the raison d'être of the Colony. Drawn up to the steps leading down to the murky waters of the river were dozens of *tongkangs* and sampans. A steady stream of coolies toted bags and lifted bales along narrow gangplanks to the quay. I threaded my way through them. They paid me as much attention as ants would have paid to an itinerant beetle.

My brain was dead from exhaustion and my feet were on autopilot. Without being conscious of it, I found myself in one of the narrow lanes near Circular Road. I rounded a corner and bumped into the brawny back of a Sikh policeman. He glared at me. In his hand were a truncheon and a wicker shield. I came to myself with a start. All around me were policemen similarly armed. In front of them was a small but noisy crowd waving red banners. The hammer and sickle was much in evidence. For a moment I stood transfixed. The sudden confrontation scared the daylights out of me. Though no one in the crowd made any overtly hostile move, I felt as though they might surge forward to the attack at any moment. My first panicky reaction was to find something to defend myself with — a dustbin cover and a stout broomstick for preference. Then common sense reasserted itself. This wasn't my fight or my place. I took to my heels. The sounds of the demonstrators faded.

I was still breathless when I got to the meeting place at last. Climbing up the narrow staircase didn't help. I was late. The venue appeared to be some sort of clan or association meeting room. There were banners on the wall that I could not read. In front was a little raised dais on which there were two empty chairs. The meeting was almost over as far as I could tell. I slipped into a chair at the back while one earnest young man was making what seemed to be housekeeping announcements. I was not surprised to see Rouse in the front row. After a couple of minutes, the assembled congregation rose and sang what I took to be a patriotic song. It reminded me somewhat of a prayer meeting.

Siew Chin caught sight of me as the meeting broke up. She came over with a shy smile. Comrade Chen came up behind her. He wasn't smiling. She held out her hand, which I took.

"How nice that you could come Dennis," she said. "Did you enjoy it?"

"Er, I came in a bit late, actually. Did I miss something important?"

She frowned a little. "Comrade Lin was telling us of the latest news from China. The fighting goes badly. The Japanese are winning everywhere. Yet the Nationalists continue to harass our comrades instead of forming a united front to resist the imperialist aggressors."

"Ah, well," I replied, embarrassed. "I'm sure I would have found it most interesting. If I'd understood it."

Chen sneered. "You do not speak Chinese? What kind of Chinese are you?"

I felt my ears redden. He had me at a disadvantage in front of Siew Chin.

"If you must know," I replied, trying to keep my tone even, "I'm a Baba. I grew up speaking Malay and English."

"So you are a Malay," he said mockingly, "or a banana who is yellow on the outside but white on the inside!" He turned to the group and made a comment, which drew a short burst of laughter. It was obviously at my expense.

"You are a duckweed without roots," he went on in an even more sneering tone. "You have forgotten your ancestors!"

My self-control broke. "Absolute rot! My family has been here since the time of Raffles. I know my grandfather and my great-grandfather. I'd be surprised if you know who your own father is!"

I was sorry the moment I had said it. The room went silent. Chen glared at me. I thought that he would strike me. I tensed, clenching my fists at my sides. Then abruptly he turned away and left the room without a word. Siew Chin went after him, darting a glance in my direction.

"Nice going," said Rouse, who had materialised next to me.

I had no desire to remain in the room. Ignoring Rouse, I followed Siew Chin down the stairs into the street. She was standing at the doorway. Chen was nowhere in sight. I called to her softly. She turned to me.

"You should not have said that to him, even if it is true," she said in an even tone that I could not interpret. Was she reproving me?

"He had it coming," I said truculently.

"He is a little rough with his words, but his heart is good. He is a good leader." She paused. "Oh, I wish that you both could get along," she said with a shake of her head. "It would be so nice if you could...if you could be part of our group."

"Why?" I asked gently.

She lowered her eyes. "Because it would be... pleasant."

"Pleasant for you?" I pressed.

She nodded, her eyes averted. She was blushing. Abruptly, she started to go back up the stairs.

"Don't go," I called out.

"I must," she said. "There are things to be done."

I wanted to put out my hand to touch her, but I stopped myself. She trotted up the stairs. I had no desire to go back.

"Come to tea," I said. "On Sunday. Come to tea with me and May."

She paused.

"It's May's birthday," I lied. "I'm giving her a little treat. Do say you'll join us. At the Adelphi. Say, around three o'clock."

"Perhaps," she responded as she disappeared into the gloom at the head of the stairs.

"Three o'clock Sunday, then," I called hopefully after her.

MAY WAS most surprised to discover that her birthday had come so soon. However, she wasn't one to pass up tea at the Adelphi, and besides she owed me one. She agreed to play along and to produce Siew Chin at the appointed hour after their shift ended on Sunday.

As it was impossible to keep a secret in that house, the rest of the family soon got to know about my assignation. June, who has an uncanny knack for detecting free food, offered to be my chaperone but I firmly declined. Julie and Augusta went round the house chanting "Denny likes a *girl*!" repeatedly until I silenced them by threatening not to bring back any cream puffs.

I spent the next two days in a state of nervous anticipation. It was ridiculous. I've done this before, I told myself. It isn't the first time. Madeline Strachan certainly didn't make me feel so unsettled. But that was Madeline. I knew how to react with her. The behavioural cues were clear. With Siew Chin...? I wasn't even sure that she really liked me, or more precisely, that she liked me in that particular way. With Madeline I had a sense of what was acceptable. Walking arm in arm with her was the most natural thing in Montmartre or along the King's Parade. I still didn't know whether Siew Chin would let me take her hand or whether she would be offended by the attempt.

I left the house in good time on Sunday to be quite sure of being on time. Sauntering through the colonnaded foyer of the Adelphi, I secured myself a table in the lounge. A doleful pianist was banging out Noel Coward tunes on a white upright piano. A Hainanese waiter materialised at my table and took my initial order for tea. I passed the time watching the comings and goings of the hotel guests — mostly white, with an occasional Asiatic. Some of the former paused to stare at me, whether out of curiosity or hostility I did not know. I ignored them.

The minutes passed. At 3:15 I began to fidget. The waiter

reappeared and sniffed at me disapprovingly when I waved him away without ordering anything else. At 3:30 I was getting positively disgruntled. Had she stood me up? May was supposed to bring her along.

May turned up shortly after four, still in her nurse's uniform. There was no sign of Siew Chin.

"What kept you?" I asked somewhat testily in my disappointment.

"We had an emergency case," replied May patiently. "The hospital is short-handed today, so we both had to stay to help."

"Where's Siew Chin? Didn't she come?" I tried to keep my voice even. Having keyed myself up so much, I felt a deep hollowness in the pit of my stomach.

"She said to excuse her. She has a meeting to attend. Look what she gave me for my birthday!"

May held up a little jade brooch. I wasn't in the mood to examine trinkets. I tried to keep my expression impassive, but May knew me too well.

"Poor Denny," she said, "do not be so disappointed. There will be other chances. She likes you."

"Really?" I said, brightening a little.

"Yes, really," said May, gently patting my hand. "I think maybe we should go home. It's not really my birthday."

I agreed readily. As we drove back I asked May, "Did she say what meeting she was going to?"

"With her Communist friends," replied May. "I wish she would not go around with them so much. They will get into serious trouble one day."

"Where did she say the meeting is?"

May looked at me. "You want to join them too?"

"Why not?" I responded lightly. "They might need a good lawyer."

"You be careful. I do not know where she is exactly. She said that they are having a protest meeting, somewhere in Sembawang. Some factory is closing down."

I had a sudden unsettled feeling. A factory in Sembawang... surely Rouse wouldn't have told them... or would he?

I dropped May at our front gate. "Thanks, May, for being such a sport. I'm sorry I'm such awful company. I'll make it up on your real birthday."

"Don't mention," she said, waving her hand. "You just be careful who you mix with."

Once out of the gate I drove off at the best speed that my old jalopy could make. The vibration nearly shook the fillings out of my teeth. By the time I got to Sembawang I could have sworn that my kidneys had changed places with my lungs.

You're a fool, I told myself, coming all this way for nothing. Even if it is the Alnilam factory, it doesn't concern you. But somehow I couldn't convince myself. Indiscretion is a cardinal sin for a lawyer. Cursing my leaky mouth, I cast about looking for the factory.

It wasn't difficult to find. For one thing, there was a clear signpost pointing the way. For another thing, there was a crowd of people with banners milling around in front of it. A couple of dilapidated buses stood forlornly on one side. The gate had been forced. Someone was addressing the throng, which numbered about a hundred as far as I could make out. Every now and then they would punch their fists in the air and shout. I didn't like the look of things. Parking my car in a convenient spot, I made my way over to the group.

I wasn't surprised to bump into Rouse by the gate. He had a photographer with him.

"Well, if it ain't my old pal Dennis," he said jovially. "Didn't know you were joining us. Quite a rabble-rouser, that guy Chen," he said approvingly, gesturing with his *kretek*. The photographer was busily snapping away.

"Mr Rouse," I said sternly, trying to keep the irritation out of my voice, "I gave you the information about the factory in confidence. You had no right to tell Chen!"

"Now, don't you go flying off the handle with me," he replied. "First place, you didn't tell me more than the name. I found out the rest myself, about how the company laid everyone off with a couple of days' notice. That's capitalists for you. Second place, if you don't want something to come out, you don't tell a reporter. Everything's fair game. Now, boy, I've got a story to file." Off he went without another word.

I was struggling to frame a suitable retort to fling at his retreating back when Siew Chin found me.

"Dennis!" she cried, smiling broadly, "I am glad that you have come to support us. How did you find us? I am sorry that I did not attend your tea for May. She was very understanding."

Before I could answer Chen appeared. He was not pleased. "What are you here for?" he demanded rudely. "We do not need you. Go away!"

The last thing I needed that day was aggravation from the likes of him.

"What the devil do you think you're up to?" I blazed back. "You might enjoy being martyred, but leave Siew Chin out of it. D'you think it's fun to be arrested and bunged into a rotten cell? She'd lose her job, have you thought of that?"

Chen however switched to Chinese and continued to hurl what I took to be imprecations at me. I regretted my inability to curse in any language but English. I should have learnt more Hindi swear words from George. Chen turned on his heel and returned to the crowd, still muttering darkly.

"Please, please do not fight," pleaded Siew Chin, on the verge of tears.

"I'm sorry," I said, though I really wasn't. "He just makes me so angry. He's not thinking of you at all."

"He is working for the cause," she said earnestly.

I made a scathing noise. "The cause!" I said bitterly. "Will it serve the cause if you're all rounded up and jailed? The hospital would never keep you on. What would you do then?"

"There is no need to worry," said Siew Chin with naive conviction. "No one will get arrested. Comrade Bill tells us it is perfectly safe. We are too far from town. By the time someone tells the police and they drive here, we will have finished. Comrade Bill has promised us good publicity in the newspapers." She gestured towards good old Comrade Bill and his sidekick, who was merrily clicking away with his camera.

"You can't go around damaging other people's property," I expostulated, pointing at the broken gates.

"But we did not do that," replied Siew Chin. "The gates were already open when we arrived. We have done nothing wrong. And there is no danger. When we have made our point, we will go peacefully."

"Come with me," I pleaded desperately.

Siew Chin shook her head.

Chen returned. "Get out! Go away now!" he yelled. Three or four toughs were with him. I felt my mouth go dry. I wasn't about to run away, not with Siew Chin there, but the prospect of a fracas with those gorillas was unappealing.

Suddenly, there was a roar and a squeal of brakes. A military three-tonner came to a halt not fifty yards from us. A dozen swarthy *sepoys* spilled from the back and drew up in a line. A young subaltern emerged from the cab and stationed himself on the right of the *sepoys*. A startled hush descended on the crowd. Chen, who had been advancing upon me with his goons, blanched visibly. At a spoken word of command the *sepoys* fixed bayonets and began to move.

I watched mesmerised as the *sepoys* marched slowly towards us, rifles at high port, bayonets gleaming. They halted literally a stone's throw from us. The crowd meanwhile had spilled out from the gates and was pressing at our back. Instinctively, I drew Siew Chin behind me. Chen was to our side, staring slack-jawed at the khaki line.

The young subaltern spoke. No doubt he meant to convey an impression of masterful authority. But his voice came out a little too high-pitched.

"Disperse now!" he commanded. "Or you will be dispersed by force!" I could see the service revolver in his hand shaking. "Leave peacefully now or you will regret it!"

What he hoped to achieve bawling in English at the uncomprehending mass heaven only knew. He might as well have been speaking Swahili. But though the words may not have been understood, the meaning was plain. An angry murmur ran round the crowd. I felt the pressure at my back as the crowd pressed forward. We were pushed a couple of paces towards the waiting *sepoys*.

"Ready!" commanded the lieutenant. Like automatons the *sepoys* brought their rifles to the ready. The metallic click of their bolts reverberated across the field.

"Present!" A dozen rifles came up, pointing straight at the crowd.

The pressure from behind eased. The crowd behind me was tense yet undecided. Some were even moving backwards. Yet there were those who still would have surged forward. Quite a number had sticks or stones in their hands. The lieutenant — who could hardly have been out of his teens — nervously licked his lips. He was clearly out of his depth. The situation was poised on the edge of a razor. I was acutely aware that one stupid move on either side could precipitate a bloodbath. Then suddenly someone shoved me roughly in the small of the back and I stumbled forward into the no-man's land between the groups. I had a vague awareness that Chen was behind me, but I couldn't swear to it.

I found myself staring down the business ends of a dozen .303 short magazine Lee-Enfields. The lieutenant was too shocked for words, which probably saved us all. The *sepoys* stood impassively, each one with his eye cocked on his sights, staring right at me.

"Sss...stay calm," I stammered. "There's ...there's no need for violence."

The lieutenant seemed taken aback by my words and accent. He recovered himself in a moment.

"Tell your people to disperse," he said sternly, his wisp of a moustache quivering. I wanted to tell him that I had nothing to do with the crowd, but the words died in my throat.

We stood suspended in time. How long we stood there staring at each other I do not know. It was probably only a few moments, but I felt the moments stretch out to eternity. I noticed the nervous twitching of his mouth, the dark matt buttons on his tunic, the sweaty streaks that discoloured the front of his uniform. I tried to swallow, but my mouth was dry.

The spell was suddenly broken by the arrival of four police Black Marias. Sturdy Sikh policemen tumbled out and began laying into everyone about them with their truncheons. The crowd broke up with shrieks. In a daze I felt myself being handcuffed and manhandled into the dark depths of the Black Maria.

OF THAT terrible journey and my subsequent incarceration I remember little. All I recall was that it was hot, cramped and uncomfortable. I was assailed by a sense of humiliation that I should find myself in police custody, arrested as part of a mob. I did not know how I would live it down. We had always prided ourselves on being upright, law-abiding people. Our social circle was a narrow and straitlaced one, not known for indulgence towards personal failings. To be arrested was a blot on the character; people in our milieu generally assumed that the police acted correctly in all cases. One might be acquitted after a trial, but society remembers the arrest and trial and generally forgets the acquittal. For me personally as a member of the Bar, as well as Mak and the family, a trial would be a continuing torment. Perhaps I might put myself in better light if I said that I was concerned also for Siew Chin and the others, but the truth is that I was consumed entirely by the consequences to my family and myself.

It was well into the night when I heard the welcome sound of a familiar voice. "Boy, where are you?"

"Here, Mak," I replied, rousing myself from my stupor.

"Mr d'Almeida has been so kind. He has arranged everything. You can go home."

The warder jangled his keys in the lock. The other inmates of the cell stared vacantly at me as I tottered out. My initial reaction of relief quickly turned into consternation. I had hoped unrealistically that somehow my employer could be kept out of this mess. Now here he was, dragged from his home on Sunday night, to spring a jackass of a junior from the slammer! I hardly relished meeting him. I stood impassively as Mak tidied me up somewhat. I collected my personal belongings in a daze. D'Almeida turned up during the process.

"Mr d'Almeida, I am truly sorry to have troubled you in this way," I began plaintively.

He held up his hand. "I think that you had better tell me the whole story," he said softly, "once your mother has been sent home."

He nodded to Mak. She would have stayed, but he politely and firmly insisted that his syce should drive her home. After she had gone, we sat down on one of the hard-backed benches in the corner of the station and I told him everything. As was his wont he listened gravely, asking brief questions on points of detail. After a quarter of an hour unburdening myself, he rose.

"Nasty business," he said. I could only hang my head.

We walked in silence down the dim corridors towards the stairs leading out of the station building. As we rounded a corner, I saw to my surprise a familiar figure sitting dejectedly on one of the benches in a side passage next to a closed door.

"Chen!" I said involuntarily.

D'Almeida stopped. "Where?" he asked.

"That's him," I said gesturing towards the hunched figure. "He's the one I told you about. The ringleader."

Chen did not appear to have noticed us. He sat with his eyes closed and his head cupped in his hands.

"Introduce us," said d'Almeida unexpectedly.

"Pardon?" I was taken totally aback by his request.

"Introduce us, if you please," repeated d'Almeida.

With some hesitancy, I approached Chen. I realised with a mild shock that I didn't even know his full name.

He looked up. "You!" he exclaimed. "What do you want now?"

I cleared my throat uneasily. "Er... my boss wants to meet you."

He stared at me dumbstruck. D'Almeida sidled up, looking around the corridor. No one was in sight. He held out his hand.

"Mr Chen I presume?" he said smoothly, "Clarence d'Almeida at your service."

Chen looked totally at a loss. He took d'Almeida's proffered hand uncertainly.

"Ah, pleased to meet you," he said uncertainly.

"The pleasure is mine," replied d'Almeida suavely, with a little bow. "Now, I am afraid that we must take our leave. I wish you a pleasant evening."

With that he strode purposefully back along the passage towards the exit, while I followed in confusion. Chen stared as if he was not quite sure that he had been dreaming.

"What was that about?" I asked as soon as we were out of the building. Its great grey bulk loomed menacingly above us, blotting out the stars.

"Curious," said d'Almeida unhelpfully. He turned down the road and began to walk briskly.

"I must think," he said to me, his mind obviously miles away. "I trust that you will not mind walking with me. I have told my syce to wait for me at chambers."

We walked together silently all the way back. I let my mind clear, drinking in the cool night air and trying not to think of what the morrow might bring.

When we got to the collapsible gate leading to the chambers, he turned to me.

"I think that you might want to take tomorrow off," he said. "I have a few matters to inquire into. Be at the office punctually at eight o'clock on Tuesday. Dress for court. I will be requiring you for the Alnilam matter. The syce will take you home."

I knew better than to question him. "I'm truly grateful, Mr d'Almeida," I said simply.

He waved away my thanks with a deprecating gesture. "I have done nothing yet to deserve your gratitude," he replied. "Well then, until Tuesday." With that he unlocked the gate and disappeared up the darkened stairs.

COMRADE BILL was as good as his word to Siew Chin and company. Pictures of the confrontation were splashed all over Monday's papers. I was told that they got even better coverage in the vernacular press.

I found myself in the centre of a dramatic shot of the demonstrators and the police. The photographer had contrived to snap the picture from a raised vantage point some distance outside the factory. There were the protestors with their banners, nicely framed by the broken gates of the factory. Facing them, the thin stalwart line of *sepoys* with their gallant officer. In between, looking a right charlie, was me, hands outstretched as if in supplication. My only consolation was that my face wasn't clearly distinguishable from that distance.

Mak didn't say anything, though I could sense that she was upset and concerned. She did not berate me for my stupidity nor nag me for my lack of consideration for the family's "face." June in contrast was quite unrestrained. She wanted to know when I would be thrown back into the slammer. Her friends would be thrilled, she said, that she was so closely related to a known felon. May was quietly concerned both about me and Siew Chin. Of Siew Chin I had no news. I assumed that she had been picked up, along with Chen and the others.

I wanted to drive straight over to the nurses' hostel, but May assured me that I would be persona non grata there. She promised to find out what she could when she went back to work.

As luck would have it however, Monday was her day off and she wasn't inclined to go back. Since Siew Chin was also off, it would not have been worth it. Siew Chin's habit was to spend her days off with relatives, returning to the hostel only after work. I was left in a lather of uncertainty. I spent the rest of the day tormented by regret at my own foolishness and a vague uneasiness about my future. I tried to convince myself that I had a cast-iron defence. After all, I had not been there as a participant, only as a spectator. But could I prove it? Would Chen back me up when it came to the crunch? Or would he be only too pleased to do so, to demonstrate to Siew Chin what a spineless cad I was when push came to shove.

Tuesday morning finally came after a restless night. I dressed and breakfasted unenthusiastically, and left without saying goodbye to anyone. D'Almeida was already at the office when I arrived shortly before eight.

"Come," he said simply, "we must see someone about your problem." I followed obediently.

To my surprise we drove right back to the Central Police Station. The syce parked the car in an inner courtyard. D'Almeida seemed to know his way around quite well. I followed him like a lamb through the maze of stairs and corridors. We finally were shown into a largish office with a view of the courts across the road. A uniformed white policeman sat behind the desk. His hair was grey at the temples. From the pips on his shoulders I surmised that he was a bigwig in the force. At his side, somewhat in the shadows, sat a civilian.

"Well, d'Almeida, what is it you want?" he snapped. He did not deign to rise when we entered.

"Good morning, Deputy Commissioner," said d'Almeida politely. "I have come about the unfortunate incident in Sembawang last Sunday. My assistant Mr Chiang was, shall we say, caught up in events and found himself in your custody."

"Caught up in events!" snorted the Deputy Commissioner, ruffling the newspaper on his desk. "Look at this! The young hooligan was leading the pack of 'em." He looked directly at me. "You're in serious trouble, young man."

"You have the discretion not to press charges," said d'Almeida calmly. "You could recommend to the Attorney-General that no prosecution should be instituted."

The Deputy-Commissioner went beetroot-red in the face. "Not press charges! Recommend to the Attorney-General not to prosecute! Have you taken leave of your senses, man?"

"Not at all," continued d'Almeida, "I suggest that it would be in the interests of justice if no charges were brought in this case."

"In the interests of justice! Let me tell you what the interests of justice require. There's too much of this damned rioting going on. Law and order, that's what justice needs. I'm going to see to it that this rabble is prosecuted to the limit of the law and put away. Make an example of 'em. Then there'll be no more of this nonsense. They're damned lucky that they came away with their skins whole. I wouldn't have blamed that young fella if he'd given the order to fire."

"Like General Dyer at Amritsar?" said d'Almeida softly.

"Dyer did his duty. And I shall do mine. Is there anything else? Otherwise don't waste my time," replied the Deputy Commissioner with some heat.

"Perhaps you would be so good as to hear me out," replied d'Almeida. "There are some curious features about the whole affair. It was, according to my information, instigated by one Mr Chen, who appears to be a Communist agitator. Mr Chen is an enigma to me. He is a Chinese Communist, but he speaks English perfectly. A labourer, but his hands are soft as a schoolteacher's. An activist of a proscribed group, who conducts his cell meetings like a Sunday school class in public and with no attempt at concealment. An agitator, who seems to desire nothing better than to be prosecuted and martyred. But you will not oblige him, will you Deputy Commissioner? I understand that Mr Chen will not be charged."

The Deputy Commissioner looked startled. "How did you know that?"

"I have my sources of information," replied d'Almeida evenly.

The Deputy Commissioner harrumphed. "It's neither here nor there what we do with this Chen fella. The rest of 'em will get what they deserve."

"Do you not find it a trifle odd that I should have met Mr Chen sitting quietly in a corner near the Criminal Investigation Department on Sunday night? Is it your practice to leave arrested offenders in the corridors of this building without guards?" d'Almeida took off his spectacles and began polishing them. He spoke almost absently. "I ask myself, why would the police let Mr Chen off? What business did he have wandering unsupervised in police headquarters while his erstwhile collaborators were incarcerated? Could it be that he had some special business here? Or to be more precise, some Special Branch business?"

D'Almeida replaced his spectacles and peered directly at the Deputy Commissioner, who seemed to have been deflated.

"Nonsense!" said the Deputy Commissioner somewhat weakly.

"I have a theory," continued d'Almeida smoothly. "Let us say, for the sake of argument, that the Special Branch wanted to infiltrate someone into the Communist movement. How would they do it? A man who appeared out of the blue asking to join would be under suspicion. But if a known agitator were to apply...? A man who had proven that he was a good Communist. Better still, one who had organised and led a couple of demonstrations by his own little cell. Even better yet, one who had been jailed by the authorities. Such a man would be useful as an infiltrator, would he not?"

The civilian in the shadows spoke for the first time. "An interesting theory. But you haven't any proof that will stand up in a court of law," he said. His voice was low and steady.

"There are many things that cannot be proven in a court of law but are true nonetheless," replied d'Almeida, looking now at the civilian. "I imagine that questions might be asked in the Legislative Council about the possibility that the whole affair was instigated by an agent provocateur working for Special Branch."

"We could detain you, you know," said the man evenly. "A matter of public order and security."

D'Almeida shrugged. "Indeed you might. But that itself might provoke questions too. One never knows where such things might lead. A Labour Member of Parliament might even pick up the matter and raise it at Westminster. Embarrassing questions. We would not want His Excellency the Governor to be embarrassed, now would we?"

The civilian gave a thin smile. "No," he said quietly, "I don't think any of us want H.E. to be embarrassed. I think your young friend here need have no further concern about prosecution."

The Deputy Commissioner, who had sat like a stuffed carp throughout this exchange, suddenly came back to life.

"What? What d'you mean no prosecution? You can't do that, man! I won't hear of it!"

The civilian stared at the Deputy Commissioner and said firmly, "It would serve the interests of justice and public order if no prosecution is brought in this case."

He turned to d'Almeida. "I trust that that is satisfactory, Mr d'Almeida?"

D'Almeida bowed slightly. "Eminently satisfactory, Mr...?" He paused. "I do not believe I caught your name?"

The man smiled his thin smile again. "I don't believe I mentioned it. Good day, sir."

MY THANKS when we left were effusive and, I fear, somewhat incoherent. I was overwhelmed by a sense of enormous relief, as though an incubus had been exorcised. A sudden thought struck me. "Will they let Chen go back to agitation?"

"I think not," replied d'Almeida. "I imagine that Mr Chen might have had his fill for the time being."

"But why not just go ahead and prosecute him, if that's what they wanted all along?"

"My dear boy," responded d'Almeida patiently, "it is one thing to be charged under the Minor Offences Ordinance and be jailed for a week. It is quite another to face a long sentence for rioting or wilful destruction of War Department property. I doubt Mr Chen would have co-operated. There are limits to martyrdom."

I subsided, chagrined at my naivety. D'Almeida hustled me into the car.

"Come, we must go quickly. We are expected in court at nine o'clock. Mr Justice Gibson has agreed to hear the Alnilam matter in open court instead of in chambers."

He explained the matter to me as we drove over to the Supreme Court. As expected, Dr Alcantra had immediately challenged Mr Alfonso's right to sue him on behalf of the company. His lawyers had applied to strike out the suit. If they succeeded, Alfonso's case would be dead without even the formality of a full trial. Normally, such an application would have been heard in the Judge's chambers. But d'Almeida had persuaded the Judge that the legal point was important enough for a hearing in open court.

We reached the door of the court just before nine. Our client Mr Alfonso was sitting just behind the counsels' desk, looking distinctly agitated. He brightened considerably when he saw d'Almeida stride through the doors. I noticed at the back of the court a dark man in a beige three-piece suit. He wore sunglasses despite the fact that the windows let in only just enough light to read by.

"Alcantra," whispered Alfonso, nodding in the direction of the stranger.

I stole a glance in his direction before the usher announced the arrival of the Judge. Mr Justice Gibson was another long-service Colonial Judge who had been on the bench since time immemorial. He was one of the better-liked of his brethren, being unfailingly courteous to counsel no matter how fatuous their arguments. He was on the verge of a well-earned retirement, much to the regret of the Bar.

Alcantra was represented by Alastair Macintyre, a competent if unspectacular advocate. Macintyre opened, presenting the law with admirable thoroughness. He had a singularly monotonous voice and my mind began to wander. I soon found myself in that catatonic state achieved by rabbits in the headlights of an oncoming car, or undergrads at a jurisprudence lecture.

D'Almeida rose to speak. I came to myself with a jerk. He made his points succinctly, pointedly and with an economy of words. There were no buttered phrases or flowery declamations. He dealt with Macintyre's arguments point by point, and point by point demolished them with surgical precision. After fifteen minutes he summed up and sat down. The Judge sat silent, seemingly far away.

At length he spoke. "Gentlemen, I thank you for your excellent submissions. I trust I will not be taken as lacking in courtesy if I do not deal with every point that you have raised. Mr Macintyre, I commend you on an excellent argument. You have admirably presented the case law, which appears preponderantly to be on your side."

Macintyre inclined his head and smirked.

"However," continued Mr Justice Gibson, "I must also pay tribute to the skill with which Mr d'Almeida has conducted his case. I find myself persuaded by his arguments."

Macintyre's smirk vanished.

"I have given the matter anxious consideration. On one hand, we have the weight of authority from England against the arguments presented by Mr d'Almeida. On the other hand, it has been forcibly impressed upon me that all is not as it should be regarding the property of the company, Sawah Nipah. Recent events involving certain young members of the Bar..."

He stared directly at me here. I sank a little in my chair, seeking to become one with the furniture.

"...have brought to my attention the fact that the property in question apparently is now owned by Dr Alcantra's company, Alnilam Properties. I would say that there is a case for Dr Alcantra to answer. I am accordingly inclined to allow this suit to be brought against Dr Alcantra by Mr Alfonso. No doubt the truth will emerge from the evidence."

My fuddled brain sought to make sense of the Judge's words.

Alfonso plucked at my sleeve. "Does this mean that we get to sue Alcantra?" he asked in penetrating whisper.

"Yes, I think so," I replied, waving him to be silent. Both counsel were now addressing the Judge, discussing in courteous tones the form that the order should take.

"Well, gentlemen," announced the Judge, "perhaps it would be best if we adjourn for half-an-hour in order for you to consult with your respective clients as to a possible settlement." He rose and left the room.

Alfonso immediately came over to d'Almeida. "Well, Mr d'Almeida," he asked somewhat breathlessly, "does this mean that we can continue with the suit against Alcantra?"

"Yes," said d'Almeida with a hint of satisfaction, "and with the company's money too. The Judge is inclined to order that the company should finance the case against Dr Alcantra. I imagine that he will be amenable to an offer of settlement."

Alfonso rubbed his hands with glee. "You cannot imagine what satisfaction this news brings," he said. "I saw the rogue in the back of the court just now. No doubt he is conferring with his lawyers."

I saw Macintyre re-enter the courtroom and beckon to d'Almeida. The two counsel were soon having a tête-à-tête. D'Almeida returned to us, smiling ever so slightly.

"Things are going better than I expected," he said. "Mr Macintyre has lost his client. It appears that Dr Alcantra has left without giving his counsel instructions. They are attempting to contact him. We shall wait."

And wait we did. Thirty minutes turned into an hour. The Judge returned.

"My Lord," said Macintyre with a hint of mortification, "I regret to say that I have no further instructions. I am told that my client Dr Alcantra has left for Batavia on the 10:45 flying boat."

"Left, Mr Macintyre? What do you mean, left?" inquired the Judge.

"Exactly as I have said, my Lord," replied Macintyre. "According to his office, he has gone without leaving word when he will return. I fear I must ask to be discharged from acting further."

The Judge was plainly put out by this turn of events. He ruled in favour of d'Almeida. When it was over, Macintyre came across to congratulate d'Almeida on his advocacy. Alfonso was all smiles.

"Well, Mr d'Almeida, a famous victory! I thank you for your efforts. I take it that this means that we have won."

"Indubitably," responded d'Almeida. "I do not imagine that Dr Alcantra will return to defend the case."

"And his defamation suit against me?"

"That will be discontinued for want of prosecution. I think you need have no further concern on that score, my dear Mr Alfonso."

Alfonso beamed and shook hands all round. He left to celebrate his frabjous day, chortling in his joy. As we packed, I thanked d'Almeida again for getting me off the hook.

"No thanks are necessary, my boy," he said. "I trust that you will choose your company with better care in future." I nodded emphatically. "I will leave you to tie up the loose ends yourself."

"Loose ends?" I asked, with some bewilderment.

He arched his eyebrows. "Surely you must be eager to have some hard words with the one who set up the whole affair? His actions might have had the most serious repercussions."

"You mean Chen?"

He shook his head. "Think, my dear Chiang. Chen by all accounts was as surprised as you when the army and the police showed up. He and your young lady friend seemed to have been counting on a bloodless coup. Someone else obviously had told the police in good time that there would be trouble. They could not have arrived in less than forty-five minutes coming from town. The inevitable conclusion...?"

My mind was racing. Forty-five minutes. "The inevitable conclusion... is that the police were told *before* the demonstration." It was as if a flash of lightning had illuminated all.

D'Almeida nodded. "Precisely. You know better than I who might have done so and for what motive. Choose your friends very carefully." With that he walked off.

I STORMED off to find my prey. Sure enough he was there, hanging around outside the court building like a vulture waiting for a corpse.

"You!" I stormed "You set us up!"

"Now hold on, son," drawled Rouse in his infuriating way. "What're you all het up for?"

"You set us up didn't you, Rouse? Called the police and told them there'd be a demonstration in front of the factory, on Navy land. You were the one who busted open the gates so that the crowd could get in."

Things were becoming clearer and clearer as I spoke. "You even had a photographer posted, somewhere where he'd get a good shot of the goings-on. You could have got us all killed!"

He clucked his tongue. "No need for dramatics. Yeah, I admit I did tell the cops that there was a little shindig up at the factory.

But I didn't reckon on the army showing up like that. But, hey, no one was hurt. We got some great pictures. I got my story. Your red friends got a good press, all over the globe thanks to me. And I heard they ain't even pressing charges. Seems to me all's well that ends well."

"All's well..." I spluttered. "You're nothing but a rampant opportunist! Have you no bloody morality, man?"

The mask of affability dropped abruptly. "Don't you go lecturing me about morality, boy. You think the world's like your fancy school and namby-pamby college? It's a dirty world out there, boy. You make your own breaks. You think I want to be a two-bit hack for a no-name rag all my life? Not on your life. I take my breaks where I see 'em and I make my own luck. If that's an opportunist, then I'm guilty."

I was almost incoherent with rage. I turned my back on him and stalked off.

"Grow up, kid!" I heard him yell as his parting shot.

That was the last time I saw Rouse. He left the Colony shortly thereafter, no doubt looking for more "human interest" stories. He was as good as his word, though. He didn't stay long with *The Newark Sapphire*. His by-line started appearing more and more frequently in the quality press. His star reached its zenith when the Germans invaded Russia. Comrade Bill was there, reporting from the front all through the Great Patriotic War. Then abruptly, like a meteorite, it fell as the Cold War froze Europe in its Arctic grip.

The last I heard of Rouse was in the early fifties. He'd gotten into a spot of bother with some American senator that put paid to him finally.

I can't quite remember the name. What was he called, now? It's on the tip of my tongue... Senator Mc-something-or-other... McCarthy, I think it was. Yes, that's right, Senator McCarthy. I'm almost certain that was the name.

CROSSROADS

MY LIFE, which had hitherto been humming placidly along with a simple harmony, now began to take on complex contrapuntal overtones. After my little run-in with the police, I found that I had acquired a certain notoriety at the Bar. I had always considered myself to be a loyal subject of the King and it distressed me that I had now gotten a reputation as a Communist. I'm not sure that it wasn't entirely my imagination, but I felt that judges and older lawyers looked somewhat askance at me. As for the younger lawyers, they ribbed me mercilessly. I even found a red rag pinned to my robe bag in the changing room. I tried hard to take it all in good spirit, but there remained a nagging fear that I had offended the powers-that-be and that my career was dead in the water before it had even begun to make headway.

Meanwhile, plans for the wedding of May and Ralph proceeded apace. As the senior male relative (indeed, the only male relative), I was intimately involved in the planning of the event.

There was some trouble as to which rites were to be followed. The full works for a traditional Baba wedding called for twelve days of celebration, something that neither our stamina nor our pockets would support. A less taxing alternative was sought.

Ralph was nominally Anglican, so it came to mind that there might be a possibility of holding the wedding at the Cathedral.

This was a splendid example of English neo-Gothic architecture set at the centre of a St. Andrew's cross formed by two avenues of saga trees. It would have been a magnificent setting for Ralph and May's wedding. The drive beneath the trees to the church portal, the long aisle, the gilded lectern, the tall stained-glass windows behind the altar.... Exactly what one would imagine for a proper white wedding. Unfortunately, it transpired that the only connection that Ralph had with the Cathedral, apart from his twice-yearly attendance at Christmas and Easter, was the fact that he had been baptised there. From the way that Ralph told it, it was clear that the occasion had been a somewhat moist experience for all the participants. We decided not to tax the Dean's tolerance. The issue thus remained unresolved.

Beyond these, however, the matter that gave me the most concern was my relationship with Siew Chin. I was attracted to her — of that much I was sure. Beyond that I could not say for certain. For some reason she made me unsure of myself. Perhaps it was the fact that I could not read her emotionally. I found her inscrutable. I was never entirely certain whether she liked me or not. Or it might have been that I felt culturally insecure around her.

This was a new sensation to me. In England I had never given a thought to the matter. All my friends spoke English and it was entirely natural to me that I should find European culture comfortable. It was to that end that Uncle had packed me off to a public school. He wanted to make an English gentleman of me. In this he succeeded to a large extent. I was brought up on a diet of *Boys' Own*, Rudyard Kipling, Rider Haggard and G. A. Henty, which I devoured with the uncritical appetite of youth. I played cricket, punted on the Cam and stood in line for the Proms like all my college mates. Even back in Singapore, I felt entirely at home within my English-speaking milieu — Bernie Higgins, d'Almeida, Cuthbert, Aziz, Ralph and George. The fact that our skins stretched over the entire spectrum from white to black made not one jot of difference to us. Ironically, it was Siew Chin, whose skin was the same colour as mine, who made me feel a foreigner. She gave me a glimpse into a world which I knew existed, but which I had hitherto dismissed as unimportant to me.

May assured me that Siew Chin was also attracted to me. I had to take her word for this, for I could not trust myself to interpret Siew Chin's behaviour dispassionately. I had a couple of chances to see her briefly at the hospital when I called to fetch May home from work, as I did occasionally. Chen's exit left the field clear for me. If she regretted the part that I played in toppling her political mentor, she did not show it. Neither did she show any animosity towards me for breaking up her cell. On the other hand, she betrayed no increased fondness towards me either. She remained demure, reserved and maddeningly unreadable.

Be that as it may, I was certain that I wanted to get to know her better. May's wedding provided the perfect excuse for this. Though the exact form of the nuptials had yet to be settled, May had determined that Siew Chin should be her maid of honour. Ralph had asked me to be his best man. I accepted with genuine pleasure. I would have plenty of opportunity to be with Siew Chin during the wedding preparations.

RALPH'S parents had passed on some time before and he had no close relatives to contend with, so he was in that sense his own master. On our side, normally a Baba wedding would have been the preserve of the mistress of the house. However, Mak felt that as the couple would be paying for the festivities, they should have the final say. She therefore firmly declined to express her wishes, knowing that the bride and bridegroom would accede to them whether they could afford to or not. So the decision was left essentially to May.

Typically, May wanted all her sisters and half-sisters involved in the decision. It was this surfeit of democracy that prolonged the process. I was asked to sit in on the discussions, but this was mere formality. No one paid the least attention to me at all, especially as my suggestion was that the happy couple should elope and save us all a lot of bother.

Finally, a powwow at the house was called in order to make a decision. Ralph was a little awkward, surrounded by so many females. I sat next to him to give him support. Siew Chin was also there. She and May arrived together after work. It was the first time she had visited us at home. She sat herself down next to May, saying nothing much to anyone. I gave her a little smile. She smiled back shyly but made no attempt at conversation. I debated whether or not to break the ice myself. The debate was abruptly terminated when Gek Neo called us all to order.

In order to bring the proceedings to an expeditious end, we resolved not to break for tea until the matter was settled. Gek Neo, in her practical way, suggested that under the circumstances the simplest way was the best — have the marriage registered under the Christian Marriage Ordinance and leave it at that. June and the other girls reacted with horror. They were looking forward to the festivities —a simple ceremony at the Registry was to them only slightly better than an elopement. In any case, they pointed out, May was the first to get married and she should have it done properly. The relatives would expect nothing less. A full-scale wedding in the old style was not necessary. Such things were getting increasingly rare in any case. Only the very rich could afford the full twelve-day feast. But at least a few days should be devoted to the nuptials. There could be a civil ceremony first, followed by the traditional rites on some auspicious date.

Ralph and I listened attentively while the ladies had their say. At length a consensus was reached on the Registry ceremony plus a single day for the customary wedding. May looked to Ralph, who signified his agreement. They duly reported the result to Mak, who received the decision with outward equanimity. Inwardly, I'm sure she was very pleased. Despite her open-mindedness, Mak was still extremely traditional. She placed great store on doing things properly. While she would have accepted a civil wedding if the couple had wanted it, she would have done so with regret. Even though they couldn't afford the full works, at least some of the customary rituals would be observed.

Siew Chin had sat through the whole discussion quietly, neither agreeing nor disagreeing with the various suggestions. As we broke up to go in to tea, she approached me.

"May I speak with you privately?" she asked shyly.

This was the first time she had spoken to me of her own accord since our little adventure with the law.

"Of course," I responded eagerly. "We can go out onto the veranda."

As I was about to lead her onto the veranda, Julie appeared and collared me.

"Where are you both going, eh?" she asked. "No disappearing now. We are going to have tea soon. You must help to carry out the tray of *kueh*, Denny. We all are not strong enough."

I glared at her irritatedly, but it had no effect. She tugged me by the wrist. I followed, exasperated.

Siew Chin smiled. "Your younger sister calls you by your name," she remarked, eyebrows raised quizzically.

"Yes," I answered, "I know it's unusual, but Julie's not really my sister. Nor for that matter is May."

I explained the whole convoluted story to her, about my father and my uncle and my uncle's wives and his daughters. She nodded her head at the end but still looked rather confused.

"Well," I concluded, "now you see why the traditional titles don't work in this family. It's easier just to call each other by our names."

Her face was impassive, but did I detect just a quick flash of disapproval? In her world, younger siblings would not have had the temerity to address their elders by anything other than the title of "elder brother" or "elder sister." I could imagine that she thought us lax and uncultured for allowing such informality. It disturbed me somehow that she might think less of us. But her face and demeanour betrayed no overt disapprobation.

Tea was a pretty raucous affair. June had taken over Ralph and was merrily laying bare all the family secrets. Julie and Augusta, catching the mood of the moment, were all over the place in their schoolgirl fashion, chattering at the top of their voices. May was engaged in what was evidently an engrossing tête-à-tête with Siew Chin and Gek Neo. Mak busied herself producing a continuous stream of goodies from the kitchen, aided and abetted by Ah Sum, who fussed about like a black-and-white bumblebee. I retreated glumly into a corner, forgotten and discarded, waiting for my opportunity to catch Siew Chin alone again.

At last Ralph managed to prise himself loose from June's remora-like grasp. Quickly swallowing the remains of his tea, he rose and thanked Mak. Siew Chin also took the opportunity to rise. There was a general bustling and a round of hugs.

As we made our way to the door, I asked Siew Chin, "How are you getting back? Can I offer you a lift?"

She hesitated. "I will be all right, thank you. I can take a bus."

"You most certainly can not," I insisted, "not when it's getting dark. And it might rain. Look, I'm taking Ralph back. It's only a little way further by car to your hostel." Actually, Ralph's place was a good half-mile in the other direction, but I was counting on the likelihood that Siew Chin wouldn't be familiar with the roads. She hesitated again, looking with anxiety at the glowering sky.

"It's really no trouble," I said, "it's on the way."

At that moment, as if on cue, a gust of wind laden with the smell of rain rustled the trees. To my satisfaction, she agreed with a small nod.

We made our way out to the car, discreetly leaving Ralph and May to say their goodbyes on the veranda. Julie and Augusta however did not possess such a fine sense of decorum. They were peering out from behind the curtains. I flicked a small pebble at the window and gestured to them to disappear, which they did in a flurry of giggles.

Ralph appeared finally and we piled into the car. He started to get in the back seat when I stopped him.

"You'd better sit in front. I'll drop you off first and then drive Siew Chin to her hostel."

Ralph's brow creased in puzzlement. "Isn't it more convenient to let Siew Chin out first?" he queried.

"No, it isn't," I said firmly. "It's much better if we go by your place first and then drop Siew Chin off later, right?"

"But..." he began. I glared at him.

He finally twigged. "Ah, yes, um, right," he said, holding up the front passenger seat for Siew Chin to enter. "Much better to drop me off first."

Ralph and I chatted about manly things while Siew Chin sat quietly in the back. After he got out, she moved to the front seat. She still showed no sign of taking up our conversation where we had been so unfortunately interrupted by Julie. Finally, I decided to seize the initiative.

"You wanted to speak to me privately?" I inquired cautiously.

"Yes," she said. A pause followed. She seemed to be trying to decide how to continue. "Would you come and meet my father?"

This took me entirely by surprise. "Meet your father?" I echoed, at a loss for any other words.

"Only if it is not inconvenient," she continued, as if apprehensive that I would decline.

"No, no, it's not inconvenient at all," I replied hastily, "but what would I say to him?"

She sighed and shook her head slightly. "It is a little difficult to explain," she said, staring through the windshield. "I must start at the beginning. It is many years since I have seen my father. He is a businessman in Ipoh. He owns a tin mine — many tin mines. He sends me money every month. I have — had — a brother. Not a real brother, but one like May and Julie."

"A half-brother," I interjected helpfully.

She nodded. "Yes, a half-brother. We have different mothers. His mother was my father's second wife. My mother was the first wife. She could not produce a son, so we came to live here while he stayed in Ipoh. My half-brother and my father ran the business there. Last year he died in an accident."

"I'm so sorry," I said lamely, not quite sure of how to respond properly.

"Yes, I am sorry also. But I did not know him so well. We did not see each other much. Not even at Chinese New Year." She paused, and we travelled a short while in silence.

"My brother died," she continued at length, "and my father became very sad. He has no other son. So he has come down here. He says he wants to live in the Colony and not in the Malay States. He will sell the tin mines. He told me that he wants to buy a big house and that I should go and live with him."

"And your mother?"

"She has passed away also, two years ago," said Siew Chin simply and without apparent emotion. "My father says that he will need someone in the Colony to advise him about business and legal matters. I thought of you. Will you meet him?"

I hesitated. It seemed like a pretty tall order, advising a *towkay* about business. "Would you like me to?" I asked, temporising.

She nodded. "Yes, if it is convenient."

"I'll do it if that's what you want," I replied cautiously. "But I'm not sure that I'm really qualified for the job."

"I think that you are the best. I do not trust anybody else. My father is not familiar with the ways of the Colony. He needs a man who can help him to deal with the *orang puteh*," she replied.

I was surprised by her use of the Malay phrase for the white man. Normally the non-Baba Chinese called them red-haired devils or worse, but I suppose that it would have sounded somewhat unsuitable translated into English.

"I am worried about my father," she continued in a softer voice. "He has... changed. I do not know what he wants. I trust you to look after him."

I made up my mind. "Of course I'll do it for you," I responded, vastly pleased at her confidence in me.

"My father is staying at the Raffles now. When can you meet him?"

"Well," I answered decisively, "what about today, if it's okay with him?"

She paused a while and then nodded. "Yes, today is all right. Can you go now? We can catch him before he goes out for dinner."

I agreed. I turned the car round in a convenient side road. Fifteen minutes later we chugged into the forecourt of the Raffles.

THE SIKH doorman gave me a look that implied that junk should be delivered at the rear door and not left standing at the main entrance. Ignoring him, I closed the car door as quietly as I could, praying that the wing mirror would not fall off, and then followed Siew Chin past the reception desk to the foyer.

"Please wait," she said and disappeared down the corridor.

I looked around the foyer. The Grand Dining Room opened out on my right. It was set in a well, illuminated by natural light streaming in from the skylights. A grand wooden staircase led up to the floors above, lined with doors leading to the guest-rooms. It was here that they held the regular cruise dinners for the hordes of tourists that debouched from the liners in the harbour. A troupe of waiters was setting the tables for dinner, meticulously placing knives and forks and spoons and wine glasses in their appointed places. I watched them for a while and then decided to have a drink at the Long Bar, which was directly across from the dining room.

There were a few guests lounging around, including one or two Asiatics. Officially, there was no colour bar in hotels. But the old Hotel de l'Europe had a way of dealing with undesired guests. They'd put them in a pokey corner near the kitchen and ignore them. The food when it came was cold and the service colder. After a while, they'd get the message and leave. None of us locals shed any tears when they pulled the Europe down to build the new Supreme Court. Fortunately, the Raffles wasn't like that.

I settled myself comfortably in a cane armchair under one of the ceiling fans. A wrinkled waiter appeared and took my order. He shambled back in five minutes with my *gin pahit* balanced on a silver salver. I sipped it slowly and looked around idly at my fellow guests. There were the usual motley crew of planters, a couple of fellows in suits whom I took to be civil servants, a prosperous looking Indian gentleman talking animatedly to a younger man and a grizzled man sitting in a corner of the bar apparently determined to sample every cocktail on offer.

My attention was drawn to a pair seated at the bar near my table. The younger fellow was about my age and had the sickly pallor of the European climate about him. He was obviously a "griffin" — fresh off the boat and still wet behind the ears. His companion was an old hand, evidently well into his anecdotage. Having secured a fresh victim, he wasn't about to let go. I heard snatches of their conversation.

"It was right there y'know," said the older fellow, "right under the billiard table. Right there, I shot a tiger in my pyjamas. Would you believe it? What I want to know is, what was the bugger doing in my pyjamas? Haw! Haw!"

He slapped the young man hard on the shoulder. The fellow grimaced and looked around desperately for an escape route. Our eyes met. I raised my glass to him and smiled in commiseration. He started to smile back but then stopped, as if unsure if this was quite the done thing. The old goat turned round and saw me. He scowled a little, then took his charge by the arm and steered him to the other end of the bar.

"Lots of riffraff about these days," he said in a voice that I could not help hearing, "Take no notice. Did I tell you about the time I hunted down a wild elephant in Rawang?"

The young man, desperate though he was to get away, spent the rest of his time studiously avoiding looking in my direction. For some reason my initial sympathy for him had died completely.

After about a half an hour Siew Chin came back in the company of an older man. I judged him to be in his sixties, slim in frame and with a small grey moustache. He wore an European-style suit and carried a black cane. All in all, he presented a very distinguished appearance and carried himself with the air of a man who was accustomed to refinement.

Siew Chin presented me to him. He put out his hand and spoke some words of Chinese. I shook it, mumbling an apology that I couldn't understand what he said but that I was glad to meet him.

The old man looked at me through his pince-nez. "You do not speak Chinese?" he said interrogatively.

"No, I'm afraid not," I replied, feeling my ears redden. Again I feared that I wasn't making a good impression on Siew Chin. I braced myself for the inevitable cutting remark on my linguistic inadequacies.

"Then, daughter, we must speak English when we are with your young friend," said the old man, without a hint of condescension.

I was taken completely by surprise by this gracious gesture and instantly warmed to him.

"You are a Baba then?" he inquired, inviting me to sit next to him. "How long has your family been in the Colony?"

"Yes," I replied, "we're Babas. I think we've been here practically from the start. At least, my grandfather's father was born here about the time that Raffles came."

"Ah, an old family," he said, nodding. "You know where your ancestors come from in China?"

I shifted uncomfortably. "No, not exactly. Somewhere from the south. Fukien Province I think."

"Ha!" he said jovially, slapping me on the arm, "then we are countrymen. I also come from Fukien, from a village on the Han River."

I smiled faintly, not knowing what to say. Siew Chin saved me by intervening.

"Pa, Dennis is the one who saved us all from jail. Not once only but twice. He is a good lawyer. He studied in England."

"So," said Siew Chin's father, "a lawyer. A man of learning. That is good. You are ready to be my... how you say?" He turned to Siew Chin.

"Private secretary," she replied.

"Yes, private secretary," he continued. "I need help when I am in Singapore. I am not used to the big city. I am a *sua ku*, from the small town." He laughed shortly, slapping his thigh.

I wasn't entirely sure I was cut out for the job. I said so, hoping that I would not give offence by appearing to be reluctant to accept the post.

"My daughter has told me much about her trouble with the law. She has also told me of the skill of her lawyer. I am sure that a man who can deal with the police and the courts so well must be very clever. If you are willing, I think that you will have no trouble to do what I need. You should not worry about the money."

He named a figure four times my current salary. My eyes nearly popped out. I was tempted to accept there and then. Cash was tight around the house. A fourfold increase in my salary would be very welcome, especially with the looming prospect of losing May's contribution. However, my innate caution reasserted itself.

"May I think about it, Sir?"

"Yes, yes," he replied readily. "You cannot decide now. Think about it one day, two days, three days. Then give me your answer when you are ready."

With that he rose and proffered his hand. I shook it and he left, heading for the Dining Room. I looked at Siew Chin, trying to summon up the nerve to ask her out to dinner. She didn't give me the chance.

She shook my hand demurely and said, "When you decide, come and tell me." Then off she went after her father.

I cursed myself for my indecision. I drove home distractedly, my head full of swirling thoughts.

MY MIND wasn't on the job for the next few days. The body might have been present in court but the spirit was far away.

In those distant days of youth I hadn't yet grown jaded and cynical. I rather enjoyed the cut and thrust of litigation. I couldn't at that time imagine myself doing anything else remotely as interesting. Yet the feeling that I had reached a dead end in my chosen career continually haunted me. I had neither connections nor — as I reluctantly admitted to myself — any special brilliance as an advocate. No doubt d'Almeida would keep me on, but could I pull my weight? I had seen enough of the aging hacks hanging around the Police Courts scrabbling for the odd running-down case to know that I didn't want to end my days like that. On the other hand, I had a heaven-sent opportunity to quadruple my salary at one go.

To be private secretary to the Towkay (as I had begun to think of him in my mind) would bring me into contact with the crème de la crème of local business. When it came to money, even the *tuan besar* of the whitest of white firms would condescend to meet a native on close-to-equal terms. My ancestors were businessmen. Surely I could do it too. Then there was the prospect of getting to hang around Siew Chin more and be paid for it. It was too good to be true. Yet still I hung back.

It was while I was in this undecided frame of mind that I bumped into Bernie Higgins along the corridors of the Police Courts. I hadn't seen anything of him since our little escapade with Comrade Chen and his merry men.

"Hello, Bernie, old boy," I said jovially. "Haven't seen you around for some time. What've you been up to?"

"Ah... hello, Dennis," he replied. He seemed distracted and none too pleased to see me. "I've been busy."

"Will I see you at the Club? We could have a couple of sets of tennis."

"No, sorry, not today. Must be off. Tons of work."

With that he practically fled from my presence. I am not as a general rule what you would call a sensitive person, but I was really miffed by Bernie's behaviour. There is a certain comradeship among those forced to queue up in the freezing cold for the same lavatory while some mental retard practises arias from *The Mikado*. Six terms of shared misery in the same college is the basis of many a secure friendship. I thought of Bernie as one of my closest chums, and his offhand manner cut me to the quick. However, after the initial irritation had worn off a little, I decided that perhaps I was too hasty in judging him. After all, the calls on a Magistrate's time were enormous. He might be — probably was — snowed under with work. I decided to give him the benefit of the doubt.

As I rounded the corner I saw him with a group of his magisterial colleagues. He seemed to be having a good time with them, laughing and chatting away. It didn't look like he was in a tearing hurry to get back to the grind. I left without bothering to greet them.

I stormed down South Bridge Road seething like a lava flow. There was no doubt about it, Bernie Higgins had just snubbed me. Come to think of it, I hadn't seen him at the Club for some time.

The Recreation Club was, strictly speaking, only for Asiatics; the Europeans kept to themselves at the Cricket Club on the other side of the Padang. Nevertheless, Bernie was a regular guest of several of the members, including myself. The more I thought about it, the more certain I was that he had stopped coming after the Chen business. I could only surmise that he did not want to continue the friendship. I could imagine what his new friends were telling him. It isn't done for a young up-and-coming Magistrate to be seen so often in the company of a Chink, and a known Commie at that. One's seniors might talk, what. Best to let the acquaintance drop old boy.

By the time I got back to chambers I was in a calmer frame of mind. I had also determined what I had to do. George and Aziz were in the Assistants' Lounge.

"George, old chap, would you happen to know a good Chinese teacher?" I asked.

George stopped scribbling and looked up from the *Times* crossword.

"When you say 'a Chinese teacher,' do you mean a teacher who is by race Chinese, or do you mean a person who teaches Chinese? If it's the former, I know a few who might suit you, including one who is quite scrumptious."

"Thanks all the same, but keep the scrumptious one for yourself," I replied. "I'm looking for someone to teach me to speak Chinese."

At this George sat up bolt upright. "To teach you to speak Chinese? What in heaven's name for?"

All of a sudden I became embarrassed. "Ah... well... I just thought it would be good to learn something of the ancestral language. Y'know, pick up a little culture."

"Culture? You?" hooted George derisively. "Hedy Lamarr and Glenn Miller and P. G. Woodhouse not good enough for you anymore?"

"Well, y'know, it's always good to know something about one's own ancestors," I responded defensively. "Isn't that so, Aziz?" I shot him a look pleading for support.

"Yes, absolutely," said Aziz, smiling affably. "Shouldn't lose touch with your roots."

"Roots!" exclaimed George. "My dear Aziz, I'll have you know that Dennis here has got wonderful, thick roots. That's why he can hardly make it across the tennis court to hit the ball!"

"No, seriously, Siew Chin's father has made me a proposition. I might just accept, but I've got to know some Chinese."

"Aha," said George, "Siew Chin's father. Now it all becomes clear. *Cherchez la femme*, as somebody or other once said. Who was it, now?"

"Dumas, I think," I replied.

"Right, spot on, Dumas it was. Look for the lady. For the

sake of a lady I'd learn Swahili if necessary. Say no more, your problem is understood. Unfortunately not solved, but certainly understood."

Aziz joined in. "You're thinking of leaving the firm?"

Put like that, it sounded rather final. I found it hard to actually say the words.

"Yes...I suppose that's what I mean," I replied hesitantly. "The Towkay has made me a very generous offer. I'm seriously thinking of accepting."

"What on earth can have possessed you?" exclaimed George in his usual unsympathetic way. "You want to chuck all this up and go off with some *towkay* as what? A clerk?"

"Have you spoken to Clarence about this?" asked Aziz quietly.

"No," I replied slowly, "but I suppose I shall have to."

George suddenly became serious when he realised that I meant it.

"Look, Dennis, I don't know what's buzzing in your nut, but think about it carefully. It's a big thing you're doing, giving up the law. You've got your whole life ahead of you, a fabulous career." He came over and put his hand on my arm. "If you want to talk about it...."

"Thanks, George," I responded, "but I have thought about it."

"Well," said George, shrugging his shoulders, "but you mind what I say. Make sure it's really what you want and that you're not just doing it for the sake of some female."

Aziz looked grave. "I think you really should talk to Clarence about this."

I nodded and left hurriedly. If I had stayed, they might have swayed me back into indecision and I didn't want that. I had made up my mind and I wasn't about to have it unmade by my well-meaning friends.

When I left the company of George and Aziz I hadn't yet plucked up the courage to actually go and see d'Almeida. However, the decision was made for me. I bumped into him practically outside the Assistants' Lounge. My heart gave a jump. How much had he overheard?

Steeling myself, I blurted out, "Mr d'Almeida, might I have a moment of your time please?"

He said nothing but indicated that I should follow him to his room. Once we were snugly ensconced in his large leather chairs, he spoke quietly, "Now, young man, what is it that you wanted to speak to me about?"

I told him in brief sentences about the Towkay's offer to me. I thanked him for the privilege of working with him and for his patience and forbearance towards me. Saying that I felt I needed to explore new opportunities, I gave him my notice. Throughout the whole experience I felt numb. It was as though some other consciousness had possessed my body and was saying the words. I did not want to seem ungrateful, but I feared that was the impression I conveyed with my stilted speech. D'Almeida listened in silence. He paused a few moments after I had finished, then said:

"Chiang, I won't judge whether you're doing the right thing and I won't try to change your mind. You must do what you think best for yourself and your family. I merely counsel that you do not act precipitately. I will not accept your notice — not yet. I realise that the last few months have been rather arduous for you. A short sabbatical would not be out of order. Take three months. Come and see me again after that. We shall speak again. If you still feel as you do now, I shall accept your resignation at that time."

I was overwhelmed. "Mr d'Almeida, it's enormously generous of you. I hardly know how to thank you."

"No thanks are necessary," he replied drily. "Use the time well."

With that he returned to his files. The interview was obviously over. I rose and headed to the door. As I reached it, he looked up at me over the rim of his spectacles.

"By the way, Chiang, a piece of unsolicited advice, if I may be so bold," he said. "Think carefully before you exchange a wide circle for a narrow one. A man's worth isn't determined by the language that he speaks."

I was at a loss as to a proper response to this. Fortunately, d'Almeida didn't seem to expect one, so I contented myself with thanking him again. It was the work of only a few minutes to clear my desk. As far as the staff was concerned, I was taking an extended break. As for George, I left a note on his desk explaining that d'Almeida had been good enough to give me a three-month sabbatical and that I proposed to spend it working for the Towkay. It was perhaps a trifle cowardly not to have faced him personally, but I didn't feel like being cross-examined on my motives at that point.

D'Almeida's handsome offer took a load of my mind. Not only was I not burning my bridges behind me entirely, I was also saved the necessity of justifying my actions to Mak. Loyalty is a virtue much prized by the Babas. Mak would not have approved of me leaving the d'Almeidas for the sake of a higher salary; especially as they had been so good to me. I hadn't yet decided to tell her about Siew Chin. I suspected that she suspected the truth. But I wasn't about to confirm it; at least not until I was quite certain about my own feelings and hers.

EARLY THAT evening, I turned up at the Raffles to meet the Towkay. I was shown to his suite by a little scamp in a bellboy's uniform, who stared with obvious disgust at the very small tip I left in his hand. Out of the corner of my eye I saw him stick out his tongue at me as I stood at the door. He was saved from retribution when the door opened. To my delight, it was Siew Chin let me in. She was in mufti, dressed in a floral *samfoo* with her hair in two braids. She invited me to sit.

"You aren't at work today?" I asked.

"No, I have left the hospital. My father wishes me to keep house for him," she answered simply.

Any opportunity for further conversation vanished with the entrance of the Towkay.

"Ah, my young friend," he said affably, "you have decided?"

"Yes, Mr Lim," I replied, "I'd be happy to be your private secretary. But could I just ask for a trial period of three months? My boss, Mr d'Almeida, has been kind enough to give me leave."

The Towkay nodded. "Yes, we will try out first. Then we will see."

We discussed various mundane details about remuneration and terms while Siew Chin unobtrusively brought us tea. At the end of the discussion, the Towkay offered me his hand and the bargain was sealed.

"I shall call you Dennis, as Siew Chin does," he said.

He poured the tea and lifted his cup in a toast. I reciprocated wordlessly, still not entirely sure in my mind that I was doing the right thing. The terms were fair, the work untaxing, the remuneration generous. Yet I could not get rid of the niggling feeling that somehow, somewhere, something wasn't right. I shook myself. Cast into paradise, here I was looking for snakes. I gulped my tea and tried to swallow my doubts.

"You can drive, Dennis?" asked the Towkay.

I nodded.

"Come," he said and motioned for us to follow.

We went through the foyer to the entrance. Parked under the stately travellers palms was a brand-new Rolls. I fingered the gleaming winged ornament on the bonnet. The seats exuded the scent of fresh leather.

"You can drive us," said the Towkay, indicating that I should take the driver's seat. He got in the back, motioning to Siew Chin to join him.

"I do not like to drive. In a small town maybe okay, but in this big city...?" He shook his head. "Too many cars, trolley buses, bicycles."

"Where to, sir?" I queried in my best Jeeves fashion.

That seemed to tickle his fancy. He laughed shortly, his eyes crinkling with amusement.

"We look for houses. Take me where I can see fine houses by the sea."

I thought a moment. "We could go east towards the Seaview Hotel, or west along Pasir Panjang," I suggested.

"West," said the Towkay, "to the setting sun."

IT WAS with a sense of déjà vu that I drove past the harbour towards the long strand of Pasir Panjang. Had it been only a year since I did this in another Rolls, with another girl? The scenery was the same, the smells familiar. I however felt a completely different person. It seemed to me that it was someone else altogether who had driven down this road all those months ago; someone who knew who he was and where he was going. Shaking off the philosophical mood, I tried to concentrate on my driving.

The mansions of the rich began somewhere around the fifth milestone. At the Towkay's urging, I slowed down as we reached them. The manicured lawns stretched from road to house and from house to the sea behind. Open windows stared like sightless eyes from the walls. Here and there we saw a *pekebun* hard at work mowing a lawn or weeding a flowerbed. The occupants were not to be seen. We passed slowly along the row of facades like a Maharajah reviewing his troops.

Just before the sixth milestone there was a break in the row of seafront houses. The waves lapped onto the beach right next to the road. A low ridge rose on the right hand side, crowned with what seemed to be a pagoda. A tall Chinese gate stood at the foot of a long drive. Beyond, the ridge was terraced and decorated with fantastic statues painted in garishly bright colours.

The Towkay told me to stop. "Whose house is that?" he asked.

"I think it belongs to the Aw brothers. You know, the Tiger Balm people," I answered. "I've never visited it myself, but I hear that they don't mind people wandering round the gardens."

The Towkay nodded and dismounted. He crossed the road to the gate. The gatekeeper let him in after a short conversation. He indicated that we should follow. The long drive snaked along the side of the ridge. Groups of figures lined the road, demons and demigods, heroes and villains.

"These show stories and legends from China. You know them?" asked the Towkay.

I admitted with a tinge of embarrassment that I did not.

"Come, I will tell you," said the Towkay.

As we proceeded up the path he explained the significance of each vignette, pointing out characters of which I hitherto had heard nothing. The groups at the bottom of the drive represented scenes from Chinese myths and legends and illustrated virtues like filial piety, loyalty and honesty. Further up, the themes got darker and the carvings more gruesome. Most seemed to have been concerned with sin and retribution. The sculptors evidently had gotten hold of a consignment of red paint cheap. The stuff was splashed liberally about on amputated limbs, impaled bodies and dismembered heads. As we progressed, the Towkay fell silent and ceased to comment on the statues.

At the top of the drive was the villa, built in western style and painted in soothing pastel tones, overlooking a swimming pool filled with carved figures. The windows were shuttered. We stood at the top terrace, looking out to sea. The sun was low on the horizon. A cool breeze was blowing inland. I positioned myself next to Siew Chin. The Towkay seemed miles away.

He stood silently, with an air of preoccupation. "The dark comes," he said softly, as though to himself.

Abruptly, he turned back and said, "We must go."

He made his way down to the road without another word. We drove back to town in silence. At the hotel, he dismissed me in a distracted way and returned with Siew Chin to his suite.

NEXT morning the Towkay seemed to have recovered his good spirits. I met him at his suite again. He introduced me to his housing agent. The agent was a fat Indian who seemed to be melting from the heat, judging from the amount of sweat that poured off his face. He had short-listed several houses in the town area for lease.

My first task was to ferry them around to examine the houses. This process took the better part of the morning. The Towkay was silent for the most part, inspecting each house carefully without comment while the agent babbled on about the virtues of each. In the end, he decided to take a largish bungalow just off Orchard Road. I was particularly pleased with this, because that made him and Siew Chin practically neighbours of ours.

The decision was made with surprising speed. The Towkay did not deign to bargain, but just accepted the landlord's terms without demur. I thought that the rent was exorbitant and was about to suggest trying to cut it down when it occurred to me that the same could be said of my salary. I decided that a judicious silence was in order.

The fat agent produced a lease from his fat briefcase. The Towkay passed it on to me to peruse. I fervently wished that I had paid more attention to my lectures on conveyancing. The document was written in the usual polysyllabic gobbledygook that passes for English in legal documents. It seemed to be all right as far as I could make out.

The Towkay signed the lease with an indifferent flourish of his pen, produced a wad of notes that he handed over to the agent, and that was that. The agent bowed and scraped his way out of the house clutching his money and beaming a smile that nearly split his head in two.

With the small matter of accommodation taken care of, the next item on the order of business was a visit to McPhee & Co., whose premises were right in the heart of town at Raffles Place. The Towkay had procured a letter of introduction from his business associates in Ipoh. I dutifully drove him over.

McPhee & Co. turned out to be a firm of rubber and stockbrokers. Their offices were plush and discreet. I handed the letter of introduction to the receptionist, who bade us take a seat in a waiting room. The managing partner himself, a Mr Strathallan, emerged to greet us. It was evident from the way he conducted himself that the Towkay was a client of great importance. To me he paid scant attention.

The business proceeded with practiced efficiency. We were ushered into Mr Strathallan's spacious office, seated in his grandest armchairs and plied with tea and biscuits. Strathallan kept the conversation going, talking of the doings of various mining and plantation companies upcountry, while the Towkay quietly sipped his tea. Occasionally, the Towkay would make a casual comment regarding a particular company or individual. I could see Strathallan filing each nugget of information away for future reference.

After a while, a peon appeared with a sheaf of documents. Again the Towkay passed them over to me to peruse. I tried desperately not to show my abysmal ignorance of matters of high finance. In a world of bulls and bears, I'm sorry to say that I'm a complete jackass. Nevertheless, I made a pretence of examining the documents carefully, asking what I hoped would be taken for pointed questions on various aspects.

As far as I could gather from the documents and the explanations provided by Strathallan, the Towkay was being accorded credit facilities to trade in tin, rubber and shares. As before, he signed the documents with complete nonchalance, as if the offer of a credit line of $20,000 was a matter of small moment to him.

To seal the deal, the Towkay produced from his briefcase a small sheaf of share certificates, which he handed to me to pass on to Strathallan. These, I gathered, were to be the collateral for his credit line. I noted that they were shares in Lipis Consolidated Mines, the Towkay's own company. Strathallan examined them cursorily, then gave them to the waiting peon. There was a round of handshakes and Strathallan escorted us to the door.

A young Chinese man about my age was waiting for us in the antechamber. He introduced himself simply as Lee. He was to be the Towkay's remisier. Lee offered to take us directly to the trading room. However, the Towkay declined.

"Not yet," he said. "I come back afterwards. Come, we must go somewhere now." I dutifully followed him downstairs.

He set off at a brisk pace across the square and dived into Change Alley. The Alley was a narrow, crowded passage full of small stalls and packed with humanity. At the turn of the century it had been the centre of the rubber trade. Now it was an oriental bazaar, full of traders of all sorts selling goods from all civilised lands and beyond.

The Towkay strode into the crowd, clearing the way with judicious waves of his walking stick. We came to a hole-in-the-wall office and ducked in. There was barely room for the two of us. At the further end sat an Indian man. The caste marks on his forehead clearly identified him as a Chettiar, a member of the moneylending class.

The Towkay produced another letter of introduction. The Chettiar read it gravely, then nodded wordlessly. The Towkay produced a little pouch from the depths of his briefcase and handed it over. The moneylender emptied the contents onto a black velvet tray and produced a jeweller's glass. He examined each item carefully — a dazzling pair of ruby earrings, four gold bracelets, a gold ring and a bangle of the deepest green jade I had ever seen. He considered the items solemnly, wrote out a chit, then delved into his jacket and counted out a pile of notes. The Towkay took them without comment. The whole business was over in ten minutes.

Emerging into the sunshine, the Towkay said, "The first rule of business is to make use of all your assets."

He rubbed his belly. "It is time to eat," he announced.

He led me to Robinson's, where we had a good lunch at the café. The place was full of Europeans and we got quite a number of stares. But the food was good and the Towkay was in high spirits, so they didn't bother me at all.

After lunch, we headed back to McPhee & Co. to pick up Lee, who conducted us to the trading room of the Stock Exchange. The Towkay took a seat in the gallery and whispered his instructions to Lee, who disappeared to execute them. The place was like a cattle market, with trading clerks and remisiers bustling all over, bellowing at the tops of their voices. The din was incredible. How anyone got anything done was a mystery to me.

I watched as clerks chalked up the prices on the big board. The

Towkay sat in his armchair, impassively watching. I soon got bored and my eyes began to glaze over.

The Towkay leaned over and said, "You do not have to wait here with me. Come back at four o'clock."

I left with great relief to savour the unaccustomed luxury of being at a loose end in the middle of the afternoon on a working day.

Any hopes of quitting early were dashed when I picked the Towkay up. He was vastly pleased. Evidently the day's punting had gone well. At the hotel, he instructed me to return for him at 7:30. I took the opportunity to head home for a shower and a bite.

Ah Sum was none too pleased to be told that I needed to be fed early. She clattered around the kitchen mumbling to herself in Cantonese, stoking up the charcoal fire. She didn't think much of a job that had me back home at five and then out again at seven. Still, she whipped up a hot meal with commendable speed.

While I wolfed it down, I watched the girls sitting at the table with Mak patiently beading slippers, handkerchiefs and other articles. These were traditionally part of a Nonya bride's trousseau.

Since May was a non-traditional bride holding a full-time job, all the girls had been roped in to help. They sat there threading infinitesimal glass beads onto strings and tying them together in delicate patterns. All the while they kept up a constant patter of gossip and news. Mak supervised each girl in turn, unpicking mistakes, praising good work, demonstrating complicated little flourishes. Baba culture depends entirely on the womenfolk; the emancipation of women has been its death knell.

I WAS back at the hotel by 7:30. Siew Chin was joining her father for dinner. On the Towkay's instructions, I drove them to New World Amusement Park.

New World was a collection of stalls, cinemas, theatres, sideshows, restaurants and booths. Throngs of people, native and white, streamed through the neon-lit gates.

As far as entertainment went, you could get everything that the Colony could offer right there, from Peking opera to the latest Hollywood offering. The noise was incredible. On one side of the entrance was a group of Malays displaying their prowess in silat, the art of self-defence. On the other side a peddler of medicated oils was bellowing at the crowd, extolling the virtues of his foul-smelling concoctions. We gravitated over to an open-air stage where a Cantonese opera was in progress. The players were decked out in fantastic costumes, their faces rouged and powdered until they looked like masks. The recitatives and arias were delivered in a loud nasal whine, which sounded to me not unlike a cat being disembowelled with a blunt instrument. The Towkay leaned over to explain the finer points but I could hardly hear him over the cacophony. After a short while he lost interest and started to move away, much to my relief.

We made our way over to a covered hall, from which drifted the sound of orchestral music. The orchestra was belting out a passable rendition of the "Continental" and the floor was covered with couples striving to be Astaire and Rogers.

We took a seat at one of the tables, where the Towkay ordered a couple of beers and some dishes. The orchestra switched over to Jerome Kern and some couples gave up. I noticed that several of the girls returned to a sort of holding pen on the other side of the dance floor. A new batch of young fellows appeared with their tickets. Some of the girls got back on their feet, having barely had the chance to warm their seats. Others stared forlornly at the floor or gazed disinterestedly around the room. Several couples were gyrating slowly on the dance floor. I summoned up my courage.

"Would you care to dance?" I asked Siew Chin.

At first I was afraid that she would refuse outright. She blushed and looked down briefly, and then stole a glance at her father. He smiled and waved his hand to indicate his consent.

"Go, go. You should enjoy life while it lasts."

She allowed me to lead her to the floor. Dancing in that crowd was not unlike participating in a rugby scrum, but for me it was a rare pleasure nonetheless. Everyone seemed to be talking, making it hard to actually hear the orchestra. I decided not to waste my breath, but just savoured the moment.

The orchestra went through a selection of Jerome Kern tunes and then on to Gershwin and Irving Berlin. Couples left the floor and new couples took their place. I didn't make any move to return to the table. To my gratification neither did Siew Chin.

At length the orchestra ran out of tunes. Reluctantly I led Siew Chin back to the table, where her father was already tucking into his repast. There was a variety of dishes, including a crisp suckling piglet. He indicated that we should join in. Though I had already eaten, the spin around the dance floor had given me an appetite. I joined him heartily while Siew Chin picked daintily at the delicacies.

At nine o'clock the Towkay indicated that we should go. When we reached the car, he said, "Drop Siew Chin at the hotel. Then we go somewhere, eh?"

I did as he instructed, leaving Siew Chin at the entrance of the Raffles. Much to my regret, there wasn't any chance to follow up on what I felt to have been a breakthrough in our relationship. The Towkay allowed her to give him a filial peck on the cheek, then told me to drive to an address in Chinatown.

Even at that hour Chinatown was still buzzing. We drove past Malay Street, which had been notorious for its brothels before the Great War. The Municipal Government in a fit of puritanism had cleaned the whole lot up, to the great disappointment of the many visiting sailors. Still, the area was far from salubrious.

I stopped at the appointed address, a nondescript shophouse. The Towkay evidently knew his way around.

"You wait here," he told me and disappeared through the swing doors.

From inside I heard the clack of mah-jong tiles and a low babble of voices. The air in the room was blue with cigarette smoke. I settled myself in the front seat of the Rolls. Despite my efforts to keep awake, I soon found myself dozing.

I came to myself with a jerk and checked my watch. It was close to 2:00 am. The Towkay was just emerging from the gambling den. His face was flushed and red, his breath smelt of rice wine. He climbed into the back seat without a word. I drove him back and helped him to his suite. We got in without disturbing Siew Chin.

He clapped me on the shoulder and said, "A good night, my young friend. We do this again tomorrow."

I bade him goodnight and hauled myself wearily back to my old banger. The house was dark when I got back. I stumbled up the stairs and collapsed on my bed without even undressing.

MY WORKING life now underwent a complete change. Late in the morning I would motor down to the Towkay's new house, into which he had now moved. There I would sort the mail into three piles: bills, begging letters and the rest. The Towkay would pay the bills promptly.

"Honour is everything," he said to me. "You should not leave bills unpaid."

The begging letters were treated with what seemed to me to be undeserved indulgence. No matter how trivial or self-serving, the Towkay would answer each letter personally, dictating each reply to me to type out. In quite a few instances he sent money to the more deserving ones; not large sums, $10 here, $20 there.

As for the rest, they went into the wastebasket. Mostly they were circulars or advertisements from all sorts of tradespeople. They came buzzing round like bees to a honey pot. The Towkay had little time for them.

After doing the mail, I would send him over to the Stock Exchange, where he would spend the day. At the end of the day, we would have a meal at one of the Worlds —Happy World or Great World or Gay World. Then it would be time for his nightly visit to the gambling den. Gambling seemed to be his passion; no doubt his fascination with the stock market stemmed in part from that obsession.

The advantage of this kind of life was that it left me free for the better part of the day while the Towkay was busying himself hunting bears and bulls up and down the stock and commodity markets.

I put this time to good use by making myself indispensable to Siew Chin. She had taken over the management of the house, which was a large, rambling villa with six bedrooms. The Towkay engaged a Malay woman to do the cleaning, so Siew Chin was left principally with the task of supervision. I pottered about as handyman and gopher — going for this, that and the other and generally being handy.

In the days and weeks that followed I attempted to ease myself past her defences. We spoke of many things, but she seemed most interested in politics. I found her opinions somewhat utopian. She seemed to have a naive faith in the perfectibility of mankind. I, on the other hand, had seen too much of the dark side even after only a year of legal practice. However, I did not think that it would do my cause much good to appear overtly cynical; I disguised my scepticism and listened with good humour as she prattled on about the evils of capitalism and the coming of the workers' revolution.

I was amazed that she had retained such an unmarked soul, considering what she had been through: abandonment by her father, exile in Singapore, the death of her mother and only brother, the loneliness of singlehood in the nurses' hostel. I found myself wondering whether her seeming naivety was in fact an elaborate pose that she adopted to shield herself from the harsh reality of a hard world. Whatever it was, I felt that I wasn't getting through to the real woman. On the face of it, we talked naturally and comfortably, but there was a reserve beneath the surface that I could not penetrate. Her innermost feelings were closed to me.

The presence of Salmah the cleaning lady meant that we were not alone together much. In any case, I felt instinctively that the time was not yet ripe to move our relationship forward. I was groping my way in the dark, trying to judge when I could venture to suggest a more intimate tête-à-tête over tea or dinner without risking a devastating rebuff. I considered asking George for advice, but discarded the idea quickly.

As far as women were concerned, George had all the subtlety of a caveman hunting a mate; a technique which brought him a surprising amount of success, though little in the way of lasting relationships. My instincts told me that the process should not be rushed; that patience was required lest she bolt. It was a more leisured and leisurely age, far removed in time and tone from the frenetic pace of life today. I felt no pressure to move faster, for I thought that I had all the time in the world to win her confidence and affection.

After about six weeks working for the Towkay, I noticed a subtle change in the atmosphere. There seemed to be a tension in the air, a vague sense of expectancy. The Towkay seemed more preoccupied, less communicative. At first I thought that the market might have gone sour, but the regular credit and debit notes showed a steady profit. Nothing spectacular, a couple of hundred here, five hundred there. Of course there were losses, but these were more than covered by the gains. In fact, in the month and half that I had been working for him it appeared that the Towkay had made more than a thousand dollars punting on the stock and commodity markets. As for the gambling, I knew for a fact that he never brought more than a hundred dollars in cash with him, and when he returned at night, more often than not the hundred dollars had increased a little. Yet he had not the same cheerful air about him as when we first met.

I discovered quite by accident that he was taking barbiturates. While waiting in the car for the Towkay one night, I decided to do a spot of tidying up. When I plumped up the cushions in the back seat, a packet of white powder fell out. I picked it up. Scribbled in pencil on the front was the word veronal. I'd read enough Agatha Christie books to recognise it at once as a sedative. I felt a tinge of concern. Barbiturates are dangerous things. I'd never touch the stuff myself. Next day, I mentioned the matter casually to Siew Chin.

"Do you know that your father is taking veronal?"

"No need to worry, I got it for him," she said. "Pa has insomnia. He cannot sleep because of the noise of the city."

"Is it safe?" I ventured cautiously.

"Yes," she answered simply. "No need for you to worry. I have told him how much to take each time. I get it from the hospital in small packets. Which I pay for."

She added the last with a small twinkle in her eye, reminding me of my previous unfounded suspicions of her. I took this gentle teasing as a positive sign that she was gradually opening up.

As she seemed not to be overly concerned about the barbiturates, I put the matter out of my mind. The Towkay's appetite for good food seemed little diminished. He still retained his passion for gambling and Chinese opera. He still flung his money around as if there were no tomorrow. On the face of it, everything was normal. I dismissed my apprehensions as groundless, reminding myself that paranoia is one of the side-effects of reading too many detective novels.

BACK ON the home front, the sewing machines were merrily whirring away. Every Nonya bride is expected to produce a complete trousseau, beaded, brocaded and embroided to the smallest detail. All the girls had thrown themselves wholeheartedly into the business. The background buzz became so much a part of the house that I no longer noticed it. So it came as something of a shock one fine morning when I awoke to silence. The machines had stopped. For a moment I had a sense of foreboding. Then June burst into my room.

"Oy, don't you ever knock?" I protested.

"Get up already! It's late!"

I blinked. "Late? Late for what?"

"You forgot or what? Today is Hari Antar Sireh," she replied impatiently. "You have to go to the Registry."

Then I remembered. We had fixed the registration of the marriage for that very day. In a quaint mixing of customs, the same day had been chosen as Hari Antar Sireh, the Day for Delivering Sireh.

According to Baba custom, invitations to a wedding took the form of a quid of *sireh* wrapped in a leaf. Since I was the only one with a car, I had been appointed to the position of driver. My job was to ferry Gek Neo around as she delivered the betel nut paste packets. My topsy-turvy working life had completely driven the matter from my mind.

Ironically much more attention was paid to the preparations for Hari Antar Sireh than to the Registry wedding. In the eyes of the law, registration was what counted. Once Ralph signed the registration book he was committed to lifelong servitude without time off for good behaviour. Yet none of us accorded any importance to that tiresome formality. As far as everyone was concerned, what mattered was the customary wedding ceremony, which was to be held exactly a week after Hari Antar Sireh.

The Registry ceremony — if one could call it that — was over in a flash. No one else was there except the bridal couple, dressed in ordinary clothes, and the witnesses, who happened to be Siew Chin and me. In, sign the book, shake hands with the rather bored Assistant Registrar, out. It was over and done with in half an hour; it would have been five minutes if the Assistant Registrar hadn't kept us waiting while he finished his breakfast.

Ralph then dashed off to the office, betraying no sign of the fact that he had just signed away his freedom. May and Siew Chin went over to the nurses' hostel, where a small hen party had been arranged. I rushed over to the Towkay's place to do my job. After dropping him at the Stock Exchange, I drove back to finish the important task of the day, delivering the sireh.

I hadn't realised till that day quite how many relatives we had. In a Baba clan each member has a precise designation; no easy titles like a simple "aunt" or "uncle." Fortunately, Gek Neo had been well-schooled in the intricacies of familial relationships. She was the one who kept track of the seemingly unending stream of 'Npek, 'Nku, 'Nkim, and Um that we met. My job was just to get her to the right door. Once there, she did the necessary business with polished courtesy. She'd prompt me by whispering in my ear, Kim Poh Cho (or whatever their name was), and I'd respond by politely greeting in the approved fashion some old biddy whom I'd never before seen in my life.

After motoring around half of Singapore island, I was so tired that my greetings became automatic. At the last house, we were greeted by a cheeky urchin who made a rude face at us as we crossed the portal.

"*Budak chelaka!*" exclaimed Gek Neo.

Automatically, I extended my hand to the scamp and said, "Hello, *budak chelaka*." Gek Neo gave me a sharp tap with her fan and shot me a withering look.

With the tiresome business of delivering sireh out of the way, the only thing left was to deliver the conventional wedding invitations to our mutual friends. Siew Chin took care of May's friends and I was to do the same for Ralph's. It was just a matter of popping down to the GPO and sticking a stamp on the invitation cards.

As I was doing so, a name caught my eye. I'd suggested inviting Bernie and Ralph had agreed. There was his card in my hand. For a moment I had the urge to toss it in the wastebasket. Then a sudden resolve gripped me.

Tucking the card into my jacket pocket, I drove over to the Police Courts. I went straight to Bernie's chambers, brushing past his startled clerk. With a perfunctory knock, I entered. Bernie was sitting at his desk reading the newspapers. He jerked up with a start at my incursion.

"Hello, Bernie, old boy," I said with a somewhat forced joviality.

"Ah...well, Dennis," he responded weakly, completely taken aback at my sudden appearance. "What... what a surprise."

It was evident that he was uncomfortable, though not hostile.

"Been busy?" I asked.

He squirmed. "Yes, rather." He avoided my gaze.

"Sorry to barge in like this," I continued, "but my sister May is getting married next week. I'd like you to come. If you want."

I tossed the card nonchalantly onto the desk in front of him. He blinked at it for a couple of moments.

"It's... it's awfully decent of you," he said at last.

"It's next Friday. The address is on the card. Come, but only if you want to," I said and left.

OUTSIDE THE court, I nearly collapsed into the driver's seat. Whatever can have possessed me, I asked myself. It would have served me right if Bernie had called the ushers to toss me right out, barging in unannounced like that. Still, the deed had been done. Somehow I felt a little better that I had done it.

Excitement at our place grew more palpable as the week wore on. The whirr of sewing machines was replaced by the hiss of frying, the thump of the mortar in the pestle and the smell of rempah, belachan and baking kueh. May seemed happier than ever and positively bloomed.

In contrast, the atmosphere at the Towkay's house grew ever more subdued. In the beginning he would talk almost constantly to me, instructing me in this or that aspect of Chinese culture. Now he said hardly a word, not even at dinner, which hitherto had been the high point of his day. I hesitated to ask Siew Chin what the matter was for fear of being considered nosey. I knew it couldn't be money, since the steady stream of bought and sold notes kept showing a pattern of small gains. Evidently something was preying on his mind, but I didn't know what. If Siew Chin knew, she wasn't confiding in me.

The day before the wedding, activity rose to a fever pitch. The girls started an orgy of cleaning. Every non-moving thing in sight was washed, polished and waxed. I decided that I had better make myself scarce and left early for the Towkay's place. To my surprise, the Towkay was already up when I got there.

"Today we take a rest," he declared. "We go to the Turf Club."

He seemed much more cheerful, though not as much as when we first met. There were dark rings around his eyes, which I attributed to his late nights.

I rather welcomed a change of routine. The new Turf Club was out in Bukit Timah, a good forty minutes' drive away. It was out of the city, in the greenery and fresh air. I thought that getting away from the stuffy trading room of the Stock Exchange would do the Towkay good. Siew Chin was informed of the decision and bustled around packing us a picnic lunch. To my regret, she could not come with us. Instead she was going to help May put the final touches in place for the morrow.

When we drew up at the imposing three-storey grandstand, the place was already packed. Only members were allowed entry, but a quick call to the Towkay's brokers had fixed that. We were given membership for the day, courtesy of Mr Strathallan of McPhee & Co., who happened to be one of the Stewards of the Club. Mr Strathallan also had his own private box, which he offered to the Towkay for the day.

We went through the main gate and up one of the lifts to the topmost level. The view of the course was magnificent. After unlocking the gate to the box, the Towkay went off to the betting windows to place his bets. A large board displayed the Grand Prize, $50,000 — a fabulous sum. $50,000 meant instant elevation from the proletariat to the leisured class. It was the dream of such riches that drew the crowd that milled below us, Europeans and Asiatics together. Everyone here was equal before the gods of fortune. When the starter's bell rang all heads — white, black and brown — craned forward alike to watch the flailing hooves.

When we got back to our box, we found two white ladies in possession. They were dressed in flowery frocks and carried parasols. One was fortyish, probably the wife of a minor civil servant or junior manager in a white firm judging from her clothes. The other was younger, still fair of complexion. She was on the plumpish side and had a certain lack of grace in her costume that pointed to a lower-middle class upbringing. A day at the races in a private box was plainly a rare treat for them. That they had no right to be there was evident, for they furtively avoided looking at me when I arrived. I cleared my throat politely, hoping that they would realise their mistake and leave. However, they paid no attention to me at all. Finally, I decided to confront them.

"Pardon me," I said, as courteously as I could, "but I believe that you're in our box."

The older woman turned to me. "Really?" she asked frigidly. "This is your box, you say?"

I showed her my badge. "Yes, I'm afraid it is."

She was nonplussed and retreated into glacial silence. I pressed on.

"If you would be so kind as to let us take our seats, I'd be grateful. Or perhaps you too have a badge allowing you access?"

"No, no, as a matter of fact we haven't," she replied with ill-grace. "Well, if you insist, you shall have your box."

She vacated the place with a dark frown, followed by the younger woman. As she left, I heard her complain to her companion, "Really, the manners of some of these natives! Imagine asking us to leave! What is this Colony coming to, I ask you?"

I bit back a reply. Noel Coward said it all when he remarked after meeting the cream of colonial society in Singapore, that he now understood why there was such a shortage of domestic servants in London.

The encounter spoilt the mood of the day for me. I had no more stomach for horse races. Making some excuse to the Towkay,

I headed for the exit. He was too engrossed in the race to really notice my absence. I hopped into the car and drove off, not really knowing where I was going.

Without consciously meaning to, I found myself on the track leading to Madeline's aunt's house. The house still had its melancholy look and the drive was still littered with red Flame-of-the-forest blossoms. I parked the Rolls and headed down the track. I plunged into the cool green depths of the jungle and walked briskly, trying to clear my head.

Throughout all the years I had lived in England I had believed in the Empire and what it stood for. I was a Baba, a King's Chinese. One year back in the Colony had frayed my faith in the ideals of Empire. As I walked through the jungle I realised that no matter how good I was, I would never be good enough. Never would I be accepted as an equal by the whites in the Colony. That realisation left me dismayed and not a little confused emotionally. The only world I knew was that of the white man. The other world, the one to which Siew Chin and the Towkay belonged, was totally alien to me. I felt instinctively that I should always be a stranger there; I would never be accepted as an equal either.

I had not resolved my emotional and intellectual turmoil by the time I got back to fetch the Towkay. I found him in the box, staring vacantly into the distance. He smiled ruefully when he saw me. I didn't ask how he had fared. The torn-up shreds of his race-card told their own story eloquently.

"Come," he said, "we should return."

WE DROVE back in silence. He didn't go out to dinner that night but dismissed me almost absently. I had a solitary meal in town, wrestling with my demons. By the time I got home, all was quiet.

It seemed like I had hardly time to shut my eyes before I was woken by an ungodly din. Fumbling for my bedside clock, I noted with dismay that it was already 5:30 a.m. I knew that it was pointless to try to get into the bathroom in a house with five young ladies all attempting to get dressed at the same time. I clamped the pillow over my head and tried to get back to sleep.

I had barely started to doze when June materialised by my side, ruthlessly snatched the pillow off my head and bundled me off to get ready. The bedlam was incredible. Friends and relatives were already arriving to help in the ceremony — the pageboy, the pagegirl, the sang khek um or mistress of ceremonies, who would instruct the bride on the proper rituals. I dodged them all and fled to the bathroom. Automatically, I washed, shaved and got dressed. To me fell the vital task of making sure the groom actually turned up.

The sun was just peeking over the house tops when I reached Ralph's flat. Dressed in a grey morning suit, complete with topper, he wouldn't have looked out of place at Ascot. However, for a wedding in the tropics...? After more than sixty years of holding my piece, I can finally say it: he looked a right charlie.

Ralph was a bundle of nerves. I pointed out to him that there wasn't any need to worry about the impending ceremony since he had already strapped on the ball and chain when he signed the Register of Marriages the week before. Strangely, this failed to calm him.

Reinforcements soon arrived in the form of George Singham. George was the other best man. Traditionally, a Baba bridegroom had to have two best men. The reason, I thought, was clear. In the old days the happy couple wouldn't have met before the ceremony. The first glimpse that the groom would get of his blushing bride was when he lifted the veil. The best men were there to ensure that he didn't make a break for the door.

The summons for us came shortly after ten o'clock. The pageboy arrived to announce that we were awaited at the bride's house. I recognised him as the same imp whom I had met the previous week when we were delivering the sireh; he banished all doubt by pulling a face at me.

Ralph, the pageboy and me piled into the Rolls, which the Towkay had kindly lent for the occasion. It was decorated with two long stalks of sugar cane. To comply with tradition, the bridegroom was supposed to have been preceded by gong beaters, flutists and cymbal players, as well as minions bearing costly gifts. However, in our straitened circumstances we had to be content with a procession of just two cars, the Rolls and my old jalopy driven by George.

We were greeted as pulled up at the house by a deafening fusillade of firecrackers. The path was red with the debris of the long strings of crackers that hung from the first floor windows. A crowd of guests thronged the verandas. In the side garden, a large marquee had been pitched. A band was playing, striving to make itself heard above the din. We made our way through the acrid cloud of smoke into the front hall. There we waited until the bride made her appearance.

After a quarter of an hour May appeared, led by the mistress of ceremonies and attended by a pagegirl and Siew Chin, her maid of honour. May was resplendent in her traditional embroidered wedding costume, shining with gold lace, a black veil over her face. On her head she wore an elaborate jewelled headdress. I knew that it had belonged to Mak when she got married. Siew Chin, in contrast, was dressed in a fetching *cheongsam* of cherry-coloured silk. May bowed solemnly to Ralph and he reciprocated with all the gravity of a viceroy receiving the submission of a native rajah. Then the wedding couple was led into the sitting room, where the *chinpang* or unveiling ceremony was to take place.

I could see Ralph's hands shaking. George and I took up our places just in case Ralph decided to bolt. But when the time came he did the deed like a man, lifting the veil with a steady movement. May was radiant. Her eyes were lowered modestly. A ceremonial bed had been placed in the room, an old four-poster that had come with the house. With a deft flick, Ralph tossed the veil into the canopy of the bed. The couple then took their seats and pretended to feed one another. The pageboy was then produced. His job was to roll from one side of the bed to the other, to induce the gods to bless the union with children — especially male ones.

This ritual completed, the newly-married couple emerged into the hall again to be greeted by the shouts and acclamations of their gathered friends and relatives. Even the more traditional Nonyas who had tut-tutted their way through the ceremony because of its compressed and hybrid nature condescended to beam at the newlyweds. Mak was close to tears, dabbing at her eyes with her handkerchief. Our job was done.

While May and Ralph held court in the sitting room, George and I mingled with the guests. The orchestra was going full blast and several people were on the floor doing the *ronggeng*. I managed to corner Siew Chin for a dance. She seemed to be enjoying herself immensely.

At the end of the dance she put her hand in mine and allowed me to lead her off the floor. My heart leapt. I steered her to a table in the corner, but unfortunately a group of her nurse friends materialised and took possession of her.

I had little time to be despondent about this reverse, as someone came up and tapped me on the shoulder. I turned round. It was Bernie O'Higgins.

"Hello, old man," he said simply, holding out his hand.

I was elated to see him, but it seemed an occasion for a dose of British reserve.

"Good to see you, old chap. Jolly glad you could come," I responded, taking his outstretched hand.

"Glad you invited me," he replied laconically.

There was no need for further words. We went and found George and had a roaring good time quaffing beer and disparaging various members of Bench and Bar.

AFTER FIVE O'CLOCK a new stream of guests appeared — friends of Ralph and May who couldn't take time off from their jobs. Mak had also invited all my office mates, so the whole gang was there, from Moraiss the chief clerk down to the peon. Aziz, my erstwhile senior in the firm, came up and pumped my hand.

"How are you doing, eh? Long time no see. Your towkay is a good boss?"

"Can't complain," I replied noncommittally, a little embarrassed at having no further pangs of guilt about my change of job.

I glanced around. "Isn't Mr d'Almeida here?"

"He said he will be late. He got a telegram just as we were leaving. Some important document is coming in."

To tell the truth, I was relieved. I was acutely conscious of the debt I owed to d'Almeida. But here I was on the verge of a decisive breakthrough with Siew Chin. To leave the Towkay's service now was out of the question. I wanted to put off the day when my break with the firm would become irrevocable. I knew that if I met d'Almeida, I would have to say something of my plans regarding my future. His absence allowed me to avoid the problem at least for the moment.

I was saved from further discomfort by June, who appeared at my elbow suddenly. June had been bouncing around the grounds like a super-kinetic ping-pong ball all day, meeting, greeting and eating.

"Nearly time," she said breathlessly. "And your Towkay is here too."

She dragged me off to the sitting room. My last job of the day was to drive the bridal couple to Clifford Pier, where they were to board a steamer for Penang. Baba weddings didn't normally include a honeymoon, but Ralph and May decided that they'd adopt this particular custom. The whole affair was such a mishmash anyway, one more change hardly mattered.

I intercepted the Towkay just at the entrance. His appearance shocked me. He seemed very tired and careworn. Nevertheless, he smiled and asked me to introduce him to Ralph and May. This I did with pleasure. He clasped May's hands in his and gave her his very best wishes. Then he shook Ralph's hands, leaving an *ang-pow*.

"I wish you long life and much prosperity," he said simply.

As I guided him out of the room, Siew Chin appeared.

"Take me home, daughter," said the Towkay.

I protested, saying that I would do so in the Rolls.

"No, no," replied the old man. "Your sister and her husband will miss their boat. My daughter can do it. I only ask that you lend us your car."

"But you can't drive, not in your state," I protested again.

"I can drive," said Siew Chin simply. "I will take my father back."

I completely floored by this revelation. "You can drive?"

"Yes," she replied. "When my mother was alive I drove her all over. I know my way around quite well."

I felt a complete fool. That day when I insisted on sending Ralph back first before bringing her home — she must have seen straight through me. Was she laughing at me all the time, secretly? What other hidden depths had she, I wondered?

The Towkay came up and took my hand in both of his. "Goodbye, my young friend."

June interrupted by tugging urgently on my sleeve.

"The boat! Come!" she commanded imperiously.

Mumbling an incoherent goodbye, I sped to the car. Ralph and May were already seated in the back, dressed in their ordinary going-out clothes. Off we went in a scrunch of gravel, the firecrackers making a *feu de joie* as we rolled out the gate.

Luckily, the traffic wasn't too heavy. We got to Clifford Pier with a quarter of an hour to spare.

May gave me a big hug. "Thank you for all you have done for us," she said.

Ralph shook my hand solemnly. "Yes, thanks for everything Dennis. And thank your Towkay. He gave us $100 in the *ang-pow*. A generous cove, but a bit solemn, if you know what I mean. 'Enjoy life while it lasts. Without honour life is nothing,' he told me. That's quite something for a man to think about on his wedding day."

My mind was uneasy as I drove back to the house. The party was still in full swing. As I made my way towards the drinks, I bumped into d'Almeida.

"Ah, Chiang," he said. "I regret that I have missed the happy couple. But something came up. Something that may concern you." He motioned me to a quiet corner. "I got this just half an hour ago. I think you should read it."

He gave me a folded piece of paper. I unfolded it with trepidation. It was a message from a firm of upcountry lawyers, based in Ipoh.

"Re: your request for current information regarding Lipis Consolidated Mines," I read, "we would like to inform you that trading in the shares will be suspended when the market next reopens. It transpires that the former managing director of the said company, Mr Lim Chin Poh, has been guilty of severe peculation. The company's auditors have today completed their examination of the company's accounts. It is their conclusion that the company is now insolvent and that its liabilities exceed its assets by approximately $60,000. It now appears likely that the death of Mr Lim Chin Poh last year was not an accident as had been initially concluded. The late Mr Lim apparently left a suicide note in which he admitted to his misfeasance. This note has only now come to light. The auditors are anxious to contact Mr Lim's father, Lim Beh, whom they feel may be able to shed more light on the circumstances. Mr Lim Senior is believed to be in the Colony at the present time…"

I could read no further.

"So that's what he was up to," I said, to myself as much as to d'Almeida. "He was trying to win enough to cover up his son's embezzlement."

An awful sense of foreboding possessed me.

"Is this news public yet?" I asked anxiously.

"Not entirely," answered d'Almeida. "The auditors completed their investigations today and issued a preliminary statement after the market had closed. The announcement will be made on Monday when the market opens again. But the business community will know by now."

I rushed off with an incoherent word of thanks to d'Almeida. On my way I bumped into Bernie and George.

"Quick! Into the car," I gasped, "I'll explain later."

As we scorched our way over to the Towkay's house I sketched out the whole affair in breathless half-sentences.

The house was in complete darkness. I pounded on the door but there was no response.

Then George exclaimed, "The garage! The car's running in the garage!"

He was right. I could hear the distinctive chugging cough of my old banger from the back. We rushed over. The doors were shut. Old rags had been stuffed under them. Praying fervently that we were not too late, I put my shoulder to the door. George and Bernie lent their weight. Fortunately the door was old and termite-ridden. After half a dozen hefty whacks it gave way.

The acrid smell of exhaust fumes greeted us. I plunged in. In the gloom, I saw a small crumpled shape on the back seat. Tying my handkerchief over my mouth, I stumbled over. She was surprisingly light. I burst out into the fresh air gasping. Out of the corner of my eye I saw George and Ralph carry a limp and lifeless form from the garage and lay it gently on the grass.

TO SAY that I was drained would be an understatement. I felt as if the very life force had been physically sucked out of me. George and Aziz and Bernie rallied round, urging me to take time off, to get away, to forget. D'Almeida sent word that my job was still waiting for me, when I should choose to come back to it. Mak in her quiet way let me know that she and the girls were there for me, come what may. But for all of them, I might have given up totally and broken down.

As it was, I could not face the prospect of either going back to the old routine or being alone with my regrets. I felt instinctively that the best thing to do was to keep busy.

The Towkay left no heirs and there was no one else I knew of who could deal with all the tedious details of the estate. I took on the task wholly without authority. It kept me from thinking too much. I did the best I could, sorting out the bills, cajoling the debtors, holding off the creditors. "Leave no debts unpaid," he had told me right at the beginning. I tried my best to keep faith with that.

Fortunately, he left quite a bit of cash around the house. That went to paying off the many tradesmen who had extended credit. Salmah too was paid and went back to her *kampong* satisfied. The car was repossessed and the deposit forfeited, and that was that.

The bank set off the debits against the credits and came out square. So did the stockbrokers. A small rally on the market allowed them to sell his portfolio at a price sufficient to offset the margin facilities and even leave a small surplus. The shares in his company were of course worthless, but that didn't matter. After a fortnight of slogging through all the papers, I found with some satisfaction that all the debts were covered and that no one was left worse off by the Towkay's passing.

It was just as well that I was kept busy twenty-five hours a day. It took my mind off Siew Chin, but only as long as I had work to do. When respite from my labours came, I found my thoughts inevitably drawn back to her.

For a while it was touch and go. Not only had she inhaled an awful lot of carbon monoxide, she had been given a dose of veronal sufficient to knock out a bull buffalo as well. I tried repeatedly to visit her in hospital, but found my way barred by a harridan with a flaming sword. She had strict instructions to stop anyone save family from disturbing the patient. I was not kin, nor had I anything more than the unspoken hope of a closer connection in my favour. They wouldn't let me see her under any circumstances. Evidently Matron considered me to be a bad influence.

Since all those who knew the truth were silent, all kinds of wild stories were circulating about the affair. Word had gotten around that I was the cad who was responsible for the mess that she was in. Some said that I had seduced her, leading to a desperate attempt at suicide. The nurses were all warned not to let me near Siew Chin. I knew that it was useless to even attempt to deny the stories. I contemplated all sorts of stratagems, even going so far as to try my peon disguise again. To no avail; they were on guard, my face was familiar and I was ignominiously escorted from the premises with dire threats ringing in my ears.

After a fortnight, May and Ralph returned from their honeymoon to be told the whole dreadful story. May rushed off immediately to Siew Chin. I offered to come with her, but she thought it would be better if I waited. Wait I did. I pottered around the Towkay's house, putting the last papers in order. At about four o'clock a rather agitated Ralph materialised at the door.

"You'd better go quick," he said breathlessly.

I dropped what I was doing. "How is she?" I asked anxiously.

"Don't know," replied Ralph. "May sent word by some idiot peon who speaks no known human language that you should go over now. I couldn't get anything else out of him."

Grabbing my coat, I leapt into my car and pushed it as hard as I could. I squealed to a halt in front of the ward in a shower of gravel, drawing disapproving stares from the nurses and patients. Taking the stairs two at a time, I almost collided into May.

"What are you doing here?" she asked with astonishment.

"Didn't you send for me? Ralph told me I should come quick."

"Ayoh, the *gobblock*!" she exclaimed. "I said you should go quick to the railway station. Siew Chin is leaving today. She is going back to Ipoh. Now. She thinks you do not care for her. You did not even visit." She gave me a reproachful glance.

The injustice of this nearly bowled me over. "Didn't visit? What a bloody load of tripe! I've tried again and again, practically every day for the last fourteen days. It's your blasted Matron and her gang of harpies that kept me out. Did you set her straight?"

"I told her you cared," said May. "Now you should go and tell her yourself."

I needed no second bidding. Off I went in a billow of smoke and scorched rubber. I pulled up at the station entrance and practically flew through the portal. I looked at my watch. My only hope lay in the habitual unpunctuality of the FMS Railways. I raced to the platform. To my relief the train was still there.

Then there was a shrill toot and a burst of steam. The carriages began to move.

Urging my legs to a superhuman effort, I ran along the platform trying to catch up. Then I saw her. She was sitting at the window in the last carriage, her face drawn and pale. I called her name loudly. She did not hear over the clacking and hissing of the train. I called again, breathless with the exertion. She turned her face, saw me. There was no smile.

"Siew Chin, wait," I huffed. "Don't go! I need... I... I...want..."

I knew what I had to say to make her stay. I willed myself to say the words. But all of a sudden, unbidden, a vision of Madeline's face flashed before my eyes. The words died in my throat.

The moment was gone. I halted despondently at the end of the platform as the train steamed out of the station.

I am surprised, looking back over the great gulf of years, how the memory of that scene still evokes such powerful emotions in me. It was as if someone had wrenched out all my insides. I stood there, totally gutted, watching as the train grew steadily smaller and the clacking of the wheels faded.

Then, just as it was about to round the bend and disappear, I saw the small window at the end of the last carriage open. A pale face peeked out. A white handkerchief waved. I raised my hand and waved back uncertainly. The train slowly vanished.

I stayed on that platform for a long time, staring blankly at the tracks that converged in the far distance.

GLOSSARY

The following is a list of non-English words used in the text. The words in parentheses
are the modern spelling of the word.

adek (adik) — younger sister/brother
almeirah — cupboard/dresser
amah — female servant/nursemaid
amok (amuk) — manic
ang-pow — gift envelope
attap — roof made from nipah palm
Baba — Straits Chinese, usually male
bangun — stand/get/wake up
barang-barang — things
bedak sejok (sejuk) — face powder
belachan — dried shrimp paste
belukar — secondary jungle
Bibik — term of respect for an older woman
bomoh — medicine man
budak chelaka (celaka) — rude child
buka — open
burra memsahib — grande dame or great lady
caravanserai — entourage
changkul (cangkul) — hoe/pick
charpoy — lightweight bedstead
cheongsam — dress
chinpang — wedding unveiling ceremony
datang — come/arrive
gin pahit — bitter gin
gobblock (goblock) — stupid
hantu-hantu — ghosts
jaga — guard/watchman
kachang puteh (kacang putih) — dried nuts
kamcheng — porcelain bowl with lid
kampong (kampung) — village
kaya bread — bread with egg-custard spread
kebun — a term used by the Babas to refer to
    the gardener
kerosang — brooch fastening the front of a
    kebaya
kretek — clove cigarette
kris — daggar with a wavy blade
kueh (kuih) — cake
kwali (kuali) — frypan
lalang — long-bladed grass

langsuir — banshee
memshahib — female master
'nkim, 'nku, 'npek, um — aunts of various
    degrees
Nonyas — Straits Chinese females
orang puteh (putih) — white man
parang — chopping knife
pawang — witch doctor
perempuan sial — dammed woman
pontianak — ghost of a woman who died in
    childbirth
puchat sa-kali (pucat sekali) — completely pale
rempah — spices
ronggeng — traditional Malay dance
saga — red sandalwood/coral tree
sahib — term of address for a white man in
    India
samfoo — jacket and trouser set
sang khek um — mistress of ceremonies
sarong (sarung) kebaya — traditional Malay
    dress
sepoy — Indian soldier
shaitan (syaitan) — Satan/devil
silat — self-defence matrial art
Sinkhek — non-Straits Chinese
sireh (sirih) — betel nut paste/leaf
songkok — male headdress
stengahs — half measure of whiskey
sua ku — small town person
Tachi — elder sister
talaq — divorce
tongkang — flat-bottomed boat/barge
topi — hat
towkay — tycoon/boss
tuan — term of address for a white man in
    Malaya and the Straits Settlements
tuan besar — big boss
tutup — closed, button-up jacket
ulu — jungle

ABOUT THE AUTHOR

Walter Woon was educated at the National University of Singapore and St John's College. Cambridge. He has been at various times the Sub-Dean and Vice-Dean of the NUS Law Faculty, a nominated Member of Parliament, a director of two listed companies, legal adviser to the President, ambassador to several European countries, Solicitor-General and Attorney-General. He is presently a Senior Counsel, David Marshall Professor of Law at the NUS Law Faculty and Dean of the Singapore Institute of Legal Education.

He is married with two sons.

The Advocate's Devil is the first installment of *The Advocate's Devil* Trilogy.